So True A Love

OTHER BOOKS BY JOANNA BARKER

A Heart Worth Stealing

So True a Love

PROPER ROMANCE

Joanna Barker

SHADOW
MOUNTAIN
PUBLISHING

To Heidi—

Ups and downs, laughs and tears, we've been through it all.

You're my person, and I wouldn't have it any other way.

Library of Congress Cataloging-in-Publication Data
Names: Barker, Joanna L., 1990– author.
Title: So true a love / Joanna Barker.
Other titles: Proper romance.
Description: [Salt Lake City] : Shadow Mountain Publishing, [2024] | Series: Proper romance | Summary: "Verity Travers, a well-connected lady and private investigator, retires after a perilous case. However, a personal attack on her friend reignites her determination to catch the assailant. Verity is forced to team up with the dashing Bow Street Runner Nathaniel Denning, and as they close in on the truth, their investigation becomes more complicated than ever as danger and passion collide"—Provided by publisher.
Identifiers: LCCN 2024008435 (print) | LCCN 2024008436 (ebook) | ISBN 9781639932948 (trade paperback) | ISBN 9781649332943 (ebook)
Subjects: LCSH: Women private investigators—England—London—Fiction. | Robbery—England—London—Fiction. | Man-woman relationships—Fiction. | London (England), setting. | BISAC: FICTION / Romance / Historical / Regency | FICTION / Romance / Clean & Wholesome | LCGFT: Romance fiction. | Historical fiction.
Classification: LCC PS3602.A775526 S68 2024 (print) | LCC PS3602.A775526 (ebook) | DDC 813/.6—dc23/eng/20240304
LC record available at https://lccn.loc.gov/2024008435
LC ebook record available at https://lccn.loc.gov/2024008436

Printed in the United States of America
Lake Book Manufacturing, LLC, Melrose Park, IL

10 9 8 7 6 5 4 3 2 1

CHAPTER 1

London, England, 1803

Mama was in fine form tonight.

"Now, one glorious effort!" she cried out as she swept to the center of the stage, her jewelry glittering in the candlelight. "A daughter's arm, fell monster, strikes this blow! Yes, first she strikes."

The Theatre Royal at Drury Lane was generally alive with whispers and gossip during a performance, but tonight, Mama held her audience captive, breathless.

Including me. I'd attended dozens of her plays over the years, been subjected to endless rehearsals at home, but when Mama took the stage, all that fell away. She became someone else—*something* else.

I managed to pull my eyes from the stage to focus again on the play-bill in my lap. My sketch of Mama stared back at me from the paper, shadowed and unfinished. I adjusted the shading, giving her face sharper angles, making her eyes dark, flashing pools.

"That is very good." Elizabeth leaned over, eyes twinkling as she looked down at my drawing. "You should showcase your skills more often. The gentlemen would surely flock."

I grinned. "What would I do with a flock of gentlemen? I'd hardly know what to do with *one*."

She laughed. "I know what you do in your spare time, darling. I doubt a few fops and dandies are much of a challenge for Verity Travers."

"Hush, both of you," Lady Harwood whispered from behind us, thankfully saving me from responding.

Elizabeth sent me a look of amused long-suffering before we obliged her mother and turned back to the play.

"An injur'd daughter's arm," Mama declared, her voice echoing as she raised her dagger high, "sends thee devoted to th' infernal gods."

In one thrilling movement—practiced dozens of times—she struck Dionysius with the dagger. The actor made a great show of dying, protesting his death with a villain's disbelief. But I watched my mother, the face I knew so well. It was a fascinating dichotomy. To me, she was simply Mama. But to all else in the theatre tonight, she was the ethereal Trinity Travers, the greatest tragedienne of her age, whose talent made ladies swoon and gentlemen collapse into fits.

I tore my eyes from the stage, and my pencil flew across the paper, filling in the missing details. The sharp point of the dagger, the shadows of Mama's draped dress. I darkened her ebony hair, the only physical trait I'd received from her. It was unfortunate because while I liked my hair, a generous figure like Mama's might have been the better inheritance.

When Mama gave her final bows, Drury Lane trembled from the thunderous applause. She curtsied graciously, catching my eye and sending me a mischievous wink. My mouth twitched to one side. Some girls had mothers who embroidered pillows or did charity work. Mine put herself on full display for the entire *ton* every Season.

The actors retreated from the stage as the curtains descended, and the crowd broke into a thousand conversations.

"Oh, she is unparalleled!" Lady Harwood exclaimed as we gathered our things. "I declare, Miss Travers, your mother is the finest actress I've ever seen. I cannot imagine a more expressive Euphrasia."

"Indeed," I said with a hidden smile. Lady Harwood needn't know that Mama was not particularly fond of the role of Euphrasia. If she had her choice, she would perform Lady Macbeth every evening. Anything less than Shakespeare was aggravating.

Sir Reginald—Elizabeth's father, who had snored through the entire third act and now looked a bit bleary-eyed—led us out into the corridor and down the stairs.

"Should you like to greet Mama?" I offered, facing the inevitable head-on. "I imagine she would be pleased to see you again."

"Oh, not tonight." Lady Harwood looked flustered at the idea. *Flustered*. And she the wife of a baronet. "I daresay she is tired after such a performance. No, I shall save my compliments until the unveiling party in a few days. Your mother is coming, isn't she?"

"You have asked Verity that three times tonight, Mother," Elizabeth said with some exasperation.

Lady Harwood sniffed. "I just want to be sure."

"Mama is coming," I reassured her. "And I would not miss it for the world. *The Woman in Red* is a favorite of mine, though I've seen only prints."

Lady Harwood had curated an expansive art collection over the years, which I had been awed by in the past, but her newest acquisition was unmatched in reputation—*The Woman in Red* by Giuseppe Romano. It was the most famous of Romano's paintings and had surely cost Sir Reginald a pretty penny. Though he had little interest in art himself, he could not resist owning such an unmistakable symbol of wealth and status. Lady Harwood had organized a dinner party to unveil the painting. I counted myself fortunate to have been invited.

"Oh, it is stunning, my dear." Lady Harwood's eyes were bright. "There is truly nothing like it in all the world."

"Come, it is late." Sir Reginald herded us through the saloon, though his eyes crinkled as he regarded his wife fondly.

As we crossed the long saloon, enormous Doric columns presiding over the open space, I found myself glancing to my right. I didn't know why—it had been more than two years since my brother, Jack, had last stood guard there, hired by Drury Lane in his capacity as a Bow Street officer to watch for pickpockets. I should have been used to his absence.

I frowned when I saw who stood in Jack's place—a great beef of a man, whose shrewd eyes searched the crowd. Nettleton, if I remembered right. I pressed my lips together, pulling my eyes away.

The cool April air enveloped us as we left the Theatre Royal, and I gratefully inhaled a deep breath. The crowd around us dispersed, escorts helping glittering ladies into carriages. Sir Reginald looked about for his own equipage and sighed when he spotted it two blocks down Drury Lane.

"A bit of a walk, I'm afraid," he said, extending his arm to his wife.

She barely acknowledged him, still lost in the glow that came from a shared experience of excellence. "Yes, yes," she said distantly.

Elizabeth linked arms with me as we trailed behind her parents, dim moonlight falling upon us. "Thank you for coming tonight," she said. "The company would have been terribly dull without you."

I laughed. "You needn't worry about wounding my sensibilities, Elizabeth. I know I was a replacement for the guest you truly desired. Let us hope your Lord Blakely recovers from his cold quickly."

Elizabeth smiled, and it reminded me again why I was grateful to have her as a friend. Not because her smile lit up beautiful features, so lauded by the gossip papers upon her recent engagement, but because of the inherent goodness that shone there. I had yet to meet her intended, the Earl of Blakely, but I certainly had my doubts about his deserving her. I could only hope he was a better match for her than that flighty Mr. Hall she'd had her heart set on last spring.

"Of course I am sad he is ill," she said, "but I am also glad you came. It has been so long since I've seen you."

"*You* are to blame for that." I tapped her arm. "Though I suppose traveling with your aunt was certainly a more pleasant prospect than wintering in Town."

Elizabeth's steps faltered. "Y-yes," she said, forcing a laugh. "It is entirely my fault. But now that I am returned, you will see so much of me that you shall wish me gone again."

"Quite likely," I said. "I do find old friends rather irritating."

We laughed together as we crossed the intersection, still following behind Lady Harwood and Sir Reginald. In truth, I'd been surprised by Lady Harwood's invitation to join them tonight—I was far beneath the notice of a baronet's wife. After all, an actress's daughter was not usually a highly sought-after social companion, and my shadowy parentage lowered my prospects even more, though Lady Harwood did not know of my true background. But Elizabeth's friendship with me must have held more sway than I'd realized.

The street was full of carriages, and the Harwoods' coachman turned onto a quieter lane ahead to escape the bustle. We went after it, the noise and blazing lights of the theatre fading behind us. It seemed silly to allow the Harwoods to see me home—I could easily walk there myself in the space of five minutes—but Lady Harwood was all propriety. I did not want to shock her by suggesting I make my way back alone.

"Spare a penny?" A beggar limped out of the shadows ahead of us, dirty hand outstretched before him. Moonlight broke over his features just enough to make out hooded eyes, a beak of a nose, and a skinny neck.

Lady Harwood stepped back, grasping her husband's arm.

Sir Reginald eyed the beggar cautiously. "I am sorry, my good fellow," he said. "I haven't any coins on me at present."

"Just a farthin'," the man pressed.

Beggars were plentiful in Covent Garden—we'd seen half a dozen when we'd entered the theatre earlier that evening—and yet, in this brief moment, a sudden awareness sharpened inside me. Jack called it instinct, Grandmama my sixth sense. I had no exact word for this twisting in my gut, but I knew I trusted it. The only time I'd ignored the feeling, I'd regretted it dearly.

Sir Reginald began to steer Lady Harwood around the man. "Good night," he said pointedly, continuing toward his waiting coach.

But the beggar stepped to block their path.

And suddenly, his hand wasn't empty.

Moonlight glinted off a pistol pointed directly at Sir Reginald. My heart stilled in my chest, and my disbelieving eyes traveled from the pistol to the beggar's face, harsh and cold.

"Give it here," he hissed. "All your lurries. Jewels, money, everythin'."

Elizabeth clutched my arm, her face white. My mouth went dry, and I could not make myself move, as though I had lead in every limb. It seemed a hazy impossibility, more like a scene from the Greek play we'd just left than reality. This man could not truly be robbing us here, a stone's throw from the theatre. Heavens, Bow Street office itself was only one street over.

"Hurry," the man snapped. "No screamin' now, or you'll not see daylight."

The Harwoods' carriage was still ahead, too far to see what was happening. I threw a desperate glance behind me. Another group of playgoers was just up the street. I could ignore the thief's warning and scream, call for help. But I discarded that plan immediately. I might frighten him and provoke his twitchy trigger finger.

Lady Harwood let loose a small squeak, and the pistol turned to her.

Sir Reginald stepped in front of his wife, raising his hands. "Please," he managed, his voice hoarse. He glanced back at Elizabeth and me. "Do as he says."

Lady Harwood and Elizabeth obeyed, their shaking hands unclasping bracelets and necklaces while Sir Reginald gave up a gold ring and cravat pin. But I stood stock still, hands gripping my reticule. My reticule, which contained a comb, hair pins, a handkerchief, my playbill— and a tiny pistol.

Jack had gifted it to me when I was sixteen. "You never know when you might find yourself in a spot of trouble," he'd said, handing me the pistol with an inlaid pearl handle. Perfect for a lady. If a lady were to need a pistol, that was.

He had taught me how to shoot, and I had practiced anytime I could, becoming rather a decent markswoman. I'd taken the pistol everywhere with me since then, always tucked into my reticule. I'd had it with me that night three months ago—when I had needed it most. The night everything had changed.

I shoved the memory away. I had to think logically. I could not possibly load *and* aim my pistol with the man already pointing his at Lady Harwood. The safest thing to do was to follow his instructions. Better to lose a few trinkets than our lives.

Still, I was loath to give up my weapon. While the thief was leering at Elizabeth, I quickly slipped my reticule behind the shawl draped around my arms. Just in time, as he jerked his pistol toward me in the next moment.

"You, lady." He stepped closer to me, weathered skin contrasting with his eyes, young and alert. "Get on with it."

I raised my trembling hands to remove my pearl earrings—the only things of value I had on my person—and dropped them into his ragged little sack, heavy with our belongings.

Satisfied I was complying, he focused again on Elizabeth. "The bag," he insisted, voice sharp as broken glass. He glanced up and down the street, shifting his weight uneasily.

Elizabeth still had her reticule on her wrist. She grasped it with her free hand, eyes wide. "No," she stammered. "Please, you mustn't."

The man moved closer, the pistol's barrel not a foot from her chest.

"Elizabeth." Sir Reginald tensed, looking ready to throw himself in front of his daughter. "Give it to him."

She stood frozen, then inexplicably shot *me* a desperate look. But there was nothing I could do to help her.

"It is all right," I managed. "Do as he says."

The man lost his patience. He reached forward and tore the reticule from Elizabeth's wrist. She stifled a yelp, clutching her arm. He stuffed the reticule inside his sack as he faced Sir Reginald.

"There, you have everything," Sir Reginald said. "Let us—"

Faster than I thought possible, the thief smashed Sir Reginald alongside the head with the handle of his pistol. The baronet staggered back and fell to the cobblestone street, Lady Harwood's scream echoing in my ears.

The thief bounded away, disappearing down the dark alley.

Shock charged through me, followed closely by anger—furious, pounding anger. Lady Harwood dropped to her knees beside her husband, holding his shoulder, sobbing. I stared. He'd *attacked* Sir Reginald. Right here on the street.

I took a step after the thief.

Stop, the voice of caution in my mind said. But I could barely hear it over the rushing in my ears. Why hadn't he just taken our valuables and fled? I would have let him. There had been no point in confronting him when he'd had the upper hand.

But now.

Now, how could I possibly stand by while such a fetid curse of a man made his escape?

I spun to Elizabeth, my body moving before I even realized I'd made a decision. She stood with both hands pressed to her mouth in unadulterated shock as she gaped at her father bleeding on the street. "Elizabeth." I grasped her shoulders. "Run to the theatre. There's a Bow Street Runner inside. He will help."

Elizabeth shook her head, dazed. "I—"

"Go now!" I crouched by Lady Harwood kneeling beside her husband in the street. He was moaning, a gaping cut on his brow seeping blood onto the stones beneath him. I tore open my reticule and found my handkerchief. Behind me, I could hear Elizabeth's footsteps running back toward the theatre.

"Help!" she shouted. "Help!"

"Put pressure on the wound," I ordered Lady Harwood, showing her how to press the handkerchief against Sir Reginald's forehead. "Hold it there until help arrives."

"Where are you going?" she cried, but I did not answer as I darted down the alley.

After the thief.

Fool, I said to myself. *Idiot. Clodhead.* Why was I doing this? I knew how this ended. I'd been here before.

But I kept running, convincing myself that this time would be different. I would not try to apprehend the man. That would be foolishness incarnate. No, I would follow him until he thought himself safe. I would discover his hiding hole, whatever dank place he called home, and return with an officer.

I pulled my pistol from my reticule as I ran, though I had no intention of firing it tonight. I certainly couldn't load it as I dashed down an alleyway. However, if the thief surprised me, *he* would not know it was empty.

The shadows of the buildings obscured all but the center of the alley, bright with moonlight. The thief could be hiding, but I doubted it. Escape was his aim. But to where?

I came to an intersection and paused, keeping to the shadows, my chest heaving, my unloaded pistol at the ready. Where had he gone?

Then I heard retreating footsteps to my left. A figure escaped toward the light of another street.

I went after him, acting on instinct alone. All I could feel was the fire in my chest, the burning indignation that had *never* led me anywhere good. I focused on the darting shadow even as I hid within the dark angles of the walls, taking light steps and quick, shallow breaths, as Jack had taught me.

The thief threw a harried glance over his shoulder, but he didn't see me. Not that he would have felt particularly threatened even if he *had* seen me. I had neither Mama's statuesque height nor Jack's intimidating brawn.

The thief reached the next street and plunged across, causing a jarvey to shout and draw up his horses. He entered the alley directly across and disappeared once again. I dashed into the street, determined not to lose—

A blurred figure at the corner of my eye, moving fast.

Then I slammed into something solid as a stone wall.

CHAPTER 2

I flew through the air, vision twisting as the cobblestones rushed to meet me. I tried to roll to lessen the brunt of the impact, but there wasn't time. My shoulder and hip crashed into the stones, the shock reverberating through my entire body.

For a paralyzing moment, I lay there, unable to fill my lungs with air. Then pain *shrieked* through me—stinging, biting pain. I gasped, inhaling a desperate gulp, my head dazed and muddled.

"Blast it," groaned a male voice beside me.

I barely comprehended it, still stunned. What had happened? Had I been run over by a coach? I'd been right behind the thief—

The thief! I forced my eyes open, the oil lamps swirling through the evening fog, my vision blurry. Horse hooves, carriage wheels, the dirty street . . .

I did not see the shadow of a fleeing thief.

"Drat." I struggled to sit up, wincing at the pain in my side and shoulder. If I could just get to my feet, perhaps I could—

"Miss?" It was the same voice as before, but now it was low and urgent and directed at me. "Miss, are you all right?"

A man crouched beside me on the street, his features dark, silhouetted against the lamp behind him.

"I am sorry," he said, his words scattering through my head. "I didn't see you. I swear you came from nowhere."

Realization struck then. I'd run into him. Or he'd run into me. It hardly mattered—the thief was long gone by now, vanished into the crooked lanes of London's rookeries.

"Are ye planning to move," a harsh voice called out, "or do ye intend to block the street till mornin'?"

I looked dazedly at the hackney stopped behind me. The driver scowled, spitting some foul liquid over the edge of the coach. A gentleman, clearly.

I tried to push myself to my feet but winced as splintering pain seemed to radiate from every inch of my body.

"Here, allow me." The man beside me stood and offered his hand. I hesitated, but it appeared I could not stand on my own at the moment, and I preferred *not* to remain splayed in the filth that coated the street. I took his hand, large and solid, and he pulled me to my feet. Dizziness claimed me, and I swayed, staggering to the side. The same strong hands caught me, keeping me from spilling once more to the ground.

"Steady on," the man cautioned, his deep voice near my ear.

I tried to gain my bearings as he guided me off the street. The driver harrumphed and whipped the reins against his horses, the coach jolting past us.

"Are you hurt?" The man held me about my waist with one hand, the other at my elbow, no doubt worried I would collapse.

I *was* hurt, but how badly? I'd abandoned my shawl in the chase, and the short sleeves of my silk evening gown had done little to protect my arms. Angry red scrapes marred my skin. I could feel the ache in my hip and shoulder, and I knew I would be sore and bruised for days yet. But . . .

Nothing broken.

"I'm fi—" I looked up at my rescuer, and my voice cut out.

His face was no longer hidden in black silhouette, and what a face it was. I made out deep-set eyes—dark but somehow bright at the same time. His features deftly cut the shadows and moonlight, a strong brow balanced with a narrow, angular jaw. Waves of brownish hair swept across his forehead, considerably unkempt, though that was likely due to our collision rather than a laissez-faire approach to styling. He was young, perhaps only a few years my senior, with a good six inches on me, if not more. His shoulders and waist were lean, but I was quite assured of his sturdiness, considering the way he'd sent me flying when we'd crashed.

A sudden heat climbed my neck. I pulled away from him, tugging my skirts straight. "I'm fine."

He inspected my arms, brow furrowed. He didn't believe me. But then he glanced toward the alley where the thief had disappeared.

"Blast," he muttered. "I had him."

My gaze sharpened on him. "Had who?"

He sighed, raking a hand through his hair. "A thief. There was a robbery just now outside the Theatre Royal. I was giving chase and—"

"*You* were chasing him?" Who was this man? Had he heard the commotion and attempted a citizen's arrest?

"Yes, but he got away during our spill." He turned back to me. "I am terribly sorry, but I must return to the theatre. Do you have anyone to . . ." He paused as he glanced around me, realizing for the first time that I was alone.

But my own eyes were fixed on where his jacket parted and a familiar gilded stave peeked out at me. I knew that stave. Jack had carried one just like it.

"You're from Bow Street," I said rather stupidly.

"Yes." He took half a step away. "And I really must—"

"You're not Nettleton." I was still utterly baffled, my thoughts scattered. Had Elizabeth not found the man?

He said nothing for one long moment, then turned to face me fully again. "No," he said slowly, "but the young lady who came screaming into the theatre did not seem to care who went after the man, and I'm a mite faster than Nettleton."

This man must be Nettleton's partner for the night. But now it was even odder that I did not recognize him. I knew all the officers, didn't I? Although, admittedly, it *had* been ages since I'd last been to Bow Street.

He took in my appearance fully for the first time, my silk evening gown and intricate hairstyle. "Did you just come from the theatre? Perhaps you saw the thief."

"Yes, I saw him," I said, unaccountably irritated. "I was following him when you ran into me."

The last word had barely left my mouth when I realized what a mistake I'd made. He stared at me, and I wished—not for the first time—that I had learned any amount of social restraint in my time at Mrs. Simmons Preparatory School for Girls.

"You were following him?" The pure disbelief in his voice was like a sliver beneath my skin.

I knew I shouldn't, but my tongue went on without my permission. "He certainly didn't make it very difficult," I said tartly. "An elephant would have made less noise."

His eyebrows arched higher. I'd made it worse.

"Should we walk back together?" I suggested quickly, hoping he might forget what I'd said. "Lady Harwood will be beside herself by now."

But a silver gleam caught my eye, and I froze. My tiny pistol lay on the street not two feet from where I stood. I sent the man a sideways glance. Had he seen it? Proper young ladies did not carry pistols, no matter how delicate or feminine this particular weapon might be.

He did not seem to be looking, turning back the way he'd come, perhaps wondering which way was the faster route. Leaving the pistol was not an option—Jack had spent a small fortune on it. And that had been before he'd married rich.

I moved quickly, bending and scooping up the pistol in one motion. I tugged my reticule open and slipped it inside. Done.

But as I raised my head again, I saw him again watching me, his eyes fixed firmly on my reticule.

"I dropped something," I said quickly. Had he seen?

His gaze lifted to meet mine, and he opened his mouth, possibly to question my sanity. Until a chill wind rustled my skirts, and I shivered. Without a word, he shrugged off his jacket and draped it around my shoulders. It held his warmth and the faintest smell of lemons.

I stood stock still, surprised, but he only gestured toward the alley. "Come on, then."

I fell in beside him, hurrying my steps to match his longer stride. The energy that had overcome me during the chase began to dissipate, and the fear and worry returned.

"Sir Reginald was attacked during the robbery," I said. "Did you see him? Is he all right?"

"Who?" he asked absently. "I came straight from the theatre."

"My friend's father," I explained. "The thief struck Sir Reginald to keep him from following."

He sent me a sidelong glance. "And so you decided to follow instead?" What was that tone he'd used? Curiosity? Reproach? I fought the urge to look at him, saying nothing. "Might I ask," he said, keeping a careful distance between us as we walked, "what you intended to do if you'd caught the man?"

I cleared my throat. "I did not intend to catch him."

"What, then, was your intention?"

"I planned to follow him until I discovered his hiding place, then fetch help."

He coughed, perhaps to hide a laugh or a snort. I shot him a glance. He quickly masked his expression, looking perfectly serious.

I quickened my steps. The less time I spent alone with this man, the better.

He did not break stride as he matched my new pace. "You are sure you are not hurt?"

"Of course I'm hurt," I said, a bit more hotly than I'd intended. "But I'm far from incapacitated."

"Clearly," he said under his breath. I opened my mouth, but he pressed on before I could respond. "How do you know Nettleton?"

"He was acquainted with my brother," I said. "I would not say I know him much at all." He was persistent, I would give him that. But the last thing I wished to discuss was my history with Bow Street—or Jack's. I parried. "How did you know where the thief would run?"

He shrugged. "I assumed he would escape toward Seven Dials. I took another route, hoping to cut him off."

Until he'd cut *me* off instead. I held my tongue.

No doubt he would have continued to question me, but we reached the end of the alley and found a crowd gathered. Elizabeth gave a small cry upon spotting us and raced to me.

"Verity," she gasped, clutching my elbows. "What in heaven's name were you thinking, dashing off like that? Mother is inconsolable. She thinks you dead, or worse."

"Worse than dead?" I said dryly. "What a notion."

Elizabeth shook her head. "You cannot be making jests at a time like this."

I winced. That had been terrible of me. It was a clear failing of mine, allowing humor into the most inappropriate of moments. "I am sorry. How is your father?"

"He is all right," she said, her voice strained but her relief clear. "A bit dazed but speaking."

I peered around her to make my own judgment. Sir Reginald sat in the center of the small crowd, holding the bloodstained handkerchief to his head, his eyes closed and his face pale. He didn't look *well*, by any means, but neither did he look to be in any danger. I let out a small sigh. No matter that Sir Reginald was a bit overbearing, he'd tried to protect the three of us tonight. I was unexpectedly moved.

The Harwoods' coach waited on the street, and Lady Harwood stood beside her husband, wringing her hands as she spoke to Nettleton, who jotted notes down in a small book. Even from here, he looked bored with the whole affair.

Elizabeth turned to my companion. "Were you able to catch the blackguard, sir?"

"Ah," he said, clasping his hands behind his back. "I'm afraid not. There was something of a mishap."

Instead of disappointment, an inexplicable flash of panic crossed Elizabeth's face. Was she worried the man might return? But her expression shifted in the next instant, and she managed a tight smile. "I thank you for pursuing him all the same, Mr. . . . ?"

She glanced at me for the answer. My cheeks heated. We had tumbled to the street together and shared an entire conversation, yet I hadn't thought to ask his name.

My mouth parted—to say what?—but he noted my distress and spoke first.

"Denning," he supplied, along with a short bow. "Nathaniel Denning."

"Miss Elizabeth Harwood." Elizabeth curtsied. "I would say it is a pleasure, sir, but perhaps you might forgive me for excluding that nicety this evening."

He gave a rather charming half smile. "I would, indeed."

"Denning!"

Nettleton stepped away from Lady Harwood and waved toward us, his face set in what I imagined was a perpetual scowl. I thought Mr. Denning might show some sign of irritation at the less-than-polite summoning, but he only dipped his head at the two of us. "Pardon me, ladies," he said and went to join his partner.

I took Elizabeth's elbow as we trailed after him. "Your father is truly all right?"

She nodded, though her hands trembled. "The doctor will confirm it, of course, but it seems to look much worse than it is."

"That is typical of head wounds," I said, trying to reassure her. "I am certain he'll be perfectly fine."

Lady Harwood saw us coming and moved to meet us. "Verity Travers," she scolded. "What were you thinking, running after him? The man could have killed you!"

I *hadn't* been thinking when I'd dashed after the thief. Not about how stupid it was or how dangerous or how it might affect my reputation. Another failing of mine—blind single-mindedness. Rare were the times when all my flaws joined together to defeat me, but tonight was clearly one of them.

"I wasn't running after him," I lied outright, trying my best to deflect. "I was looking for help. I thought I saw a carriage coming down the alley."

She did not seem entirely mollified by my answer, but then Sir Reginald made a noise of pain behind us, and both she and Elizabeth turned to help him, faces painted in concern.

I stayed back. Sir Reginald did not need another pair of hands to fuss over him. I spotted my abandoned shawl a few paces away from where the two officers stood, their heads bent together. I moved to pick it up, conveniently within earshot.

"—assume from your lack of a handcuffed thief that he escaped your pursuit?" That was Nettleton, snide and sarcastic.

Mr. Denning did not respond immediately, his hands on his hips. Would he blame me?

"He got away." Mr. Denning spoke evenly, without trying to explain himself.

Nettleton frowned but only consulted his notebook. "I haven't gotten anything useful from the ladies. They are both at their wits' end."

"You can hardly blame them," Mr. Denning said with a touch of annoyance now, if I wasn't mistaken. "They've had a trying night."

Nettleton ignored him. "I've the barest description of the thief but not enough to go on."

I could not help myself. "What description do you have?"

They turned, and Nettleton noticed me for the first time. I'd thought he might recognize me—Jack had introduced us before—but apparently, I hadn't made much of an impression.

"Who's this?" he grunted at Mr. Denning, his eyes taking in the man's jacket slung over my shoulders.

Mr. Denning hesitated, and I realized he didn't know *my* name. But I wasn't about to spout it out with Nettleton standing there. I was perfectly aware of what he thought of my brother. Knowing who I was could sour both of them toward the Harwoods and solving this crime.

"I am a friend of Miss Harwood," I said quickly. "The description?"

Nettleton's eyes narrowed at my prodding, but he glanced down at his notebook again.

"Average height, large hat, dark eyes," he read off.

I blinked. "That's it?"

He gave a *hmpf.* "Lady Harwood was not in a particularly descriptive state of mind."

"No, no, dear, you must sit!" Lady Harwood commanded, drawing our attention. Sir Reginald paid her no mind and balanced himself against the brick wall as he found his feet.

"I am well enough," he said irritably, shaking off her helping hands. "I must speak to the Runners." He started forward to join us, his steps teetering.

Mr. Denning met him halfway, inconspicuously taking his elbow to steady him.

"Thank you," the baronet muttered, clearly not wanting his wife and daughter to know how affected he was. He straightened and looked at the two officers. "He's gotten away, has he?"

Nettleton sent Mr. Denning a pointed look.

Mr. Denning sighed. "Yes," he said, not beating around the bush. "I had him in my sights, but I lost him during an unexpected . . . collision."

Sir Reginald squinted like he was trying to see through his pain. "Well, what is our next step? How do we catch the miscreant?"

Nettleton and Mr. Denning exchanged a glance. Their thoughts were clear. In cases like this, the chances of finding the culprit, let alone convicting him, were little to none.

"It is late, sir," Nettleton said, clearly wishing to go home. "You've suffered a brutal blow, and a doctor needs to take a look at that wound. You might come by Bow Street in the morning."

Sir Reginald frowned, realizing they were putting him off.

"Sir Reginald," I said. "Lady Harwood and Elizabeth are tired. We shan't drag them to the magistrate's court at this hour. There is little we can do until morning."

He considered that, then exhaled. "Very well." He addressed the officers again. "We shall be at Bow Street at nine o'clock. I expect you both to meet me with a plan of action."

"As you say," Nettleton said, irritation hiding beneath a false smile.

Lady Harwood took Sir Reginald's arm despite his insistence that he was perfectly able, and Elizabeth hovered anxiously behind her parents as they moved toward the coach, as though her delicate frame would be any help if the man *did* decide to fall.

I did not immediately follow. Although I'd hopefully waylaid Lady Harwood's suspicions about my pursuit of the thief, she wasn't the only one I worried about. As soon as Nettleton's back was turned, I slipped the jacket from my shoulders. "Mr. Denning."

He started, likely forgetting I was there. His eyes focused on me. "Yes?"

I carefully straightened the arms of the jacket and held it out to him. "Thank you for this."

"Of course." He took it, laying it over one arm.

"Mr. Denning." I toyed with the fringe on my shawl. "Could you—that is, if it isn't too much trouble—would you please not tell anyone that I pursued the thief?" He faced me fully, curiosity hiding in the angles of his face. His distractingly handsome face. I tried to focus as I continued. "I truly never meant to *catch* the man. It was instinct alone that made me follow him. The Harwoods wouldn't like it, I am sure. And I daresay Society in general would not look kindly on me either."

He raised one eyebrow. "Are you asking a principal officer of Bow Street to lie, miss?"

I was taken aback. "No, not lie. Only, if you find no reason to mention it . . ."

It was then I realized he was teasing me. At least, I *thought* he was. The corner of his mouth twitched, and his eyes seemed to hold an amused glint.

Interesting.

He crossed his arms over his jacket. "And what of the pistol I saw you slip into your reticule? I imagine you wouldn't like anyone to know about that either."

My heart stuttered. He *had* seen it.

"Do you often carry a weapon to the theatre?" he asked. "Perhaps to ward off overeager suitors?"

He thought me foolish. Which I *was*, to be sure. But his opinion of me did not matter. I needed only his word that he wouldn't tell anyone.

"Please, sir. I would consider it a favor." I raised my chin. "And I do not owe those lightly."

Mr. Denning inspected me. "Very well. And what name should I assign to this secret?"

I *could* tell him my name now; Nettleton was not listening. And yet I hesitated. So rarely did I have this chance, this tempting anonymity. The Travers name was both famous and infamous. Was it so terrible of me not to want this man to immediately assume things about me because of my family?

"Verity!"

Elizabeth chose that very inopportune moment to call from the coach.

Mr. Denning raised one eyebrow. "Verity? An interesting name for someone determined to hide the truth."

Well, at least he did not know my surname. That was the one that mattered.

"I am sorry," I said, my voice a bit clipped. "I must go."

I began to move around him, but he took the smallest sideways step to stop me. "You'll come to Bow Street in the morning with the Harwoods?" he asked. "We will need your account of the theft."

"Of course." Elizabeth would want me there. And though they did not know it yet, Bow Street would need my help if they wanted a halfway decent description of the thief.

He nodded. "You know the address?"

Now I did smile, quite mischievously. "As it happens, I do. Good night, Mr. Denning."

I stepped into the coach with the help of the driver, then we started off, Lady Harwood fussing over Sir Reginald. I allowed myself the scantest look back.

Mr. Denning stood in the center of the street, hands in his pockets, his returned jacket draped over one arm as he watched us depart. Our eyes met, and he nodded. A farewell.

We turned a corner, and he vanished from my sight.

CHAPTER 3

Even with all the commotion of the robbery, I still managed to arrive home before Mama. It was fortunate—I wasn't prepared to answer the questions she would send my way.

My hands shook as I undressed, and I knew they did not shake from the cold. No. It was the familiar fear that crept in, an unwelcome visitor.

Why had I run after the man? Had I learned nothing? I'd behaved like the old Verity, who acted without thought. That Verity had learned hard lessons about risk and reward, and the difference between bravery and foolishness. They were not lessons I was keen to repeat.

I took a steadying breath. I knew I had to be more careful, but tonight could have ended much worse. We'd all lived, at least. And yes, the thief had gotten away, but that was the reality of life. Sometimes injustices could not be fixed.

If only injustice didn't burn in my chest like the whiskey I'd once "borrowed" from Jack's room, then had vowed never to drink again.

There was also the matter of Mr. Denning. Would he keep my secrets? I was inclined to believe he would. There had been something in his eyes there at the end . . .

A familiar urge tugged at me, and I knew myself well enough to realize I would not sleep until I'd put a pencil to paper. I climbed from bed and lit a candle, then sat at my desk, where my drawing supplies waited for me.

I should draw the thief. His face was fresh in my mind, and a sketch might prove useful to Bow Street. But here in the darkness of night, with the cold air wrapped around me, I had no desire to re-create the man who scowled at me from my memories.

Instead, I pictured Mr. Denning's deep-set eyes, the emotions caught in their depths, and my pencil roamed free. Within ten minutes, I set it down and inspected my sketch. Not perfect, yet there was a fascinating discernment in those eyes. It stirred within me a knowledge of this man that I had no reason to have.

Now I was being absurd. As Grandmama often said, "Logic leaves after midnight."

I returned to bed and closed my eyes. I settled into my breaths, into the comfort of the familiar, and I slept.

"Good morning, dear," Mama chirped when I entered the dining room the next morning. "You are up early."

She sat across from Grandmama at the table, a teacup perched near her mouth, her dark eyes taking me in. Grandmama did not acknowledge my entrance, fixated as she was on her porridge.

"I might say the same to you." I skipped the covered trays of food and moved straight for the tea. Little sleep and a heavy dose of Mama's dramatic energy never went well together. I loved my mother, but the woman could be downright exhausting, particularly early in the morning. Not to mention that my body ached from my collision with Mr. Denning last night. I needed fortifying.

Mama smiled. Somehow, even at eight o'clock in the morning, her hair was intricately arranged, her emerald-green morning dress perfectly pressed, and her cheeks and lips touched with rouge. One would never know she'd had even less sleep than I.

"I've an appointment with Mr. Webb," she said, naming the manager of the Theatre Royal. "The man keeps ungodly hours."

"As do actresses," I observed.

"Speaking of, did you enjoy the performance last night?" Mama tipped her head as I added an obscene amount of sugar to my tea.

How strange to think that even a decade ago, no one in London had known Mama's name. She'd spent the first half of my life touring with small country troupes, and it had been pure luck that the manager of the Theatre Royal had seen her perform in York and hired her on the spot. Mama's sudden rise to fame might have bothered some, but I was quite used to it. I had no desire for attention, which Mama could *not* account for, and I generally watched the results of Mama's success with passive amusement.

"Oh, it was most disappointing," I said, pretending sincerity. "No fainting ladies that I could see, and not one shouted proposal. What *will* the papers write about?"

Mama laughed. "You are wretched. Who raised you?"

I took a sip of my too-hot tea to hide a smile. "Only the triumph of Drury Lane."

Her eyes gleamed with amusement. "At least the news sheets have that correct."

My stomach soothed by the tea, I filled a plate with toast and jam. I sat beside my grandmother, kissing her softly on the cheek. "Good morning, Grandmama."

"Is it?" she grunted. "Perhaps you might not think so when your back aches as if you just brought in the harvest."

"You never did say why you are awake so early," Mama interrupted. "And after such a late night."

I avoided her eyes. I would tell Mama about the events of last night eventually—I'd never been good at keeping secrets from her; she always ferreted them out somehow—but now was not the time. She hadn't yet recovered from the incident in January, and there was no point in worrying her.

"I couldn't sleep," I said instead. "There was a bird outside my window."

"What kind of bird?" Grandmama interjected.

"A magpie," I improvised.

She stabbed her fork at me. "Was it alone? How many were there?"

It was always a gamble with Grandmama. One never knew what the right answer was, depending on the folklore she clung to.

"Two," I lied, taking another sip of my tea. "Yes, there were two."

Her eyes lit up. "How interesting."

"What is interesting?" Mama looked lazily amused.

"Two magpies denotes marriage." Grandmama eyed me closely. "You haven't been hiding a beau from us, have you, girl?"

I laughed. "Hardly."

She sniffed and turned back to her porridge. She did not like it when I poked fun at her superstitions. "Just be glad it wasn't one magpie."

I dared not ask why. Sometimes it was best to leave things be.

Mama sent me an appraising look over her tea, as if she knew something was not quite right with me. Thankfully, she left soon after, instructing me to keep an eye on Grandmama. It wasn't that Grandmama wasn't able—it was that she was *mischievous*. One never knew what sort of trouble she might get into. Just last week, she'd embroiled herself in a quarrel with a neighbor, something about a missing basket of biscuits.

I, however, had an appointment as well. I passed Mama's instructions on to our housekeeper, Pritchett, who knew well enough how to handle Grandmama, and at a quarter to nine o'clock, I slipped out of the house.

Bow Street was only a few minutes' walk from our home, a convenience Jack had enjoyed when he'd lived here. I sighed as I started down the street. Had it been only a year since he'd married and left London? I adored Genevieve, my sister-in-law, and heartily approved of Jack's choice. But if I'd known what a hole his absence might leave in our lives, I might not have been quite so eager in encouraging their romance.

Jack and I were two of the same. Though he was a few years older than I, we'd always been close. Mama was perpetually absent, working and touring, and our father . . .

Well, we did not often speak of our father, the Right Honorable Earl of Westincott. What was there to say about a man whose only continuing connection to me was financial obligation? But illegitimacy had had the unintended effect of bonding Jack and me together more than most brothers and sisters. The secrecy, the whispers, the story that our navy captain "father" had died twenty years ago. Who else could understand as well as Jack?

While his marriage was a good thing—a wonderful thing—it did not help the absence I felt in my heart.

I arrived at No. 4 Bow Street, the redbrick facade looming over me, just as the Harwoods' carriage came to a stop on the street. Elizabeth descended, looking pale and perhaps a little ill, but she approached with a smile. "Thank you for coming. It's a relief since you know so much more about all this than I do."

"Of course." I glanced at Sir Reginald helping Lady Harwood from the carriage. He had a white bandage wrapped around his head, mostly hidden by his topper. "Your father is well?"

She made a noise of annoyance. "Perfectly well. He's been snapping at Mother's fussing all morning."

"Miss Travers." Lady Harwood approached, looking around in some confusion. "Did you come alone?"

I quickly assumed a look of naive innocence. While Mama had spent years meticulously crafting her public persona—rejecting the stigma of a London actress by portraying herself as the loving mother, the grieving widow—*I* was far less concerned with my reputation. I had too much to do to bother with a chaperone.

And fortunately for me, with Mama perpetually absent because of performances or rehearsals, Grandmama had taken on the role of indifferent guardian, and she far preferred the comforts of home to trailing about London after me. But I had to tread carefully with Lady Harwood.

"Yes, most unfortunate," I said, sighing. "Mama had a meeting at the theatre, very important, not to be missed. And I live only a short walk from here."

I did not bother to add that I thought it ridiculous that a woman of my age—a sage, old twenty-one years—and my relatively low social status needed a constant chaperone. Neither did I explain that Covent Garden was one of the tamer locales I frequented.

Lady Harwood's brow dipped in disapproval, but she had no chance to protest as we followed Sir Reginald inside the Bow Street magistrate's court. I looked cautiously about. It was strangely quiet inside the main office, most of the officers undoubtedly out seeing to their individual cases.

"Ah, Mr. Nettleton," Sir Reginald proclaimed, spotting the hulking man across the office.

"Sir Reginald." Nettleton moved to greet us. "How is your head?"

"Fine, fine," Sir Reginald said brusquely. I had to stop a smile. Men. Heaven forbid they admit a weakness.

"Good." Nettleton waved forward. "If you'll come this way."

We followed him to an interview room off the main office. The others filed in, but I paused at the doorway. I had so many memories of this place. Bringing Jack lunch, laughing with the other officers, dreaming of one day being like them. At least, in my own way.

I swallowed hard. How easily things could change.

"Good morning."

I spun. Mr. Denning stood just behind me, and if I was not mistaken, there was a glint of amusement in his eyes at startling me. How had he? I was usually quite alert. I blamed my night of tossing and turning.

"I trust you are well this morning," he said, his gaze traveling my face. "Miss . . . ?"

I'd forgotten he still did not know my name. I could hardly avoid it forever, but a little intrigue never went amiss.

"Very well, Mr. Denning," I said, indifferent and aloof. "And 'miss' will do nicely, thank you."

He exhaled a short laugh and opened his mouth.

"Denning," Nettleton barked from inside the room, interrupting quite perfectly.

I offered Mr. Denning a polite smile and breezed through the doorway.

Mr. Denning followed me inside and closed the door. I sat beside Elizabeth but turned my attention to Nettleton.

"Thank you for coming." He sat behind the table and placed his hands flat on the surface. "I—"

"What news have you?" Sir Reginald interrupted.

Nettleton stopped. "News?"

"Of the thief," Sir Reginald said impatiently.

"Since last night?" Nettleton raised his brows. "We've not been so fortunate."

I understood his amusement. Short of the thief turning himself in, there were few developments that were possible in such a short amount of time.

Sir Reginald frowned. "But we *will* discuss our plan of action."

Mr. Denning leaned back against the closed door, crossing his arms as he observed the conversation, expression difficult to read.

It was only with curiosity that I eyed him, of course. Not with female interest, certainly, even if I noticed that his brown hair had a hint of auburn to it or that his crossed arms caused his waistcoat to stretch over his long and narrow chest.

"Yes, indeed." Nettleton cleared his throat. I wondered if he'd hoped we would not come at all. He consulted the notebook before him. "I daresay you are hoping to reclaim the goods that were stolen from you. A gold watch, cravat pin, a ruby necklace—"

"My reticule," Elizabeth cut in, sitting forward.

He glanced at her, irritated at the second interruption. "Was there anything of substantial value inside?"

She flushed but did not look away. "Well, no. But it was sentimental."

Nettleton gave a dismissive shake of his head. "We can try to track down your belongings through rewards and advertisements, focusing on the items of greatest value. Then—"

"I don't care about my cravat pin." Sir Reginald sat at the front of his chair, indignant. "I want to catch the man responsible."

Nettleton looked as if he wished to handcuff the next person who interrupted him. "Unfortunately," he said sharply, addressing us as though we were all unintelligent goats that had wandered into the magistrate's office, "we've limited resources, and—"

"Surely you cannot have more pressing cases than that of a violent madman attacking innocent people in plain sight." Sir Reginald seemed truly baffled as to why Nettleton was not falling over himself to solve this case. "We were all nearly murdered last night. Such despicable thieves should not be allowed to freely wander the streets."

Nettleton glared back, taking offense where it was likely quite intended. Mr. Denning pushed himself away from the door and moved toward the table.

"Of course, Sir Reginald," he said. "We have no intention of doing nothing."

His voice was so perfectly calm and steady that Sir Reginald was caught off guard, his mouth parted.

"However," Mr. Denning went on, "there are certain obstacles in this case that make it more challenging."

"What sort of obstacles?" Lady Harwood spoke for the first time, clutching her reticule in her lap. "What is so challenging about finding a common thief?"

Mr. Denning paused as if to gather his thoughts, and I understood. Investigating a crime was never as straightforward as the wronged parties wished it to be.

"Lady Harwood, Sir Reginald," I said soothingly, thinking they might understand better if it came from me. "The difficulty is that the thief *was* common. In a robbery such as last night's, it is hard to even know where to begin. We have very few clues, and he might have left Town, for all we know."

Everyone turned to me with varying expressions of surprise and disbelief. Oh no. I'd meant to explain, to clarify, but instead, I'd made myself an object of curiosity to these acquaintances who hardly knew me. Well, save for Elizabeth, whose eyes were wide and slightly alarmed. She, at least, knew some of my history.

I coughed, hoping she would keep quiet. Her parents need not know that I'd spent many of my formative years engaged in helping Jack with his cases—and taking on a few of my own.

"That is to say," I amended, "we should be thankful for any help the officers might give us in locating our stolen things."

Sir Reginald did not seem satisfied in the least. "Is it not your duty to pursue such criminals?" he demanded of the two men. "No matter the difficulties?"

Nettleton stood, thick knuckles braced on the table. "Our duty is to pursue what the magistrates and the chief officer assign us to pursue. We've more cases than you can imagine and little time to waste on such as this."

He left something to be desired in his manners, but let it not be said that Nettleton was cowed by a title.

"A magistrate." Sir Reginald latched onto the word. "I demand to speak to a magistrate."

Nettleton's eyes burned, but Mr. Denning looked unfazed. "Yes, certainly," Mr. Denning said pleasantly. "Mr. Etchells just arrived for morning hearings. I am sure he'll have a few moments."

"I'll fetch him," Nettleton muttered under his breath, no doubt grateful for any chance to escape. He gathered his papers and stomped from the room.

"While we wait," Mr. Denning said, fixing his gaze on me, "perhaps I might interview the young miss? We did not have the chance last evening."

Lady Harwood waved her hand absently, turning to speak to Sir Reginald in a whisper, their faces tense. Though I understood Nettleton's reluctance to take on the case, neither could I blame Lady Harwood or Sir Reginald for their reactions. I'd been there last night as well. I'd felt the cold cut of fear as the thief had watched us with those hardened eyes, finger light on the trigger. Death had been a moment away.

"Miss?"

I tore my eyes from Lady Harwood. Mr. Denning waited expectantly at the door.

I stood and followed him to the main office. He gestured for me to sit at a small desk, and I did, clasping my hands in my lap and trying to look like a genteel young lady who would never touch a pistol, let alone carry one on her person. Appearances were everything, after all, and people were quick to believe what they wished to believe. If Mr. Denning was like most men, he would be keen to put me back inside the box labeled "Proper Miss."

I would let him. Better to be underestimated.

I looked up at him, still standing on the other side of the desk. His eyes were fixed upon me, his irises a dark brown that brought to mind a collection of manly things—stained mahogany desks, a bottle of aged scotch, worn leather saddles. It made me wish to dabble more in paints so I might try to capture the exact color.

"What would you like to know?" I asked, straightening.

He prepared paper and ink to record my answers. "A great many things, but perhaps we might start with your recollection of the theft."

As he sat, a middle-aged gentleman strode by, bespectacled and distinguished. Mr. Etchells, no doubt. He seemed not to notice us, absently smoothing his waistcoat before he entered the room where the Harwoods waited. I could hear the murmur of voices inside before the door closed. Perhaps if I hurried this interview, I could return to listen in.

"Very well," I said, facing Mr. Denning again. "I daresay my account is similar to the others'. We were leaving the theatre and walking to our carriage when the thief stopped us with his pistol and demanded our valuables. I thought of calling for help, but the risk seemed too great."

"Did you consider using *your* pistol?" He spoke indifferently, but the way his pen hovered over the paper made me think him quite the opposite.

"No, of course not." I refused to be embarrassed. "It wasn't loaded. Besides, I assumed he would leave us be once he had our goods. A pair of earrings is not worth one's life."

"A proverb to live by," he said dryly as he scratched away at the paper. "What happened next?"

I eyed him. Had that been a joke? "After he took our valuables, he struck Sir Reginald with his pistol and ran. I instructed Elizabeth to go for help and told Lady Harwood how to tend the wound. Then, as you know, I followed after the thief."

"Indeed," he said, still writing. "And did you get a good look at the man?"

This was where I was eager to help. I knew it was a near impossibility for Bow Street to track the thief down, but an accurate description would at least give them a chance.

"Yes." I sat forward in my chair. "He had a weathered face, like a sailor or coach driver. Someone who spends much of his time out of doors. I would place him in his middle thirties. He wore a large hat, so I cannot guess at his hair color, but he had a rather prominent nose. Large and bulging. And a thin neck. Surprising, with the weight of that nose. And his eyes—" My voice cut out. Mr. Denning had stopped writing and was staring at me. I pulled my chin back. "I am sorry. Was I speaking too quickly?"

He shook his head, sitting back in his chair as he inspected me. "No. I simply don't know if I've ever heard such a detailed description of a criminal."

My cheeks warmed, though I wasn't embarrassed. Was I pleased, then? That seemed odd, considering the strangeness of his compliment—if it *was* a compliment.

"I am observant, that is all," I said.

I'd allowed the comings and goings of Bow Street to fade during our conversation, but now my ears picked out a familiar voice from behind me.

"As I live and breathe. Can it be little Verity Travers?"

CHAPTER 4

I twisted in my chair. Coming in the front doors were two men, one tall with broad lines, the other shorter but built heavy like a blacksmith.

A smile burst onto my lips. "Little?" I repeated loftily as I stood. "I am nearly five and a half feet, Mr. Drake. And perfectly able to fetch a ladder should I need anything on a high shelf."

As they stopped beside us, Drake laughed that contagious burst that always lifted my spirits. "A ladder, indeed."

Drake had been Jack's friend while in the army, and the two had come over to Bow Street together a few years ago. It had been months since I'd seen him, and I'd missed the great bear of a man. I beamed at him, then turned to his taller companion. "Mr. Rawlings. So good to see you again."

Rawlings nodded in greeting. He'd always been the darker, grumpier foil to Drake's cheerfulness, but if I looked closely, I thought I saw a hint of gladness to see me in his eyes. "Miss Travers."

Jack and Drake had met Rawlings at Bow Street, the two more sociable men forcing the reticent officer to accept their heavy-handed overtures of friendship. I'd once fancied the dark and handsome Rawlings as a girl, taken in by his slight Scottish brogue, but it had lasted only as long as it had taken me to realize that brooding, silent gentlemen were not the thing for me, even if the romance novels favored them.

A chair scraped behind us, and I turned to find Mr. Denning standing, staring at me. "Travers?" he repeated. "As in Jack Travers?"

I'd forgotten my little ruse. All the euphoria I'd felt at seeing Jack's old friends withered away.

"The very one," Drake said brightly.

"He's my brother," I supplied, attempting to keep my voice steady. It had been over two years since Jack had been dismissed from Bow Street, but it appeared the stories would persist far longer than that. Every Bow Street officer knew what had happened to him. Jack had been investigating the murder of a Society lady and, based on the evidence he'd had, had accused the woman's betrothed. Falsely accused, as it turned out. When the true murderer came to light, Jack had been dismissed by the magistrates.

"Your brother is Jack Travers," Mr. Denning repeated in disbelief. I could not help but try to read the thoughts behind his eyes. Opinions about Jack varied greatly among the men of Bow Street.

"Aye," Rawlings said in that deep, rolling accent of his as he removed his worn leather gloves. "And her mother is Trinity Travers."

I shot him a sharp look. He merely shrugged, as if to say, *Better to have it over and done with.*

"The actress?" Mr. Denning drew back his chin.

"Yes, Verity is the epitome of well-connected," Drake said, plopping down on a nearby chair.

"Unless one counts you lot," I said.

"Oh, we count double." Drake flashed a grin. "How long has it been since we last saw you? Blast, if it hasn't been months. Since Jack went and chained himself to a wife."

He was right. In the past, Drake and Rawlings and many of the other officers had been frequent visitors to our home for dinners and parties. With Jack gone, those evenings had fallen by the wayside, Mama busy at the theatre and me with my own ambitions.

"A lovely wife," I admonished him. "Something you might consider for yourself before you end up a lonely curmudgeon."

"He's already a lonely curmudgeon," Rawlings said, face buried in his newspaper.

"Oh, pull a punch every now and again, Rawlings." Drake sounded unruffled.

I shook my head with a laugh as I took my seat, but I found myself glancing again at Mr. Denning. Would he be angry that I'd hidden my name and family from him?

He eyed me with something new in his expression—but not what I'd expected. Sometimes I saw fascination or calculated interest when a person learned who my mother was. Sometimes I saw judgment when they knew my connection to Jack.

But Mr. Denning's eyes held none of those. No, it was wariness that filled his expression.

Drake nodded at Mr. Denning with a grin. "I see you've met Sir Chivalry."

"Sir Chivalry?" I echoed.

"Oh yes," Drake went on. "You see, the ladies are quite keen on Denning here, and—"

"It's only an unearned nickname," Mr. Denning interrupted. Was that a touch of pink on his cheeks?

"What brings you to Bow Street?" Rawlings asked me, ignoring Drake's nonsense.

"What brings anyone to Bow Street?" I said. "I'm reporting a crime."

"Truly?" Drake leaned forward. "What crime?"

Mr. Denning spoke for me. "Miss Travers and her companions were leaving the Theatre Royal yesterday evening when they were robbed. The thief escaped."

Drake's carefree expression vanished in an instant, and Rawlings's eyes sharpened as he set down his newspaper.

"Any leads?" Drake asked, his voice serious.

It shouldn't have surprised me how easily they switched from pleasant conversation to serious questioning. I'd known them for years, after all. But while Drake could be a bit outrageous, and Rawlings was still something of a stormy enigma, they were both talented investigators and dedicated officers. Duty came before all else.

"We don't—" I said at the same moment Mr. Denning said, "No, it—"

We both stopped.

He waved for me to continue, and I nodded. "We don't have anything substantial. I was just giving Mr. Denning my description of the criminal in the hopes it might help."

"What of the stolen items?" Rawlings asked. "Perhaps they'll be fenced and we can track them back to the thief."

"I'd considered that," Mr. Denning said. "But Nettleton doesn't seem particularly intent on following this case through."

Drake made a noise of disapproval. "Nettleton *never* wants to follow a case through. He prefers his suspects to surrender of their own free will. Less work, you see."

Mr. Denning shook his head. "I hate to agree with Nettleton, believe me, but this case does seem a needle in a haystack. At best, we would apprehend a street thief, of which there is no shortage in London. At worst, we waste time that could be applied to more serious cases."

I sighed. "I'm afraid Sir Reginald believes differently. His pride was quite wounded."

As though summoned by my words, Sir Reginald stepped out of the interview room behind us, followed by Mr. Etchells.

"Denning," the magistrate said, moving toward us. "There you are."

Mr. Denning straightened, more than a little apprehensive. "Yes, sir?"

"After speaking with Sir Reginald," Mr. Etchells said, "I am convinced of the need to track down this thief. Considering his attack on the baronet, the criminal seems bent on violence, and we cannot allow it."

Sir Reginald nodded in agreement, looking far more satisfied than when we'd left him.

"He also insisted," Mr. Etchells went on, "that *you* be the one to take the case."

Mr. Denning's jaw dropped. "Me, sir?"

"Yes," Sir Reginald cut in. "You've proven yourself willing and able, unlike *some*." He cast a disparaging glance behind him and seemed disappointed not to see Nettleton.

Mr. Denning shook his head. "But I am already handling the Winters robbery."

My ears perked up. I'd read about that theft in the *Hue and Cry*. A valuable Greek vase had been stolen from a home in Mayfair, with no sign of a break-in.

Drake stepped forward. "Mr. Etchells, I would be happy to take this case on."

Yes, that would be ideal. Drake was an excellent investigator. Sir Reginald could hardly complain.

"Not only am I already acquainted with Miss Travers here," Drake said, gesturing to me, "but I—"

"Travers?" Mr. Etchells seemed to notice me for the first time.

My stomach sank. He wore the same bewildered expression that Mr. Denning had sported just a few minutes earlier. Mr. Etchells might be new to Bow Street, but of course he knew the name. Everyone knew it.

Mr. Etchells shot Rawlings a look, and Rawlings nodded, confirming the magistrate's suspicions. I was Jack Travers's relation. Mr. Etchells considered that as he glanced between Drake and me. "No," he finally said. "Denning will take it."

I blew out a breath. His reasons were obvious. I was a Travers, which equated to *trouble*. Drake was clearly connected to me, and to Jack, which could compromise the case.

Mr. Denning was not ready to give in. "Sir," he said, stepping forward, "what of Nettleton? He knows the details of the case as well as I do, and—"

Sir Reginald made a noise, but Mr. Etchells spoke first. "No," he said firmly. "Nettleton has other duties. Denning, you are to give your full focus to this case, and Drake will take over the Winters investigation."

Mr. Denning looked about to protest yet again, but then he pressed his lips together and offered a curt nod. "Yes, sir."

I felt for the man. To be taken off such an important case and assigned to our paltry street robbery was akin to riding an purebred Arabian, then trading it in for a donkey. Ours was not the sort of case that propelled a man's career forward. It was the sort of case that drowned a man in useless interviews, false leads, and wasted hours.

But the magistrate's hands were tied. Sir Reginald was wealthy, powerful, and well-connected. This was simply how the game was played.

Mr. Etchells looked sympathetic. "Sir Reginald has offered a reward," he said as reparation.

"Yes," Sir Reginald said. "Fifty pounds for the capture of the thief."

Fifty pounds? *Fifty pounds?*

Mr. Denning blinked, and I swore I could see the immediate calculations in his mind. A Bow Street officer was paid a weekly salary, but it was not nearly enough to live on. They often took on private work to supplement their income. But fifty pounds? It was almost absurd. Heavens, for fifty pounds, even I would—

No. No, I wouldn't.

"A generous offer." Mr. Denning sent a glance at me, though he looked away in the next instant.

"See that you make every effort," Sir Reginald instructed. "I am determined that this man be punished to the full extent of the law."

"I will do all I can, sir," Mr. Denning said, resigned to his fate.

Sir Reginald nodded and, seeming to think his business finished, started for the door.

"Sir Reginald." Mr. Denning moved to intercept him. "I am sorry to take any more of your time, but I shall need to interview you all and record detailed descriptions of each stolen item."

Sir Reginald sighed. "Yes, very well."

He followed Mr. Denning back inside the interview room. Mr. Etchells disappeared almost as quickly, no doubt to begin his morning hearings.

I turned to Drake and Rawlings with a grimace. "I see Jack's reputation hasn't changed much."

"Hogwash, is what it is," Drake muttered. "Jack didn't do anything the rest of us haven't done before. As if any investigation is perfect."

Rawlings shook his head. "Etchells doesn't mean anything by it, lass. He has no ill will toward Jack or you. He is only being careful."

My hands tightened into fists. No doubt the account was whispered as a warning to new officers eager to prove themselves. Never mind that it could have been anyone. Never mind that the magistrates in power then had never liked Jack. Never mind that the man he'd accused was smarmy, horrible, and rich—and had been the one to insist upon Jack's dismissal.

Many officers, like Nettleton, believed it to be a just decision, that Jack had gotten what he'd deserved. Others—Drake and Rawlings included—held that the punishment far exceeded the mistake.

I couldn't help but wonder to which camp Mr. Denning belonged. "And if it's not Etchells I'm worried about?" I murmured.

Rawlings seemed to read my thoughts. "He's a good man, Denning," he said in a gruff voice. "He'll not hold it against you."

"Unlike Nettleton," Drake said sourly.

"How long has Mr. Denning been at Bow Street?" I asked, curious. "I don't remember him."

"Only a few months," Rawlings confirmed. "Just promoted from the patrols."

"You needn't worry," Drake told me. "Sir Chivalry is sharp—and eager. He'll do well enough."

I shot him a querying look. "Why 'Sir Chivalry'? You aren't torturing the poor man, are you?"

Drake grinned. "He won't be poor if he can manage to track down that thief of yours." He propped his feet on the corner of a desk. "And you'll have to ask him about the nickname. The story is *extremely* amusing."

"I sincerely doubt I will have the opportunity," I said dryly. "I do not plan on involving myself in the case more than necessary."

Drake rubbed his hands together. "I recall you being a great help to Jack with his cases before he left. You could wrap this up quicker than Denning if you put your mind to it."

My breath caught in my lungs, sharp and painful. I'd never been more grateful that I hadn't told them about my aspirations, wanting to prove myself a success before declaring my dreams. They didn't know about my failure.

"No," I said quickly. "I am certain he will do well enough."

"But you'll come to us if anything is amiss," Rawlings said, more an order than a question.

I nodded. "Of course."

With a small wave, I reentered the interview room. Mr. Denning glanced up, his eyes following me as I seated myself beside Elizabeth. He finally looked away, asking Lady Harwood a question, and I was grateful. I didn't like guessing what went on behind those eyes now that he knew who I was. Elizabeth offered me a wan smile, waiting her turn to be questioned.

I, however, had a task of my own to complete.

As Lady Harwood detailed the size and number of the rubies on her necklace, I slipped a piece of paper from the table and settled back in my chair. I retrieved the stub of a pencil in my reticule, and I began sketching. I had an excellent memory, but more than that, I had a special knack for remembering *faces*. For as long as I could remember, I'd been able to recall with perfect clarity any face I'd seen, no matter how briefly. My sketchbooks were packed full of my family, friends, acquaintances, people I'd passed on the street.

I was lost in my drawing for nearly a quarter of an hour while Mr. Denning conducted his interviews with the others. When I finished, I quickly scribbled a few sentences on the back of my sketch. After Elizabeth finished recounting her stolen belongings, Mr. Denning turned to me.

"Miss Travers?" he asked politely. "Have you anything to add to the list of stolen items?"

"Just a pair of earrings," I said. "I've written a description for you." I placed my paper on the table so that my sketch was down, my writing facing up. Better to let Mr. Denning find the drawing after we left. I'd already brought enough unwanted attention to myself today.

Mr. Denning furrowed his brow, but there was no chance for argument. Sir Reginald was already standing, assisting Lady Harwood to her feet. I followed as Mr. Denning escorted them to the front entrance.

"I should like to be informed of any progress you make," Sir Reginald said sternly to Mr. Denning. "Any development, no matter how small, I want to know of it."

"Of course," Mr. Denning said, though he couldn't be excited at the prospect of traipsing to Mayfair with every new bit of information. But for fifty pounds, I imagined Mr. Denning would be more than willing to swallow his protests.

Lady Harwood and Elizabeth trailed Sir Reginald outside. I paused beside Mr. Denning in the antechamber, tying my bonnet ribbons in a neat bow under my chin. He watched me, arms crossed.

"I have learned my lesson, Miss Travers," he said, putting a slight emphasis on my name. "The next time I collide with a young lady on the street, I will immediately insist upon learning her name."

He did not seem angry, at least. "I am sorry to have deceived you," I said. "It is only that I have learned to be cautious. Names have power, and mine has more than most."

The rough edge of his expression began to soften, though his crossed arms remained tight against his chest, and his eyes still held that new guardedness.

"I do not feel deceived," he said. "Though perhaps a little foolish."

"Not because of Drake, I hope."

He gave a short laugh. "No, I can handle the likes of him. It is pretty young women with famous names I cannot keep up with."

"Pretty?" I put one hand on my waist. "Sir Chivalry, indeed." I hadn't pegged him as a flirt, but a man had to earn the nickname somehow.

His brow dropped. "I am not particularly fond of that appellation, Miss Travers."

"A shame," I said. "It's quite catching."

He shook his head, though his lips seemed to fight a smile.

I took a step past him. "You needn't bother searching for my earrings. Focus on the Harwoods' goods."

"You don't want your earrings back?"

I shrugged one shoulder. "I am not terribly attached to them."

"Still," he said. "There is no information too small. One never knows what will provide a lead."

"True enough," I agreed. "My brother Jack often said—" I stopped. I still did not know what this man thought of Jack, and I wasn't at all ready to open that line of discussion. "That is, I certainly agree."

We stood in an awkward, drawn-out silence until I gathered myself together and moved toward the front door. "Best of luck, Mr. Denning. I daresay you will need it."

"I shall take your luck, Miss Travers," he said after me. "And I will find your stolen earrings, whether you care for them or not."

There was such a surety to his deep voice, such a masculine confidence, that I almost believed him. My stomach took a tumble.

I immediately brushed it off. Ridiculous to get worked up over a man I hardly knew. Even if he *did* have a sharp wit—and an even sharper jaw. But it wouldn't do to form an attachment.

I knew better.

CHAPTER 5

"Sugar and cream?" Elizabeth paused as she prepared my tea, glancing to where I stood beside the parlor window.

I'd been drawn to the window immediately upon entering the room. Harwood House was right in the center of Mayfair, and their street bustled with strolling ladies and gentlemen, governesses scolding naughty children, and servants about their tasks. It was the sort of busyness one could watch quite contentedly for hours, imagining the possible stories behind each and every face.

I turned to Elizabeth with a grin. "As much sugar as you'll allow me without seeming greedy. I'm afraid I've a terrible weakness."

"One mustn't do anything halfway." She returned my smile, but it left her face quickly.

I sat next to her on the sofa, watching her as she added a small mountain of sugar to my teacup. Elizabeth was acting odd. As soon as we'd left Bow Street, she'd invited me for tea. I'd gladly accepted, hoping to distract her from the trauma she'd endured the night before. But it was proving to be a difficult task. She'd been unnervingly quiet during the carriage ride, and since we'd arrived—Lady Harwood claiming a headache and taking herself away to lie down—Elizabeth still had not spoken more than a dozen words. She was jumpy and distracted. It *could* be that she was still suffering ill effects from the robbery. But I did not think it was so, and my instincts were rarely wrong about such matters.

Elizabeth handed me my teacup, and I sipped it, eyeing her over the top. She focused entirely on preparing her own cup, pouring the tea with such delicate precision that one might think it was a task of vast importance.

I set my cup on the saucer. "Elizabeth," I said quietly. "Are you quite all right?"

Her eyes leaped to mine. "Of course." She paused. "Well, I am still shaken, to be sure, but I imagine I will be well soon enough."

"You only seem . . ." My voice drifted as I tried to find the right word. "I wonder if there is something else bothering you."

Her hands gripped the teapot tightly, and she sat without moving for a long moment. Finally, she set it back down on the tray. Leaving her poured tea untouched, she clasped her hands in her lap. "You are right," she said quietly. "Verity, I have not been honest with you."

Concern grew inside me. Elizabeth had always been so carefree and light. What was it that burdened her now?

She finally lifted her eyes to meet mine. "Verity, I need to hire you."

I stared. "Hire me?"

"Yes," she said, suddenly looking uncertain. "You are still taking cases, are you not?"

I was at a loss for words. I had not expected this in the slightest.

Elizabeth was one of the few people who knew I'd been involved in Jack's thief-taking business he'd started after the fiasco at Bow Street. She also knew that upon his leaving London after his marriage, I'd struck out on my own. I had a knack for it. Besides my excellent memory, I also had a boundless determination and a network of contacts, thanks to my work with Jack.

It had certainly helped that it was still my task to collect and sort Jack's mail, sending him what I deemed important. I knew he would never notice if I helped myself to a case every now and again. Just the ones I could handle, of course. A stolen horse, a dishonest maid, the like. I mostly took female clients because they were far less inclined to make a fuss when they learned I was also a woman. In the few months I'd worked on my own, I'd managed to close a modest amount of cases.

All for a price, naturally. I couldn't work for free. Not when I had very clear dreams of escaping the *patronage* of my father. A man who paid for everything in my life—my home, my schooling, my clothes— and yet knew nothing about me.

Because what earl took any interest in an illegitimate daughter who had no aspirations of a good marriage?

In any case, when I'd begun this venture, I'd been sure of myself. I'd been full of that reckless spontaneity that only inexperience and youth seemed to inspire. Of course I would make a name for myself. I would build my clientele until I earned a decent living. I wouldn't have to depend on anyone, not Jack or Mama or my absent father.

Oh, how that confidence had fallen, a brick wall built with cracked and crumbling mortar.

I looked at Elizabeth, my lungs tight. "No," I managed. "No, I'm no longer taking cases."

Her expression slowly changed from one of hope to surprise. "But why?"

She knew so much about me, but not this. She'd been traveling when the incident had occurred, and I had little desire to tell her now.

I countered with a question of my own. "Why do you want to hire me? Mr. Denning seems competent enough. I've no doubt he'll make a valiant effort to find the thief—"

"I do not care about the thief," she interrupted. "I care about the contents of my reticule."

My brows knit together as I ran through my memories of the last day and night. How Elizabeth had fought to keep her reticule even when the thief had trained his pistol on her. How she'd insisted that Nettleton include her reticule on the list of stolen goods.

"Elizabeth, what was in your reticule?" I asked. She'd told the officers it was of sentimental value only, but Elizabeth's reaction now seemed far beyond that.

She hesitated. "A letter," she said finally.

"What sort of letter?"

"I—I cannot say."

I squinted. "Whom was it from?"

She closed her eyes. "Oh, Verity," she whispered. "I truly cannot tell you that."

I sat in bewildered silence, trying to understand. Elizabeth wished for me to find her stolen reticule that held a mysterious letter, the contents of which were secret. It all pointed to the letter containing something of an illicit nature. But Elizabeth was all that was upstanding and proper and good.

What was in that letter?

I wanted nothing more than to pry an answer out of her, but I tried another line of questioning instead. "Am I to understand you do not wish your parents to know about this? Is that why you did not tell the Runners?"

She nodded fervently. "Mother and Father cannot know. They *cannot.*"

I exhaled a long breath. "Elizabeth, all of this is beyond the point. I haven't taken a case in months. I've—I've moved on."

Elizabeth shook her head. "I don't understand. Before I left to travel with my aunt, it was all you spoke about. You loved your work."

"I did," I admitted, my heart taking a beating at her words. "But things change. Faster than we can ever anticipate."

She bit her lip, eyes glistening. "There is more truth in that than you know."

We looked at each other, silence stretching between us. What was she not telling me?

"Please, Verity," she whispered. "I cannot share what is in that letter, but I can tell you that it would destroy me. If someone were to find it and realize its significance, I would never recover."

"Your name is on it?" My natural curiosity took control of my tongue.

She nodded guiltily.

"Why on earth were you carrying such a letter to the theatre, of all places?" I rubbed my forehead. I didn't often get headaches, but if anything could cause one, it would be the events of the last twenty-four hours.

Elizabeth sighed. "I was reading it in my room last night before we left. Mother came in unexpectedly, and I was forced to hide it in my reticule. I never imagined I would not come home with that letter."

A sudden knock came at the door, and a maid popped her head inside. "Miss? Do you have a moment?"

Elizabeth sat up, forcing a pleasant smile. "Yes, do come in, Marianne."

The maid stepped inside. She was pretty and slight, her honey-colored hair neatly pulled back. I guessed her to be a few years older than Elizabeth and me.

She bobbed a curtsy. "Begging your pardon, miss, but Lady Harwood says your new dress has arrived, and she wishes you to come see it."

"Oh." Elizabeth looked a bit startled, as though new dresses and insistent mothers were part of a different world from the one she currently occupied.

I tried to cover for her. "You are Elizabeth's abigail, are you not?"

Marianne's eyes lifted to mine, surprised. It was a common enough reaction. Most women of status refused to acknowledge servants even in their own houses. But I was far from a woman of status, and besides, a little kindness went a long way.

"Yes, Miss Travers," she said. "It is a pleasure to meet you. Miss Harwood speaks of you often."

"I imagine as the center of her better stories," I said. "We had a jolly time of it at school."

"Indeed, we did." Elizabeth managed a smile, a halfhearted affair. "Marianne, please tell Mother I will come up after my tea with Miss Travers. Thank you."

Marianne curtsied and left.

Elizabeth turned once again to me, her eyes filled with desperation. My polite smile faded, and the soberness of our conversation returned like an evening fog.

"Please, Verity," she said quietly. "I need your help. Even if the Runners find my reticule, they might see the letter and inform my parents. It must be you who finds it. Please, help me."

Help me. The words echoed in my head like church bells. But I had to refuse. I'd learned my lesson, hadn't I?

And yet . . .

Elizabeth had no interest in finding the thief. I simply had to find her reticule and the letter. I'd done it before, located stolen items. I could do it again. Still . . .

"The thief likely discarded your reticule," I said, my last-ditch effort. "And the letter."

"I cannot take that chance," Elizabeth said, weariness claiming her voice. Had she slept at all last night? "I'll pay you anything you like. Please."

Did she think my hesitation was based on payment?

I exhaled, wrapping her cool hands in both of mine. She clutched onto me, and I felt the weight of her fears like a physical thing. And it was decided. I couldn't let her face this alone—whatever *this* was.

"You needn't pay me a penny," I told her firmly. "I'll help."

She stilled, then exhaled a relieved sigh. "Oh, thank you, Verity. You cannot know how grateful I am."

"You may pay me in sugar and gossip," I said, pretending an optimism neither of us felt. "The two most valuable currencies, as everyone knows."

She nodded, sporting a weak smile. "Indeed."

She excused herself to find a handkerchief for her watery eyes and left me alone in the parlor. I sat still, back straight and heart thumping.

Was I truly going to do this? Delve back into that world that had nearly swallowed me whole?

I had to. For Elizabeth, one of the few true friends I had.

It was just one case, I told myself. Simple. Straightforward. If I felt it grabbing ahold of me, clawing at me, this time, I would know when to abandon ship.

With experience came wisdom.

I hoped.

CHAPTER 6

The next morning, I set out, determined to put my plan into action. It was two-pronged, as any worthwhile plan was. First: question my network of contacts to see if they knew my thief. Second: search the nearby pawnbrokers for the stolen valuables.

During my time working alongside Jack, I'd made dozens of connections among those in London's less . . . respectable professions. First on my list to question: the "incomparable" Wily Greaves.

Not that I called him that, of course. That was how he'd described himself the last time I'd seen him.

I had no address for him, and neither would he have ever given me one. But that was hardly a challenge. Within two hours, I was promenading through Hyde Park, looking for all the world like a young miss out to impress the *ton*. But my eyes were keen, inspecting all the paths that branched from mine. It would need to be a relatively private spot but public enough to make all the parties comfortable.

A flash of crimson. There. Not a dozen yards away, a man in a bright-red jacket strolled down a walking path that crossed into a small grove of trees. I followed after him.

I trailed him for a minute or two, watching to ensure he was alone. He wouldn't be pleased if I interrupted a meeting with clients. Just as I decided the time was right, he rounded a curve in the path behind a stand of trees. I hurried to catch him, reached the curve, and—

He was gone.

I stopped short. Where had he gone? My eyes darted about. There weren't *that* many trees, yet he'd vanished like a drop of water on a hot day.

"Dare I hope you were looking for me?"

My mouth twisted into a lopsided grin as I turned to face the man now standing on the path behind me, hands stuck in his pockets, mischievous eyes twinkling.

"One would have to be blind *not* to spot you," I said. "Really, Wily, could you have a more conspicuous wardrobe?"

Wily snorted, straightening his jacket over the green-checked waistcoat he wore, both perfectly tailored to suit his wiry frame, though they'd been patched several times over. "Conspicuous? Surely you mean dapper."

"Certainly," I said dryly. "Dapper."

He gave a little bow. "You are too kind, Miss Travers." Then he squinted at me as if realizing something. "Now, then, how did you find me? I make it a point not to be findable."

"I do not think that is a word," I pointed out.

He waved that off. "I'm a fence, not a wordsmith. But apparently not a very good fence if just anyone can track me down."

"I am not just anyone," I countered. "I went to that tea shop you favor and asked around for you. A kind gentleman with truly terrible breath pointed me in the direction of your rented rooms. When the landlady tried to frighten me off, a few coins loosened her tongue, and she happened to recall you had a meeting today in the park." I spread my hands wide. "And here we are. All in a day's work."

Wily whistled. "Well, don't you rule the roost. I will, of course, be changing rooms immediately."

My grin grew wider. Wily was a scoundrel of the first order, but I liked him.

"Now," he said, clapping his hands together. "I do have a client arriving any minute, and I doubt you went through all the trouble of tracking me down for a bit of prittle-prattle."

I almost asked who his client was, then decided it was best if I did not know. Working with those of Wily's profession was a necessity when pursuing criminals, but a lady could pretend some ignorance.

I quickly explained about the theft two evenings previous and about my need to locate Elizabeth's reticule with the letter inside, though I omitted her name. He listened with a furrowed brow, foot tapping incessantly as I described the stolen items.

"Have you come across any of them?" I asked hopefully. Wily was rather a good fence. If anyone were trying to sell the Harwoods' things, he would likely know about it.

"No," he said, "but with loot such as that, I'm not surprised the thief hasn't spouted them yet. Likely waiting for his trail to cool."

"I thought the same thing," I said. "And I doubt the thief would bother to sell the reticule."

"Right," he said. "If it's the letter you need, then you'll have to find the thief. Assuming he hasn't ditched it by now."

I sighed. "That would certainly solve all my problems, but I must be sure." I opened my own reticule and pulled out the folded drawing I'd worked on the night before, re-creating the image I'd given Mr. Denning to use. I held it out to Wily. "Do you recognize him?"

He sent me a scandalized look. "You know me better than that, Miss Travers. If I start snitching, no one will trust me with their business."

I gave a short laugh. "Believe you me, this man is far beneath the notice of your associates."

He looked unconvinced but took the paper and inspected it. He shook his head. "Never seen him. Even if I had—"

"I know, I know." I held up one hand. "But it might interest you to know there is a reward of fifty pounds for the capture of the thief."

Wily's eyes sharpened. Ah, money. The true way to a fence's heart.

"You don't say," he said, studying the sketch a little closer.

I tugged it back. "A reward that I would happily split with you if you were to prove helpful."

"I'm always helpful," he said with a waggle of his eyebrows.

I hid a laugh as I folded the sketch and placed it back in my reticule. "So, you'll ask around?"

He huffed. "Ask around. As if it's that simple."

I cast my eyes to the clouds above. "It never is with you."

He winked as he tipped his hat, a sorry-looking black topper. "Give me a few days," he said. "I'll see what I can find."

The bell above the door jingled as I entered the pawnbroker's shop. My nose wrinkled immediately. This one smelled even worse than the last, which was perplexing. The shelves of the crowded shop teetered with items—broken lamps, hat boxes, walking sticks, clocks, dusty portraits—but nothing that ought to smell like something had died.

I'd visited a few other contacts in the area after Wily, including Tommy Rutkins, the butcher who collected Jack's mail. But no one had any leads for me, either about the stolen goods or the face of the suspect I'd sketched. So I'd set my mind to searching the nearby pawnshops. It was quite as boring as it sounded, and this being my fourth shop, I was quickly wearying of the task.

A low counter ran along the back of the shop, displaying a variety of jewelry, snuff boxes, and silverware. A man with wild side whiskers and a thick neck stood behind it, polishing a gilded hand mirror with a cloth. He eyed me suspiciously as I approached.

"Can I help you, miss?" he asked as he took me in. I'd worn my plainest dress, a simple straw bonnet, and no jewelry, but even if I looked like a tradesman's daughter, generally tradesmen's daughters did not frequent pawnbrokers.

Which was why I had not come unprepared. I pushed away my weariness and forced a smile to my face. "Oh, I do hope so." I pitched my voice a touch higher than usual and added a dose of desperation. "I've lost something, you see, and I'm terribly desperate to find it again."

The man frowned. "This ain't a place for lost things, miss. Everything here is for sale."

I waved a hand, the gesture almost wild. "No, no, of course not. But, you see, I borrowed my mother's earrings without her knowing. They were her prized possession, and I was foolish to do it, but . . ." I paused, leaning forward as if to enter him into my confidence. "I was so hoping to impress a man. The things a girl will do."

I gave a slightly mad laugh, and the man pulled back, no doubt fearing my mania might be catching. I went on as if I hadn't noticed. "But I lost the earrings. The posts must have been loose, for when I returned home, they were both gone from my ears."

I allowed my eyes to fill with tears, and I sniffed, fishing about in my reticule for a handkerchief. I would never tell Mama how often I used the acting skills I'd learned from her—she would be unbearably smug.

"After all that, the man hardly even looked at me! Oh!" I dabbed at my nose, forcing a hiccup. "So you see, I must find the earrings, or Mama will be positively irate with me. I was hopeful someone might have found them on the street and brought them here to sell."

It was a far-fetched story, one that would have given most people pause. But when added to my hysterics and crying, the man seemed to have no desire to prolong our interaction.

"Earrings," he repeated, squinting at me. "What kind, then?"

"Pearl earrings," I said. "The lightest shade of cream with gold settings."

I'd meant what I'd told Mr. Denning yesterday. I had no attachment to my earrings—tiny things indeed, the gold fake and the make precarious. Mama had offered to lend me some of her jewelry to wear to the theatre, but I disliked the feel of baubles about my neck and wrists. I used the earrings now only because I thought they might be my best chance at a lead. Lady Harwood's and Elizabeth's jewelry was far more valuable, and most pawnbrokers would never touch it, not wanting to bring the law down upon them with such obviously stolen goods. But my earrings were different. If the thief was desperate, he might try to pawn my simple jewelry while using a proper fence for the more expensive items.

The pawnbroker gave a sigh of irritation. Clearly, he was busy, what with all the mirror polishing, but he gestured at the counter before him. "Do you see them here?"

I'd already given the counter a cursory glance and hadn't seen my earrings. Still, I pretended now to inspect each item closely, moving up and down the counter.

"Oh, I don't see them." My voice rose in a slight wail. "Is there anywhere else you might have them? Please, sir, do help me."

He looked as though he would do anything to escape me at the moment. "We—we might've bought some things yesterday but haven't put them out yet. I could check in back."

I clasped my handkerchief to my chest. "I would be most grateful. Thank you!"

He backed away and practically ran through the door behind the counter.

I dropped my act immediately, turning to inspect the shelves nearest me. I'd made my own list of the Harwoods' stolen goods with Elizabeth's help, and now I scanned the items as quickly as possible. The broker would return quickly, eager to be rid of me. I bent to examine a cravat pin, but it was silver, not gold like Sir Reginald's.

"That was quite the performance," came a voice from behind me.

I jolted upright, nearly smacking my head on the shelf. A tall figure stepped around a teetering longcase clock, hat tucked beneath his arm and dark eyes fixed on me.

"Mr. Denning." The words came out incredulous, but it *was* Mr. Denning, looking far more at ease in this dusty old shop than he had any right to. What was he—

No, that was a stupid thought. He was doing the same thing I was, looking for the stolen goods. I just hadn't imagined we might stumble upon each other, what with how many pawnbrokers there were in London.

He shifted his weight to one leg, eyeing me from head to toe. "And here I thought you did not care about your earrings. Your exact words, if I recall correctly."

"Oh," I said dumbly. "Yes, you see—"

Approaching footsteps announced the return of the pawnbroker. He stepped out from the back room, empty-handed.

"Sorry, miss," he said. "We haven't anything of the sort."

I conjured a disappointed sigh. "Oh bother. What dreadful luck."

Then the man's eyes narrowed on Mr. Denning behind me. "You're still here, then? Find anything?"

"Sadly not, Mr. Puce," Mr. Denning said evenly.

Puce? An unfortunate name, indeed.

"I told you we don't buy stolen goods," Mr. Puce said doggedly, not bothering to mention the fact that there was hardly a way to tell if an item was stolen or not.

"Well, if you should come across any of the items I described to you," Mr. Denning said, handing him a card, "I would be grateful to hear of it."

Mr. Puce took the card. "How grateful?"

Mr. Denning smiled. "Enough to make it worth your time." The pawnbroker grunted and began turning away, but Mr. Denning stepped forward to the counter. "Just one more moment, sir," he said, withdrawing a familiar paper from his jacket pocket. "Have you seen this man before?"

The man gave the paper a cursory inspection. "Can't say that I have," he said. "He your thief?"

Mr. Denning folded the page. "Just let me know if you see him."

"Yes, sir," Mr. Puce said under his breath.

Mr. Denning turned back to me. "Are you leaving, miss? Might I hold the door for you?"

His expression was pleasant enough, but the glint in his eyes was anything but. I would not be escaping from him anytime soon. My stomach took a twirl.

"Um, yes, thank you." Nodding politely at Mr. Puce, I followed Mr. Denning to the door.

As soon as we were outside, he took my elbow and pulled me out of sight of the pawnbroker. I should have disliked being manhandled, but he managed it with such finesse that my pulse actually leaped at his firm direction.

He released my arm and turned on me in the same instant. "Miss Travers," he said, tone gravelly. "Care to explain what just happened?"

I had hoped that in the few minutes since he'd seen me, I would come up with some clever excuse for my ploy inside the shop, but as of yet, such brilliance eluded me. I had only the truth or denial.

I chose denial.

"What do you mean?" I said. "I was simply looking for my earrings."

"And that story you concocted?"

I waved a hand. "Oh, I knew he would ignore me if I didn't give him a reason to help me. No one likes a crying lady."

"Shocking, to be sure," he said. "But you have yet to explain *why* you were looking for your earrings."

I tried distraction next. "Is that my drawing there?" I plucked the paper from his clasped hand before he could protest. I unfolded it, my sketch greeting me—the thief's hooded eyes and hooked nose. "I'm glad you're putting it to good use. A description can only go so far; a visual aid, though, jogs the memory a bit more than a list of banal characteristics."

He tugged the paper back and slipped it inside his jacket. "Miss Travers, as amusing as this is, I've things to do. If you'll not answer my question, I'll wager a guess."

"Certainly." Perhaps he might do me a favor and provide an excuse I hadn't yet thought of.

He crossed his arms, lowering his head to look me in the eyes. "You've decided to investigate this case yourself."

I'd prepared a perfectly innocent expression, but it fell away immediately, overtaken by surprise.

He gave a slight smile. "I thought as much," he said. "Drake mentioned that you sometimes aided your brother in his thief-taking cases. That, combined with your penchant for following criminals down dark alleyways, made it fairly simple to guess."

I took a deep breath. He knew, and there was little I could do about it. "You don't seem nearly as shocked as you ought to be, sir."

"About what?"

I squinted at him. "Me being a woman, of course."

His lips pulled to one side. "I'm afraid that fact was quite obvious from the moment we met, Miss Travers."

I flushed, thinking of our tumble in the street. What *had* his first impression of me been?

I clasped my gloved hands before me. How to admit the truth without telling all of it? I couldn't tell him about the letter. "Yes, you are right," I admitted. "I am investigating the theft. I want to ensure no stone is left unturned."

He raised an eyebrow. "The faith you have in me is astonishing."

"Forgive me if I have little faith in Bow Street in general." I'd meant to say it dryly—a joke—but there was too much bitterness in my voice for it to possibly be construed any other way.

"I see," he murmured, glancing away for the first time.

I shifted my weight. "I am sure you are an excellent investigator. Drake and Rawlings vouched for you, and I trust their opinions. But Elizabeth asked me to—"

"Miss Harwood?" He sounded skeptical.

"Yes," I said. "She knew of my work with Jack and asked that I make my own inquiries. I never imagined it would be a problem. Many hands make light work, as they say."

"It is only a problem," he said, "if I haven't any idea there are other hands involved, or if I might unexpectedly run into said hands while doing my own work."

I narrowed my eyes. "I know what I am doing, Mr. Denning."

He shook his head. "Your abilities are not the issue here, Miss Travers. I was given this case, and I am determined to solve it as swiftly as I can. Your involvement will complicate matters."

I crossed my arms. "You want to solve it quickly so as to return to the Winters investigation."

He appraised me for a long moment, his eyes moving over every inch of my face.

"It is understandable," I said. "Certainly, an unsolvable theft on Grosvenor Square is more interesting than a common street robbery."

His brow bent. "How do you know so much of the Winters case?"

"I have a subscription to the *Hue and Cry*."

If that surprised him, he hid it well. He eyed me closely. "Yes, of course I want to return to the Winters case. But thanks to *your* connection, I am saddled with this one, which only proves my point."

His words cut me to the quick. He was right. Because of me— because Jack was my brother—Mr. Etchells had refused to allow Drake to take the case and had instead assigned Mr. Denning. It wasn't my fault, not directly, but the result was the same.

"I wonder," I said stiffly, "if you imagine I exhibit the same flaws in my investigative work as my brother did. Might I guess that you side with those who view my brother in a less than favorable light?"

"No," Mr. Denning said shortly. "I have very carefully not formed an opinion on that matter."

I looked up at him, my irritation softening to curiosity. "Why not?"

He shrugged. "All I've heard are the rumors. Who am I to judge a man I've never met?"

Oh. Well, now I felt a ninny. I looked across the busy street as I gathered my thoughts. "I . . . I am sorry. I assumed you were of the same mind as Nettleton."

"Rarely are Nettleton and I of the same mind." He sighed and uncrossed his arms. "But this is all beside the point. I must ask you to let me do my job, Miss Travers. I understand that Miss Harwood is anxious for her things to be found, but there is a proper way to do this."

"Proper or not," I said quietly, "I promised my friend that I would help her. I shall do my best not to interfere with your investigation, Mr. Denning, but you haven't any say as to whether I continue mine." He stared at me, the midday sun above burnishing his red-brown locks a dark copper. "Now, if you've said your piece, I'll be off." I nodded in farewell, then moved around him.

His hand caught my forearm, stopping me. His touch was light—I could break away if I wished to. But his face was so very near mine, those brown eyes of his so focused, that I quite forgot I was trying to make a dramatic exit. My pulse tripped.

"Do be careful, Miss Travers." He bent to speak in my ear. "I would hate for you to get in over your head."

He smelled of lemon. Why did he smell of lemon? I tried not to breathe. "Is that an entreaty or a warning?"

He released me and stepped away. "Both. I'm a busy man. Despite what Drake might say, I have little time to rescue damsels in distress."

I tried to collect myself. "A common occurrence for you, Sir Chivalry?"

"Be careful," was his answer as he took several backward steps. "Please." Then he turned and strode away, stealing the chance for me to have the last word.

Rude, indeed. Though it was difficult to feel too much annoyance, what with my heart still pounding like a war drum and my skin alive with heat.

I spun and marched away, determined not to linger on how decidedly unsettled I felt. Mr. Denning had surprised me in more ways than one, and all within the space of a single conversation.

And I could not help but wonder what else I did not know about him.

CHAPTER 7

My continuing search of nearby pawnshops proved fruitless. All the theatrics and clever thinking in the world could not produce evidence when there was none.

In the late afternoon, I found myself a few minutes' walk from the Harwoods' home and decided to update Elizabeth. Not that there was much to tell her since I'd seen her the morning previous, but perhaps I could ease her mind a little.

The footman let me in and went to find Elizabeth. I waited in the entry hall, familiar to me now but no less impressive. Marble floors, elaborately carved woodwork, gilded mirrors. It was all very untouchable.

I tugged open my reticule and retrieved my sketch of the thief, leaning against the wall as I inspected it again. It was odd that no one had recognized him. All those I'd spoken to today were local to Covent Garden and the surrounding area. Did that mean the thief was a newer resident?

My eyes moved over the sketch, taking in the details of his eyes and jaw, then I paused. I let my thoughts drift back to the night of the theft. Hadn't the man had large bags beneath his eyes?

I fished in my reticule for my pencil and bent over a small table nearby. My pencil flew across the paper, adding drooping shadows beneath the man's shrewd gaze. It was a small change, but every detail was important. I was so involved in my sketch that I did not hear the footsteps from within the drawing room until the door opened behind me.

"Miss Travers!"

I straightened, paper and pencil in hand, to see Lady Harwood standing in the open doorway, looking at me in surprise. "What a pleasure to see you. Elizabeth did not tell me you were coming."

I hid the sketch behind my back. "Oh, it was a spontaneous visit. I wanted to look in on her, see that she was well."

Lady Harwood's eyes dimmed slightly. "Yes, of course."

Then she glanced behind her and made a tutting noise. "Dear me, I'm being terribly rude. Mr. Allett, do come out, and I shall make introductions."

I furrowed my brow. Allett. How did I know that name?

Lady Harwood moved aside, and a man stepped into the doorway. He was smartly dressed in a fawn jacket and green waistcoat, all impeccably tailored, but my eyes were drawn to his face. Oh, but it was a *fascinating* face. Intelligent eyes, clear blue and focused. A short, sharp nose, slightly off center, and a slight jaw sporting a neatly trimmed beard. His dark hair was speckled with gray, and I guessed him to be around forty-five years of age. He adjusted a leather case in his hand, his long, slender fingers dappled with . . . paint?

"Miss Travers, might I introduce Mr. Lucas Allett," Lady Harwood said, gesturing to her guest. "Mr. Allett, this is Miss Verity Travers, a dear friend of Elizabeth's."

Mr. Allett bowed smartly, his movements crisp. "A pleasure, Miss Travers."

I curtsied in return. "The same to you, sir."

Lady Harwood clasped her hands before her. "Mr. Allett was here working on Elizabeth's portrait. I've just sent her upstairs to change."

"Portrait?" Suddenly, his name collided with all the details I'd gathered. "Oh! You are *the* Lucas Allett, the portraitist?"

Mr. Allett smiled politely. "The very one."

That explained the beard. I'd heard he had studied in Italy, so perhaps he'd adopted their styles before returning to England to pursue his career.

"We were ever so pleased to snatch him up," Lady Harwood said. "He is always booked months in advance. But I was determined to have this portrait finished before Elizabeth marries."

"Indeed," Mr. Allett said. "Her ladyship was quite persistent."

As he spoke, my ears caught on the slightest inflection in his voice, as though he were trying to hide a less respectable accent with a smoother, more genteel one. It made me appraise him differently. If I guessed correctly, he wasn't born to wealth and privilege like the Harwoods. He was like me, attempting to hold a mirage long enough to be accepted.

"Mr. Allett, if you'll just wait a moment," Lady Harwood said, "I'll fetch that book I mentioned. Perhaps you might speak with Miss Travers."

She was gone in a flutter of skirts, leaving the two of us alone in the entry. It was an opportunity I would not squander.

"It is truly a pleasure to meet you, sir," I said sincerely. "I've seen your work before. It is astounding. The way you capture light, and the brush of silk against skin . . ."

Mr. Allett watched me curiously. "You speak like an artist yourself."

I gave a skitter of a laugh. "Oh, goodness no. That is, I sketch every now and again. I certainly would never call myself an artist."

"And a sketch is not art?" he asked.

I drew back my chin. "Well, not like your work."

"It is not work." He spoke matter-of-factly, gaze unrelenting. "It is a passion, no matter the medium or subject. If you create, you are an artist."

I swallowed hard, his words piercing. I'd never thought of my drawing like that. It had always been a simple pastime, a parlor trick, a luxury if I found the time for it. I'd certainly never considered myself an artist, not like him.

It was then that I looked down at myself and remembered what I was wearing. Heavens, if I'd known I'd be meeting one of London's premier artists today, I surely would have changed before coming. I tugged at my plain walking dress, the sketch in my hand crinkling as I moved.

His eyes flicked to the sketch. "Is that one of your drawings?"

I froze. "No. No, this is—"

He stepped forward without warning and pulled it from my fingers. He held it up to the afternoon light, inspecting the lines of my sketch with critical eyes. My mouth dropped open, but I closed it abruptly and waited, not breathing.

Mr. Allett looked at me. "This is very good, Miss Travers. Very good, indeed."

I let out my breath all in a rush. Did he truly think so, or was he being polite?

He returned the paper to me, eyeing me with interest. "Have you had any formal training?"

I shook my head, folding the sketch. "Only briefly at school. Nothing substantial."

Lady Harwood reappeared with a smile. I counted myself lucky that she'd been gone while he'd inspected my drawing, or else she might have wondered as to the reason I had sketched the thief.

"Here you are, Mr. Allett," she said, handing him a book. "We will see you tomorrow night for the unveiling?"

"Of course," he said. "Will the young Miss Travers be attending as well?"

I nodded eagerly. "Oh, yes. I am most eager to see *The Woman in Red*. It has been a favorite of mine since I purchased a print of it a few years ago."

I did not tell Mr. Allett how often I'd tried to re-create the famous painting, my print tucked carefully into a leather-bound album with the rest of my collection. He did not need to know of those disastrous attempts.

Mr. Allett tipped his head slightly, peering at me as if to see beyond my words and into my thoughts, but said nothing.

"Wonderful." Lady Harwood clapped her hands together. "It will be a happy gathering, I've no doubt."

She turned to speak to a passing footman about fetching Mr. Allett's things, and he took the opportunity to step closer to me, hands clasping his case behind his back. "Perhaps, Miss Travers," he said, "you might bring a few of your other sketches tomorrow night. I am always looking for bright young minds to mentor."

I nearly choked. Lucas Allett wanted to see my work? "I . . . I should be honored, sir."

He leveled a serious look at me. "Your very best, mind you. Pieces that are representative of who you are as an artist."

What on earth did that mean? "Naturally," I managed.

The footman returned with Mr. Allett's hat and gloves, and he donned them, bid Lady Harwood farewell, and turned to me. "Until tomorrow, Miss Travers."

After he left, Lady Harwood sighed. "What a gracious man. And such talent."

"Indeed," I easily agreed.

"Come now," she said, ushering me into the parlor. "I will send a maid for Elizabeth, and we shall have tea, yes?"

I could hardly refuse, even though I wanted to speak to Elizabeth in private. As we seated ourselves and she chattered on about the portrait unveiling tomorrow evening, I could not seem to focus on her words. All I could think of was that Mr. *Lucas Allett* had seen my drawing and thought it "very good." He wanted to see more. He was considering mentoring me.

I tried to contain my excitement, rein it in before it made a fool of me. Mr. Allett had expressed a desire to see more, that was all. He hadn't promised anything. And yet my mind leaped ahead, picturing a new path for me, wherein I became a famous portraitist, capturing images of England's elite and rich, claiming my own space in the world.

I couldn't help but linger on that vision. What a life that could be, even if it weren't the one I'd imagined for so long.

After all, when I finished this case for Elizabeth, I would be done. I'd promised myself and Mama. I would need something else to grasp on to, to keep me afloat.

Perhaps this chance with Mr. Allett was precisely what I needed.

CHAPTER 8

Lady Harwood was a frustratingly attentive hostess during our tea, and I found only a few moments to speak with Elizabeth when a friend of her mother's fortuitously came to visit.

"Any news?" she whispered urgently, eyeing her mother across the room.

I winced. "I am sorry. I did not mean to raise your hopes by coming." Her face fell. "Oh."

"That is not to say I won't have news soon," I tried to reassure her. "I've already whittled down my list of pawnshops, and I have several contacts on the lookout for our thief or any of your stolen items."

"I see." She tugged at a curl. "I know I must be patient, but I am finding it rather difficult."

Once again, the urge to ask what was in that missing letter rose inside me. But I tamped it down. If she wished to tell me, she would.

"It could be very good news that we haven't found anything," I said, setting my teacup down. "Likely, the thief abandoned the letter the night of the theft."

She shook her head. "I know I am being stubborn. I know it. But, Verity"—she fixed me with her gaze, weary and worn—"I have not slept in two days. I cannot seem to breathe normally, knowing that letter is somewhere out in the world. Please, do not give up."

I softened. "I shall persist; you know I shall."

Elizabeth exhaled. "Thank you."

I returned home as the sun began dropping behind the rooftops, setting the windows aglow with golden light. I let myself inside, quieting when I spotted Grandmama asleep in an armchair near the fire, her cap askew as she gently snored. I smiled, straightening the blanket that slipped down her lap and setting her mending aside.

"*Naps are for babies and the dead*," she'd snapped on more than one occasion. That was, of course, a slight against Mama, who often napped on the days she had late performances. But Mama only laughed and called Grandmama a cantankerous old woman, and they would continue squabbling as I gave exaggerated sighs of long-suffering.

I left my grandmother and went upstairs. It had been an exhausting day, and all I wanted to do was fall atop my bed.

But as I passed Mama's door, she called out. "Verity?"

I stepped inside. Mama sat at her dressing table, in the midst of dabbing rouge on her lips. She had another performance tonight, no doubt.

She looked at me in the mirror with a smile, then replaced the lid of her rouge and turned to face me. "There you are, dear," she said. "I was wondering where you'd gone off to. Busy day?"

"Oh, just errands here and there." I plopped down on her chaise lounge.

"Errands?" Her brows dropped. "Nothing more?"

"No?" I said, more a question than a statement.

"Then, why did Mrs. Perkins see you outside the Bow Street office yesterday morning?"

Blast our nosy neighbor and her loose tongue. I'd planned to tell Mama sooner or later. I had just hoped it would be much, much later.

I opened my mouth to speak, but she pointed the jar of rouge at me. "Only the truth, Verity."

It was a well-used refrain in our household. Often, it was teasing, considering my name, but now there was no trace of amusement in Mama's voice.

I sighed. "I was going to tell you."

"Tell me what, precisely?"

I toyed with the tassel of a cushion. "There may have been an incident as I was leaving the theatre with the Harwoods the other night."

"What sort of an incident?" Her voice was suspicious.

I winced as my gaze met hers. "Just the smallest of robberies."

"Verity Travers!" She flew to her feet, her mouth wide. "You were *robbed*, and you didn't think to mention it?"

"I wasn't hurt," I protested, though I immediately decided not to tell her that Sir Reginald *had* been. "The lout only took my pearl earrings. I did not want to worry you."

"Worry me?" Her hand fluttered to her forehead. "Heavens, darling, I worry no matter what." She gave a long exhale and peeked at me between her fingers. "That's why you were at Bow Street. You're after the thief."

"No," I said quickly, then paused. "Well, yes and no."

Mama sank back into her chair, though her posture was still impeccable. "You told me you had given this up."

"I did," I assured her. "I have. I went to Bow Street to report the crime. I was perfectly happy to leave it to the officers."

"Until?"

"Until circumstances changed." I chewed on my lip. If I told her about Elizabeth and her secret, Mama might report it to Lady Harwood. I could not break my friend's trust. "I need to find this thief, Mama. I cannot tell you why exactly. But please trust that I am doing it for good reasons."

Mama sat in silence, eyes locked on me as she evaluated my words. "It is not a matter of trust, Verity. It is a matter of safety."

"I know." My voice croaked a little. "But I am taking precautions. What happened in January won't happen again."

She said nothing, chewing her lip.

"And by no means do I intend to continue down that path again," I said, my voice finding a bit more confidence. "I swear. After this case . . ."

How did I think to finish that sentence? After this case, I would go back to pretending my future hadn't disappeared in the space of one night? Go back to trying and failing to find something that ignited my soul as much as my investigative work did?

Mama still looked dubious. I played the only card I had left. "I saw Drake and Rawlings at Bow Street. They said they would help me with the case should I need it."

It wasn't a lie, not really. I knew they would help me if I asked.

A ghost of a smile touched Mama's lips. "I do miss those two. We should invite them to dinner soon." She tugged on one of her ebony curls hanging over her shoulder, then exhaled long and slow. "Oh, very well. I doubt there is anything I could say to stop you. But *please* be careful."

Her words brought back a memory of Mr. Denning the day before, his face close to mine. *Do be careful, Miss Travers. I would hate for you to get in over your head.*

I shook myself. *His* words had filled me with annoyance, but this was my mother. She was begging me to take care because of love, not because of any personal motivation.

"Of course," I said. "I promise."

She eyed me a moment longer, a look of doubt about my assurance, then nodded and turned back to her mirror. "I am sorry to miss dinner again tonight," she said, picking up her small vial of perfume.

"I am quite old enough that you needn't worry about that," I said. "Although it *would* be nice to have another at the table besides Grandmama. She will undoubtedly question me again on the magpie situation outside my bedroom window."

Mama's motions stilled. "It has been rather lonely for you without Jack, I imagine."

It was a topic we hadn't broached before. Neither of us had realized how much his leaving would affect our day-to-day lives. When he'd joined Bow Street, we'd grown used to having him near. And now that he was gone again, everything was . . . incomplete. A missing piece of a puzzle.

"I am sorry for it," she said, not moving. "I know I am absent far too often."

I knew she meant her words. She was not a distant or unkind mother. And yet . . . and yet she *could* take on fewer performances, spend more time with Grandmama and me. But she did not. And she'd been like that as long as I could remember.

"Never mind that." I stood and moved to the door. "What would I do with you constantly underfoot?"

"Ha!" she scoffed. "So says the child who followed me about day and night, begging for stories and treats and toys."

Because I had wanted her attention. Because I wanted her to see me.

"I shall try to be less of a handful in the future," I managed to say lightly.

She laughed. "Yes, well, you'll marry soon enough, and then your husband can keep you out of trouble."

Mama knew very well I had no intention to marry, and yet she kept up this facade as though she might wear me down and convince me. But I knew better. After all, *she* had been the one to teach me to protect my heart.

I slipped from her room and closed the door behind me. Sometimes, the most personal lessons were the hardest.

I woke bright and early, wishing to make progress on the case before the Harwoods' party tonight. I visited more pawnshops and tracked down several of my contacts. It was an exhausting business . . . and fruitless. The pawnbrokers were useless as ever, my contacts even more so, and I had yet to hear from Wily.

But I had high hopes for Mrs. Webb, who ran a public house in Seven Dials with her husband. I'd met the older woman two years ago when she'd been taken in by a swindler who had promised grand returns on investments in his "health tonic." As one might gather, the crook left Town before his investors grew wise of his false promises, but Mrs. Webb hired Jack to find him. I'd helped with the case and, upon meeting Mrs. Webb, had struck up an immediate friendship with the sharp-tongued matron. A friendship that had proven handy many a time, as she kept her eyes and ears open to anyone who entered her establishment. Since Jack and I had recovered her ten-pound investment from the swindler, she was more than happy to help with my investigations here and there.

I found her in the kitchen of The Stag and the Crown, stirring some foul-looking stew over the fire. When I showed her the sketch of the thief, her hawk-like eyes darted over each stroke of my pencil.

"That's done to a cow's thumb, that is," she exclaimed, her stirring paused. "A right likeness. Did you draw it yourself?"

My heart skipped a beat. "A likeness of whom?"

"Why, that's Tobias Higgs," she declared. "I'd know that sneaksby anywhere."

"You're sure?" I pressed her.

"Sure as anythin'. He used to come by on the daily."

Tobias Higgs. My thief had a name, and I had a lead. I tried to calm the leap in my chest, the fire in my veins. Oh, but it was *addicting*. "What can you tell me about him?"

She shrugged, resuming her stirring. "Always up to some mischief, Higgs. Likes to break my mugs, so I kicked him out a few weeks back and haven't seen him since."

"Any friends? Acquaintances?"

Mrs. Webb pursed her lips. "Aye. What was his name? The slippery fellow."

That could apply to a great many in the London area.

She snapped her fingers. "I've his name on the tip of my tongue. He's a slyboots, like a fox in a henhouse. And dresses like a fop to boot."

I froze, my hands clenched around the paper. "You can't mean Wily Greaves?"

Her eyes lit up. "That's the one! I used to see the two of 'em together. A rotten pair, they are."

Wily. My lungs tightened. I stared down at the sketch, now wrinkled and worn from countless foldings. Wily had seen this same drawing. It was nearly impossible that he wouldn't have recognized the man he apparently broke bread with on the regular. Not when Mrs. Webb had named him so easily.

She shot a glance at me. "What you want Higgs for?"

"Theft," I said distractedly. "And assault."

She snorted. "The sapskull."

"I don't disagree." I rubbed my forehead. "You said you hadn't seen either of them in a few weeks. I'm assuming you don't know where they are now?"

Mrs. Webb shrugged. "When he wasn't gettin' himself into trouble, Higgs sometimes worked as a lumper down at the Wapping docks."

That wasn't particularly helpful. London's docks were expansive. Even if Higgs was currently working on any ships, it would be close to impossible to find him.

"Anything more specific?" I asked hopefully.

She shook her head. "Sorry. The man was an oaf. I ignored him when I could."

I could hardly blame her for that. I thanked her with a shilling and kindly refused a bowl of stew, from which I was quite certain I would never recover. My stomach was already a twist of knots as I left the public house. How could he? I'd known Wily was less than honest on the best of days, yet I never imagined he would outright *lie* to me. Apparently he not only knew Higgs, but it also seemed they were friends, or even accomplices.

Was Wily involved in selling the very goods Higgs had stolen from us?

Anger swept through me, and I wanted to swear. I settled for kicking a broken crate on the side of the road, and it gave a satisfying crunch. I gave it one more kick for good measure, then leaned back on the wall, the cold from the stone leeching through my body.

I'd been foolish. Already, I'd made an enormous mistake in trusting someone I shouldn't have. I'd never imagined Wily might be working with Higgs. But then, he *was* good at his job. And if Higgs wanted the best return on his stolen jewelry, Wily was an obvious choice for a fence.

My heart stilled. Had Wily tipped Higgs off after I'd spoken with him yesterday? I had to assume so. Likely, they'd both left London, looking for greener and less dangerous pastures to sell their goods.

But what did that mean for me? For Elizabeth? I'd told Wily that the letter was important. Would he seek out the letter and try to discover why Elizabeth wished to keep it a secret?

I closed my eyes, leaning my head back. I took long, slow breaths, trying to calm my racing pulse. I had to decide what my next move was. But a plan evaded me. I could not settle my thoughts, let alone organize them in any useful way.

I pushed away from the wall and started for home. Mama and I were leaving for the Harwoods' party in less than an hour, where I would have to face Elizabeth, knowing what I did about Wily and Higgs. How could I admit I'd made such a mistake?

But the prideful part of me reared its head. I did not *have* to tell her. I could still fix this. Perhaps I could track Wily down again. I'd done it before. But I did not think it would be so easy next time. He knew I would be after him, and he would take precautions.

I'd been working this case for all of two days, and I was already in over my head.

Mr. Denning had expected this of me. And I'd proven him right.

How perfectly wretched.

CHAPTER 9

Our coach bumped along the cobblestone streets, the buildings around us fading into shadow with the coming night. Mama sat across from me, dressed in a gold-silk evening gown, her dark curls arranged in an elegant coiffure. She seemed as distant as I felt, for which I was grateful. I did not want her questioning my black mood, not when I'd assured her just the evening before that I had everything well in hand regarding my case.

I'd been so looking forward to the party tonight—particularly to seeing *The Woman in Red*—but anxiety had replaced anticipation. I had no answers for Elizabeth and only doubts for myself.

"What is that you have there, darling?"

Mama had been staring out the window absently, but now her eyes fixed upon the portfolio I held in my lap. My hands tightened around the worn leather, but I'd prepared a reason.

"Just a sketch of Elizabeth," I said lightly. "I promised I would bring it tonight."

I wasn't sure why I didn't tell Mama of Mr. Allett's interest in my art. Perhaps because it might give her a false hope that something would catch my interest as much as my investigative work. Painting was certainly a more acceptable occupation for a woman such as I.

I tried to keep my own hopes bundled close, sure that if I let them rise at all, the fall would be all the greater. I had sorted through my sketches after I'd dressed tonight, trying to understand what Mr. Allett had meant. Pieces that represented me as an artist? All my sketches seemed trite and simplistic—Mama on stage as Lady Macbeth last Season, Grandmama knitting before the fire, Jack walking the street, head bent and expression serious. But I had little else to show. I was never interested in drawing landscapes or architecture. It was *faces* that fascinated me, that drew me in and made me wish to capture the secrets I saw in my subjects' eyes.

I had stacked a few of my drawings, chewing my lip. It wouldn't be enough, of that I was certain.

Right before I had closed my portfolio, I'd paused. I hadn't had much time to work on my latest sketch—the wavy brown hair and unyielding eyes of a certain Bow Street officer—though I'd been unable to rid my mind of his face or his expression when he'd caught my arm and pulled me close on the street yesterday.

The sketch was far from finished, and yet there was something in it that felt . . . alive. I had slipped it inside my portfolio before I could second-guess myself.

Which I was doing plenty of now as I climbed the front steps of Harwood House behind Mama. Mr. Allett would be kind, I was sure. But whatever he'd seen in me wouldn't be enough after he saw the rest of my work. And that would be perfectly all right, I told myself. It would.

Yet I could not deny that his words kept coming back to me. *This is very good, Miss Travers. Very good, indeed.*

We handed our things to the footman, though I kept hold of my portfolio, of which I was suddenly very self-conscious. Was I to walk about the entire party with it in hand?

While Mama instructed the footman on how precisely to handle her silk shawl, I slipped my portfolio into the drawer of the sideboard to my left. I could retrieve it when Mr. Allett was ready.

The butler escorted Mama and me inside the drawing room filled with milling guests and conversation. Sir Reginald and Lady Harwood waited to greet us near the door.

"My dear Mrs. Travers," Lady Harwood exclaimed. "How pleased we are you could come."

Mama swept forward, smiling grandly, and I followed behind, as I always did.

"But of course," she said, curtsying. "How kind you are to invite us both. I should never refuse an invitation from the foremost hostess in all London."

Lady Harwood waved her off, her cheeks pinking. "Heavens, how you flatter me when it should be I complimenting you. Did Verity tell you how very much I enjoyed your performance the other night? Oh, I was in raptures, to be sure."

Mama sent me a playful smile. "No, she did not, but then, daughters enjoy keeping secrets from their mothers."

"Secrets?" Lady Harwood repeated as though she'd never heard the word before. "Elizabeth tells me everything. What could she have to keep from me?"

A great many things, it would seem, though I would be mad to say anything.

"Indeed," Mama said with amusement. "How lucky you are to have such an obedient daughter."

Mama was teasing me, of course. She was far from an obedient daughter herself, reminded daily by Grandmama, but her teasing struck me differently tonight. Mama did not know that my nerves were already on edge.

"Elizabeth is just over there," Lady Harwood said to me, nodding across the room.

I took a deep breath and released my irritation. "Thank you."

She led Mama off to a group of her friends gossiping in the corner, and I turned to inspect the room. A small frame hung in the place of honor above the mantel, though it was covered by silk wrappings. Undoubtedly, the Harwoods intended to unveil the Romano painting later in the evening in dramatic fashion. They'd certainly invited quite a crowd, with close to two dozen guests mingling about the drawing room.

Because of Mama's fame, I often rubbed shoulders with the *ton*. I knew which fork to use, which dance step to take, which topics to avoid in conversation. Yet I still never felt entirely comfortable at Society functions. If these people truly knew me—the illegitimate, thief-taking me—they would not be so eager to seat me at their tables.

I spotted Elizabeth near the fireplace, its flickering glow painting her even more beautiful than usual. It was unsurprising that the man beside her could not keep his eyes off her. He was a handsome fellow, with light hair and an easy smile. This must be her Lord Blakely.

I stepped toward them but paused when my gaze caught on another familiar figure—this one far more surprising. Mr. Denning watched me from the corner, glass in hand, eyes narrowed.

My stomach jolted. What on *earth* was he doing here? Surely his duties did not extend to attending his clients' parties.

He took a sip of his drink as he watched me, perfectly at ease, uncaring that his plain black jacket and unadorned green waistcoat were far simpler than any other in the room. Not that it mattered. He was handsome enough that he could have worn rags and still attracted the gazes of the several young ladies who eyed him now. Including me, apparently.

He nodded a greeting, though he made no move to join me, quite thankfully. The last thing I needed was another lecture about how I would get myself into trouble.

I pulled back my shoulders and returned Mr. Denning's nod—there was no need for rudeness, but neither did I need to be overly friendly—then promptly turned away and marched to Elizabeth's side.

"Verity," she greeted me, smiling brightly. Too brightly. "There you are. I thought you'd never arrive."

"Mama believes no party begins without her," I said, "and thus has developed a terrible penchant for tardiness."

The man beside her laughed. "Ah, you must be the much-lauded Miss Travers."

I curtsied, focusing on Lord Blakely as I rose. I was glad for the distraction—my eyes kept trying to wander toward Mr. Denning playing the part of mysterious, handsome stranger in the corner. "Not so lauded as you, my lord," I said. "Assuming, of course, that you *are* Lord Blakely and not some interloper intent on stealing away Miss Harwood."

He grinned. "I *am* he, though I shall certainly be on the lookout for interlopers."

"Yes, one must be prepared," I said quite seriously. "Especially with such a diamond at your side."

Lord Blakely nodded with equal sobriety. "I primed my dueling pistols this morning."

"Oh, hush." Elizabeth shook her head. "So much for my practiced introduction. I might have guessed with the two of you."

We chatted a few minutes more, our conversation moving easily. Lord Blakely was a pleasant man, well-read and intelligent. I liked him immediately and understood why he'd been one of the most eligible men of the Season. Although a title and fortune had not hurt his appeal.

Elizabeth was quiet throughout, seeming content to listen. I tried several times to catch her eye, wanting to give some sign of my approval, but she seemed distracted, her gaze never settling on anything longer than a few seconds.

I turned to inspect the room again, avoiding Mr. Denning's corner even as I tried to catch a glimpse of Mr. Allett's clever eyes. But the artist was nowhere to be seen.

"Has Mr. Allett arrived yet?" I inquired.

Elizabeth said nothing, and when I turned to her, she stared off into the crowd, not seeming to hear me.

"Miss Harwood?" Lord Blakely touched her arm, and she jumped, nearly spilling her drink.

"I am sorry," she said, wide-eyed. "What is it you asked?"

I examined my friend. She had been different since that night outside the theatre, that much was certain. But tonight, she seemed worse. Not even a room full of people, including her betrothed, could draw her away from whatever thoughts brought such worry to her eyes.

"I wondered if Mr. Allett had arrived yet," I prompted gently.

"Oh." Elizabeth passed her glass to her other hand. "No, he sent a note this afternoon saying he'd come down with a cold and was unable to attend."

My disappointment was fierce. Mr. Allett wasn't coming. Likely, he'd already forgotten about me and my sketches. He was a busy man, after all, one who certainly did not have time to mentor the likes of me. I managed to keep a smile on my face even as my stomach fell to the floor.

"Let us hope he does not remain ill for very long," Lord Blakely said. "I am anxious to see this portrait of yours. I cannot, after all, think of a more beautiful subject than my bride."

He took her hand and settled it on his arm, his movement tender and sweet. Elizabeth forced a smile as she looked up at him. Lord Blakely did not seem to have noticed Elizabeth's strange behavior.

Dinner was announced, and I was escorted to the table by an elderly man named Mr. Falsey, who, based on his sour expression alone, would have gotten along rather well with Grandmama. When we were also seated together at the table, I sighed and gave up any hopes for stimulating conversation.

That was, until the chair on my left scraped backward. I looked up, hoping to see some mildly intelligent middle-aged man who did not smell too strongly of tobacco.

I should have known better.

"Miss Travers," Mr. Denning said as he sat beside me, the lines of his figure taking up far too much of my space.

I focused on removing my gloves one finger at a time. "Mr. Denning," I managed finally, laying my gloves across my lap.

He did not look at me as he adjusted his chair to his left. I frowned. I hadn't worn any particularly offensive perfume. "I hadn't thought to see you here tonight."

"Neither did I think to come." He looked up the table, inspecting every guest. "But Sir Reginald is a difficult man to refuse. He hired me to attend tonight as security for the unveiling."

"You are fortunate," I said as a servant filled my wine glass. "The rest of us must suffer through dinner without compensation."

If I hadn't been eyeing him so closely, I might've missed the twitch of his mouth.

We sat in silence as the food was served, the chatter of the table around us filling the air. Mama sat across the table and to my right, and she sent me a curious glance, eyes flicking to Mr. Denning. I sighed. I had to say something or risk provoking her interest in the man.

"Are you an admirer of Romano?" I asked him.

"Who?" His hand rested on the table between us, large and manly and uncomfortably close.

"Romano. The artist of the painting you are being paid to protect."

"Oh." He shrugged. "No, I cannot say I've seen any of his work."

I blinked. "Surely you jest. Not even *The Woman in Red*? It is his most famous piece."

Mr. Denning gave a dry laugh. "I am afraid I'm terribly uncivilized, Miss Travers."

He still did not look at me, and I found my annoyance growing. I was no beauty like Elizabeth, but I wasn't so terrible to look at. Besides, common courtesy demanded *some* eye contact during a conversation.

"I doubt that very much, Sir Chivalry," I said shortly.

His eyes cut to mine. Ha. I knew his weakness.

"I would very much appreciate you not calling me that," he said, his voice clipped.

My fingers traced the bottom of my glass. "I might abstain from doing so, *if . . .*"

"If what?"

"If you tell me how your investigation is going."

He turned to face me, and almost immediately, I regretted claiming the full force of his penetrating gaze. Those deep chestnut eyes seemed to see far beyond what they ought, drilling into mine with leg-trembling intensity.

Thank heavens I was seated.

"I think," he said, voice low, "that I am already keeping too many of *your* secrets to consider sharing any of my own."

My cheeks heated. What with the events of the last few days, I'd almost forgotten about my pursuit of the thief, my *pistol*.

I attempted to parry. "Or perhaps you simply have no leads to share."

"I'd like to believe you hope for the opposite," he said, "so that I might catch the thief and we could all move on. Or are you so determined to solve it on your own? Prove yourself?"

My chest filled with cold air. "No," I said thinly. "No, that is not my intention at all. I only wish to help my friend." I turned my shoulder away from him, spearing a bite of roast pheasant with my fork.

"Miss Travers, I . . ."

I could see movement from the corner of my eye as he shifted uncomfortably. I said nothing, chewing with determination. No matter what he'd said the other day, he *did* think I was like Jack. Or who he believed Jack to be, at least. Despite my refusing to tell him my name—or perhaps because of it—he still could not allow me to be my own person.

He sighed and sat back in his chair. "One of the pawnbrokers recognized the thief from your drawing."

I straightened. This was an unexpected olive branch. "Oh?"

"Yes," he said. "He knew him almost immediately. Said the drawing was 'right useful.'"

"Did he now?" I tried not to grin too smugly. "What luck."

Mr. Denning pressed on. "The broker said the thief comes into his shop occasionally, though he hasn't seen him recently."

That went along with what Mrs. Webb had said. Higgs seemed to be lying low after the robbery. But Mr. Denning hadn't said his name. Did he not know it yet?

"And the thief's name?" I edged, curious to see if I'd discovered something he hadn't yet.

Mr. Denning did not speak, so I turned to look at him. He eyed me, something like suspicion building in his expression.

"You already know it," he said suddenly.

I drew back my chin. "What?"

"You already know his name. You are simply trying to see how far I've gotten."

I considered denying it. I was working for Elizabeth, after all, not for Bow Street. He hadn't any right to my hard-earned information.

But something made me pause. I'd been assuming that I had to be the one to find the thief first so that if the letter *had* survived, I could recover it without anyone the wiser. Yet, did I really think Mr. Denning was the sort of man who would read a lady's private correspondence?

Besides, he'd shown good faith by telling me what he knew. He certainly hadn't needed to. I ought to reciprocate.

"Yes, I know his name," I finally said. "Tobias Higgs. Though I learned it only today."

He bent an inch closer, eyes slightly narrowed. "And I assume you would have passed on that critical piece of information to me even if we hadn't been seated beside each other at a dinner party?"

He did not seem angry or upset. More . . . resignedly amused.

"Of course," I said, pretending offense. "I want the man caught as much as anyone."

He leaned back, and I took a relieved breath, a bit too gulping for my taste.

"The pawnbroker had little other information for me," he said. "I'd never heard of Higgs, and there was no record of his name at Bow Street." Mr. Denning rubbed his chin and eyed me. "Any other useful tidbits you wish to pass on?"

I tried not to wince, imagining what he might say if I told him the truth. *Oh, just that Higgs's only known associate is Wily Greaves, the same man I trusted with nearly every detail of the case.*

"No," I said, trying for nonchalance. "But I do hope that next time, you won't be so hasty to dismiss my work. My brother used to find me quite helpful, you know."

He lifted one brow. "I don't make it a habit to work with young ladies. Especially ones who constantly interrupt my investigation."

I ought to be irritated with him. Except it did not seem that he truly meant what he'd said. There was an edge of respect to his words that I could not have anticipated.

"And here I thought we'd begun to trust one another, Mr. Denning," I said lightly.

"Trust is a valuable thing, Miss Travers," he responded. "One mustn't give it away too easily."

"Very well. I suppose I shall settle for you telling me your next step." I took a sip of wine, eyeing him over my glass. If I knew what his next step was, perhaps I might know what mine should be.

He chuckled. "An excellent attempt, Miss Travers, but I won't be sharing *that* with my competition."

I splayed a hand across my silk bodice and fluttered my eyelashes. "How flattering that you consider me so, Mr. Denning." If he thought me silly and vain, all the better.

He peered at me. "Does that ever work? Like your act with the pawnbroker the other day?"

"A girl must use all the skills at her disposal," I replied. "You would be surprised how often I am underestimated."

"Then it is fortunate I am a quick study." Mr. Denning hadn't smiled at me since before he'd been assigned this case, since before he'd learned who I was. But he smiled now, his mouth quirked into a charming half grin, his dark eyes glittering. "I'll not be so foolish as to underestimate you in the future."

My stomach took an alarming tumble.

I forced my eyes from his, my cheeks pricking with heat. A smile like Mr. Denning's could get a girl into a world of trouble.

Thankfully, a footman came between us at that moment, allowing me to collect myself. He refilled the wine glass I'd been sipping from, though, strangely, Mr. Denning's glass was still full. The footman noticed as well.

"Is the wine not to your liking, sir?" he asked Mr. Denning. "I can bring a different refreshment."

Mr. Denning waved him off. "No, thank you."

The footman nodded and moved on, leaving an interesting silence between Mr. Denning and myself. I sent Mr. Denning a sidelong glance, toying with my gloves in my lap. He took a bite of potato, not looking at me as he chewed.

"I do not drink while working," he said eventually, his voice almost *too* steady. As if he'd offered this explanation many times before. "I prefer to have my wits about me."

"I see," I said, trying not to show how very intrigued I was. "Wits are rather hard to come by. Best not to frighten them off."

"Indeed." Amusement hid in his voice.

The lady to his left soon claimed his attention, and I could not help a sigh of relief. Every moment I spent speaking to him felt like an appraisal, like he weighed and measured every word I said. Our conversation had been both intimidating . . . and exhilarating.

In truth, I'd enjoyed it. There, I could admit that much. I often felt somewhat lonely at these events, not quite fitting in with my middling social status and average looks. But with Mr. Denning, I hadn't felt out of place. I'd felt rather *in place*, if such a state existed.

When dinner concluded, there was no separating of the genders. Instead, we all returned to the drawing room together, excitement building among the guests as the unveiling of *The Woman in Red* drew near. In the commotion, I slipped away from Mr. Denning, intent on avoiding him for the rest of the evening.

I looked about for Mama, but before I could spot her, Elizabeth appeared at my side.

"Verity," she said, voice tremulous. "I need to speak with you."

She pulled me with her to the outskirts of the group, and I watched her with growing concern. "Elizabeth, what is it? You're making me nervous."

She cleared her throat. "Oh, there is nothing to be anxious over."

That did not help anything. "Please, tell me."

"It's silly," she said. "Only I—well, I've decided that you needn't pursue the case any further."

I stared. "What?"

"Yes," she said more firmly. "I've been rather foolish about it. Of course the thief wouldn't have kept the letter, and really, there is nothing too bothersome in it anyway."

I fought back all the words that leaped to my tongue. What of her worries and sleepless nights? What of her insistence that she could be utterly ruined by the contents of that letter? I took a deep breath. "Elizabeth, this doesn't make any sense. Has something happened?"

She shook her head almost violently. "No, I've simply had more time to think. I would hate to waste your time."

"But I—"

"Thank you all for coming tonight." Sir Reginald's voice boomed from across the room. He stood beside Lady Harwood, both of them beaming, the covered painting hanging above them.

Elizabeth and I turned to face them, though her words still rattled through my mind. I felt shaky. Call off the investigation? What did she mean by it?

"As the Bible teaches us," Sir Reginald went on, "talent should never be hidden under a bushel. And so, we are determined to share this beautiful painting with anyone who crosses our threshold." He gestured to the butler next to the mantel, who nodded and reached up to tug on the corner of the silk draping. It slipped away, eliciting a collective gasp from the watching guests.

The Woman in Red was beautiful. Stunning. Even from across the room, I could see the details that had so captured the attention of the art world—the subtle smile on her lips, the grace in the curve of her hands as she grasped a bundle of wildflowers in her lap, the titular red silk dress flowing in crimson lines to pool around the lady's ankles.

The story behind *The Woman in Red* was more myth than truth, but everyone knew it. It was said that Romano had loved the woman he'd painted, and when she'd died tragically—falling from a seaside cliff during a storm—he had immediately sold the painting, too distraught to ever see his lover's face again. He'd died soon after of a broken heart, if the rumor mills were to be believed. In the eighteen years since his death, the painting had passed through many hands, its story and significance building with every sale.

The painting itself was not much larger than my leather portfolio, but it held such power, such entrancing emotion. Because though the woman smiled, though the Italian countryside around her was bright and idyllic, there was a darker depth to her eyes that seemed to foreshadow the tragic turn her life would soon take.

"It is beautiful," Elizabeth said, her voice quiet. "No matter how many times I see it, I am stunned anew."

A chill raised the hair on my arms. Not because of her words but because the look in her eyes—the subtle shadow that spoke of a hidden agony—was far too similar to *The Woman in Red*.

"Elizabeth." I took her arm. "You are not telling me the truth."

She turned away but not before I caught the glimmer of tears in her eyes. "Please, Verity, do as I say. You must stop investigating." Then she slipped away and went to join her parents, a smile pasted on her face as she accepted the glowing compliments from other guests.

I could only stand there, dazed and absolutely certain that my friend was in terrible, terrible trouble.

CHAPTER 10

I wanted nothing more than to leave, to be alone with my thoughts as I tried to make sense of what Elizabeth had said. How could I pretend nothing was amiss? Talk and laugh and admire the painting as though every part of my life weren't in baffling disarray?

My knees felt weak. I put one hand on the wall behind me to steady myself. First Wily's betrayal, then Mr. Allett's absence, now this with Elizabeth. Yesterday, I'd felt in control, ready for anything. Now it had all spun out of my grasp like a ribbon pulled along by a devilish wind.

Some force drew my gaze upward. Mr. Denning stood across the room, and while the rest of the guests were still exclaiming over the painting, he watched me. His expression, so difficult to read in our other interactions, now seemed . . . worried?

I turned away. The last thing I wanted from him was pity.

My eyes settled on Mama, laughing with a group of friends. She would not like to leave. But if I told her I had a headache, she might let me leave while she stayed. I would fetch my stashed portfolio, then make my excuses to the Harwoods.

I slipped into the entry hall and moved to the sideboard, where I'd hidden my sketches earlier. I pulled the drawer open and picked up the thick leather portfolio but then could not seem to move. I closed my eyes, feeling the weight of the collection in my hands. My throat filled with a painful lump. Why did nothing ever turn out as it should? I worked hard, tried my best—and for good causes too. Why should success be so difficult?

Do not cry, I ordered myself. But one tear dropped hot to my cheek, and I angrily swiped it away.

"Miss Travers?"

I jolted. "Oh!" My portfolio went flying from my hands, skidding across the marble floor and scattering several of my drawings about.

Mr. Denning stared at me as one of my drawings settled at his feet. Half of his face was shadowed, the other alight from the flame of a nearby sconce. He looked even more startled than I felt, his mouth parted and posture frozen.

"I—I am sorry," he said, stumbling a bit over his words. "I did not mean to—" He shook his head and seemed to collect himself. He dropped to one knee to gather the pages nearest him. "I wanted to see that you were all right. You looked rather . . ."

An irrational surge of annoyance swept through me. "Rather what?" I snapped, snatching up the drawing of Mama to my left.

Mr. Denning paused, not looking up at me. "Shaken. Upset. I am sorry, it is not any of my business."

I immediately regretted my sharp response. He was only being kind. I took a deep breath. "No, I am sorry," I said softly. "I have had a very trying day and did not intend to have an audience for the end of it."

He picked up another sketch and stood. If he wondered why I'd brought a variety of drawings to a dinner party, he did not mention it. "Was I part of what made your day trying?"

I scooped up a drawing of Jack. "Perhaps a little, but not in the way you might imagine."

He straightened the papers in his hands. "A very careful answer that reveals nothing important. You are quite adept at that."

I straightened. "Pardon?"

"We have had several conversations, Miss Travers," he said, "but at the end of each one, I only feel like I have more questions and less understanding. You hold yourself apart while managing to appear completely involved."

I clutched the drawings in my hands, my heart pounding. "I . . ."

I could not think of what to say. I'd spent the better part of a decade crafting the versions of myself to show to others—to Society, to my friends, to my family, to my network of contacts. Yet he'd summed me up in a sentence, brisk and to the point.

I'd never felt more seen. Nor more vulnerable.

I needed to leave.

"I'll take those," I said hurriedly, holding out my shaking hand for the pages he held. "Thank you."

His lips pressed into a line as if he were holding himself back from saying more. He went to hand me the stack—until his gaze dropped to the sketch on the top.

And he stopped, staring.

"Is this . . . ?" He squinted. "Is this me?"

I knew before I even looked. Sure enough, my unfinished sketch of Mr. Denning peered up at me, his graphite eyes seeming to laugh. Oh, *why* had I decided to bring that sketch?

"No," I said quickly, stepping forward to take it from him. "Of course it isn't. I—"

He pulled the sketch back, looking closer. I could not stand it. It was incomplete, imperfect, and revealed far too much. I'd meant that drawing for Mr. Allett's eyes, not for this man who tugged on my emotions and nerves like a determined fisherman.

"Mr. Denning, please." My words were a choked begging.

His gaze shot up to mine, taking in my distraught face. Without another word, he bent to pick up the leather portfolio from the floor between us, tucked his stack inside, and handed it to me.

"Good evening, Miss Travers." His voice was softer than it had ever been before. Then he disappeared back inside the drawing room without another word.

One would think I might struggle to sleep after such a day, but thankfully, my body knew I needed a reprieve. After Mama and I returned home—she had insisted on accompanying me, for which I felt terrible—I fell into bed and slept until clouded daylight woke me. I allowed myself to lie in bed, the memories and realities of the last few days slowly drifting through my head.

Elizabeth. Her strange behavior. Her insistence that I stop investigating. Why would she not tell me the truth? I did not want to be hurt by this, but we'd been friends for years. I trusted her. Did she not trust me?

I took a long, deep breath. No, my heart said. That was not it. She had not looked at me with wariness or doubt. But what, then?

For a wild moment, I entertained the idea that Lord Blakely might have something to do with the whole affair. If Elizabeth had some horrid secret, would he not have much to lose as her betrothed? But that was ridiculous. He was a gentleman in every sense of the word. Besides, he clearly adored Elizabeth.

My thoughts turned to Mr. Denning, as they'd been fighting to all along. Our tête-à-tête at the dinner table, the shadow in his eyes when he'd handed me the drawing of himself.

His words.

You hold yourself apart while managing to appear completely involved.

I hadn't imagined that a man like him could be so perceptive of human nature. But perhaps that came with working at Bow Street. When one spent every day neck-deep in criminals, evidence, and testimonies, I supposed it shaped the way one viewed the world.

But Mr. Denning hadn't any idea why I did it—why I protected myself. If he did, I guessed he would look at me very differently than he had last night.

I heard Pritchett bustling about in the corridor. I needed to move, to dress, to do something. But what? Elizabeth had asked me to stop investigating. If I were a good friend, I would do as she wished.

And yet I did not think it was as simple as that. She was hiding something from me, something that made her act irrationally. And it had to do with this case.

Besides that, my irritation at Wily was growing. He'd fed me a stream of bald-faced lies when we'd met in the park. He and Tobias Higgs were up to no good wherever they were, likely cackling that they'd tricked me—thinking they'd gotten the upper hand.

I was trapped in indecision. Part of me desperately wanted to give up, move on. This was the life I'd broken from three months ago, for good reason. Yet another part of me—my intuition, perhaps—insisted that I had to see this through. I stood on the edge of a ravine, with surety and safety behind me, danger and the unknown before me.

It was my memory of Elizabeth's face that pushed me from the cliff. The broken darkness in her eyes, the tonelessness of her voice.

Determination lit like a fuse beneath me, and I knew I would keep pushing, keep searching for the letter. Even though I was also fully aware of how easily a simple case could turn unpredictable, dangerous even, I had to see it through. Elizabeth needed me, Higgs deserved a trial and swift sentence, and Wily . . . well, I was not certain what he deserved, but I would face that problem when I came to it.

I threw off my covers and went to my wardrobe. I had no time to waste. Not when the barest makings of a plan had already begun forming in my mind.

CHAPTER 11

I dodged around a heavy-laden cart pulled by two work horses, careful to step over the muddy puddles last night's rain had left behind. Thick clouds hovered overhead, threatening another downpour, but I was far from deterred. I would go about my task rain or shine.

I reached the door, checking the sign beside it. The Nag's Head, it read in peeling letters. I grinned. I'd found it.

The execution of my plan had taken all morning, but it had been well worth it. I'd dressed once again in my plainest, hardiest clothing and traveled to the Wapping docks. I'd gone from one shipping office to the next, claiming I was looking for my brother, Tobias Higgs. I pleaded with the clerks to tell me if anyone by that name had ever worked as a lumper for their company, because our father had died and left Tobias an inheritance. There was no reason to hide from an inheritance, I reasoned.

I had little luck at the first half dozen offices but struck gold at Watson's Trading Company. The clerk there had seemed rather taken with me, so I'd made certain to smile and toy with my hair a great deal. He'd spent a quarter hour poring over their ledgers, looking for any record of Higgs.

"Ah," he'd said, squinting his eyes. "Yes, here he is. He was paid for unloading a shipment not a fortnight ago."

My pulse had quickened. "Have you any means of contacting him?"

He'd shaken his head. "We hire men when we need them. He hasn't come looking for work since then, it seems."

I must have looked disappointed, because he went on eagerly, as if to placate me. "But," he'd said, "the ship your brother helped unload is still docked. Undergoing repairs, it appears. Perhaps the captain might know something."

The captain hadn't, but the boatswain had. He'd pointed me in the direction of a nearby public house, The Nag's Head, which he'd said many of the other lumpers frequented.

A public house I now stood in front of, the narrow windows clouded and dirty. I took a deep breath. Would I find Higgs inside?

I tightened my grip around my reticule. My pistol was inside, but I would try not to need it. I had to take only a quick glance around inside. If Higgs was here, I would fetch Mr. Denning to make the arrest. If not, I would retreat and watch the tavern from outside. I wasn't terribly worried that Higgs would recognize me. The last person he would expect to see in such a sordid establishment was the lady he had robbed a few days prior.

I stepped inside, the door creaking. The plaster-and-wood ceiling of the taproom seemed to scrape the top of my bonnet, sagging at several points. Worn tables and chairs crowded nearly every inch of the space, though only a few were occupied at this time of day. The smell of woodsmoke and roasting meat filled my nose, along with other less pleasant aromas.

A skinny stick of a man in an apron glanced at me from where he served a round of drinks near the fireplace. He eyed me from head to toe. "You lost, girl?"

My eyes darted about, but the men hunched over their food and drinks, many with their backs to me or tucked away in shadowy corners. It was impossible to tell if any of them was Higgs. I hedged. "Oh. No. I was looking for my brother."

The barkeep set down mugs of ale, the liquid sloshing out onto the table. "Your brother have a name?" he asked, moving around me to clear another table.

I took a few hesitant steps after him, casting quick glances at the patrons I passed, but none looked familiar. What was I to say? If Higgs was present, I could hardly give out his name and alert him. I hadn't anticipated such an inquisitive barkeep.

"His name is . . ." I swallowed hard. "That is, I am—"

"There you are, Patience," said a voice behind me.

I froze. I knew that voice. Knew it well enough that my stomach flipped like a fish on dry land.

I turned. And there he stood—Mr. Denning. His forgettable brown wool jacket and cap failed at their jobs quite miserably, what with that imposing figure and those knowing eyes now fixed on me.

Then I realized what he'd said. Patience?

"My sister," Mr. Denning explained to the barkeep, taking my elbow.

What was he doing? He was ruining my cover story. Because if *he* was the brother I was looking for, I had no reason to ask around after Higgs.

The barkeep nodded vaguely, not seeming to care in the slightest as he half-heartedly wiped the sticky surface of the table.

Mr. Denning tugged on my elbow, guiding me toward a table near the window. Why was he always tugging me somewhere?

"Patience?" I shot under my breath.

"Well, I could hardly use Verity," he muttered. "Patience seemed close enough."

As soon as the barkeep looked away, I pulled my arm from his grasp. Mr. Denning sat at the table and looked pointedly at the chair across from him. "Sit."

"I am not a puppy." I kept my voice low but did not bother to hide my flare of vexation.

"No, we've already discussed that you are quite clearly a woman," he said mildly.

I considered leaving. Mr. Denning had stated plainly last night that he did not wish to work together. But my stubbornness refused to surrender. This was *my* lead. I'd done the work, and I would not give in.

I pulled out the chair and sat.

"Now," he said, crossing his arms on the table, "as flattered as I am that you followed me here, I really cannot—"

"Followed you?" I stared. "Are you mad?"

He seemed unconvinced. "How else would you be here?"

"I made my own inquiries." So far, this conversation was not at all to my liking. I glanced over my shoulder, but the barkeep was occupied behind the bar. "Inquiries which you just interrupted and likely ruined."

"Me?" He bent forward, his large frame impossible to ignore. "I was here first, if you'll recall."

"And what is your plan?"

He tapped his fingers on the table. "Watching the pub for Higgs, clearly. But now I've a wandering sister to explain away."

I narrowed my eyes. "A wandering sister who is *not* leaving. I've every right to be here, same as you."

We were both leaning over the small table, eyes locked, our faces only a few inches apart. I refused to back away. But the way his gaze traced over me, evaluating, inspecting . . . My skin suddenly felt too hot, my pulse quickening.

He pulled back. I forced myself to breathe, to act natural. He did not seem affected—not like I was.

"Very well," he said shortly. "We shall say we are waiting for our ship to depart. No one should ask too many questions."

His acquiescence took me aback. I was still up in arms. "That is it? I expected more of a fight."

"At least this way, I know where you are. Better than you appearing when it least suits me." He shrugged out of his jacket and slung it on the chair behind him. My eyes lingered on the firm shape of his chest beneath his waistcoat and shirt. I snapped my rebellious gaze away just as he settled back in his chair.

"So, we are working together, then?" I asked, peering determinedly out the window.

"Working together?" From the corner of my eye, I watched as he rubbed his chin. "For now, I suppose. Surveillance is always easier with two people."

He was right about that. I grew restless easily. It would be good to have another pair of eyes.

"I assume Higgs is not already here?" I allowed myself another quick sweep of the tavern, but I saw no hint of black eyes or a hooked nose.

"An astute observation, Miss Travers," he said dryly. "We'll make an officer of you yet."

I gave a short laugh. "I assure you that is not my life's ambition, Mr. Denning."

He opened his mouth, likely to ask *what*, then, was my life's ambition, but I had little desire to discuss the subject, considering *I* did not even know that.

"Did you truly think I tailed you here?" I asked, more to distract him than anything.

Mr. Denning shifted uncomfortably. "You do seem to pay very close attention to me."

Something clicked inside my mind. I stilled. Was this because he'd seen my sketch of him last night? Did he think . . . Did he think me obsessed with him? That I followed him about London like a lovesick schoolgirl?

My expression was no doubt horrified, because his eyes leaped from wary to alert in seconds. "What is it?"

"I am not . . ." But my voice failed, mortified by the words it was trying to convey. "You mustn't think that I . . ."

"Think what?"

I closed my eyes briefly. "I sketch everyone I meet, Mr. Denning. I promise it is no sign of any—any *special* regard for you. Though I am embarrassed that you saw my sketch before it was finished, because my skills were not fully represented, I assure you."

He stared at me. Then he gave an unexpected laugh. "I must say, that is something of a relief."

"A relief?" Ought I be offended by that? "Am I so repugnant?"

He coughed. "No, it isn't that."

I eyed him curiously, recalling what Drake had said about ladies being keen on Mr. Denning. "Has this something to do with your unwanted nickname?"

"What did Drake tell you?" he asked, grimacing.

"Nothing, I promise," I said. "He is not one to break a confidence."

He crossed one leg over the other. "It's silly, really. Slightly amusing at best."

I sat forward on my chair. "Do tell."

A serving maid appeared beside our table, wiping her hands on her apron. "Somethin' to eat?" she asked abruptly.

"A meal for my sister," Mr. Denning said, placing the slightest emphasis on the last word.

The maid nodded and left.

"I'm not hungry," I said archly.

"We must keep up appearances."

"Appearances?" I was wholly skeptical. "I think we are already in trouble there if we are to be brother and sister. The two of us look nothing alike."

Once again, his eyes flicked over me. "No," he agreed, "we certainly do not. But I doubt you would prefer the alternative."

"Which is?"

"In a place like this, what else might our fellow patrons assume you to be?"

Now it was my turn to redden as his meaning became clear.

"You are simply trying to distract me." I leaned my forearms on the tables. "I do believe you were about to share an amusing anecdote."

"Was I?"

"Come now," I said. "We might be here for hours. I could do with a laugh."

"And laugh you shall," he said dryly.

I raised my eyebrows expectantly.

"Oh, very well." He sighed. "It was a few months ago, right after I was promoted to officer. I was crossing Blackfriars Bridge when I heard a scream. A party was out on the river for a pleasure cruise, and one of the young ladies had fallen overboard."

I was immediately interested. "And she could not swim, of course."

Mr. Denning's cheek tugged as if he hid a smile. "No, she could not swim. And apparently, neither could any of her companions. I went in after her and pulled her to shore."

"I see. A damsel in distress." I struggled to keep a straight face. "I imagine she was most grateful."

"Ah, well, yes," he said, tugging at his cravat. "I'm afraid that she . . . she took a *liking* to me."

"A liking?"

He exhaled. "Yes. It was rather absurd. I cannot think why."

I certainly could. If Mr. Denning had saved *my* life—pulled me from the river, knelt beside me with eyes filled with concern, handsome and dripping—well, I could not think of any woman who would not be affected. The image alone was enough to send heat curling into my stomach.

"In any case," he went on, "she began appearing at the most inopportune moments, bringing me food and small gifts, insisting on showing her gratitude. Drake was at the office when she came once and heard the whole story from her." He grimaced. "He was the one to coin the name 'Sir Chivalry.'"

I grinned. "It all makes perfect sense now. But forgive me if I cannot feel too terrible for you, having a young lady dote upon you."

"I am not opposed to doting in general," he said. "But it did get tiresome once the others—"

He stopped, aghast. But it was too late.

"The others?" I asked, positively delighted. "There were more?"

"Deuce it all," he muttered.

"Did you save *all* of their lives?" I propped one hand under my chin.

"No, of course not," he said. "One had her reticule stolen by a footpad. Another had a missing cat—"

"A cat!" I had trouble keeping my voice down. Oh, but it was so amusing. "I did not know Bow Street dealt with stolen cats."

"We don't," he said rather flatly. "But apparently, it became a pastime among a certain set of young ladies to distract me from my real cases."

I could easily see it. I knew the type, spoiled and bored girls of the *ton* with nothing better to do. They would love the challenge of flirting with a handsome Bow Street Runner, a forbidden temptation to ladies of their status.

"And are you still tripping over these damsels?" I asked. "I saw no sign of any at the office the other day."

"No, quite thankfully, that nonsense seems to have faded away." He crossed his arms over his chest, the fabric of his shirt pulling against his muscled forearms.

I tipped my head. "Is that why you were so alarmed thinking I'd followed you here?"

He looked a bit chagrined. "Perhaps."

"Well, you have nothing to fear from me," I said. "Romance is the farthest thing from my mind at present. Even if it weren't, I daresay there are better ways of catching a suitor."

"Perhaps running men down on the street while pursuing a thief?" His eyes glinted.

"Ha," I said dryly. "That usually creates the opposite effect, I'm afraid."

"Only for those of a weak constitution, Miss Travers."

"Oh, none of that formality," I said. "Please, call me Patience."

He laughed, and the sound was so unexpected that I had to catch my breath. His laugh came from deep within him, full and unbounded—a laugh I might have heard much sooner had our first few meetings not been so very complicated. But it was his face that held me captive, brought to life by his wide smile and the fine lines about his eyes. Handsome, to be sure. But something more. Something real.

My heart clenched, and I had to look away.

The maid returned and set a plate and mug before me, leaving without so much as a word. I lifted my fork and poked what I thought was a meat pie, its crust hard and dense. The drink—perhaps a watery switchel?—appeared little better, seeming to have bits of . . . *something* floating on the surface.

"Eat your fill, dear sister," Mr. Denning said, eyes bright with restrained mirth.

I pushed the plate away from me. "Thank you, but I have no desire for an early grave."

"You might have fooled me," he muttered under his breath as he pulled my plate to him.

"You cannot eat that," I protested. "It will make you ill."

"I hate to let food go to waste." He picked up the pie and took a bite. He chewed, then coughed.

"As bad as it looks?" I asked pointedly.

"No, no," he said, taking a swig of switchel to wash it down. "It is delightful. Do have some."

"One of us must be well and able if Higgs shows up," I said. "You'll be incapacitated if you eat any more."

"You would be surprised what I've learned to stomach over the years."

"A strange thing to take pride in."

"One does what one must. Not all of us have such talents as you." He leaned his elbows on the table. "Speaking of talents, I must ask . . ."

I grew unaccountably nervous. "Oh?"

He paused before continuing, his expression curious. "Why did you have those drawings with you last night?"

I balked. It was not the worst question he might have asked me—there were so many things I was keeping from him. But it struck close to my heart, a personal disappointment I hadn't yet had time to examine, considering all that had happened since yesterday.

The front door opened, and my neck twisted to look, glad for a reason to avoid Mr. Denning's eyes. But it was an older gentleman, hunched and gray—not Higgs.

I turned back, clearing my throat. "The drawings were . . . That is, I brought them for an acquaintance."

"Not me, I assume."

I gave a little laugh. "No, though that was likely clear from my reaction last night."

"Indeed." He paused. "Who were they for?"

I sighed. He'd told me about his nickname. I supposed I owed an answer in return. "Do you know Mr. Lucas Allett?" I asked. "The portraitist?"

He nodded. "Lady Harwood has mentioned him."

"Well, he was to be a guest last night," I said. "We met a few days ago, and he saw my sketch of Higgs. He seemed to think I showed promise and asked me to bring more of my work to the party."

Mr. Denning leaned back in his chair, one arm stretched forward on the table. "I didn't know you had such aspirations."

"I don't," I said quickly. "That is, I *didn't*. But when an artist like Mr. Allett takes an interest, it is difficult not to want . . . more."

And I had wanted more. Even in the space of one day, my thoughts had begun to shift and change, wondering if this was *it*—a new path for my life. I could be an artist like Mr. Allett. I enjoyed drawing, even if it did not quite fulfill me as much as investigating.

Mr. Denning appraised me, his eyes soft. "But he did not come."

"No." I tugged at the sleeve of my pelisse, restless. "I missed my chance."

But he immediately shook his head. "Life does not work like that. Your future is not dependent on a single chance meeting."

That captured my interest. "Then what does it depend upon?"

"Your choices. Your abilities. Your determination." His lips bent up. "The last of which you seem to have in spades."

I did not know how to react. I hadn't expected such a sentiment from him.

"Besides," he said, "I've seen your talent firsthand. Mr. Allett would be a fool not to seek you out."

Oh, how I tried not to blush, to stop the heat spreading up through my neck and cheeks. My first instincts were to bat his compliment away, make a jest, change the subject. But there was something so sincere in his expression that I did none of those things. "Thank you," I said instead, my voice quiet. "That is kind of you to say."

He looked into my eyes for another second, a second that felt longer than it should have. His brow was furrowed as though he was trying to see beyond what I was showing him to the truth beneath.

But the odd thing was that I wasn't hiding any truth. Not about this. He knew something about me that I hadn't told anyone else, not my mother or grandmother or Elizabeth.

It was the strangest feeling, the realization that this man whom I'd known for less than a week had seen one of the most intimate pieces of my life. I ought to feel the edge of panic that came whenever I shared any part of my true self with another. Yet my nerves remained steady, my emotions calm.

"I teased you earlier," he said, "about becoming an officer. But from what Drake has said about you helping your brother with his thief-taking cases, perhaps that is not far from the truth."

Dash it all. *Now* I was panicking.

"It was a foolish dream," I said quickly. "Never serious. I simply wanted to be like Jack."

"And yet you've managed to dog my steps every second of this investigation." Mr. Denning spoke matter-of-factly. "That is no accident."

I did not meet his eyes. He knew too much. He would not be satisfied with a lie. "I did have ambitions," I managed. "I thought I could make a future."

"A female thief-taker?"

I quirked my lips to one side. "Yes. I know it sounds ridiculous. But for a while, I was successful. I had a growing clientele, mostly women, and I was good at what I did. I enjoyed it."

"But no longer?"

My lungs tightened. *This* I would not tell him. "No," I said, my voice holding a ragged edge. "I've since learned that it is not the life for me. I took this case for Elizabeth's sake, but I won't be taking any others."

I examined the taproom again, though no one had entered or left in several minutes. But it was something to occupy my eyes instead of darting them to Mr. Denning like I desperately wished to.

He said nothing for a long minute, the hum of voices and clattering dishes from the kitchen filling the space between us.

"She is lucky to have a friend like you," he finally said.

I had no response to that. I'd run out of words. I'd spoken too many truths and almost-truths, and it frightened me. It had never been like this before with anyone else. But there was something in the intensity of his eyes and voice that made me trust him. Made me want to tell him more.

Which was why I pushed back my chair and stood, heart pattering.

"I am going to check the street," I said, tightening the ribbons of my bonnet. "A short walk. I'll be back."

Mr. Denning stood as well, and I thought for a moment that he would protest, insist that he be the one to patrol, but he only asked, "You have your pistol?"

I raised my wrist, my reticule swinging with the weight of my small pistol. "Yes."

He nodded. "Keep a close eye." Then he took his seat again without another word. Heavens, if that didn't make me like him more.

Fresh air, I told myself. That was the cure for this warmth that spread like melting butter throughout my body. A brisk walk in the spring air would do the trick.

What a liar I was.

CHAPTER 12

We kept watch at the tavern for the rest of the day, until the gloomy daylight drifted toward the blackness of night. I was careful to keep our conversation focused on the case. Mr. Denning shared that he'd been led to The Nag's Head by a contact who'd had dealings with Higgs before, and I held my breath, thinking he might know about Wily's connection to our thief. But he said nothing of it, only detailing some of Higgs's past crimes.

"Petty theft and homebreaking, for the most part," he said as the serving maid lit the lamps around the taproom, chasing away the growing shadows. "He's spent the last few years in and out of Newgate."

I frowned. "Anything violent?"

"Not that I could tell."

A group of rowdy sailors spilled through the front door, and Mr. Denning took a pretend swig of his ale as he inspected them. He had a better view of the front, while my vantage point included the kitchen and back entrance. He shook his head. Still no Higgs.

"Does it not strike you as odd?" I asked, moving my spoon about the stew I'd barely touched. Next time I sat through a long surveillance, I would bring my own provisions.

"What, precisely?"

"That Higgs has no record of violent crimes," I said, "and yet he not only threatened us with a pistol but also struck Sir Reginald."

Mr. Denning looked thoughtful. "Perhaps he was desperate. Desperate people are unpredictable."

"Perhaps." I was unconvinced.

The tavern grew increasingly crowded, with dockworkers and sailors coming in search of a drink. And the later it grew, the more leering looks the men sent my way, even with Mr. Denning right beside me.

I did not think he had noticed until I realized his chair had slowly shifted, blocking me from most of the room. That, and the fact that his jaw tightened more and more with every whistle sent my way.

"I think I've become somewhat of a liability," I said under my breath. "I should leave and let you continue to keep watch."

Except I did not want to go. The longer we stayed, the more certain I grew that Higgs would walk in at any moment and we could end this.

But Mr. Denning shook his head. "You cannot go by yourself. Not at this time of night."

"Neither can I stay," I pointed out. "I am drawing far too much attention. And you needn't worry; this is not the first time I've traveled through London after dark."

"But—" Then his eyes caught on something behind me. Or someone. He straightened.

I froze, not wanting to turn and give away our interest. "Is it him?"

"I cannot tell for sure," he said. "Stay here."

Before I could point out that *I* was the one who had seen Higgs before and, therefore, would be able to identify him, Mr. Denning had slipped away into the rambunctious press of tavern-goers. I could not help a quick glance over my shoulder, watching Mr. Denning's lean shoulders work through the crowd. He headed for a table in the corner, shadowed and out of the way. I could just make out two figures seated there. What had he seen to provoke his suspicion?

"What's a pretty thing like yourself doing here alone?"

My attention snapped back in a heartbeat. A rangy, disheveled man had slid into Mr. Denning's vacated chair, grinning at me with crooked teeth. He ran a hand through his greasy hair, slicking it back against his head.

"My business is my own," I said, eyes narrowed. "And that seat is taken."

"Don't look taken." He winked, no doubt thinking himself quite the wit.

"My brother is here." I allowed a threatening note to enter my voice. "He'll not be pleased."

"What your brother doesn't know won't hurt him." The man's eyes roved down over my body, and I resisted the urge to kick his leg.

I stood, intending to go after Mr. Denning.

But the man was quick, on his feet in an instant and blocking my path. "Come now," he said, his breath reeking of ale. "Give a fellow a chance." He grasped my forearm in one hand, the other snaking out to catch my waist. He pulled me against him, eyes dark with desire.

My pulse hammered in my ears, but I remained calm. I'd prepared for this. Jack had insisted on teaching me a dozen different ways to escape such a situation. I was readying myself to act—a swift kick to his shin, then a jab at his eyes after his grip on my arms loosened—when the man was jerked roughly away from me.

"What—" But he didn't get out another word before Mr. Denning's fist smashed into his nose.

The man collapsed into a shrieking fit, holding his bleeding nose. Everyone turned to look at him, conversations falling off as the fiddler stopped in the middle of his song.

But I could only stare at Mr. Denning, his eyes dangerous as he loomed over the man.

"Don't you dare touch her," he growled, his voice a thunderstorm.

Another man rushed him from behind, face twisted in menace.

"Denning!" I cried.

Mr. Denning spun, ducking the oncoming attack and using the man's own momentum to send him crashing into our table.

The crowd was jeering and shouting, and a few ruffians were forcing their way through the gathering, revenge in their eyes. Apparently, our new friends were popular.

Mr. Denning saw them too. He grabbed his hat from where it had fallen to the floor, then swept up behind me. "I think it's time we were going," he said in my ear as his hand pressed into my lower back, urging me forward.

I threw a glance behind us as he jerked open the front door. The two men he'd fought still lay moaning on the ground, the remnants of our paltry dinner scattered about. But then we were out onto the dark street, strangely quiet after the ear-shattering din of the tavern.

"Can you run?" he asked, taking my hand.

I came to myself. "Yes."

We broke into a sprint, me struggling to keep pace with Mr. Denning's longer strides, and were halfway down the street before our pursuers burst out onto the street after us.

"There they are!" one of them cried.

A sudden blackness gaped to our right—a small lane. I pulled on Mr. Denning's hand, and he followed me without hesitation, the two of us dashing into the dark together.

Until he skittered to a halt, stopping me with him. The lane ended abruptly just ahead, closed off by the thick stone walls of a warehouse.

Shouts echoed behind us, and figures appeared against the moonlight at the end of the street.

"We need to hide," he said in a whisper, barely winded by our run.

I searched our surroundings, hoping to spot a wagon or crate to crouch behind. There was nothing. Footsteps behind us, voices growing louder—

Mr. Denning took me roughly by the shoulders and pushed me backward. My back met a rickety wooden door, the overhanging stone around it encasing us in deep shadow.

I could barely see his face, so I felt more than saw his finger move to his lips, urging quiet. But I could not have spoken even if I wanted to. My heart seemed to have taken up permanent residence in my throat, beating with a ferocity that left my mind muddled and my knees weak.

His body pressed against mine, keeping me between him and the door. His hands moved to my waist, holding me firmly, and I swore I could feel the heat of his skin through my stays. My own hands were trapped against his chest, and he ducked his head to hover beside mine, crowding my space.

Considering what that scoundrel in the tavern had attempted to do, I should have felt panicked, intruded upon. But I didn't. Instead, all I could think of was how Mr. Denning smelled of smoke and salt, how his strong frame molded around mine, protecting me.

Footsteps and shouts from the street. "This way!"

My pulse leaped yet again as they came closer, into the lane. We both held our breath, the two of us frozen together.

If the fools had thought to bring a lantern, they would have seen us in an instant. But the men ran right by, all clearly deep in their cups by their slurred shouts and stumbles. Mr. Denning's fingers dug into my waist, holding me tight.

The men seemed as surprised as we had been at the dead end, though their language was decidedly less appropriate. Cursing, they hurried back the way they'd come.

"Split up," one man ordered, sounding like the least drunk of the bunch. "They're here somewhere."

They faded into the night, their voices becoming distant shouts.

We stood there in silence, our ragged breathing filling my ears. Mr. Denning waited another moment, his jaw brushing my hair, the wool of his jacket warm against my cheek. A whirlwind, deep and engulfing, swept up through me, claiming my chest. I did not recognize the feeling. I had no name for it.

He leaned back, glancing both ways before stepping away without looking at me. The chilly night air swept in, a sharp contrast to the blood that raced hot through my veins.

"Come on," he murmured.

We crept back to the start of the lane. We could still hear the shouts of our pursuers, seeming to come from every direction. How many blasted friends did that reprobate have?

"We could make another run for it," I whispered.

As if the weather had a sense of humor, it began to rain as the words left my mouth. I gasped, the cold raindrops splashing against my face.

Mr. Denning pulled me under the eaves of a nearby house, jaw set rather grimly. "We need to lie low for a couple of hours."

"Where?" I managed. I did not bother to protest because he was right. We would never make it back to Covent Garden without being seen—or soaked to the bone.

"I know a place." He held out his hand again.

I did not hesitate. I went with him.

His hand was warm and reassuring in mine as he led me down the street, waiting at each corner and checking for drunken vigilantes before guiding me across. He changed direction twice when we heard shouts yet again, but he never spoke, and I followed his lead.

Finally, after a quarter of an hour, he stopped before a line of small, rough townhouses. They sagged to one side as if held up by pure hope, the shutters splintered and windows dirty. But the door before us was newly painted, candlelight reaching out to us from underneath, and he pulled it open, ushering me inside.

"Where are we?" I asked as he shut the door behind us. I took in the cramped corridor, narrow stairs leading upward.

He swept his hat from his head. "It's safe," he assured me, not answering my question.

"Nathaniel?" a female voice called from another room.

"Come." He moved toward the open door at the end of the corridor. "Meet my parents."

His parents? I managed to convince my feet to move and followed him to the kitchen, where a woman stood beside a small hearth, stirring a bubbling pot. I paused in the doorway. She had fair hair touched with gray, a plump figure, and a wide smile as she spotted her son.

"I wasn't expecting you today," she exclaimed, Mr. Denning swooping in on her and kissing her cheek. "I thought you were working."

"I was," he said. "We ran into a spot of trouble and needed a place to hide."

"We?" Her eyes flicked to me, then widened. "Oh!"

I bobbed a curtsy. "Ma'am."

She stared at me another moment, then back at Mr. Denning. I got the distinct impression this was *not* a common occurrence. "What have you done to get this poor girl into trouble?"

"'This poor girl' hardly needs my help to find trouble," he said dryly. "She does well enough on her own."

Mrs. Denning whacked her son with a kitchen rag. "Hush, you. Now be polite, Nathaniel, and introduce me."

Mr. Denning grinned and waved a hand from his mother to me. "Mother, meet Miss Verity Travers. Miss Travers, my mother, Miriam Denning."

She came to me and took my hand, her hold gentle. "I am very pleased to meet you."

"Thank you for taking us in," I said, a bit taken aback at her friendliness.

"I could hardly send you off into this rain," she said. "Are you hungry?"

"Near to starving." Nathaniel—no, Mr. Denning—peered into the pot. "I do think the cook at that tavern was trying to poison us."

Mrs. Denning tutted. "Go and keep your father company. Supper will be ready in a few minutes."

I followed Mr. Denning to a tiny sitting room, squashed with two armchairs, a small sofa, and overflowing bookshelves. An older gentleman with silver hair sat by the narrow fireplace, a thick blanket tucked over his lap. He glanced up from his book, curiosity in his eyes as he took me in.

"Who is this, Nathaniel?" he asked, lowering the book to his lap. He wore spectacles, which he removed with shaking hands.

"Miss Travers, meet my father, George Denning," Nathaniel said. It was difficult to think of him as anything but Nathaniel now, what with his parents' voices in my head. "Father, this is Miss Verity Travers."

I dipped into another curtsy. "Mr. Denning."

The older Mr. Denning smiled widely, and it was clear from whom Nathaniel had inherited his broad grin. "A pleasure, Miss Travers. Do come sit, please."

I hesitated, casting Nathaniel a questioning glance. How long would we be staying? I did not mind warm fires and cozy rooms as a generality, but neither did I wish to take over his parents' home for longer than necessary. He offered a short shrug, not having an answer for me.

So, I sat on the small sofa across from the older Mr. Denning, Nathaniel taking the spot beside me. The room wasn't overly warm, but when his arm brushed mine, it seemed like the fire flared against my skin.

"I must say, this a surprise." Mr. Denning leaned forward. "Nathaniel never mentioned he had befriended any beautiful young ladies."

Nathaniel ignored the sly insinuation in his father's words. "Miss Travers has been assisting me with a case."

"Assisting you?" I narrowed my eyes. "That is one way to phrase it."

He gave a short laugh, propping his elbow on the arm of the sofa. "I tried to pick the least offensive."

"Ha," I said wryly.

Mr. Denning looked back and forth between the two of us. "I must admit to some confusion."

I paused, then realized there was nothing for it. "Your son and I happen to be investigating the same theft."

He glanced in surprise at Nathaniel, who only shrugged. "It's a modern world, Father," he said quite soberly. "Ladies investigate crimes now, and we must learn to live with it."

I knew he was teasing, but my defenses still rose. "And it would be a better world if such an idea were not so opposed. Ladies have much to offer and little chance to do so."

Mr. Denning sat back in his chair, eyeing me curiously. "I don't disagree, Miss Travers. But is it not dangerous, the work you do?"

A flash of memory, a bolt of fear through my heart. My eyes flitted to Nathaniel's, and his expression shifted infinitesimally. But before I could respond, Mrs. Denning bustled into the sitting room, holding a tray filled with steaming bowls and a loaf of freshly baked bread.

"This will taste a mite better than whatever you ate at that tavern," she said, setting down the tray. "Miss Travers, you shall have to excuse our informality. We are accustomed to eating round the fire."

That was curious, considering I'd seen a perfectly adequate table inside the kitchen, but I did not protest as she pressed a bowl of steaming soup into my hands. I took a bite. It was simple but delicious, bursting with seasoned meat and tender vegetables.

"Now," she said, handing Nathaniel a bowl, "am I allowed to ask what brought you both here?"

I cast Nathaniel an appraising look. "Unfortunately, I must admit that your son was right. It was my fault that trouble found us tonight."

Nathaniel made a noise of disagreement as he settled back on the sofa with his soup. "Trouble found us, but it was hardly your fault. One must instead blame the drunken lecher who decided to lay his hands on a woman."

Pride filled Mrs. Denning's eyes as she looked at her son. "I am hardly surprised. Nathaniel never could let an insult to a lady pass without consequence. Why, when he was only eight years old, he challenged a man on the street to a duel in my defense."

"Did he now?" I said, curiosity rising.

"Mother," Nathaniel said warningly.

She seemed not to notice, smiling in remembrance. "The man had knocked into me and spilled the contents of my basket. Nathaniel could not abide the rudeness. Oh, I can still picture him, demanding an apology or satisfaction."

"Truly?" I turned to look at Nathaniel with an impish smile. "A champion of women indeed." I barely restrained myself from adding *Sir Chivalry*.

Nathaniel ran a hand over his face. "Surely there are other less embarrassing topics for us to discuss."

"No, no," I said, laughing. "I am *quite* content."

"What is that you are reading, Father?" Nathaniel asked loudly, turning the subject himself. Mrs. Denning and I exchanged a grin but allowed it.

"*Tom Jones*," Mr. Denning said.

Nathaniel sighed. "Again?"

"One can never read a favorite novel too many times," Mr. Denning said, completely undeterred.

"*Tom Jones* is written by Henry Fielding, is it not?" I asked.

Mr. Denning looked pleased at my comment. "It is indeed! You know your authors, Miss Travers."

"Generally not," I said as Mrs. Denning seated herself after serving everyone. "I haven't read the book. But I know a fair bit about the Fielding brothers."

Nathaniel eyed me appraisingly. "Do you, now?"

It seemed there was a challenge in his words. "Yes, I find them rather fascinating."

"And why is that?" Mrs. Denning asked, seeming to have forgotten her own bowl of soup.

"Henry Fielding founded the Bow Street officers," I explained. "He did much to promote London's police force, though in truth, I am much more interested in his brother, John."

"The Blind Beak," Nathaniel said with a grin.

"Yes!" I said, perhaps a bit too excitedly. But how often did I get the chance to speak of my interests?

"The Blind Beak?" Mrs. Denning repeated in bewilderment. "What on earth are you two on about?"

"John Fielding took over as magistrate after his brother, Henry, died," Nathaniel explained.

"John was blind," I added, "but had a keen ear. It was said he could recognize upward of three thousand criminals just from their voices alone."

"Indeed?" Mr. Denning looked rightfully impressed.

"A useful skill to have, I imagine." Nathaniel winked at me. "Not unlike your own, Miss Travers."

"Mine?" I asked skeptically. Was he teasing me?

"Your sketches," he said. "Your ability to remember faces and re-create them. I've never seen anything like it. It is—" He stopped suddenly, seeming to remember we were not alone. "It is exceptional."

My cheeks pricked, no doubt pink. "Thank you."

He turned back to his father, and I had to take a breath. We were acquaintances. Partners, at best. No matter how my body reacted to him.

Nothing good would come from allowing myself to think otherwise.

CHAPTER 13

Mrs. Denning began pressing me about my drawings, curious and kind, and our meal passed far more pleasantly than I could have imagined. The simple food filled my belly with warmth—or perhaps that was because my body flushed with heat every time I met Nathaniel's eyes. It was a peculiar thing, being in this home with this man. He relaxed against the sofa beside me, one arm settled across the back, his hand only an inch or two from my shoulder. It was a closeness I was *very* aware of, though I made no effort to move away.

When I looked at the clock, I was shocked to see that two hours had passed. When was the last time anything had felt so effortless? Especially a conversation with strangers. But with the Dennings, it seemed not to matter. It was clear they would welcome anyone into their home and treat them as warmly as they'd treated me.

Mrs. Denning stood and began collecting our dishes, and I hurried to help.

"No, no," she insisted. "Please sit. You are a guest."

"I've never been good at sitting still," I said as I took Nathaniel's bowl.

"Or following instructions," he muttered under his breath, though with a twitch of his lips.

I shot him a superior look and followed Mrs. Denning to the kitchen.

"Thank you, dear." She took my dishes. "You really needn't."

"It is no hardship, Mrs. Denning."

It was nice, truly. Not that I didn't love my family or our time together. But there did not seem to be holes in this house, not like in ours. Jack. My father. Both absent, but for very different reasons.

Mrs. Denning chattered on as she washed the dishes, and I dried them with a rag, putting each piece where she instructed. How strange not to hear a commentary of a recent performance of *The Fatal Marriage* or a lecture on the proper way to rid oneself of warts—from Mama and Grandmama, respectively.

When she finished washing, Mrs. Denning shooed me away as she finished a few last things. I approached the sitting room, hearing the men's voices.

No, just one voice. I paused in the doorway. Nathaniel had moved to sit beside his father, the ragged copy of *Tom Jones* in his hands. He tilted the pages toward the fire to catch the light as he read aloud, his deep voice filling the room.

"For I hope my friends will pardon me," he read, "when I declare I know none of them without a fault; and I should be sorry if I could imagine I had any friend who could not see mine. Forgiveness of this kind we give and demand in turn."

Mr. Denning laid his head back on his chair, eyes closed as he listened. The two looked so at ease together that I knew they'd done this many times before. I leaned against the doorframe and closed my eyes as well, letting Nathaniel's voice fill my ears, allowing his words to settle in my chest.

"There is, perhaps, no surer mark of folly," he went on, "than an attempt to correct the natural infirmities of those we love. The finest composition of human nature, as well as the finest china, may have a flaw in it; nevertheless, the pattern may remain of the highest value."

There was a steadiness in Nathaniel's voice—a surety in which he commanded the language I'd known all my life. It awakened a part of me I hadn't realized existed. I knew about the oral traditions of some cultures, passing on knowledge and wisdom through stories before they'd had the tools to write them down. I could not help but think that speaking something aloud gave it a power it might otherwise lack as simple words on a page. As Nathaniel's voice rose and fell, it wove emotions through every syllable, tugging at my heart and filling my mind.

He continued reading, and I listened for several minutes more, feeling no desire to make my presence known. But then his voice faded and fell silent, the room emptier for it.

I opened my eyes to see Nathaniel regarding his father, now softly snoring. Nathaniel set the book aside and stood. He saw me in the next instant and stilled.

My cheeks heated. "I'm sorry," I said softly. "I did not mean to intrude."

"You are not intruding, Miss Travers." He moved quietly to join me. "I brought you here."

He had. When he'd needed somewhere safe, he'd thought of the place he knew best, the people he loved most. And he'd brought me here without hesitation.

"Verity," I said. "Please, call me Verity."

I wasn't sure where the request had come from. I only knew that tonight, after what we'd been through and what I'd learned of him, the formality of *Miss Travers* sounded false to my ears.

His dark eyes reflected the glowing embers of the fire as he regarded me, serious and curious all at once. He mirrored my crossed arms as he leaned against the wall beside me, our faces but a few inches away.

"I should like that," he said, his eyes never leaving mine. "Verity."

I could not hold his gaze any longer. I looked away. "You seem to know the book well," I said. "I imagine this is not the first time you've read it."

"My father's eyes are growing weak." He cast a fond glance at the sleeping Mr. Denning. "I try to ease the strain as often as I can."

It was strange how learning one small fact about a person could change an entire perception. And I'd learned so much about Nathaniel today. He read aloud to his aging father. He cared for his mother. He would cuff a man for touching an unwilling woman.

"Oh dear, has he fallen asleep again?"

We both jolted at Mrs. Denning's voice behind us. Nathaniel coughed and shifted away.

Mrs. Denning seemed not to notice as she moved past us toward her husband. "My love," she said, touching his shoulder. "I do believe it is time for bed."

Mr. Denning slowly stirred, eyes blinking rapidly.

"Come on, then." She reached around his chair and fetched a plain wooden cane.

"Let me, Mother," Nathaniel offered, moving forward.

She waved him off. "I manage without you most nights. You stay with Miss Travers."

Then she took the blanket from Mr. Denning's lap, and I could not help but stare. Where his left leg ought to have been, there was only empty fabric pinned back above the knee to keep it out of the way.

I felt Nathaniel's eyes on me, and I immediately looked away. I hadn't meant to gawp. I just hadn't expected to see it. Not once over the course of the evening had I wondered why Mr. Denning hadn't moved from his chair.

Mrs. Denning helped her husband to stand, supporting him with one arm under his shoulders as he took the cane in his free hand.

"Good night, Miss Travers," he said with a tired smile. "It was lovely to meet you."

"You as well, Mr. Denning."

They slowly made their way from the room, and when the tap of Mr. Denning's cane had faded, I finally allowed myself to meet Nathaniel's eyes.

"I . . ." I shook my head. "I am sorry I stared. I hadn't expected—"

He sat again on the sofa. "You did not know."

"Might I ask what happened?" I sat beside him.

Nathaniel lifted a shoulder. "It was an accident. Father is—was—a carpenter. But two years ago, his apprentice lost control of his blade and cut Father's leg. The wound became infected, and the surgeon had to . . ." His voice fell away, tired. Defeated.

"How awful," I whispered.

"And entirely preventable." He sighed. "You see, the apprentice had been drinking before he came to work. Father didn't know until it was too late."

My lips parted. The selfishness and uncaring of some people.

Nathaniel looked at the fire as he rubbed his jaw. "I told you I don't drink on the job," he said quietly. "But it's more than that. I haven't had a drop of liquor since the accident. I never want to lose control. I never want to be the reason someone's life is irrevocably altered."

I tried not to feel it. I did not *want* to feel more for the man who sat beside me. But I could not help the admiration that rooted in my chest, the respect that held me in its grasp. I'd never met anyone like Nathaniel, for whom goodness seemed so natural.

He looked at me, eyes searching. I'd been silent too long.

"Is he all right now?" I asked.

"Well enough, although he never recovered his full strength." He paused. "We were lucky he did not die. We know that."

"But that does not lessen his challenges," I said. "Or yours."

He shook his head. "It is my mother who feels the strain the most. She cares for him day in and day out and never complains. She takes in laundry and mending, but . . ." His face tightened. "Money is tight."

"You support them," I realized aloud. "Both of them."

He shifted forward to rest his elbows on his knees, dropping his clasped hands between his legs. "I have an older sister and brother, and they send what they can. But they've families of their own. I am more than willing to share all I have, though it's never enough with doctors' bills still piling up."

I bit my lip. "I imagine a fifty-pound reward would go a long way in helping."

His eyes flicked to mine. "Yes."

I looked down at my hands. "Did you think I pursued this case for the reward? That we competed against one another for it?"

"The thought did cross my mind," he admitted. "It is no small amount."

"No, it is not." I straightened my skirts, and it took me all of a moment to decide. "But I have no need for it. I took this case as a favor to Elizabeth. When we find Higgs, the reward is yours."

In truth, I had great need of fifty pounds. Independence beckoned to me like a siren on the waters. I'd so long dreamed of confronting my father and telling him I no longer needed his money. But what was my independence compared to the Dennings' well-being?

Nathaniel did not speak for a long moment, and I knew he was looking at me. But we sat far too close on the sofa for me to dare meet his eyes.

"That is a kindness I never thought to expect," he said finally. "Thank you."

I nodded briskly, as if it were nothing. As if I were feeling nothing.

But I felt too much. The light inside me pulled at my seams and filled my lungs.

I changed the subject. "In truth, I should be thanking you. For coming to my defense earlier."

He leaned back, amusement toying with the shape of his mouth. "Yes, I did wonder why it took you so long."

Ha! Insufferable.

"Though," I amended, "I did not *need* your help. Drunken cads are plentiful in all levels of Society. I've a range of experience."

"Oh?" he said, arching a brow. "And how would you have extricated yourself from tonight's situation?"

"A swift kick to the shin and a jab at his eyes," I said without hesitation.

He stared, then let out a chuckle. "You cannot be serious."

I crossed my arms. I fully realized that I looked like a petulant child, but sometimes, a situation called for petulance. "Quite serious."

He straightened. "Show me."

"Show you?" I looked around. "Here?"

"Certainly," he said, his lips still holding a smile. "Perhaps you might teach me something."

A challenge beckoned in his words. And I was never one to refuse a challenge.

"Very well." I stood and moved to the open area before the fire. "Come, you shall play my unwanted admirer."

He followed me over, anticipation written all over his face.

"Now," I said, "take my arm like he did."

Nathaniel's eyes narrowed as if he thought I was testing him, daring him. But he stepped forward and slowly wrapped his strong fingers around my raised forearm. His touch sent a spiral of sparks up through my chest.

"And my other hand?" he asked.

I gulped. I was just realizing that perhaps—*perhaps*—I hadn't thought this through. "Around my waist," I said, not sounding quite like myself.

He slid his right hand around my waist, his large palm flat against my back. He pulled me against him, and my skin lit like kindling.

"Like this?" His voice was low, deep.

I cleared my throat. "Yes," I managed. "I believe that's how it was."

We stood so close, knees brushing, hearts pounding. Or at least, mine was. I couldn't have heard his if I had tried, what with the rushing in my ears.

"And do you plan on escaping anytime soon?" he asked. I could feel the rough tumble of his voice through his chest.

"Only if you're sure. I don't wish to hurt you." I meant to sound confident and assured but instead came across as girlishly breathless. Horrible.

"I think I can handle it."

Indignation lit inside me. He thought me silly. So instead of following my previous plan of attack, I adapted.

Without any warning, I spun into him so my back was against his chest. I raised my right elbow and drove it toward his stomach—

He moved, dodging left to avoid my elbow. Before I could recover, he grasped my free arm and held it tight against my stomach, pressing my back firmly against him.

"Your move," he said in my ear, his breath stirring my curls. I knew he was grinning.

He wouldn't be grinning in a moment.

I stomped my foot down on the top of his boot, and he grunted, his grasp on me weakening just enough for me to slip one arm free. I whirled and aimed a fist at his jaw, hoping for a glancing blow. But he recovered and caught my wrist, holding it above my head as he pressed my other arm against my side.

I made the mistake of looking up at him. The firelight did favors to his features that he hardly needed—shadowing the planes of his sharp jaw and setting his auburn hair aglow.

But it was his eyes that undid me. They were inescapable, dark reflections of heat and desire that threatened to trap me and never let me go.

His chest rose and fell—mine did as well. But I knew it wasn't the physical exertion. This was . . . this was something else.

"A valiant effort." His gaze raked across my face. "I am impressed."

I narrowed my eyes. "And *I* am not finished." I twisted my wrist so that I grasped his, then tried to swing his arm down and back. The intent was to force him to the ground, his arm bent behind him. But he was too quick. He moved with me, then broke away just before I had him trapped.

We paced apart, both of us still breathing hard. He eyed me with what I thought might be respect—or perhaps it was a trick of the light.

"I see yours are not only drawing-room talents, Miss Travers," he said.

"Verity," I reminded him with a saucy tip of my head.

"Verity." One side of his lips curled up. "And where did you learn all that?"

"Jack," I said. "He insisted on teaching me."

"Why?" he asked curiously.

I hesitated a moment. "He was haunted by certain cases, ones that might have turned out differently if the victims could have defended themselves."

Nathaniel was silent a long moment, and I knew he must have had similar cases. A Bow Street officer was no stranger to pain and suffering.

"He was smart to teach you," he said finally. "Would that all brothers could be so concerned."

"I am lucky in that regard, at least."

"And in what ways are you unlucky?"

His question caught me off guard. No matter what had happened today, I wasn't about to tell him everything about myself. "I've lived a very fortunate life," I said instead.

He moved closer, crossing his arms as he inspected me. I held my ground with a stubborn jab of my chin.

"Always one step forward and two steps back," he said in a soft voice. "But I am undeterred."

Undeterred? What on earth did he mean?

His eyes dropped to my lips. It was only for a second, just the barest of flickers, yet all thought flew from my mind. My lungs ceased to function, my heart caught in a leap.

I'd been kissed before. I'd seen the look in a man's eyes, felt the tempting lure of anticipation that strung between a couple. And I was quite certain that Nathaniel Denning wanted to kiss me.

My heart rebelled.

This could not happen.

Before I could pull away, footsteps met our ears. Nathaniel moved quickly to the fireplace, and I turned, pretending to inspect a framed embroidery nearby.

"Heavens," Mrs. Denning exclaimed as she entered the sitting room, and for a moment, I thought she could sense the blazing energy that radiated between Nathaniel and me. "Look at the time. It's nearly ten o'clock."

I let out a sigh of relief as I faced her. She hadn't noticed, or if she had, she was tactful enough not to mention it. I tried my best not to look at Nathaniel, who'd braced a hand on the mantel as if he'd been standing there all along instead of being a heartbeat away from kissing me a few seconds ago.

"Your parents must be worried, Miss Travers," Mrs. Denning said.

"Just my mother, Mrs. Denning." Though Mama had a performance tonight and would never know I'd been gone.

"Oh," she said, a hand to her heart. "I am sorry for your loss."

I stared at her, uncomprehending, then coughed. Blast, I'd almost forgotten—forgotten the lie I'd told since I was old enough to understand it. "Thank you," I managed, my voice faint. "It was long ago, before I was born."

I did not want to lie to Mrs. Denning, who had been so kind to me. I did not want to lie to Nathaniel, who eyed me with such intensity that I was certain he could see right through my words. That my father was not a dead navy captain but a very-much-alive earl who lived only a few miles from here. Though he might as well be dead, considering our relationship—or lack thereof.

"Even still," she said, patting my hand. "Loss never leaves us, does it?"

I pushed away my guilt. The deception was necessary, I told myself. "Yes," I said. "Yes, how right you are."

"We must get you home to your mother," she said firmly. "Surely the trouble outside has calmed by now. Come, let us gather your things while Nathaniel finds you a hackney. There are usually one or two near the tavern on the corner, dear."

Nathaniel nodded and left, the front door closing behind him a few seconds later. The room felt smaller.

Mrs. Denning fetched my things, and I followed her to the tiny entryway.

"It was so lovely to have you with us tonight, Miss Travers," Mrs. Denning said, handing me my gloves. "I—well, I don't leave the house often these days, what with . . ." Her voice drifted off. "In any case, I so enjoyed meeting you. I hope you'll stop by if you ever find yourself in the neighborhood."

I took her hand. "Of course I will, Mrs. Denning. Thank you."

"And," she said, clasping my hand, "if I am not too bold to ask, would you keep an eye on Nathaniel? He has the folly of the young—believing he is invincible. But a mother knows better." Her eyes dimmed. "And a mother imagines the worst with a profession like his."

"I will do my best," I promised. "Though I had better not mention it to him."

Mrs. Denning laughed. "Indeed not. How he would squawk if he knew I'd asked you."

The front door opened then, Nathaniel half stepping back inside. His eyes met mine. "The coach is waiting."

I bid Mrs. Denning good night, then followed Nathaniel outside. A hackney stood in the street, the mismatched team clopping anxiously as the driver held them in place.

Nathaniel opened the door but paused. "Tomorrow, I plan to watch the tavern again. From the outside, that is. We made too much of a ruckus tonight to continue that ruse."

"I agree." Where was he headed with this line of thought?

He still held the door, one thumb running over the edge. "If you are not otherwise occupied, your help would be most welcome."

I appraised him. "Do you mean that? Or are you simply trying to keep me from—how did you say it—appearing when it least suits you?"

That quick smile again. "Does it matter?"

"No," I said. "I suppose not."

He held out his hand, large and masculine. It should have been foreign, considering I'd known him only a few days. But when my hand settled on his, they formed around each other with a familiarity that shot straight to my heart.

He helped me inside, releasing me when I was settled on the bench. Pulling back, he offered a slight bow. "Until tomorrow, Miss Travers."

"Verity." Why was I so insistent?

"Verity," he agreed. He shut the door, and the coach started along the cobblestones, leaving my thoughts in just as much disarray as my heart.

CHAPTER 14

My mind was a whirl the entire ride home. How could so much have happened in one day? Finding Nathaniel at the tavern, calling a truce, dashing through the streets, meeting his parents. And those last minutes together, when I'd practically wrestled the man to prove a point. To prove myself. Just the memory sent a rush of heat to my belly—and my cheeks. He'd had his arms wrapped around me, holding me firmly against him, and I hadn't minded one bit. I'd had to force myself to pull away.

It was absurd. I hardly knew Nathaniel Denning.

But you know some things, a small voice inside me said. *You know enough.*

Enough for what? To care for him? To kiss him?

No.

I could not let myself get involved with anyone. I knew what I wanted, and love did not factor into my future.

It wasn't that I did not believe in love. I did. It was a force to be reckoned with, a force that could build and grow into something beautiful. But it could also destroy a heart. I'd seen it firsthand, and I would not wish such sorrow on anyone.

Why, then, did I find that so hard to remember when Nathaniel looked at me with knowing in his eyes?

It was just because I was lost, I decided. Only a few months ago, I'd had a plan. I'd known how to achieve my goals. But now that thief-taking was no longer my path, I needed a new road to independence. Once I found that, it would reaffirm my determination. These feelings I had for Nathaniel, they were fleeting. He was a means to an end: solving this case for Elizabeth. And once we did that, our acquaintance would cease, surely.

I arrived home at half past ten o'clock. It was fully dark, the hackney's lanterns flickering as I descended from the coach. I tried to pay the jarvey, but he said Nathaniel already had. I frowned as I closed my reticule. Nathaniel had a family to support. He did not have money to spare for a hired hack. My resolution strengthened. I would help him earn that reward.

I let myself in the front door and closed it silently behind me.

"Verity?"

Apparently *not* so silently. I furrowed my brow, following Mama's voice to the parlor. Should she not be at Drury Lane? I had been certain no one would notice my late return. Grandmama always retired early.

I slipped off my bonnet as I entered, more than a little apprehensive. Mama stood near the window, arms crossed as she watched me. Her face was difficult to read, hidden in shadow, and she did not speak.

"I thought you were performing tonight," I said to fill the silence.

"No," she said stiffly. "Not tonight. And you can imagine my surprise when you did not show for dinner . . . or for hours after."

"I am sorry I am so late," I hurried to say. "I was with Elizabeth, and—"

"That was not the Harwoods' coach."

I blinked. "No, I—I hired one, because—"

She held up one hand. "I have spent the last few hours pacing and worrying. I had no idea where you were, Verity. Whether you were dead or alive. So what you say next had better be the truth."

"I was working my case," I said, my voice holding an edge I'd never heard from it. "The one I told you about."

"And where did this case take you?"

I hesitated. "The docks."

She stared at me. "You were down at the docks after dark, *alone*?"

"I am quite used to my own company these days," I said a bit shortly.

Mama stilled, staring at me. "What?"

I shouldn't have said that. I hadn't meant to. But the long day was dragging at me, my emotions worn and frayed at the edges. "Nothing," I said. "I'm sorry. I'll send a note next time."

Mama shook herself from her stupor. "There won't be a next time, Verity. I've tried to allow you your space, your independence, but this goes too far."

"And I have no say in my life?" I asked hotly.

"When you are foolish enough to put it in danger, then no."

"I wasn't in danger," I insisted. Not very much, at least. Nathaniel had ensured that.

She threw her hands in the air. "This is just like last time."

"No. No, it isn't."

Mama didn't hear me. "You've gotten in over your head again. You must see it. You must stop."

A strange anger clawed up my throat, but I pushed it back. Mama and I never quarreled. We had disagreements but nothing like this.

"You don't know anything about this case," I said, trying to keep my voice even. "Besides, I've learned from my mistakes. What happened three months ago won't happen again."

"You cannot know that." She took a step closer. "Verity, this is foolishness. Why can't you see that? This is not the life for a young lady."

Oh, but that was the wrong thing to say.

"A familiar admonition," I said tightly. "Is that not what everyone told you about becoming an actress?"

Mama was shaking her head before I finished speaking. "That is entirely different. There is no danger in what I do."

"Save for libertine earls."

"We've talked about this," she insisted. "You know the whole story."

I did. She'd told me herself when I was a girl, how the handsome earl had seen her on stage and fallen in love with her. How he'd wooed her and promised to marry her. How she'd fallen for his false sincerity and found herself pregnant. How she'd borne him a son and then a daughter. He'd broken Mama's heart countless times, but then he'd shattered it when he'd eventually married—a widowed baroness with a fortune.

The first memory I had of my father was when I'd been four or five. Mama had dressed me up like a doll, every perfect curl in place. He'd looked me over, declared me a pretty, pleasant girl, and that was it.

The second had been when I was sixteen. Mama had wanted to introduce me into Society—not as my father's daughter, of course—never that—and had brought me to see him. He'd asked me all sorts of questions about my schooling, my skills, my connections, and had seemed satisfied.

"She'll make a decent wife," he'd said to Mama as I'd been dismissed.

A decent wife. All my years of life boiled down to that.

I knew then I would be no one's wife. And I'd made certain my father knew it too.

"You must give this up," Mama said, bringing me back to the present. "This hopeless aspiration of yours. You've opportunities I could never have dreamed of. You can find a good match, settle down—"

"I don't want to settle down," I said. "And I don't want the opportunities you've forced upon me. They are all based on lies."

A quick intake of breath, as if she could not believe I'd said it. "Lies to protect you," she said. "To safeguard your reputation."

"And if I *did* marry?" I asked. "Am I to continue lying to my husband? Pretend my father died young when in truth I am the illegitimate daughter of a peer who refuses to acknowledge me? How could I do that to anyone, let alone someone I might love?" I shook my head. "That is not the life I want, trapped by a falsehood."

She sank heavily on the sofa. "That is not—" But her voice broke off. She shook her head and tried again. "I never meant—"

"I am tired," I whispered. "Good night, Mama." I hurried from the room, my emotions chasing after me, tears clouding my vision. I darted up the stairs to my room, throwing my bonnet in the corner as I swiped at my blurry eyes. Why must everything be so complicated? Why could my life not take the course of so many young women's—simple, sweet, happy?

I fell into bed and covered my face with my arms. I hadn't meant to fight with Mama. I knew how much she had done for me, and I knew she worried for me. But she did not seem to know what *I* wanted, and neither did she care to learn.

I closed my eyes, taking long, deep breaths to calm my rapid heartbeat. Sleep, I told myself. I needed a good night's rest. Everything was better after sleep.

I was only partly right. When I woke at first light, my emotions had thankfully settled. But my head pounded with a rapid staccato, a reminder that crying did not suit me in any way. My eyes were still red and puffy when I faced myself in the small mirror above my dressing table.

"What a stunning creature you are, Verity Travers," I muttered as I pinned my hair into a hasty bun. "A diamond of the first water, indeed."

Mama was not yet awake when I descended the stairs. Neither was Grandmama, though I could hear the movements of Pritchett and Cook belowstairs, preparing for the day. My stomach rumbled, but I did not want to risk meeting Mama before I knew what to say to her.

I opened the front door and slipped outside, the chill April air clinging to me and filling my lungs. I pulled my pelisse tighter about me as I started along the street.

And came to a sudden halt.

Nathaniel leaned against the gate two doors down, reading a newspaper and looking far more like a painting than he had any right to. The hazy light of dawn brushed his features with gold, and he held himself with such easy confidence. Heavens, the man was handsome. Perhaps it might have been better if the magistrate *had* appointed Nettleton to the case—at least then I wouldn't have to fight my blasted attraction every step of the investigation.

Nathaniel straightened when he saw me, folding his newspaper. "Good morning."

"Oh," I said, rather inventively. "I—I thought we would meet at the docks."

He gave a rueful smile. "I *had* thought the same, but Mother nearly boxed my ears last night when I mentioned it. She insisted I accompany you." He ran a hand through his hair, as though self-conscious. "My rooms aren't far from here. It wasn't a hardship."

I furrowed my brow. "Why did you not share my carriage last night? We might have returned together."

He shrugged. "I needed the walk."

I almost asked why but only just stopped myself. I wasn't sure I wanted to know.

We fell into step together and walked a minute in silence before he cast me a sidelong glance. "Did you not sleep well? You look tired."

I gave a little laugh. "One would think that you of all people would know how to flatter a lady, Sir Chivalry."

I'd meant to say it dryly, with humor, but his nickname came off too soft.

He caught my eyes with his. "I am not aiming at flattery today," he said. "I thought to try concern."

Concern. For me.

"I am fine," I said, though his words spun a fragile thread around my heart. "It's nothing to do with the case."

"And that means I cannot help?"

"No, it's just—" I took a steadying breath. "It is a family affair. A somewhat complicated one."

"I see."

He said nothing more, which was for the best. We needed to focus on our work. The sooner we found Higgs, the sooner Nathaniel could claim his reward and I could stamp out the threat against Elizabeth's reputation.

"How should we go about our task today?" I asked.

"There was a coffee shop on the corner near the tavern," he said. "We can likely see well enough from there."

"Let us hope our friends from last night don't return," I muttered.

"That is the benefit of them being ridiculously foxed," he said. "They likely don't remember a thing. Though I wouldn't mind another go at any of them." He flexed the knuckles of his right hand and winced. "Or perhaps not."

"You hurt yourself last night," I realized rather belatedly. "Fighting that man."

Why had I not noticed during our time together at his parents' home? Likely because I could not keep my eyes from his face.

Nathaniel grinned. "Fighting is a generous term. For him, I mean."

"You should have told me," I said. "My grandmother makes a very effective poultice for bruises."

He raised an eyebrow. "Does she?"

"It also wards off evil spirits," I said. "As a bonus."

Now he laughed. "A veritable cure-all, is it?"

I smiled for the first time that morning, though my heart warned me through it all. *Take care*, it whispered. *Take care.*

"Let's cross here," Nathaniel said, offering his arm as he looked down the street for any oncoming carriages.

I hesitated, then wrapped my hand around his arm, and he tightened it against his side.

"Miss Travers!"

My head jolted up. Who was calling my name?

I saw her in the next instant, running toward us down the street. It was Marianne, Elizabeth's maid, her bonnet dangling from its ribbons around her neck, her skirts tangled in her legs.

"Miss Travers," she gasped as she reached us, nearly bowling me over. "Thank goodness I found you. And Mr. Denning too. They already sent a message to Bow Street."

I grasped her elbows to steady her. "What on earth, Marianne? Are you all right?"

Marianne waved me off, still catching her breath. "It's not me, Miss Travers. It's Miss Harwood."

"Elizabeth?" I shot a bewildered look at Nathaniel hovering protectively nearby, eyes alarmed. "What's happened?"

"Have you seen her?" she asked, her voice desperate. "Please say you have seen her."

I shook my head. "Marianne, tell me."

"She's missing." Marianne was pale as the early dawn. "Elizabeth is gone."

CHAPTER 15

I stared open-mouthed at Marianne, but Nathaniel did not waste one second. He waved down a hackney, and we were on our way to Harwood House within the space of a minute.

"Tell us everything," he demanded, leaning across the coach toward Marianne.

She took a shuddering breath. "The family retired to their rooms last night as usual, including Miss Harwood. After helping her prepare for bed, I went to sleep."

"What time?" Nathaniel pressed.

"Around eleven," she said. "Perhaps half past."

"Then what?"

"This morning, a chambermaid went to stoke the fire in Miss Harwood's room," she said. "The maid noticed the bed hadn't been slept in, so she alerted the housekeeper, who told Lady Harwood." Marianne shook her head, eyes filled with tears. "They searched the entire house and could not find her anywhere. There is no note. She's simply gone. Vanished into the night."

Her words didn't make any sense to me. They entered my head, and yet, I could not comprehend them.

"Have her parents contacted Lord Blakely?" Nathaniel asked, his voice steady. Calm. Just hearing it helped settle the racing of my pulse. Yes, Lord Blakely. Perhaps Elizabeth had gone to her betrothed.

"Yes," she said, her eyes red-rimmed. "They sent a message to him, but I left before he responded."

I managed to clear my head enough to pose a question. "Was she acting strangely last night? Anything suspicious?"

Marianne shook her head. "No. Well, no more strange than normal. You know as well as I that she has not been right since the robbery. I thought it was lingering fear, but now . . ." She closed her eyes. "I am ever so worried, Miss Travers. I know she trusts you, and so I came for you straightaway."

Trusts me. Those words hit me hard. She'd trusted me enough to hire me to find her missing letter yet not enough to tell me what was in it. But I had to believe she had a reason.

I consoled poor Marianne until we arrived at Harwood House a few minutes later. When the coach rumbled to a stop, Nathaniel helped us both down, then led the way up the front stairs. The door was opened before he could knock, and by none other than Lady Harwood.

I nearly did not recognize her. She wore only her dressing gown, knotted messily at her waist, and her hair was a mass of graying waves about her shoulders. But it was her face that drew my eyes—lines of desperation and tight fear across every inch.

"Verity," she cried. "Please, tell me you have seen Elizabeth."

Marianne's words hadn't felt real, but now, with Lady Harwood's plea, the gravity of the situation hit me full force. Elizabeth was truly missing. She could be in danger. She could be—

No. I could not allow myself to spiral into vague possibilities and terrifying guesses. I had to manage this one minute at a time.

"Lady Harwood." I grasped her hands. They were cold and shaking. "I haven't seen her. I am so sorry."

Her shoulders bowed, and she looked smaller, like a frightened child.

"Come inside, Lady Harwood," Nathaniel said gently, one arm around her shoulders. "It is cold."

The house was in a riot, whispering servants gathering on the stairs as voices came from the open parlor door.

"—and you are certain the doors were locked?"

That was Sir Reginald's voice, more thunderous than I'd ever heard him.

"Yes, Sir Reginald, the house was secured for the night." That must be the butler. Poor man, to come under such scrutiny.

Nathaniel escorted Lady Harwood inside the parlor, and Marianne and I followed. I took in the scene all at once. Sir Reginald paced before the fireplace while Lord Blakely sat rigidly on the sofa, his handsome features creased with worry. The butler stood at attention nearby, and an older woman I presumed to be the housekeeper lingered at the back of the room.

Sir Reginald whirled as Nathaniel helped Lady Harwood to an arm-chair. "What news?" he demanded. "We sent word to Bow Street nearly an hour ago."

Nathaniel straightened. "I'm afraid I know nothing more than what Miss Harwood's maid has told us. She only just found Miss Travers and me."

If anyone wondered what the two of us were doing together, no one voiced their curiosity. Instead, Sir Reginald strode to Nathaniel and gripped his shoulder. "But you know what to do, yes? You can find her?"

Nathaniel's eyes flicked to mine. We both knew it was not a promise he could make.

"I will do everything in my power," he promised instead. "Now, please, sit. Tell me everything you know."

As Nathaniel began questioning Elizabeth's parents, I stepped to the housekeeper beside the door. "Some food and tea for Lady Harwood, I think," I said. "She needs to eat."

The housekeeper dabbed at her eyes with a handkerchief. "Right away."

I gestured to Marianne to join me on the settee near the window, out of the way but close enough to hear everything the others said. Nathaniel had brought out a little book and was jotting down notes as Lady Harwood and Sir Reginald spoke, telling him everything they knew, which was, essentially, nothing.

It was as Marianne had said. They'd all gone to bed around eleven o'clock, and when the maid had gone into Elizabeth's chambers this morning, Elizabeth was gone.

"No signs of an intrusion?" Nathaniel asked, his tone brisk.

"None," Sir Reginald insisted. "Her windows were locked. So was every window and door in the rest of the house."

"And Elizabeth said nothing about leaving to meet anyone? No appointments?"

"In the middle of the night?" Lady Harwood said with no small amount of disbelief. "Of course not."

"Not even to see her betrothed?" Nathaniel asked, sending a curious glance Lord Blakely's way, no doubt wondering if the two had arranged some sort of assignation.

But the earl shook his head. "No. We had no such plans, I swear."

I believed him, mostly because I knew Elizabeth. She would never do such a thing. But then, where *was* she?

Nathaniel tapped his pencil against the leather cover of his book, his brow furrowed.

"Is anything missing from her room?" I ventured. "Anything that might tell us where she went?"

Lady Harwood looked affronted. "I do not understand this line of questioning. Elizabeth did not *go* anywhere. She was abducted, quite clearly!"

But even Sir Reginald seemed to realize that theory made no sense. He shook his head, patting his wife's knee. "We would have heard if anyone had forced their way into the house. There would be signs."

Lady Harwood's lower lip trembled. "But . . . but why? Why would she leave?"

Her husband could only shake his head. I stared glassily past them as I wrestled within myself. They did not know about Elizabeth's missing letter or that whatever was in that letter was enough to make her panic at the thought of anyone finding it. Was it enough to make her want to disappear?

Then, of course, there was her admonition to me two nights ago. She'd asked me to stop investigating, with fear in her eyes even as she'd pretended nonchalance. But I hadn't stopped. In fact, I'd done the opposite and had thrown myself into finding Higgs, as if that would solve everything. But if I had instead told Nathaniel or her parents, Elizabeth might be sitting here today, just like any other morning.

This was my fault.

"I may know why she left," I said softly.

They all turned to stare at me.

"What do you mean?" Sir Reginald said. "Did she speak of this to you?"

"In part," I admitted.

Nathaniel's gaze was piercing from across the room, but he did not speak.

I took a deep breath. "Elizabeth knew my brother had been a Bow Street Runner. She thought I might be able to help."

It wasn't the whole truth, but I did not think Sir Reginald and Lady Harwood ready to accept a lady investigator, and it would only distract from finding Elizabeth.

"Help how?" Lord Blakely repeated, brow furrowed.

For a moment, I hesitated. Should I be speaking of this in front of Elizabeth's betrothed? Her parents were one thing; her intended was quite another. But it was too late now. I had to hope Elizabeth had put her trust in the right man.

"After the robbery outside the theatre," I said, "Elizabeth told me about a letter in her stolen reticule. She was afraid that the thief would read it and asked me if I had any ideas as to how she might recover the letter."

"But . . ." Lord Blakely shook his head. "But what was in the letter?"

"I do not know," I said. "She refused to tell me. But I cannot emphasize enough how worried she was. Anxious. Upset."

Lady Harwood and Sir Reginald stared at one another, seeming to have a conversation within a simple glance. What must that be like, to know someone so long and so well?

"She did seem different," Lady Harwood stammered. "I thought it was the robbery. I did not realize it was something more."

"And did you find the letter?" Sir Reginald asked me urgently.

I shook my head. "The night the painting was unveiled, she told me to stop looking into the matter. She attempted to laugh it off, but I knew better. Something spooked her, I am sure of it."

I could not bring myself to look at Nathaniel. What did he think of my revelations? Was he angry? Hurt that I had not told him sooner?

"And so she ran away," Lady Harwood whispered. "Am I so terrible a mother that she could not come to me?"

Sir Reginald dropped his head into his hands, no doubt feeling the same. I ached for them.

"Elizabeth loves you both," I said quietly. "Whatever her motivations, I believe she was trying to protect you. But I am sorry I did not tell you sooner. She asked me not to, and I thought I was doing the right thing, keeping a friend's confidence. But it grew beyond us so quickly." I swallowed hard. "I should have said something."

Lady Harwood shook her head and reached out for my hand. She was all that was prim and proper, but now, with tears in her eyes and her features so pale, she looked nothing like the feared Society matron most people saw. "I am simply glad she had a friend to call upon for help," she whispered.

I squeezed her hand, unable to speak.

Lord Blakely stood suddenly, clasping his hands behind his back and pacing to the window. "Are we certain," he said, "that she was not taken by someone? You say, Miss Travers, that the thief has the letter from her reticule. Could he have read it and come back for her for some reason?"

I shook my head. "Without knowing the contents of that letter, I cannot say."

Nathaniel spoke for the first time since I'd begun my confession. "It is very unlikely Miss Harwood was taken, considering that no servants sounded the alarm and no locks were forced or windows broken. I cannot see how a kidnapper would have managed it."

"Still," Lord Blakely said, "it is a possibility. And if so, should we not gather a search party?"

Nathaniel considered that. "Yes," he agreed. "It is better to be sure. She could very well still be in the city, whether she was taken or left of her own volition."

Lord Blakely did not wait another moment. He strode toward the door. "I can have a dozen carriages out searching for her within the hour," he promised.

I could not help being impressed. Lord Blakely seemed unfazed by the revelations about Elizabeth and only wished to do everything in his power to find her. His actions spoke well of his character.

After the earl left, Nathaniel sat forward on his chair, his face all business as he looked at the Harwoods. "If she did run away, we need to know where she might have gone. I will ask Bow Street to assist in the search here, but can you think of who she might call upon for help outside of London? Or a place she might feel safe?"

Lady Harwood and Sir Reginald looked at each other. "Perhaps Augusta?" she ventured, and he nodded.

"Augusta?" Nathaniel repeated.

She turned back to him. "My sister, Augusta Howard. She and Elizabeth are quite close. In fact, they spent a few months recently touring the south of England together." Then she gasped, sitting up straighter.

"What is it?" I sat forward on my chair.

"Elizabeth spoke of her aunt last night," she said, eyes dim. "After dinner. She mentioned how she missed Augusta after having traveled so long with her."

"And where does Mrs. Howard live?" Nathaniel's gaze took on a new sharpness.

"Bath," Lady Harwood said eagerly. "It is entirely possible that Elizabeth would run there. In fact, I think that very likely indeed." Her voice still shook, but her shoulders lifted with a dash of hope.

It was then that Marianne's expression caught my eye. She glanced between Nathaniel and me, chewing her lip, as if she wrestled with something in her mind. She caught me watching her and ducked her head. Whatever it was, she did not wish to share it.

"We'll go to Bath," Sir Reginald said firmly. "We'll find Elizabeth."

But Nathaniel shook his head. "You and Lady Harwood should stay here in case she returns. I will go to Bath. I'll leave as soon as I arrange everything with Bow Street."

Sir Reginald started to argue, but Lady Harwood rested one hand on his arm. "He's right," she said resolutely. "Let Mr. Denning do his job, and we will continue the search here."

Sir Reginald hesitated, then sat back wearily. "Very well," he conceded.

I was surprised the baronet gave in so easily. But I could see the fear behind his eyes, the worry for his daughter. He was out of his depth and trusting that Nathaniel knew best.

"I'll send word the minute I learn anything," Nathaniel promised.

I noticed he made no mention of me. No matter. I would bide my time.

"May we search Elizabeth's bedroom?" I asked Lady Harwood. "Perhaps we might find something useful."

"Of course," she said. "I can show you up myself."

"No," I said gently. "You must try to eat something, Lady Harwood. Marianne can take us."

Lady Harwood nodded in clear exhaustion and sank back into the sofa as Nathaniel and I followed Marianne from the parlor.

As soon as the door closed behind us, I faced Nathaniel. "I am coming with you to Bath."

He did not even look at me, starting up the stairs after Marianne. "No, you are not."

"And why is that?" I managed to keep my voice cool as I took the first few steps.

He let out a frustrated sigh. "For a great many reasons, Verity. It could be dangerous. We haven't any idea what Elizabeth is mixed up in. Then there is the issue of your reputation. We can hardly travel together."

"My reputation is fine," I snapped. "It is the last worry on my mind at a time like this."

He turned, eyes flashing. Considering that I stood on the step beneath him, he towered over me. "And what of the fact that you hid the truth about Elizabeth's letter from me? Did you not think that I should know something so critical to this investigation?"

"Considering I hardly knew you a few days ago," I retorted, "I think I had every right to keep my friend's secret."

"Yes, but after yesterday? After we—" He stopped, jaw tight as he glared over my shoulder. "I simply thought," he finally said, his voice low and sharp, "that I might have earned such a confidence. You must know I only wish to help."

"I know," I said in a soft voice. "Of course I know that. But I could not have known Elizabeth would run away. I was trying to do my best, and now we must press forward with the information we have now."

"*We* are not doing anything," he said. "There is no reason for you to go to Bath."

"There is every reason." I crossed my arms. "I know Elizabeth better than you do. You must acknowledge that I will be useful."

"That doesn't matter. I have to consider—"

"I am *going*," I said firmly. "Either with you or on my own. I'll leave it to you to decide."

Our eyes drilled into one another. Nathaniel's mouth was clenched, his shoulders stiff, but I did not back away.

"I'm going," I said once again, quiet but steady.

"Blast it." He groaned and raked a hand through his thick hair. "Fine. We'll go together. Heaven only knows what sort of mischief you would find on your own."

I bit back a grin of victory. But before I could say anything, Marianne spoke from the top of the stairs.

"Actually," she whispered, "I do not think either of you should go to Bath."

I'd forgotten she was there, so involved in our argument I had been. Nathaniel took one step toward her. "Why should we not go to Bath?"

But Marianne beckoned us up the stairs, eyes wide. We followed her to Elizabeth's room, and once we were all safely inside, she closed the door and faced us, wringing her hands and avoiding our eyes. "Elizabeth isn't in Bath," she said.

"How do you know that?" I asked, baffled. "Has she contacted you?"

"No," she hurried to assure me. "No, I haven't heard anything from her. But—but I know where she would go." She took a deep breath. "Bibury. It's a village in the Cotswold Hills."

"Bibury?" I shook my head. "Why would Elizabeth go there instead of to her favorite aunt?"

Marianne raised her eyes to mine. "I promised Elizabeth I would not tell. But you must believe me. If she is running, she ran to Bibury."

Part of me wished to disbelieve her. Bath seemed the surer option. But there was no doubt in her eyes, and the certainty in her voice spoke more than her words. How many secrets was Elizabeth keeping?

Nathaniel looked less convinced. "We cannot abandon a solid lead for a hunch. I need more information than that."

"It's no hunch, sir." Marianne looked to me for support, her features pained. "I won't break Elizabeth's confidence, but I will admit I know more than her parents do. They have no knowledge of any of this. Elizabeth did not go to Bath, I swear on my life."

I took her hand. I believed her. "How are we to find her there?"

"Ask for Rosemont Cottage," she replied, relief crossing her expression. "Someone can direct you. 'Tis a small hamlet."

A cottage in Bibury. I'd never been to the Cotswolds, but clearly, Elizabeth had. Perhaps during her months of traveling with her aunt? And if she had visited the town before, then Marianne likely had as well, as Elizabeth's maid.

Nathaniel and I looked at each other, each trying to gauge the other's reaction.

"It does make more sense for Elizabeth to go somewhere we wouldn't immediately suspect," I said finally. "Besides, the Cotswolds are not so very far from Bath. We can travel there after if we do not find her in Bibury."

Nathaniel paced away a few steps, then stopped and braced his hands against his waist. "You are sure?" he asked Marianne, glancing over his shoulder.

"As sure as can be," she said, her voice trembling. "Please, you must help her."

Nathaniel blew out a long breath and turned back at me with resignation. "It appears we are going to Bibury."

I nodded, trying to force away the apprehension that kneaded through my chest. I'd never been so personally attached to a case before, and it changed everything. I wasn't simply trying to earn a bit of money or build my clientele. I was searching for *Elizabeth*. She could be in danger or, at the very least, in a great deal of trouble.

I had to find her, even if it meant casting my own fears away. I had Nathaniel's help this time, after all. Things would be different.

They had to be.

CHAPTER 16

We searched Elizabeth's room to no avail, finding nothing useful beyond a few missing dresses and some personal items, which lent credence to the thought that she had indeed run away. A kidnapper was not likely to allow his victim to pack first. After arranging to meet Nathaniel at Bow Street, I hurried home to pack for our trip to Bibury.

I slipped inside the front door and padded up the stairs. I hoped Mama was still sleeping. If she saw what I was up to, it would only cause another quarrel, and I had no time. I hadn't any idea where Grandmama might be. Likely spying on the neighbors with her opera glasses again.

I packed quickly, stuffing everything into a portmanteau I'd pillaged from the small attic room. I was half afraid Nathaniel might try to leave without me. He was still frustrated with me for keeping the letter a secret, and I could not blame him.

Even frustrated, though, he'd kept a clear head. He'd asked me to bring any sketches I had of Elizabeth, so I carefully placed those on the top of my full bag. Then I left a note for Mama on my pillow, and I crept down the stairs with the portmanteau in one hand, my half boots in the other. I stepped carefully, not wanting to alert anyone to my escape. When I reached the front door, I carefully pulled on my boots, knotting the laces securely, then picked up my bag once again.

"And where are you off to?"

I whirled. Grandmama sat before the fire, her eyebrows arched.

"Drat it all." I leaned against the door. How had I not seen her when I'd come in? "Heavens, Grandmama, were you waiting just so you could frighten me?"

"Yes," she said dryly. "I've nothing better to do than terrorize my granddaughter."

"It would not surprise me."

"You didn't answer my question," she said, stabbing at the carpet with her cane. "Where are you going? I may be old, but I know you haven't any plans to travel."

The blasted portmanteau had given me away. "I'm working a case," I said. "I wrote Mama a letter explaining everything."

"Hmm." Grandmama stood, wizened arms shaking as she braced herself on the cane. "And will that handsome gentleman who met you this morning be joining you?"

"Grandmama," I accused. "Have you been watching from the windows again?"

She cackled. "As if I have anything else to occupy my time with."

I rubbed a hand over my closed eyes. "And here I thought I was rather inconspicuous."

"Ridiculous?" she said, pretending to mishear me. "Yes, quite."

I sighed. "Mr. Denning *is* coming with me. We'll be gone a few days at most. Please tell Mama not to worry."

"That is like telling the clouds not to rain." She shuffled toward me, cane clattering loudly against the floorboards. I tried not to wince. "She'll be furious I let you go."

"Then don't tell her."

A wicked grin caught her lips. "The two of you are more alike than you think, you know."

I didn't want to think of it now. My quarrel with Mama seemed so long ago. I had to focus on Elizabeth. "I must go." I moved for the door. "I'll be home soon."

"Wait."

I turned back to see her pulling a gold chain from around her neck. A brass pendant swung at the end, encasing a dark stone. She held it out to me.

I eyed it warily. "What is that?"

"A bezoar," she said. "A talisman against bad fortune."

I stared at her. "You wish me to take a stone from the stomach of a goat for good luck."

Grandmama shook the pendant at me. "It's not doing me any good. You need it."

I sighed. I knew it was her way of telling me to take care. That she loved me. "Thank you," I said, taking the chain from her. I made to slip it into my reticule, but she tsked and pointed at my neck. I looped the chain over my neck and tucked the pendant beneath my pelisse.

"There you are," she declared. "I feel better already."

I stepped forward to kiss her cheek, her skin papery soft. "Do keep out of trouble while I'm away."

"I make no promises. Trouble is the only sort of fun I have these days."

I left a moment later, my heart lighter. Grandmama often had that effect, though she didn't mean to.

I hurried down the road, determined not to be late and give Nathaniel any more reason to be cross with me. My bag knocked into my knees every other step. I cast a quick look over my shoulder as I prepared to cross the street . . . and I paused.

I'd seen a figure—or I thought I had—from the corner of my eye. But now as I looked, I saw only two maids with baskets and an old man with a cane, none of whom paid me any mind. Nonetheless, a skitter ran up my spine.

Crossing the street, I tried to push away the feeling, but it persisted, drawing lines of ice through me. I walked another minute, listening for footsteps behind me, but the noise of the street covered anything I might hear. I slowed and pretended to look in a shop window, peering back as surreptitiously as I could. There. I saw it, a shape in the shadows two buildings away.

Starting off again, I waited until the street was nearly clear. I could barely hear the scuffle of footsteps, but I knew he was there. I set my heel and whirled about. "If that is you, Wily, you'd better show yourself before I pull my pistol."

A moment passed, then he stepped from the darkened doorway of an apothecary, eyes glinting. He held up both hands as he grinned. "You're a difficult woman to surprise, Miss Travers," he said, sauntering forward.

"If only that were true." I narrowed my eyes. "But no, I was plenty surprised when Mrs. Webb told me you were in league with Tobias Higgs, the very man I was trying to find."

Wily's hands lowered. "Ah," he said. "You know about that."

"I know," I said tightly. "And I've half a mind to turn you in."

"It was just a job," he said, hands in his pockets. "Higgs came to me needing to sell off the larger pieces he'd lifted. Once I'd sold them and taken my cut, I was going to tell you where he was."

"How kind." My voice was dry. "You make a hefty commission while my friend is missing."

"Missing?" Wily repeated, confused. "What do you mean?"

"Miss Harwood, the friend whose letter you were supposed to help me find." I took a step closer. "She's gone. We think she's run away. At least, we hope she has."

He stared at me, his ruddy cheeks growing redder by the second. "You can't be blaming me. I had nothing to do with that."

I set my jaw. "No, it was my fault. For trusting that you might care more for helping me than for profit."

"I never . . ." But his voice faded off. He shook his head. "Did she run because of that letter?"

I lifted one shoulder. "I have to believe so. She was consumed with finding it." Then my eyes focused on him. "Why? Do you know what became of it?"

Wily shifted uncomfortably. "Perhaps."

I took a step closer. "Tell me," I demanded.

"All right, all right," he stammered. "After you and I met in the park, I asked Higgs why he'd thought it a brilliant idea to rob a baronet right outside a theatre. The man's no fool, no matter what you think." Wily paused. "He said someone paid him to do it."

My brow furrowed. "Someone paid Higgs to attack a random group of theatre-goers?"

"No," he countered. "Someone paid him to attack your friend and her parents."

I stared at him. "The Harwoods? But why?" I knew they were wealthy, and their jewelry had likely been worth a small fortune, but why them among all the extravagantly rich at Drury Lane that night?

Wily shrugged. "Haven't the foggiest. But Higgs said the fellow told him to take everything from them. When Higgs brought the loot to him, the man only kept the young miss's reticule."

"With the letter," I said, stunned. "But who was it? Who was the man who hired Higgs?"

"I don't know," he said. "I never met him, and Higgs didn't know him. Didn't care to either, especially not after the man let him keep the jewelry."

Someone had paid Higgs to rob the Harwoods, to take their things and attack Sir Reginald. Because of the letter? Had this mystery man known Elizabeth would have it?

I held one hand to my head, trying to think. "Why are you here now? Why did you seek me out?"

"I finished my business with Higgs." He scuffed his boot along the stones.

"So now that you're finished with him, you'll sell him out." I scowled. "No honor among thieves, indeed."

His head jerked up. "I'm not a thief, Miss Travers," he growled. "I'm a fence."

I snorted. "I am finding that distinction impossible to see at the moment."

"A man's got to eat," he said, squaring his shoulders. "I'm sorry I didn't tell you I knew Higgs, but I didn't see the harm at the time. I'd get my money, and you'd get your man, eventually."

"Oh? And where is he, exactly?"

"St. Giles," he said promptly.

My stomach dropped. St. Giles was a rookery north of Covent Garden, with crime so abundant that even Bow Street rarely ventured within its boundaries.

But it was not the danger that worried me. St. Giles was an intricate maze of twisted lanes and narrow passages. It was known to disorient even those born and bred there. What chance did we have of finding Higgs among its crowded lodging houses?

"Anything more specific than that?" I asked, disheartened.

"He was trying to lie low." He blew out a breath. "I couldn't very well ask for an address. A bit suspicious, don't you think?"

I crossed my arms, bumps rising along my skin even though the sun shone overhead. Higgs had simply been a front man. Who was the stranger who hired him? Had Elizabeth somehow made an enemy?

So many questions raced through my mind, but one resolution clarified like a strike of lightning. I had to tell Nathaniel. If we found Higgs, perhaps he could lead us to the man who had hired him.

"I have to go," I said abruptly.

"To Bow Street?"

I shot a look at him. "Yes. Someone has to find Elizabeth."

Wily coughed. "Perhaps you might not tell the Runners about me."

"We'll see," I said, allowing a hint of a threat into my voice.

He held up one hand. "I came in good faith to help you."

"And for a share of the fifty pounds." I didn't bother to mention that I'd already given up the reward to Nathaniel in my mind.

He took a backward step. "I don't want it," he said, more serious than I'd ever seen him. Wily was always flighty and ridiculous, but now I thought I heard a touch of regret in his voice. "I'm sorry about your friend. Truly."

I nodded, glancing up the street. When I looked back, he was gone.

CHAPTER 17

I arrived at Bow Street to find it bustling with officers and patrol-men. It seemed Nathaniel had called upon the vast resources of the magistrate's court, all on behalf of Elizabeth. I stood there a moment in the thick of it, my eyes touched with tears. No matter that he was frustrated with me, he was doing everything he could to find Elizabeth.

I spotted him across the room, addressing a group of patrolmen. He spoke calmly but assuredly, his expression serious. There was such confidence in his every aspect. How easily he commanded their attention—and mine.

The group around him began breaking up, and I stepped toward him just as someone moved in front of me.

"Pardon me," I said absently. Then I looked again at the man's trimmed beard. "Mr. Allett?"

The portraitist stopped, surprised at my recognition. His blue eyes squinted at my face, trying to place me.

"Miss Travers," I reminded him, bobbing a curtsy. "We met at Harwood House a few days ago."

He nodded. "That's right. The young lady with the sketch."

"Yes." I peered up at him curiously. "Might I ask what brought you to Bow Street today?"

He tightened his cravat with a soft sigh. "It's this business with Miss Harwood, I'm afraid. I was asked to bring my sketches of the young lady, from the portrait I was painting of her. They would be the most recent likeness of her, and useful in a search."

"Oh?" That was odd. Nathaniel certainly wouldn't need mine if he had Allett's sketches.

"Miss Travers." Nathaniel appeared at my side.

Immediate awareness of him swept through my body, lighting up my spine. "Mr. Denning," I managed.

"I see you've found Mr. Allett," he said, giving the slightest raise of his eyebrow.

A *suspicious* raise of his eyebrow. My mouth parted slightly. Had he . . . had he remembered what I'd told him about my hopes for working with Mr. Allett? Had he brought him here on purpose so I might see him again?

"Yes, indeed," I said slowly.

"And did you bring your sketches?" Nathaniel asked.

"I did," I said, though I held my portmanteau closer. I hadn't imagined Mr. Allett would see these.

Nathaniel held out a hand for them, daring me to refuse him in front of Mr. Allett.

"I hardly see why you need mine," I said, cheeks pricking. "You have Mr. Allett's sketches, which are no doubt superior."

"We have several search parties," Nathaniel said evenly. "The more, the better."

Mr. Allett waited expectantly, so I reached inside my portmanteau and extracted the sketches.

"Here you are," I said quietly, handing them to Nathaniel.

He flipped through them, Mr. Allett glancing unobtrusively over his shoulder. Nathaniel nodded. "These will do nicely. One moment, please." Without another word, he strode away.

"Miss Travers."

I turned to look at Mr. Allett, swallowing hard. "Yes?"

He gave a gentle smile. "I know this is certainly not the right time, what with Miss Harwood's plight. But I owe you an apology."

"An apology?"

"Indeed. I asked you to bring your sketches to Lady Harwood's party the other night, and then I fell ill. I am sorry if I disappointed you by not showing."

"Oh." I shook my head. "You needn't apologize, sir. It was hardly your fault."

"Be that as it may," he said, "I likely dashed your hopes, and I am sorry for it. But based on what I've seen of your work, you have true talent. I should be interested to see more and to discuss a possible apprenticeship. You need only to send a note round, perhaps when things have . . . calmed."

It took me a few seconds to recover enough to speak. "Thank you, Mr. Allett. That is very kind."

He tipped his hat. "I wish you the very best of luck in finding your friend, Miss Travers."

I curtsied as he left, and when I rose, I could not help the tugging at my lips. I had an offer from Mr. Allett. What that offer entailed, exactly, I wasn't sure. But it was something. A start.

Nathaniel appeared back at my side, his own large valise in hand. He had apparently finished distributing the sketches. "Are you ready?"

I did not beat around the bush. "Did you bring Allett here because of me?"

"I brought him here to help with the search," he said briskly. "If you happened to speak to him, that is your affair." He took my bag from my hand and started for the door.

I wasn't sure which to protest, his casual appropriation of my bag or his unexpected meddling in my affairs. I decided upon the latter. "You do not owe me any favors," I said, starting after him. "Why help me after I kept information from you?"

He stopped and turned to face me, head tilted. "Is that how you view the world, Verity? As favors owed and gained? Transactions rather than relationships?"

I was taken aback. "I—"

"I helped you," he went on, "because it is entirely possible to care about someone even when they enjoy testing the limits of one's self-restraint."

I blinked.

"Now come," he said, his eyes softening. "We have a coach to catch."

I trailed after him, trying to decipher his words. *Cared* could mean a great many things. One could care about a horse, a favorite book, a family heirloom. But the way he'd said it almost made me think he meant more.

But it did not matter. I could not let it matter.

Besides, I had more important issues to discuss.

"Nathaniel," I said, again hurrying to catch him before he stepped outside. "Considering I have the utmost respect for your patience"—he scoffed—"before we left, I thought to tell you something I just learned from an informant."

"An informant?" Nathaniel faced me again. "And what did this informant say?"

I took a deep breath. "That Higgs had been hired to rob the Har-woods. That the man who hired him wanted none of the jewelry—only Elizabeth's reticule."

His expression shifted. "With the letter inside."

"Yes," I said. "I cannot help but think it's all connected. It must be. Elizabeth didn't want anyone to read the contents of that letter, but someone found it. Someone *knew*."

Nathaniel frowned. "Things just grew infinitely more complicated."

"More still," I said. "My informant says Higgs is hiding in St. Giles."

"Of course he is." Nathaniel exhaled. "I need to pass this on to the officers searching for Elizabeth. I'll only be a moment."

He spoke quickly to another officer, then joined me again. We left Bow Street and walked together in silence. I sent him a sidelong glance, trying not to admire his profile. I should be trying to fight the fire in my stomach, not fan the flames.

I cast about for a topic. "I admit, I half expected you to leave for Bibury without me."

"I gave you my word." He sounded somewhat insulted that I would doubt him. "Besides, I am quite aware that you would follow on your own, and I could never abide that."

"Because you've taken it upon yourself to become my protector?" I teased.

"If you'll let me," he said rather seriously.

I'd thought he would grin, make a joke, wave off my comment. But he hadn't. And something strange happened. The fire inside me didn't flare in a rush of sparks. It smoldered, flickering and safe, filling me with warmth.

"I know, I know," he said with a sigh. "You can take care of your-self."

I fiddled with my reticule. "Heaven forbid I refuse Sir Chivalry an opportunity to help a lady."

Now he did grin, and it spread across his face like sunlight. "You do it often enough."

We arrived a few minutes later at the Gloucester Coffee House on Piccadilly, from which our mail coach was set to depart. The equipage was waiting in the yard, its horses being readied while passengers pre-pared to board. I moved toward the coach office to purchase tickets, but Nathaniel shook his head.

"I've already secured tickets," he said, leading us toward the coach.

My brows knit together. "I can pay my own way." I knew very well that coach travel was expensive—too expensive for a Bow Street officer supporting his parents.

He only shrugged. "You can pay for the inn tonight."

The inn?

Logically, I'd known that we would not be able to reach Bibury today. But I hadn't realized what that might entail as to our sleeping arrangements.

Nathaniel handed our bags to a porter, who loaded them atop the coach, then he helped me up the step and inside. Two gentlemen had already taken the forward-facing bench, perfectly content to ignore me as I sat opposite them. Nathaniel settled on the bench beside me, his long leg brushing mine. I hitched a breath. Our journey to Bibury would take the better part of two days—two days of sitting beside Nathaniel, his arms and legs pressed against mine, his masculine scent filling my head.

The other passengers found their seats atop the coach, and we started off with the sound of a horn, winding through the London streets.

"I must say, I am astonished your mother gave her permission for this venture," Nathaniel said quietly, bending toward my ear so as not to be overheard by our two companions. "Even if Elizabeth is a friend."

I shifted my weight uneasily. He had insisted on this condition this morning as we'd made our plans, and I'd lied quite baldly when I'd agreed. "Ah, well." I'd hoped to avoid this topic until we were out of London. "I did not ask her, precisely. I left her a note."

"A note?" Nathaniel stared at me. "Blast it, Verity, you promised me."

"I am one and twenty," I said tightly. "I can make my own decisions."

"Yes, but now she will think me an indecent rogue who whisked you away."

Indecent was right. Everything about him was downright indecent—that deep voice, those flashing eyes, the way he consumed space.

"She'll think nothing of the sort," I managed. "I explained everything in my note."

He scrubbed a hand over his face. "You'll make a fellow go mad, Verity Travers."

"Then it is a good thing I never intend to marry. I can hardly condemn a man to insanity."

I wasn't sure why I said it. Perhaps I meant to make light of the situation, draw his ire away.

But instead, he turned to look at me, his expression impossible to read. "You never wish to marry?" he asked. Curious. Careful.

Why had I said it? "Matrimony holds no appeal for me."

His brow settled low over his eyes, and he looked as if he wished to press the point.

I shifted uneasily. "I—I should not have said anything. Please, forget you heard it."

Nathaniel's eyes raked over my face. He exhaled a long breath, shaking his head. "I find it quite impossible to forget anything about you."

He was so close. I couldn't escape his penetrating gaze, his mystifying interest in me. I knew I wasn't imagining it. Nathaniel did not bother to hide his emotions, at least when he wasn't working. What I saw in his eyes when he looked at me was enough to make any woman dizzy—and I wasn't any woman. We'd grown closer this past week, and what I'd learned about him only made this pull between us stronger. More intoxicating.

I dragged my eyes from him, a physical pain. I tried to think of something—anything—to say, and I toyed with the pendant hanging from my neck.

Nathaniel glanced down at the pendant in my hands. "What is that?"

"Oh." I looked down at it, my thoughts still fuzzy. Rational thought was rather elusive when seated beside Mr. Nathaniel Denning. "My grandmother gave it to me. It's a bezoar."

"A bezoar?"

I smiled at his baffled expression. "Grandmama is a great believer in superstition and folklore. Like her poultices, it's meant to ward off bad fortune."

"And does it work?" he asked, clearly amused.

"Well, you've yet to insist the coachman turn around and take me home, so I shall answer a tentative yes."

His lips twitched. "It's a mail coach. They would laugh in my face."

"Thank heavens for the Royal Mail."

One of the men across from us eyed us strangely. I wondered if he could hear our conversation above the noise of the coach. Apparently Nathaniel thought the same, because we fell into silence.

We spoke little for the rest of the morning. Nathaniel pulled out a book from his pocket while I contented myself with gazing out the window at the passing landscape. I did not often leave London, save for a visit every now and again to Wimborne, Jack's new home. If the bumping of the coach wouldn't have rendered my efforts disastrous, I might have attempted a sketch of the lovely countryside.

The distraction certainly would have been welcome. As it was, I could not stop myself from thinking constantly of Elizabeth. I hadn't any idea what we might learn tomorrow. Perhaps she had committed some terrible crime and was hiding from the authorities. Or perhaps she had been kidnapped after all, and she wasn't even in Bibury. If we *did* find her, would she speak to us, or would she refuse?

It was nearly two o'clock in the afternoon when we stopped yet again to change horses in a small village. Dark clouds threatened as passengers piled from the coach—mail coaches only stopped for minutes at a time—and hurried to stretch their legs or see to their needs. Several people hawked their food for sale, and I purchased a few potato pasties for us to share.

We were walking back to the coach when the rain began to fall. It wasn't torrential, by any account, but it was enough that Nathaniel put his hand to my back, hastening our steps. That was, until I brought us both to a halt.

A young mother stood beside the coach, a babe in her arms and two rosy-cheeked children clutching her skirts. They'd boarded with us in London and had traveled atop our carriage. It was a vastly inferior option, but the fare was much cheaper. And based on the worn state of her clothing and those of her children, it had likely taken all her funds.

Now she pulled the children around her, shielding them and the baby from the rain as best she could, her face tired and distraught.

I did not have children, but I knew a woman in distress. I went to her, touching her arm gently. She looked at me, startled. "Take our places inside," I said, peeking at the baby in her arms. The child could not be more than a few weeks old and fussed with a scrunched-up face. "None of you should be in the rain."

The woman stared at me. "I couldn't, ma'am," she stammered. "We didn't pay for that. The coachman—"

"Never mind the coachman," I said. "Now, hurry in before you all get wet."

"I—" She shook her head in disbelief, her eyes shiny as she looked down at her little ones. "Thank you," she whispered. "I wasn't sure how I would manage."

Nathaniel stepped forward. "Here, allow me."

He helped her inside, then lifted both of the wide-eyed children to
sit on the bench beside her. If he had any objections to my giving up our
seats, he didn't say.

"Thank you both," the woman said sincerely. "Truly."

I was taken aback by her gratitude. "It is nothing," I said, my voice
a bit raspy.

Nathaniel closed the door, then turned to face me, his eyes discern-
ing. He gestured to the steps leading atop the coach. "Shall we?"

With Nathaniel's help, I managed the high step up and settled on
the bench behind the driver, barely wide enough for the two of us. It
must have been miserable for that poor woman with three children
hanging off her. I wished I'd thought to offer our seats sooner.

Nathaniel climbed up behind me, the shoulders of his coat already
damp from the misting rain. It would be a long afternoon, no doubt,
but I could not bring myself to regret my decision.

Especially not as Nathaniel settled beside me, the coach swaying
beneath us with his movements. He was even closer now than inside
the coach. There was positively no space between us, our sides pressed
together, his warmth reaching to me.

I shivered, but it had little to do with the rain.

He noticed, of course. "I suppose you've nothing warmer than that
pelisse?"

I shook my head. I'd not thought we'd spend much time exposed to
the elements, and I'd packed so quickly.

The coach jolted forward, and nothing but Nathaniel's firm arm
behind me kept me from toppling right over the back of the bench.

"Hold on," he said and waited until I grasped the railing before
reaching for his bag, which the porter had fortuitously stowed on the
roof of the coach behind us. Unbuckling the top, he searched around
before pulling out a gray wool scarf, thick and dry. He held it out to me.

"No," I said, pulling back slightly. Very slightly—I truly had nowhere to go on this tiny bench. "That is yours."

He sighed. "Obviously. I am offering it to you."

"I was the one who gave up our seats."

"And it should have been me," he said gruffly. "Here, take the blasted
scarf."

When I hesitated, he began wrapping it around my neck himself.
I opened my mouth to protest yet again, but then his hands grazed the
delicate skin of my neck, and my stomach tumbled like a leaf on the
wind. I lost all ability to speak.

His eyes met mine as he coiled the scarf once again. His breath caressed my cheek, which was no doubt red and flushed. He finished, his hands pausing briefly to adjust the scarf before dropping to his lap.

"Thank you." My voice did not belong to me. It belonged to some breathless, lovesick girl.

Nathaniel nodded. The hair peeking from the bottom of his hat was damp, curling around his ears rather boyishly. It was altogether charming and attractive—alarmingly so.

A brisk wind picked up as we left the shelter of the little town where we'd stopped. Nathaniel again rifled through his bag.

"Here we are," he said as he pulled out a folded lump of fabric. "One never regrets being prepared." He unfolded a blanket, small and worn but quite cozy looking. "May I?"

He draped it around both of our backs, offering me one side to hold while he took the other.

"Do you always travel with your own bedding?" I asked.

"Let us simply say that I've learned not to trust the supposed comforts a roadside inn provides," he said.

We pulled the blanket up over our heads, creating a canopy of sorts.

"That should keep off the worst of it," he said. "Though I hope you haven't any plans to attend a ball tonight."

I laughed, and it was a relieving sound, breaking the strange tension that had crept between us since he'd so gently brushed my neck. "Are you insinuating that limp curls and sodden skirts are *not* the height of fashion these days?"

"A pity, if not so," he said, looking straight ahead even as his cheeks colored slightly. "You do wear them well."

Pleasure slipped through every inch of me. He meant his words, even as bedraggled as I knew I looked. He always meant his words.

Nathaniel shifted his weight. "We ought to establish a story for ourselves. Why we are traveling together."

I'd thought the same thing earlier, inside the coach, but hadn't dared broach the subject within earshot of those two gentlemen. "Can we not simply be brother and sister again?"

"I am not entirely sure such a ruse would be convincing."

He had a point. Just the way he looked at me—boldly, burning— was enough to set off anyone's suspicions.

"What, then?" I curled my fingers around my edge of the blanket, peeking out into the dreary rain. "You could be my cousin."

"I thought perhaps husband."

I nearly choked, whipping my head to look at him. He grinned.

"No," I sputtered immediately. "We cannot do that."

"And why is that?" he said, somehow—impossibly—leaning closer, teasing in his every feature. "Of course, someone *will* wonder what a lout like me is doing with a woman like you, but perhaps you can tell them I am incredibly clever or fabulously rich."

"No," I said again, heat spreading across my neck and cheeks. "I only meant . . ." I paused. "We certainly could not convince anyone we are married. We hardly know each other."

"*That* is not true," he said. "I know you are picky about your food and enjoy boxing with drunkards in your spare time."

"Only ones with ill intent," I said, hiding a grin. "Besides, those are hardly the things anyone will expect a husband to know."

"And what might those things be?"

"How I take my tea, for example," I replied. "My habits. My likes and dislikes."

"True enough." He nodded knowingly. "There is an obvious solution, you know. I shall simply learn everything about you in the next few hours."

I laughed. I could not help it. The stress of the last few days had worn my nerves to their breaking point, and his lightness, his teasing, was precisely what I needed to escape—if only for a short while. "Very well," I said, shifting under the blanket to look at him more closely. "What would you like to know?"

"Well, you made your tea preferences sound like a critical bit of information."

My lips seemed stuck in an upward turn. "You mustn't judge me too harshly."

"Meaning?"

"The more sugar, the better," I said. "And drowned in cream."

"I see." His mouth twitched. "You prefer not to taste the tea."

I wrinkled my nose. "If at all possible."

Now he laughed, and the sound bounded through my chest, filling me and forming me. I did not think I could ever tire of his laugh. It was a kite lifting through the clouds, a glimpse of brighter and better days.

"Very well," he said, still grinning. "A little tea to go with your sugar. That is a start."

"What else do you wish to know?"

He paused, thinking. "Your favorite flower?"

"You shall be disappointed," I said. "I haven't one."

"You haven't a favorite flower?" He widened his eyes as if positively perplexed. "But every lady loves flowers. I think you all must be born with a natural adoration."

"I don't *dislike* flowers," I said, nudging him playfully with my elbow. "It is only that none stand above the others in my estimation. Can't a girl like roses and marigolds equally?"

"Not when our pretend marriage is on the line, I'm afraid," he said quite seriously.

I sighed. "Very well. For the sake of our ruse, I shall say daisies."

"Daisies?"

I fought the urge to cross my arms. "Why not daisies? I think they are rather underestimated."

He arched a brow as if unconvinced.

"They are simple and steadfast," I insisted, not entirely sure why I felt so defensive, "but still beautiful in their own way."

"Hmm," he said. "Telling."

The meaning behind his words was clear. "Are you calling me simple?"

He laughed. "I would never accuse *you* of simplicity. But the rest . . . Yes, I think they do nicely."

The back of my neck warmed. He thought me beautiful?

"Another question," he said, not letting me dwell. "Do you prefer to burn the midnight oil or rise with the sun?"

I made a face. "That is a question designed to make a person appear lazy."

Nathaniel looked amused. "How so?"

"If I admit to preferring both a late night and a late morning, you shall think me rather unambitious."

"I would think no such thing. But I would ask why."

I lifted one shoulder, an awkward movement considering the blanket draped over us and the fact that my shoulder still pressed firmly against his. "I love the quiet of night. I do my best work then."

"Your drawing?"

I nodded. "When I'm not so distracted, I can focus easier. I've always had a mind for faces. I draw other things, of course, and I do enjoy a variety, but nothing sharpens my skills more than a portrait." I paused. "I think it is the eyes. One can tell a great deal from a person's eyes. The sort of life they've lived. The good and the bad. It is a very difficult thing to capture, but when I do . . ." I sighed. "The feeling is unparalleled."

Nathaniel was quiet a moment. "The sketch you did of me," he said slowly. "The one I saw at the Harwoods' party."

I did not move. "Yes?"

He glanced at me, then away. "The rest was yet unfinished, but my eyes were . . . well, it was like staring at myself. Rather disconcerting, really."

I said nothing, biting my lip. What was he getting at?

"I only wondered," he said, "how you did that. How you captured me so well when I was little more than a stranger."

I looked again at the rainy countryside, my insides a fluttering mess.

"I—" I paused. "It does not happen often. Never, really. But from our first meeting, I was drawn to you. I wanted to know more of you. Your story."

I could see from the edge of my vision that he watched me, fully focused on my words. And suddenly, I felt ridiculous. He was going to think I was like those other ladies who followed after him, charmed by his manners and good looks.

"It is silly," I said quickly. "I am rambling. That is what happens when I spend too much time on the road, I'm afraid."

He allowed me my retreat. "It could be a great deal worse. I generally spend my time with men who seem to abhor bathing. You are a pleasant change, to be sure."

"Because I smell better?"

He smiled. "I don't ask for much in a traveling companion, but that is high on my list."

It was easy, being with him. He made our conversation a living thing, coaxing out answers from me like crocuses popping up from a snowy bank in the springtime. I should not want to talk with him like this. I should be thinking about Elizabeth, not enjoying the sound of his voice in my ear, the pressure of his body against my side.

But I did.

Very much.

I peeked at Nathaniel. He gazed forward, a trace of a smile still on his lips. A shadow was just beginning to appear against his jaw, disappearing beneath his cravat, and the wind toyed with a lock of his hair. I had to resist the urge to smooth it back.

Blast.

Oh, Verity, I groaned to myself. *What have you gotten yourself into?*

$\mathscr{C}$HAPTER 18

We talked for hours, our conversation flowing surely and easily. The rain grew heavier throughout the day, and we huddled closer, the blanket doing its best to keep us dry.

Nathaniel seemed not to mind our close proximity, speaking in my ear as he told me of his childhood, of growing up the youngest of three children. He spoke more of his parents, of their industry and diligence. He shared stories from his youth, making me laugh at his boyish antics and wish I had known him then.

For all he told me, he pressed me for stories of my own, so I told him of my childhood, my family. I carefully avoided any mention of my father, and he did not pry. The minutes flew past us, blurring together countless moments of laughter and sincerity.

When the coach came to another stop—we'd halted several times to change horses—I looked up in a daze. It still rained, but the heavy clouds had darkened even more with the coming night. How had the day passed so quickly? I'd never experienced anything like this before. I'd never lost myself so thoroughly in someone else.

"This is our stop for tonight," Nathaniel said, glancing around the small town, the rain still falling as the other passengers disembarked. "This coach continues on north. We'll take the morning coach west to Cirencester."

Nathaniel climbed down first, then I placed one foot on the step and paused, eyeing the gap between the step and the ground.

"Here," Nathaniel said, moving to help me. I reached for his hand, but he instead took me around the waist. He lifted me with such ease that my heart swooped, then he set me gently on the ground. His hands lingered at my sides.

"Thank you," I said, more hoarsely than I would ever care to admit. Surely it was a known fact that a lady was prone to lose her voice when being held by a handsome man? It seemed like sound science.

He released me and turned away, taking our bags as the porter handed them down and giving me a moment to collect myself. I spotted the young mother and her children off to one side. Her two oldest had their arms wrapped around a kneeling man, and the woman was beaming, rocking her babe. She caught my eye and gave me a grateful smile. I smiled back and nodded.

When Nathaniel had both our bags, I gestured toward a building to our right, a rather rickety establishment with a barely legible sign in the window advertising rooms for rent.

"Perhaps we might try our luck there," I said, eyeing the rest of the town. "It may be our only option."

Several of the other passengers were already making their way to the inn, and we were last in line when we stepped inside. The taproom was warm and cozy, filled with travelers and locals alike enjoying meals together. We waited patiently, glad to be out of the rain that now pounded on the roof above us.

The man ahead of us finally took his key and shuffled off to the stairs. I stepped forward to greet the innkeeper while Nathaniel handled our bags.

He looked at me from behind spectacles, smiling kindly. "Good evening, Mrs. . . . ?"

"Travers," I said without thinking.

His eyes moved to Nathaniel. "You must be Mr. Travers, then."

Nathaniel's mouth dropped, and it was all I could do to stop myself from bursting out laughing.

"Yes," I somehow managed, my grin as wide as the Thames. "This is my husband, Mr. *Travers*." I slipped my arm through Nathaniel's, looking up at him with mischievous eyes.

He coughed to cover what I was certain was a laugh of his own.

"Ah," the innkeeper said with a knowing gleam to his eye. "Newly married?"

"Very," Nathaniel said, his voice dry. "So new it doesn't quite feel real."

"I knew it," the man said triumphantly. "I've an eye for that sort of thing."

"Indeed?" I asked. "Well, you've pegged us right. We are desperately in love."

I glanced up at Nathaniel, expecting to still see that barely concealed smile. But his expression had frozen, and he looked away when I met his gaze. Was it something I'd said?

"As you should be," the innkeeper said, flipping through his ledger. "Let me see what room I have available."

"Oh." My eyes snapped back to him. "Do forgive me, but we shall need separate rooms. Still adjusting to marriage, you see."

The innkeeper raised his brow, no doubt wondering what "adjusting to marriage" meant.

"Very well." He consulted his ledger once again. He frowned and flipped another page. "Oh dear."

"What is it?" Blast, was there only one room available?

"I'm afraid I gave my last room to the fellow before you," he said apologetically.

"Your last room?" I repeated, not comprehending.

"I do apologize." He looked truly abashed.

"No matter," Nathaniel said from behind me. "Would you point us in the direction of the nearest accommodations?"

The innkeeper licked his lips. "I'm afraid we are the only inn for miles."

Nathaniel and I exchanged a baffled glance. What on earth were we to do? There were no coaches leaving until dawn, and we had nowhere to go. Not that we could leave anyway, with the rain beating down outside.

"Surely you've other rooms," Nathaniel pressed the innkeeper. "Perhaps a small closet, tucked out of the way."

I did not even allow my mind to drift toward that possibility. Nathaniel and I, together in a *closet*.

But the innkeeper shook his head. "I am terribly sorry, I don't—" Then he paused. "Well, perhaps there is one option."

"Yes?" I asked.

He gestured to the taproom behind us. "When the crowds leave, I could lay two mattresses before the fire. It would hardly be private, but it would be warm and dry."

I hesitated. Sleeping in a public room? But it was a better option than wandering in the rain, looking for someone to take us in.

I glanced at Nathaniel, and he nodded.

"Thank you, sir," I said to the innkeeper. "We are most grateful for your offer."

He guided us to a table in the corner, assuring us dinner would be ready soon, then left.

"I suppose it could be worse," Nathaniel said, his good humor not abandoning him now. He draped his coat over the back of his chair to dry. "He might have put us up in the stables."

I grinned as I removed my gloves and bonnet. "How very biblical."

As promised, the innkeeper brought us a hearty meal of roast chicken and potatoes, which soon filled my belly with warmth as the fire dried the dampness from my skin. Nathaniel and I spoke quietly as we ate, sharing observations about the other patrons, listening to the ebb and flow of a dozen conversations.

It was . . . comfortable. Familiar, somehow, though I supposed we *had* spent the better part of a day at The Nag's Head in London. But this inn was far less rowdy and considerably more pleasant.

As the evening went on, the tap room slowly emptied, travelers retiring to their rooms while the locals lingered for one more pint. It was after eleven o'clock before the innkeeper, Mr. Rutts, locked the front door and applied himself to the task of our beds. Nathaniel helped him carry two spare straw mattresses from upstairs and set them before the fire, moving tables aside to make room.

Mrs. Rutts, a sweet, matronly woman, insisted the men hang a blanket to block off the main part of the tap room, giving us a modicum of privacy. I could hardly protest, so I thanked her with an embarrassed smile as I avoided Nathaniel's laughing eyes. While the men rigged up the blanket, Mrs. Rutts invited me to their private rooms to change. I gratefully slipped out of my still-damp dress and stockings, then stood with my hands on my hips, considering my options. I certainly could not wear my night rail. I could never be so undressed in front of any man, let alone Nathaniel.

I decided to sleep in my second traveling dress, a dark-blue muslin. I kept my stays on, though I loosened them slightly. I wouldn't be terribly comfortable sleeping in them, but it was better than the alternative.

When I emerged, Mrs. Rutts handed me a stack of blankets and pillows. "Here you are, dear. I am sorry we could not offer better accommodations."

I smiled. "We are grateful, truly."

I bid her good night and reentered the taproom, now split into a smaller section by a threadbare blanket. I stepped around the temporary wall, feeling the warmth of the fire again. Nathaniel stood near the mattresses, one hand rubbing the back of his neck. He looked up at my entrance, and I did not think I imagined the flush in his cheeks.

"Mr. Rutts insisted on setting them up like this," he muttered.

The two mattresses were pushed together, the cozy glow of the fire settling on them. Without waiting, Nathaniel bent and pulled one to the side, leaving a two-foot gap between the beds. There wasn't room for anything more.

"Lady's choice, Mrs. Travers." He gestured at the two mattresses.

"Why, thank you, Mr. Travers." I chose the bed on the right and set the blankets beside it, then sat down, almost moaning at how good it felt to sit upon something so soft after the hard benches in the mail coach.

Nathaniel cleared his throat. "I—I need to change."

It was then that I noticed he still wore his traveling clothes, dirty and damp. Mrs. Rutts hadn't thought to offer him a room to change in, apparently imagining a man would have no qualms changing in a public room, considering he had only his *wife* for an audience.

"Oh." Now my face flushed, hot and prickly. "Of course. I—I'll wait behind here."

I retreated behind the blanket once more, blessing my lucky stars that I hadn't had to change in the same room as him. I did not think I would have been able to look at him again.

I heard rustling behind the blanket, and my mind strayed. I snapped it back to attention, the back of my neck warm, and cast around for a topic to distract the both of us. "What time do you think we will arrive in Bibury tomorrow?" My voice was pitched just a touch higher than normal.

"Midafternoon, I imagine." His voice was slightly muffled.

"Good," I said determinedly, trying very hard not to watch the shadows he cast against the firelit ceiling as he dressed. "The sooner we find Elizabeth, the better. I am certain she will have answers for us, and then we can put this entire ordeal behind us." I decided to busy my hands and began pulling hair pins from my messy coiffure.

"What will you do when it is behind you?" he asked.

"Return to my quiet life, I suppose," I mused, curls falling loose around my shoulders as I worked. "Or as quiet as life with my mother allows."

"And is that what you want?"

There was something in his voice—a subtle surety that he knew the answer before he had asked the question.

"Why should I not?" I asked lightly.

"Because," he said, "you are not the sort of woman who pines for a quiet life."

I straightened, clutching my handful of hair pins. "Pardon?"

"You told me once that you had wished to become like your brother," he said. "A thief-taker of sorts. It is not a dream that one gives up easily. But you did."

My jaw tightened. "I did."

"Why?"

"That is not—" I had to stop and take a breath. "I don't wish to discuss it." I set my hair pins on the nearby table.

"Of course you don't." He spoke low, but his voice was no longer dampened by the blanket between us.

I turned in surprise. "I am not—"

Then I froze. Nathaniel held aside the edge of the blanket, wearing clean breeches and a new shirt. His sleeves were rolled up to his elbows, muscular forearms taut. He wore no cravat, so his collar hung limp, his top buttons undone, revealing the smooth curve of collarbone beneath.

I should look away—his feet were bare, his shirt untucked. But he met my gaze with an unyielding one of his own, so I straightened my shoulders. "I have my reasons for keeping such things to myself."

He said nothing, only watched me with those shadowed eyes that seemed to see the barest part of me. I moved around him, snatching up my bundle of wet clothing from beside my mattress. I went to the fire to drape them over nearby chairs, as if that might help. A useless endeavor. The image of him standing there would surely be emblazoned on my mind forevermore.

"I am sorry. I . . ." He paused, then sighed, and I imagined him running a hand through his hair. "Everything I've learned about you, Verity, only makes me want to know more. I cannot seem to help myself."

I was holding my sodden stockings, though I suddenly could not remember *why*. My mind was entirely consumed in the words he'd just spoken, words that hovered between us, alive and aware.

"I am sorry," he said again, more softly. "I won't pry anymore."

My hands tightened about my stockings, and my stomach tumbled—because I already knew I had given in. "There was an incident," I said, my voice scratchy.

He said nothing and made no movement behind me. I made myself lay my stockings over the chair with unsteady hands, then crossed my arms around my middle.

"I was investigating a case," I said. "A lady had engaged me to find a man she'd hired as her new butler, who had then robbed her blind a fortnight later."

The quiet between us grew, surrounding me.

"I found him," I said, "and was following him home one night. He was dangerous, wanted for many violent crimes, but I was certain I could handle him. I had my pistol and a fool's confidence." I had to take a deep breath before continuing. "I had a feeling something wasn't right, but I ignored it. He—he led me down an alley and waited until I turned the corner. He had me by the throat before I could so much as scream." My hand rose unbidden to my throat, to that fragile column of flesh.

"He was enormous," I whispered. "And strong. I hadn't a chance, even with the tricks Jack had taught me. I fought against him, but it did nothing. I could not breathe."

A footstep sounded behind me, as if Nathaniel moved closer.

"It was a very near thing," I somehow managed. "My vision went black. But then I heard a shout. We'd been seen from the street. The man dropped me and ran. That is the only reason I am still alive." I wrapped my fingers around my neck. "I could almost feel the bruises there, the faintness of my pulse. "I was in terrible condition. My throat was so swollen, I couldn't speak for nearly a week. I could barely eat or drink. The bruises lasted far longer."

I stared into the fire, the emotions of that night gripping me, tearing me apart yet again. Death had hovered like a crow over me, eyeing me hungrily. I had defied it, but that did not mean I had forgotten its cold, grasping claws.

I finally turned to Nathaniel, my hand dropping to once again fold over my stomach. "There you have it," I said quietly. "The reason I abandoned my dream. I am too afraid. A coward."

"A coward?"

The edge in his voice made me look at him. To my surprise, Nathaniel's face was set in a murderous expression, his shadowed jaw tight, his eyes aflame. "A man tried to strangle you in a dark alley, and you think *you* are a coward?"

I gulped. I hadn't imagined this reaction. "If not a coward, then a fool, certainly. Imagining that I could do it alone. That I did not need anyone's help."

He shook his head vehemently. "He simply got the jump on you. *He* is the coward, attacking a woman like that."

"He likely did not know I was a woman," I said for some reason. "I was cloaked, and it was dark."

Nathaniel threw up his hands. "As if that makes any difference." He paced away a few steps, then returned, a scowl on his face. "Did you ever catch him?"

I shook my head. It was one of the greatest regrets of my life. "I never saw him again. I imagine he took his bounty and skipped town that night." I was suddenly and irrevocably exhausted. The long day of travel, the spent emotions of the past week—my legs no longer wished to hold me. I lowered myself to the foot of my mattress, near the fire. I needed that warmth.

A minute later, Nathaniel seated himself beside me, his elbow propped on one bent knee, his other leg stretched toward the fire. I glanced sidelong at him. His mouth was pressed into a dark slash, though his jaw had lost some of its tension.

We sat together in silence for a few minutes as Nathaniel weighed what I'd told him. I could hardly sort out my own feelings. No one but Mama and Grandmama knew what had happened that night. I'd begged them not to tell anyone, especially Jack. I could not bear to think that my brother would know of my failure. He'd always been proud of me.

But telling Nathaniel now . . . While it did not change my fears nor ease my memories of that awful night, his reaction—his fury at my assailant, the fierce protectiveness in his eyes—made me breathe fully for the first time in months. He hadn't written me off as some dotty woman in over her head, as almost anyone would have.

My mother included.

"I was engaged once," Nathaniel said.

His words were like a stone dropped into still water. I turned to stare up at him.

"Her name was Hannah," he said. "A childhood friend. We were well suited, everyone said. I thought so too."

A hot bolt of jealousy shot through me. I did not even try to pretend it *wasn't* jealousy. I felt it to my core, this world-tilting realization that Nathaniel had once asked another woman to marry him. I tucked my knees to my chest, clasping my arms around them. "What happened?" I managed.

He absently ran his knuckles against his jaw. "I was shot."

"Shot?" The disbelief in my voice was tangible.

He grinned ruefully. "The criminal I was attempting to apprehend did not take kindly to my interference. I ducked, but not quickly enough." He pulled down the collar of his shirt to reveal a scar, a white line slashing across the slope of his shoulder. "I was fortunate. It was a glancing blow, though it hurt like the dickens."

He pushed his collar back into place, which was probably for the best. My eyes had already started to wander along the shadowed lines of his chest.

"It wasn't a serious injury," he said, "but it frightened Hannah. She insisted I leave Bow Street, follow my father into his carpentry business instead. I was just a lowly member of the foot patrol at the time, not an officer, and she couldn't comprehend why I felt such a draw to my work." He shot me a wry smile. "As you might have surmised, I chose not to leave."

"So she left you?" It was inconceivable. What sort of woman would ever leave Nathaniel Denning once she had him?

He sighed. "It was not quite as simple as that, but yes. She did not want to live a life of fear, and that I could understand. But neither could I sacrifice what I saw as my calling. And so we broke our engagement." He lifted one shoulder. "She's married now, these last three years. Has two children. Happy, I think."

I eyed him. "And are you happy?"

He considered that. "Yes," he said finally, "though I have certainly had moments over the years when I've doubted my decision. When I think of what I might have had."

That jealousy again. A bitter pill.

"But," he said, still not looking at me, "I've since realized I did not love her as I should have. If I had truly loved her, I should have given up anything for her. So I believe it was for the best. She is loved and appreciated, and I finally have the post I've been working for since I was a boy." He shook his head. "I only shared because . . ." He paused. "Verity, you are not alone in feeling afraid. It is part of what we do. It's something we must confront every day."

We. As if we were equals.

"But choosing *not* to confront it," he said, "is a different sort of bravery. Choosing what is best for you and your life, even if it goes against everything you thought you wanted."

Like he had. Choosing between his betrothed and his desire to help people at Bow Street.

"Allow yourself some grace," he said. "And some time. You might be surprised how different things can seem with just a little of both." He bent his head to look me in the eye. "I think you have a gift, Verity

Travers. I've worked with dozens of officers, and you rival even the best in cleverness, in grit, in talent. But no matter what you choose to make of your life, it will be exceptional."

He made me wish to cry—for joy, of gratitude. For letting me see the other side of what pains I had suffered and assuring me that he felt them too.

"I've never known anyone like you," I said quietly. "You say what you feel, and you mean it. No guile or deception." I shook my head. "You are a good man, Nathaniel."

I wasn't sure when in our conversation we'd moved closer to each other. An unknown force had drawn us together, inch by inch, breath by breath. Our hands, propped on the floor between us, did not touch, but I swore I could feel the brush of his fingers, the surge of energy that sparked whenever he touched me.

My gaze rose until I met his eyes. I could see the fire reflected there, an orange haze of heat. His gaze consumed me. My curls fell over my shoulder in a wild wave of ebony, and his hand lifted, trapping a ringlet between his thumb and forefinger. I caught my breath.

"Am I still a good man if I wish to kiss you?" His voice was husky as he rubbed his fingers over the strands of hair. Every inch of my skin felt hot, as though I sat under a brilliant summer sun.

"If I want you to," I whispered.

He swallowed hard, watching me intently, then he bent toward me, every movement deliberate and steady. His large hand moved to cradle the back of my neck, his thumb caressing my jaw. The feel of his rough skin against mine made my blood race through my veins. This man would make my heart give out.

He did not pull me to him. He came to me, allowing me every chance to retreat.

I did not. I wanted this. I wanted it like I'd never wanted anything before. My eyes fluttered closed.

His mouth hovered even closer to mine, and then he paused. Waiting. I could feel him there. My hand moved of its own accord, touching his shirt, the thin muslin the only thing separating us.

Then he kissed me, his lips capturing mine, and it was everything. Light and dark, heart and soul, hot and cold. There was nothing possessive in his kiss, yet I felt utterly *his*. And I wanted him to be mine.

I tugged on his shirt, pulling him closer. He went a step further and wrapped his arm tightly around my waist, bringing me firmly against his side. He wasn't about to let me go now. Our lips danced a rhythm only our hearts knew. We parted to breathe, then came together again.

My hands found his jaw, the coarseness of his unshaven skin. I felt lightning wherever he touched me—a skimming up my arms, a graze of knuckles across my cheek, his fingers in my hair. I never wanted to stop. Kissing Nathaniel Denning made the world disappear. He made me feel like I *was* the world—or at least his world.

There was nothing to stop us, save our own consciences, which I was eager to ignore. I preferred blissful escape.

He did not seem quite as keen. He suddenly pulled back, breath ragged. "Verity."

My chest rose and fell rapidly, and I scolded my lungs. What was it about kissing that made one forget to breathe?

"We can't . . ." His cheeks were flushed, eyes heavy. "I shouldn't have done that. You're under my protection. You're—" He broke off, shaking his head and releasing me. "I'm sorry."

I wasn't, though I should have been. I'd kept secrets from this man and kept them still. I should not want his kisses so desperately when I knew they could lead us nowhere. I couldn't allow myself to go down the path I'd sworn off years ago.

Even if his kisses made me wish I'd never made such a promise to myself.

He sat back on his mattress, elbows on his knees, and raked a hand through his hair—which was already quite mussed, thanks to my attentions. Though that was hardly my fault. He really shouldn't have such touchable hair.

I moved away as well, trying to hold myself together. "No, I—" My voice was hoarse, thin. "I understand."

"I *want* to kiss you," he said as if he were afraid he hadn't made that clear in the last few minutes. "Heaven knows I do, but . . ."

A smile found my lips, even amid the turmoil of my mind. "I know," I said softly.

We sat in a still silence for a few moments, then he stood, regarding our space with a critical eye. He lifted his mattress into his arms.

"What are you doing?" I stared up at him.

"I've acted quite the rogue tonight," he said, moving toward the blanket that separated us from the rest of the tap room. "I'll try to be a gentleman for the remainder." He disappeared, a soft thump revealing he'd set his mattress just on the other side of our makeshift wall. When he came back, he began gathering his things, not looking at me.

"You'll be cold away from the fire," I managed.

"A fitting punishment," he said with an exhale.

He hardly needed to punish himself for kissing me. I certainly hadn't tried to stop him. But I did not think that was truly his reason. We had crossed a bridge tonight into foreign territory. He was allowing me some space, as much as he could give me in our current circumstances, and I was grateful.

"What will Mrs. Rutts think if she comes across you out there in the middle of the night?" I asked.

He smiled wryly. "We may have to pretend a lover's spat come morning." He straightened, arms filled with blankets, clothes, and his bag. He looked at me for the first time since he'd broken our kiss, his eyes seeming to shout a million emotions, each more baffling than the last. "We should sleep," he said finally. "It's late."

I nodded, though I knew sleep would be impossible. How could I drift off to oblivion when my heart still beat staccato in my chest and my lips felt the lack of his?

I had the feeling he felt the same, considering how his eyes followed me as I turned away to prepare myself for bed. But he said nothing more, only slipped back through the blanket. We did not speak as we settled onto our beds.

I stared up at the shadows the fire cast across the ceiling. I was in a strange town, a strange bed, traveling with a man I'd known only a short time. But he *wasn't* a stranger, and I felt safer and more at peace than I had in months, lying near him in the quiet.

I hesitated, then slipped my left hand under the edge of the blanket that separated us, my palm up and fingers open. A moment passed, then his hand found mine, our fingers twining together.

I gave a soundless sigh, and he ran his thumb across the inside of my wrist. It soothed me, made my heartbeat steady and my thoughts slow.

"Good night, Nathaniel," I whispered.

"Good night, Verity," he said, his deep voice a soft rumble.

I closed my eyes and let myself drift off.

CHAPTER 19

The sounds of pots and pans clanking from the inn's kitchen woke me the next morning. I squinted, the dim light slowly bringing the tap room to life around me—the ceiling beams, the crackling fire, the blanket hanging beside me. Other than the noises of the kitchen, though, I heard nothing from the rest of the tap room.

I sat up, not daring to peek beneath the blanket. "Nathaniel?"

"I'm here," he called from the other side. "I haven't abandoned you at some wayside inn, I promise."

I pushed aside my covers and stood, straightening my dress. Then I drew back the edge of the blanket and peered out. Nathaniel stood at the window overlooking the street. He offered a small smile when he saw me.

"We are the first awake?" I asked. His mattress had already been stowed, his bedding a neat pile on a nearby chair.

"Well, *I* was," he clarified with a mischievous glint in his eyes. "You do snore ever so much."

My mouth dropped. "I do *not*."

Did I?

He laughed and made his way toward me through the tables and chairs. "No, you do not. You slept rather peacefully, in truth."

Now my face heated for a different reason. I silently prayed I had not talked in my sleep. Heaven only knew what I might have said, considering the dreams I'd had. Dreams that heavily favored Nathaniel—and his lips.

But then my eyes widened, and my hands flew to my dark curls, so disorderly that they had begun to overtake the edges of my vision. I knew very well how I looked when I slept without braids or curling papers. But I'd been a bit distracted last night and hadn't remembered to tend to my hair. Likely, the back of my head was a mass of tangles, which was *not* charming, no matter how I tried to convince myself.

Nathaniel followed me as I stepped back inside our little room. I knelt beside my portmanteau and pulled out my brush and a small hand mirror. I tried to prop the mirror on a nearby chair, but it kept falling.

"Allow me?" Nathaniel took the mirror and sat on the chair, holding the mirror at eye level.

I met his eyes briefly, then looked away. "Thank you."

I wrestled with my hairbrush, trying to tame my chaotic curls. All the while, Nathaniel watched, quiet. When at last I could pull my brush through without snagging, I began pinning up a tolerable coiffure.

In the light of day, the events of last night seemed impossible. Had we truly kissed, right here where I sat? Had I fallen asleep with his hand in mine, his voice a whisper in my ear?

"Nathaniel." My voice was creaky. "About last night."

I hadn't yet formed my next words. How could I tell him nothing could happen between us when every illogical part of me was begging for another kiss?

"It won't happen again," he said softly. "It should never have happened at all, especially while working a case involving your friend."

He was right, of course. What a terrible friend I was, wrestling my feelings for this man—*kissing* this man—while Elizabeth remained missing.

I grasped onto his words. "Yes," I said firmly. "We must focus on Elizabeth. We cannot allow any . . . distractions."

He hesitated, searching my face. Did he sense there was so much more I was not telling him? "Agreed," he said.

I nodded as I placed my last hair pin, though I felt more unsettled than before. I should have told him the truth—that I did not think I could ever share my heart with another. Except, *was* that still the truth? My heart campaigned against my mind, railed against the logic of my long-held convictions.

But I refused to allow it any purchase. Nathaniel and I felt something for each other. That much was clear. I could not think beyond that now, though, not when I had too much else to preoccupy my mind— Elizabeth and the mystery surrounding her disappearance. I had to put her first. My confusing feelings for Nathaniel had to be second.

At least for now.

I reached to take the mirror from him, and my fingers brushed his. My skin seemed to remember him, welcoming his touch. "Thank you."

"Of course," he said. "I hardly want to travel with a madwoman. What an improvement a few pins make."

I threw my hairbrush at him, but he caught it, laughing. I found I was grinning.

The inn came alive soon after, Mrs. Rutts serving us a thick porridge accompanied by sweet bread dappled with raisins. When the mail coach arrived, we claimed our seats inside, no lone mothers needing shelter from the rain this time. We sat across from an older couple, who seemed perfectly content to snap at one another.

Beyond a few exchanged looks of amusement, Nathaniel and I said little to each other throughout the morning. I was glad for it, in truth. I did not know what more I could say to a man the night after we'd kissed each other breathless. And I was terrified of what he might say to me.

The morning passed quickly. I spent most of the drive peering out the window, entirely enchanted by the passing scenery. We wound through gentle hills and wooded coverts, the sky a brilliant blue after the rain of yesterday. I loved London, but there was something about the country in springtime that made a girl's heart yearn to make flower crowns and walk barefoot through the grass. It made me miss those years as a child when we'd traveled with Mama's many acting troupes, Jack and I always together, running about the countryside, causing mischief.

We arrived in Bibury just before three o'clock. We claimed our bags from atop the coach while fresh horses were hitched and new passengers boarded. Then the mail coach was off with a plume of dust.

Bibury was a little village settled into meandering green hills. Thatched-roof houses perched on either side of the road, sleepy and quaint even in midafternoon.

"Turn right at the corner, then follow the lane over Hawker's Hill," the barkeeper instructed when we stopped at the tavern for directions. "There be a sign. Ye can't miss it."

Nathaniel headed up the lane, and I trailed behind him, heart in my throat. We'd traveled two days for this. We'd given up the lead in Bath to pursue Marianne's urging. We'd trusted her, but would her information prove correct? Or had this all been a wild goose chase?

I stopped right there in the middle of the shaded lane and closed my eyes, trying to push down the wave of crushing fear, clutching my portmanteau in both hands.

"Verity?"

I shook my head. "We've come all this way, Nathaniel. What if she's not here?"

Gentle hands tugged the bag from my grip. I opened my eyes to see him take my bag in the same hand as his valise, then he held out his free hand to me. "There is only one way to be sure," he said quietly.

I took the deepest breath I could summon and slipped my hand into his. We continued, birds twittering in the thickness of the trees above us. A low rock wall ran along both sides of the lane, overgrown with ivy and speckled with purple flowers I could not name. Every so often, a gate would interrupt the wall, but none bore the name we sought.

Until we turned a bend, and there it was. A few uneven steps led up to an iron gate, and on a stone plaque were etched the words *Rosemont Cottage*. A small yard in the front burst with color, flowers of every shape and size, and as I stood there, I heard laughter.

I knew that laugh.

I released Nathaniel's hand and rushed up the stairs, desperate now. As I came to the gate, I grasped the top, the iron warm in the sun.

A young woman sat in the tiny garden, a blanket spread beneath her skirts. Her back was to me, but her golden curls gave her away.

"Elizabeth?" My voice was barely above a whisper.

She turned. Her mouth parted. "Verity?"

Then she was on her feet and running to me. With the gate still between us, she flung her arms around me, clutching me tightly. I held her in return, my face pressed into her neck.

"How did you find me?" she breathed.

"Marianne," I said, my words muffled.

"Oh, that girl." She sniffed and pulled away, crying unashamedly.

"Oh, Elizabeth." I touched her face. "Are you all right? Are you in danger?"

She shook her head. "No. Not here, at least."

I grasped her shoulders. "What happened? Why did you run?"

"I'm sorry, Verity," she said, swiping tears from her cheeks. "I did not know what else to do."

"You must tell me everything," I said. "We will face this together."

She began to nod, then noticed Nathaniel for the first time. She froze. "Mr. Denning."

"Miss Harwood," he said with a slight bow. "I cannot say how relieved I am to see you."

Elizabeth looked back at me, her eyes once again afraid. "Are you working with Bow Street?"

"I know you did not want them involved," I said apologetically. "I am sorry, but after you went missing, I could not think what else to do." She closed her eyes a moment and inhaled. "Of course. I don't blame you. Only . . ."

"Only what?"

A high, gurgled laugh came from the blanket behind Elizabeth. Elizabeth turned immediately, taking a step before pausing. She looked at me, apprehension filling every inch of her face.

I could not seem to breathe. I opened the gate and moved forward, staring at the blanket on the grass where a little cherubic arm flailed.

Elizabeth bent and picked up a beautiful baby in a white gown, hair as fair as the sun, cheeks pink. She turned back to us, her eyes guarded as she tucked the babe into the crook of her arm. "Verity," she said, "I should like you to meet Rose. My daughter."

"Your daughter?" I wasn't sure how I managed to form the words. "Are you certain?"

She managed a half smile, though it faded quickly. "Quite certain, I assure you. Very difficult to make that mistake."

A daughter. A baby. *Elizabeth's* baby. My lungs struggled to hold air. This was what she had been hiding all this time? But how? Why had she not told me?

My mind raced, trying to connect so many thoughts that I could not voice them. So instead, I stepped forward, meeting the baby's curious blue eyes, and reached out a bent finger. She looked at it, then grasped it tightly in one fat little fist. I exhaled a laugh. "Good day, little Rose. I am very glad to make your acquaintance."

She blew a bubble and released my hand, her fingers finding her toes instead.

My eyes lifted to Elizabeth, my throat dry.

"Let us go inside," she said quietly. I saw the shadow of weariness in her eyes. "Then we might talk."

CHAPTER 20

Inside the cottage, she introduced us to a plump, middle-aged woman named Mrs. Spencer. She greeted us pleasantly, and when little Rose began fussing, she took the baby from Elizabeth and went upstairs to put her to sleep. Elizabeth bade us sit in the little parlor overlooking the garden while she fixed tea.

"Did you have any idea?" Nathaniel asked in a low voice after Elizabeth had disappeared into the kitchen.

I shook my head. "None. Truly. I cannot imagine how she concealed it."

My mind leaped forward, finally finding the questions I needed answers to. Who was the father? How had she kept her pregnancy a secret? Why had she run?

I did not have to wonder *why* she had kept such a secret. Society would have torn Elizabeth to pieces, no matter that her father was a baronet. Some things simply were not done, and that included a child born out of wedlock. My stomach wrenched, and I had to take a long, deep breath. I knew all too well what could lie ahead for Elizabeth and her child, the shame and the scorn, the same challenges that had haunted me and my mother my entire life.

When Elizabeth returned, she set the tray on the table near the window and served us all, though none of us was eager to eat or drink. But simply having a teacup in hand seemed to strengthen Elizabeth, and she finally raised her eyes to meet mine as she sat on the chair beside mine.

She opened her mouth as if to speak, then closed it again. She shook her head. "I cannot believe that you are here. I have kept this secret for so long, I hardly know how to speak of it."

That I understood completely, though I could not say so now.

"You can tell us," I said, leaning forward. "Please, Elizabeth, we want to help."

Elizabeth chewed on her lip, and her eyes moved from me to Nathaniel, sitting near the window.

"Anything you say," Nathaniel said, "I will hold in the strictest of confidences, I promise. I only mean to help."

Elizabeth considered that, then gave a short nod. She looked down at her feet.

"It began a year ago," she said. "Last May. I don't know if you recall when I went away to that house party in Kent."

"I remember," I said.

"It was just a few days. A short party." She fidgeted with her teacup. "Phillip Hall attended as well."

My stomach tightened. Elizabeth had held quite a tendre for the man last Season, though nothing had ever come of it. Or so I'd thought.

"He was a charmer," she said softly. "A master at persuading away doubts."

She stopped, eyes flicking to Nathaniel.

He met her gaze with one of sympathy. "I am sorry," he said, "to make you speak of this in front of a near stranger."

Elizabeth bit her lip, then shook her head. "No, it is all right." She looked back at me, shame filling her eyes. "He—he made me promises. And fool that I was, I believed him."

I was gripping my teacup fiercely. "The cad," I hissed. "The blackguard."

She exhaled deeply. "I wish I could blame him for everything, but I made a choice that night as well, stupid as it was." She closed her eyes. "I quickly learned that Mr. Hall cared nothing for me. By the time we'd returned to London, he had found another lightskirt to chase."

"Oh, Elizabeth." Now I understood why she'd seemed so brokenhearted after he'd slighted her. I did not tend toward violence naturally, but at that moment, I would not have hesitated to plant a facer on Mr. Hall had he wandered nearby.

"I did not realize I was expecting for nearly three months," she whispered, her voice frail. "Our time in London was busy, and I was so . . . ignorant in the ways of motherhood." She stared down at her hands, avoiding my eyes. "When it finally became clear, I was aghast. How could I have allowed this to happen? What would I tell my mother? My father?"

Nathaniel and I stayed silent, letting her pace the story.

"I went to my aunt," she said. "My beloved Aunt Augusta. She had always loved me as a daughter, and she would know what to do. She helped me enact our scheme: we would tell my parents we would be traveling together for several months before the next Season. Mother and Father easily agreed. They knew I'd been heartbroken over Mr. Hall and wished to see me happy."

Her voice cracked on that last word, and she had to clear her throat. "My aunt's only condition was that I would give up the child as soon as it was born. I agreed, and we came to Bibury. Mrs. Spencer is my aunt's former housekeeper, and Aunt Augusta trusts her beyond measure. I do as well, after all she has done for me. She not only helped with the birth, but when I returned to London, she also took Rose in, cared for her." Tears again crowded her eyes. "Oh, it has been so difficult being away from my darling child. I love her, Verity, so very much. One might think the way she came into being would affect my feelings, but it does not. Not in the least."

I found tears in my own eyes, though I blinked them away. Was this how Mama thought of me? She loved me now, I knew that, but had she always felt that way? I was a constant reminder of the man who had abandoned her. "Rose is beautiful," I said quietly, fighting my rising emotions. "Truly."

"I am sorry I did not tell you sooner," she whispered. "I could not bear to have you think badly of me."

I shook my head. "I would never be your judge, Elizabeth." Not when I had so many mistakes of my own.

Nathaniel leaned forward, elbows on his knees, fingertips pressed together. "May I ask what you planned to do?"

"I planned to lie," she admitted. "I planned to return to London and marry the first decent fellow I could find before any hint of my scandal could leak out. I know, it is not very kind of me. Tricking a man into marriage with a ruined woman."

"You were frightened," I said. "No one can blame you for that."

She gave a slight smile. "I know it was despicable. I almost did not go through with it. But then I met Lord Blakely." Her smile grew and softened all at once. "I began to wonder if I could still have the life I dreamed of. Only, I hated to deceive him. I hated that he did not know about Rose." She shook her head. "I was still trying to decide whether to tell him when we went to the theatre that night."

I set my teacup down. "Might I guess that there was something about Rose in that letter?"

Elizabeth nodded. "Mrs. Spencer and I exchanged letters through my maid, Marianne, who knew everything, having attended me during my confinement. Marianne had just given me a new letter that night, and I was so desperate to hear news of my sweet baby. But then Mother came into my room, and I hid it in my reticule."

"Which was then stolen," Nathaniel filled in.

"Yes." She closed her eyes. "That was why I implored you to help me, Verity, because I knew if the contents of that letter reached anyone in Society, I would be done for. And all my fears came true."

"Someone read the letter," I said.

"I received an unsigned note," she confirmed. "A few days after the robbery. That was why I told you to stop investigating, Verity. I did not want you involved anymore."

"What did it say?" My voice was hardly above a whisper.

Elizabeth chewed on her lip, and her eyes moved from me to Nathaniel sitting near the window.

"You needn't worry about Mr. Denning," I assured her. "You can trust him."

I could feel his eyes on me, but I focused on Elizabeth.

"I wish I could," she said, voice shaking. "But the note specifically instructed me not to tell Bow Street. I am so afraid, Verity. What am I to do?"

Silence claimed the room, broken only by Elizabeth's short breaths as she fought tears.

Then Nathaniel spoke. "I dare not promise that all will be well," he said, his voice steady. "But I can tell you that we will have a much better chance of helping you if we know all the details. Otherwise we are shooting blindly into the dark. If you tell us what you know, Miss Harwood, then perhaps we might find a solution to your troubles."

My heart swelled at the compassion in his words, the care with which he spoke them.

Elizabeth stared out the window into the garden, considering. Then she nodded. "You are right. In any case, I could hardly keep it from the both of you once you saw Rose."

"The unsigned note," I urged gently. "What did it say?"

She stood and went into the bedroom opposite the sitting room. When she returned, she held a folded paper in her hands. She handed it to me and found her seat again as I opened the note, Nathaniel leaning to read over my shoulder.

Miss Harwood,

You do not know who I am, but I know who you are. More importantly, I know the secret you would do anything to keep. You see, I was fortunate enough to come across a missive addressed to you which revealed that you are not, in fact, the pure and proper miss you pretend to be. My, what a surprise this would be to your parents if they were to learn of it. Not to mention your betrothed—I daresay the Earl of Blakely would not be terribly pleased to learn that his wife-to-be is far from virtuous.

That is, unless you wish to keep this secret and continue your deceitful gambit. If so, perhaps you and I can come to an arrangement.

You have in your own home a painting in which I am most interested, The Woman in Red. *In exchange for my silence, you will deliver the painting the day after tomorrow at midnight. There is a certain tree in St. James's Park that was struck by lightning a few years ago. You will find it near the eastern entrance. Place the painting against the tree and leave.*

There now, that is not so bad. A painting for a future.

One last thing.

When you are questioned, which you undoubtedly will be, you must reveal your suspicions that your lady's maid might be involved. You need only give enough to lead to a search of her rooms, where there shall be evidence found to shift the blame entirely onto her. You leave that to me, of course.

If I do not see that painting at that tree at the time specified, your secret will be known to all of London by the end of the next day.

Tell no one. If you inform Bow Street, I will know.

Nathaniel and I finished reading at the same moment, and he sat back, shaking his head in stunned amazement. I looked up at Elizabeth, my breathing shallow.

"So you see," she whispered, "that is why I had to run. No matter what I did, someone I loved would be harmed. If I obeyed, Marianne would have been arrested for a theft she did not commit. If I did not, my future—and Rose's—were forfeit. This was the only way that I could buy some time."

Nathaniel blew out a long breath. "The blackmailer might still follow through with his threat, Miss Harwood. It is a risky gamble."

"Not so risky." She lifted one shoulder. "Marianne has stood by me through everything, helped me through the most difficult time of my life. It was *never* an option to betray her. Knowing that, I decided to call the blackmailer's bluff. I fled, assuming word of my disappearance would quickly spread throughout Town and he would hear of it. I hazarded a guess that he would not spill my secret, at least not yet. Not when it was the only leverage he had over me."

"We cannot say for sure if it worked," I said, rather impressed with my friend's ingenuity. "But your parents certainly did not know when we left them."

Elizabeth was quiet a long moment. "My parents," she managed. "How do they fare?"

"Their daughter is missing," I said, setting the letter aside. "They are distraught."

She closed her eyes in regret. "I planned to write to them in a few days. I did not want to hurt them, but I could see no other way forward. I cannot imagine how they will react to learning about Rose."

Such pain crossed her face that it made me wish to cry. To think that she had been suffering this alone—the fear and the uncertainty. She'd had a child, and I hadn't even known. She was a *mother*.

I bit my lip, realizing I had a confession of my own to make. "Elizabeth," I said. "I should tell you that your parents know more than you think. Upon your disappearance, I told them everything I knew about your missing letter and the secret you were trying to keep. I am sorry."

"Oh." She looked surprised but then shook her head. "You needn't apologize. Of course you would tell them. And perhaps it will make this all a little easier if they have some warning." She looked between the both of us with dread in her eyes. "I do not know what to do. I have lost hope that I can find a way out. I care not for my own reputation anymore. I only think of Rose. I cannot imagine what people would say about her if they knew the truth."

I pulled back, my lungs caught in a vise. The words I wished to say hung on the tip of my tongue, and yet . . . How could I tell her? Nathaniel sat not three feet away. That familiar fear tore at my chest. Would he reject me?

But the fear Elizabeth felt for her child pushed me forward. I could help, even in a small way.

"I understand better than you might realize," I said, my voice raspy.

Elizabeth's fair brows pulled into a crease. "What do you mean?"

My throat was dry. "I mean that I know very well what it is to be the illegitimate daughter of a prominent gentleman."

It had been years since I had spoken such words. I had to rip them from my very center, where I'd hidden my secret for so long. Memories rushed through my head from when I was a child—superior looks sent my way, whispers in church, rejection and exclusion. The memories were faint, from the time before Mama had insisted upon our cover story, but they were powerful. A reminder of what I'd been through, of what Rose might suffer.

I did not look at Nathaniel. I could not bear to see what might be in his eyes, whether surprise or judgment or sympathy.

I focused on Elizabeth. She sat still, staring at me. Then her entire expression shifted into sweet understanding. "Oh, Verity. I did not know."

"How would you?" I said. "I never speak of it, not when my mother has tried so hard to convince the world of a lie."

"Your father did not die when you were a child?" she asked softly.

I shook my head. "No. He is alive and well. At least, I assume he is well. We are not on speaking terms."

Finally, I could bear it no longer. My gaze flicked to Nathaniel. He sat with his hand grasping his chin, as if deep in thought. His eyes met mine, and I tried to see beyond his staid countenance, but he looked away in the next moment.

"My mother invented the story when I was very young," I said, staring down at my hands in my lap. "I have long assumed it was to protect herself, her career. But I am beginning to think it was far more than that." My eyes clouded with tears. "Because I am beginning to see just what a mother would do for her child."

I looked up at Elizabeth, and she gazed at me with so much compassion that I barely kept control of my voice as I spoke. "I am proof that a good life can come from a difficult beginning. You mustn't despair, Elizabeth. Rose can, and will, be happy."

Elizabeth embraced me, and I closed my eyes, grateful for her warm arms around me. "Thank you," she whispered. When she pulled back, she wiped the tears from her eyes and looked between Nathaniel and me. "What is our next step?"

"First and foremost," Nathaniel said, "we must see you safely returned to your parents."

I nodded my agreement. "They must know you are safe."

Elizabeth balked. "But if I return, the blackmailer will learn of it. He will demand the painting again, I am sure of it, and then there will be nothing I can do to stop him from spreading my secret, if he hasn't already."

"Perhaps not," Nathaniel said thoughtfully. "You will have our help this time. In fact, if he insists upon your delivering the painting, that might present us the perfect opportunity to catch him in the act."

"Catch him?" Her eyes widened.

I nodded, following Nathaniel's logic. "It is a good idea. However, the blackmailer cannot learn Bow Street is involved. We will have to be careful."

Elizabeth shook her head frantically. "That sounds far too dangerous. I cannot ask either of you to—"

"Elizabeth," I said, my voice firm but gentle. "You do not need to ask us."

She stared at me, her eyes growing glossy once more. She looked away and took a deep breath. "Very well," she said, collecting herself. "But I will do my part. I can pay for a hired carriage for the return trip. I sold several pieces of jewelry before I left London, so we needn't worry about funds."

"We'll be passing near Wimborne," I said, realizing suddenly. "We might stay the night there now that we won't be at the mercy of the mail coach."

"Wimborne?" Nathaniel arched a brow.

"My sister-in-law's estate," I explained. "Perhaps Jack might even have some suggestions for us. This wouldn't be the first time he's dealt with an extortionist."

Nathaniel nodded, though there was a shadow of doubt in his eyes. He still was not certain about Jack. It was difficult to shake an opinion formed through gossip and rumors, even if Nathaniel professed neutrality.

I could only imagine what his opinion of *me* was now that he knew the truth about my father. And it was not through gossip or rumors but my own words. He watched me, his expression a puzzle I could not solve.

I focused back on Elizabeth, who looked toward the stairs with trepidation in her eyes. Her thoughts were clearly with Rose and their uncertain future. I leaned forward. "We'll catch the rogue responsible," I said fiercely. "I promise."

Elizabeth nodded, her expression growing determined. "Yes," she said, straightening her back. "We will."

CHAPTER 21

It was decided that we would leave at first light, and we spent the afternoon preparing for the journey home. Nathaniel went into the village to secure a carriage for the next morning. I helped Mrs. Spencer assemble a basket of food, insisting Elizabeth spend time with Rose, playing with her toes and cooing at her little noises. I smiled to see it even as my heart hurt. Despite my reassurances to her earlier, I did not know what their future held.

When we finished preparing the food, I slipped out the front door. I needed some air. Some space to think.

I rejoined the lane that had brought us to Rosemont Cottage and continued farther west. A charming row of cottages with cheerful thatched roofs and blooming flower boxes ran to the right of the lane, while a lazy brook wound along the left. A small stone bridge arched over the stream, shielded by the thick foliage of the trees around it. I stopped here, perching on the edge of the bridge as I stared down at the slowly moving water.

Elizabeth had a child. An illegitimate child.

Even as shocking as it was, my mind did not struggle to accept what I'd learned. It made too much sense. It explained everything that had happened over the last few weeks and months. But even as my mind accepted it, my heart wrestled. How could something so beautiful and joyous as a child come from such pain and heartbreak? I ached for Elizabeth, imagining the last year of her life: keeping her pregnancy a secret from her parents, hiding in the country and delivering the child, leaving Rose to return to London. I wished she had told me, but I could not blame her for it. A secret like that burned a hole in one's heart.

I heard footsteps. I looked over my shoulder to see Nathaniel walking the lane toward me. He spotted me in the same moment and removed his hat, riffling a hand through his hair. In this dusky light, his auburn hair took on the hues of the sun, his skin golden. I felt a mess in comparison. I hadn't so much as washed my face in two days.

"I found a driver willing to take us as far as Wimborne," he said, setting his hat beside me on the bridge wall.

I nodded. "Genevieve will no doubt lend us her carriage for the remainder of the trip."

"Your sister-in-law seems a generous sort."

"Indeed," I said with a smile. "She is a very good influence on Jack, and he needs all the good influence he can get."

Nathaniel returned my smile, though it soon faded as he gazed at me. I did not like the look in his eyes—a look that warned that I was not prepared for the conversation to come.

"You should not have promised Miss Harwood we would catch the blackmailer," he said quietly, half sitting on the bridge as he crossed his arms.

"I know," I said. "But I could not help it. She is so afraid, I wasn't sure she would even agree to return to London with us."

He nodded, seeming to accept that. Then he turned and sat fully on the wall, facing away. The silence seemed to hover around us, heavy and full.

I broke it first. "You did not seem surprised."

He scuffed his boot along the stones. "About your father?"

"Yes."

He sighed. "I've had suspicions for a while now. The way you spoke of it with my mother."

I should have expected this. After all, his life's work revolved around discovering the truth. But my stomach still lurched, and I felt the mad desire to run and hide in the trees beyond the bridge.

Nathaniel sent me a searching glance. "Will you tell me about him?"

I stared across the meadow, where a few cows idly grazed. "I know very little myself," I admitted. "He met my mother early in her career, and she fell in love with him. But he was too well-placed in Society to consider marrying an actress." I fidgeted with the long sleeve of my dress. "Jack was born, and then I came a few years later. My father has since married, and Mama invented the story of her widowhood to maintain her reputation—and mine." I exhaled a long breath. "I've met him but twice, and he seems to have very little desire to know me better. The feeling is quite mutual."

"I cannot imagine that."

I snorted. "The man is a puffed-up aristocrat. You would feel the same, I assure you."

"No," he said. "I cannot imagine why anyone would not want to know you better."

It felt like a warm breeze stirred inside me, lifting my heart.

"I am sorry I did not tell you sooner," I said, shifting my weight on the bridge, not allowing myself to try to read his expression. He knew who I was now, my history. "I . . . well, you know better than most that I am the cautious sort."

"You generally have good reason," he said.

"Especially in this case." I gave a sad smile. "I've told a few people over the years, friends I thought I could depend upon. But I only ever found myself abandoned or whispered about, and so I learned to keep it to myself. It was safer."

"But lonelier," he mused.

I lifted one shoulder. "It might have been worse."

"Ah," he said. "A properly British refrain."

That coaxed a smile from me. "But it is true. At least my father provided for me. I daresay many girls in my situation are not so fortunate." I bit my lip. "That is one reason I wished to become a thief-taker. I hate depending on his money."

"Or upon anyone?" he asked. "Is that perhaps also why you find yourself opposed to marriage?"

I closed my eyes. Oh, how this man seemed to see straight through me. "My mother waited for him for so many years," I whispered. "She had her heart broken again and again. I have no desire to subject my own to such torment."

He did not speak for a long moment, and the air around us filled with birdsong and the smell of moss and the slant of the lowering sun. "I cannot say I blame you," he said finally. "A heart is a fragile thing without trust." He reached for my fidgeting fingers, slipping his hand around mine, holding it softly like he feared to break me. "Do you trust me, Verity?"

I looked up at him, pulse stuttering. How did he do that? Pull me apart by the seams and then stitch me back together in the same sentence. I had no defense.

He was asking so much with that simple question. Oh, how I wanted to answer him. But that was akin to declaring myself, and my throat seemed to close over.

It was too much, telling him all that I had over the last day and night. I couldn't calm my racing heart, the panic that gripped me. For years, I had told myself I would never be swept away by love or passion, never marry, for the man's sake as well as mine. Now, the possibility tormented me, made me doubt everything.

Nathaniel was like a sudden burst of wind spinning wildly into my life. And while he brought light and hope, he also threw everything I thought I knew and wanted into terrifying disarray. I did not want to promise anything now, not when I did not fully know my own mind.

I stood, pulling my hand from his. "I must go," I said, my voice somewhere between a croak and a rasp. "Elizabeth needs me."

I thought I might see disappointment cross his face or perhaps hurt. He only watched me with a steady expression, as if he had expected my response. But then, I'd always retreated from him. Of course he would expect this.

"I am not going to give up," he said in a low, deep voice that reached into the very center of me. "Even if you tell me that my pursuit is hopeless and your mind is set. Because my mind is just as decided, just as certain. There is something between us that I cannot deny, and neither can you." He smiled crookedly, a slow spread of his lips that made my insides melt like butter in a hot pan. "And I have no intention of letting you get away, Verity Travers."

His words lit inside me, tugged at the barricade around my heart. I wanted so badly to tell him I felt it, too, that I wanted to trust him. But the wounds my father had left on my life were still healing. Too many years of holding myself back had locked such words deep inside me. They weren't ready. Yet.

I stepped back to him and pressed a soft kiss to his cheek. His hands came to my elbows, holding me there. I let my lips linger for as long as I dared, then I pulled back.

He let me go, staying behind as I disappeared into the twilight.

CHAPTER 22

We left Bibury at dawn and traveled all day. Elizabeth was pale and quiet, no doubt thinking of the moment she had kissed Rose goodbye in the cradle, the gray light of dawn draped over the sleeping babe. I could not imagine how she felt now, leaving her child and not knowing if she would ever see her again.

I did not know what would come of it. Even if the situation with the blackmailer was resolved, the fact remained that Elizabeth had some difficult truths to explain to her parents and Lord Blakely. Would he still wish to marry her? Would her parents reject her? I hadn't any idea, and that unknown felt like ice lodged in my chest.

Elizabeth sat beside me in the carriage, Nathaniel facing us, and I found it difficult to keep my eyes from him. Our knees brushed with every jolt of the carriage, and neither of us moved away. His words from the night before played endlessly through my mind.

There is something between us, he'd said. He was certainly right in that, though I'd tried to ignore it, assign it little significance. Of course I would feel attraction to such a man as he.

But I saw it so clearly now. This wasn't mere attraction. A seed had been planted the moment I'd met him, when he'd helped me up from the London street. It had taken root when he had treated me with the calculating respect one reserves for a colleague. It had blossomed when he'd run with me from the tavern, protected me, and taken me to his childhood home. And now it filled every shadowed place in my heart when I recalled his whispered words from last night—and remembered the feel of his hands around my face as he'd kissed me before the fire at the inn.

I have no intention of letting you get away, Verity Travers.

There was nothing more certain in life than change, but I felt myself stumbling to keep my feet beneath me. I hadn't wanted this. Love, if I could call it that. I'd learned firsthand from my parents that love could be both selfish *and* caring.

And yet I could feel myself changing. Nathaniel was changing me, somehow making me both more of who I already was *and* who I wished to be. He knew the truth about me, and instead of it frightening him away, he seemed only more determined to remain at my side.

I peeked at Nathaniel across the carriage. His forefinger and thumb circled his chin, elbow propped on his crossed arm, and his eyes were on me, contemplative and intent. He shifted slightly as he caught my gaze, dropping his hand as we looked at one another. Words danced upon the tip of my tongue, things I had been too cowardly to say last night.

Elizabeth's presence kept me in check, for which I was grateful. A private carriage was too tempting a prospect for a woman who had just discovered how very much she enjoyed kissing her Bow Street companion. And kissing him again would simply muddle my head more.

Nathaniel questioned Elizabeth sporadically throughout the day—whether she recognized the handwriting on the letter, if there was anyone who held a grudge against her—but she could think of nothing beyond what she had told us the day before. We worked out more details of our scheme to catch the blackmailer, and my confidence grew with every hour. It was a good plan, and with Bow Street's help, it had every chance of success.

It was nearly dark when the familiar shape of Wimborne approached on the horizon. I'd been to my brother's new home twice in the year since he'd married, and I'd come away both times dazzled by the beauty of the estate. The house itself was an elegant, three-story brick, with wandering ivy and white-painted shutters at every window, and the grounds were expansive and stunning in their wildness. The eastern wing was still in the process of being rebuilt after a fire last year, a complication from the case Jack had been working for my future sister-in-law, Genevieve.

As our carriage neared the manor, I saw two figures descending the steps to meet us. Genevieve's vivid red hair caught the last gleams of sunset, while Jack's dark locks seemed to swallow the light. I straightened, unaccountably nervous. What would my brother think of our arrival?

Our carriage stopped before the front steps, and Jack moved to open the door. He grinned, not looking surprised to see me.

"Ah," he said, speaking loudly enough for Ginny behind him to hear. "Here is our runaway. She must have missed me terribly to have come all this way."

I took his hand and stepped down to the pebbled drive. "I can't imagine anyone missing you." But my voice lacked any sharp edges, and my frown threatened to stand on its head.

"Really?" he said. "Do you not recall Ginny chasing me all the way to London before we married? She seemed to miss me quite desperately."

Ginny laughed behind him. "Only because I needed you to clean up the mess you'd left behind."

He pretended not to hear and turned to Elizabeth, who had scooted to the edge of the bench. He held out a hand. "May I?"

She took his hand, and he helped her to the ground. "Thank you." She moved to my side, and I took her arm to reassure her.

Nathaniel stepped down directly after Elizabeth and straightened his jacket, eyeing my brother apprehensively. But Jack seemed not at all alarmed by Nathaniel's presence. Guessing by his "runaway" comment earlier, Mama had written to him upon finding my note, and he likely knew precisely who both Nathaniel and Elizabeth were.

After the requisite introductions and bows and curtsies, Ginny stepped forward and took my hands. "So lovely to see you again, Verity."

I squeezed her hands. My sister-in-law could be just as determined and obstinate as I when she wished to, but gentleness and sincerity were her true nature. "Thank you. I am sorry to come upon you so unexpectedly, but I gather you've had some warning from Mama."

"Indeed," she said. "We received a letter this morning."

I wished to ask her what Mama had said—was she utterly furious with me?—but Ginny turned next to Elizabeth, eyes kind.

"Miss Harwood," she said. "I hope you will feel very welcome here at Wimborne."

Elizabeth managed a smile. "Thank you, Mrs. Travers. I am sorry if we are imposing."

Ginny shook her head. "Not in the least. We are more than happy to have you."

"Mr. Denning," Jack said to Nathaniel. "I must thank you for accompanying my sister. A rambunctious sort, is she not?"

Nathaniel's lips twitched. "That is one word for it."

"Quiet, you," Ginny ordered her husband. "They've had a long few days, and they deserve rest and quiet, not your teasing."

"As you say, my dear," Jack said, though his eyes twinkled.

Nathaniel moved to take his bag, just unloaded by the coachman, but Ginny waved him off. "Never mind your bag, Mr. Denning; my men will see to it. Come, I will show you and Miss Harwood to your chambers. Once you've washed up, dinner will be served."

Ginny took Elizabeth's arm and guided her inside, telling her about the room being readied for her. Ginny was not the chattering sort, yet she seemed to sense that Elizabeth needed some distraction. Nathaniel sent me a searching look, but I only shrugged, so he followed after the two women.

Jack watched his wife leave with Elizabeth and Nathaniel, then turned to face me, his teasing grin slipping from his face. "You've been busy," he said simply.

I sighed. "What did Mama say in her letter?"

"A great deal," he replied. "Shall we walk? I imagine you'll wish to stretch your legs."

"And I imagine you'll wish to rake me over the coals for running away without a chaperone."

He grinned. "Then, you do not know me very well."

I made a noise of disagreement as we moved off together, aiming toward a meandering stream. "Mama will have insisted upon a lecture, I daresay."

"No lecture," he said. "In fact, Mama said nothing of the sort. She was just worried. Asked that I look out for you since your journey would lead you fairly close to Wimborne and she had an inkling you might seek my help."

Mama knew me better than I thought.

"And did she tell you of our argument?" I said quietly.

"She did not mention an argument." He paused. "She told me something else though."

"What?" My pulse quickened.

His steps slowed. "She told me what happened in January."

I stared at him. "She should not have. It was my story to tell."

He cast me a hard look. I hadn't seen much censure from my brother over the years, but I felt it now. "Yes, and *you* should have told me."

"I . . ." I bit my cheek. "I did not want you to think less of me."

"Less of you?" He gave an exasperated shake of his head. "Blast it, Verity, how can I help you if you do not confide in me? Why did you not tell me?"

"Because . . ." My voice caught. "Because I chose to stop," I finally managed. "I refused to take cases anymore. I thought you would be disappointed in me after all you did to encourage me."

He blew out a long breath. "Verity," he said slowly, as if to ensure I understood him. "I taught you because you showed such an interest and aptitude. I think you have the makings of an extraordinary investigator. But not once did I push you toward this profession because I thought you *should* follow after me. Your life is your own, and I should be proud of you no matter what."

My eyes pricked with tears, and I looked away. "Even if I were a half-wit cheat? Or a smuggler? A tavern wench, perhaps?"

He grinned. "Only if you were the very best tavern wench in all England. We Traverses do not do anything by halves."

I laughed, a weak sound, but the soberness of our conversation fled.

"I was glad you found your friend Miss Harwood," he said as we began walking again.

"A blessed relief," I agreed.

"Do you know why she disappeared?"

"Yes," I said, "and I now understand why she took such drastic action."

"Tell me everything," he insisted. "Perhaps I can help."

"I've little doubt you could," I said, "but I cannot break her confidence."

Jack did not press me, nodding once. "But you are helping her? You and Mr. Denning?"

There was another question within the one he spoke.

"Yes," I said. "He has been a true friend." That, at least, I could say without worry.

"Just a friend?"

Of course he would press me about *this*. "What did Mama say in that blasted letter?" I muttered under my breath.

Jack winked. "That is between the two of us, I'm afraid. Personal correspondence and all that." He shoved his hands in his pockets. "He seems a decent fellow."

"He is more than decent," I defended, though I wasn't sure why. Jack hadn't insulted Nathaniel, after all.

"I *see*." He drew out the word, lips tugging upward. "You know, dear sister, you would not be the first to catch feelings in the midst of an investigation. I am quite familiar with the process myself. I do hope you will come to me if you should ever find yourself wondering what this new emotion is—"

"Hush." I scowled at him.

"—why your heart is pattering on so—"

I turned and stalked away, and Jack laughed behind me, hurrying to catch up.

"Come now," he said robustly, falling into step beside me. "You must allow me to tease you now, or I will be forced to do so around Mr. Denning, and then Ginny will be angry with me."

"Perhaps I should like to see you in your wife's black books for once," I muttered. "I cannot understand how she endures your nonsense."

"Ah, love," he mused. "That great equalizer."

"Do you not mean *death*?"

"Heavens, no," he said. "It was love that blinded Ginny to my faults and convinced her to marry me. Dying would not have helped me in the least."

A short laugh burst from me. "The poor woman."

We started back toward the house, the sunset turning from brilliant orange to a deep purple.

I hesitated a minute before I spoke. "Might I ask a question?"

"Certainly."

"Do you trust Wily Greaves?"

"Wily?" Jack looked surprised. "Is he mixed up in this whole affair?"

I exhaled. "Yes, unfortunately. I'd like to believe the best of him, but he makes it so difficult."

"I'm not terribly surprised," he said. "He doesn't like anyone to know he's a good man at heart. Rather enjoys his reputation."

"But can I trust him?"

Jack shrugged. "*I* do. But then, we've gotten each other out of enough scrapes that we have little choice *but* to." He paused. "You'll have to decide for yourself. It is part of the job, learning whom to trust and whom to watch. You've always been a good judge of character, Verity. Hold to that, if nothing else."

I mulled that over as Jack led us into the house, the grand entry familiar from my previous visits, and we parted to ready for dinner. After changing my dress and fixing my hair, I looked at myself in the mirror above the dressing table. I should have looked tired and wan. But instead, there was a spark in my eyes and a flush in my cheeks that I could not account for.

Though perhaps it had something to do with the gentleman whose knees had brushed mine for the majority of our journey today.

The same gentleman who paced the bottom of the staircase when I descended a few minutes later, one hand rubbing the back of his neck. I reached the bottom of the stairs as he turned back, and he stopped, his eyes finding mine. I hadn't brought anything very fine to wear, not anticipating a formal dinner, but he didn't seem to mind.

"You look lovely." He came to join me, brushing the fronts of his breeches self-consciously.

"Not like a madwoman, I assume?"

He grinned. "Not even slightly."

I straightened my skirts. "We are the first to come down?"

"I'm not sure." He gave a sheepish smile. "I wasn't certain where to go." His eyes slipped from me, flashing across the gilded ceilings and elaborate damask wallpaper and delicate glass vases. "I didn't realize your brother had married so well."

"Oh yes, he's always been something of a fortune hunter," I said, careful to keep my voice serious. "The richer the lady, the better." When Nathaniel's eyes snapped back to mine, wide and surprised, I laughed. "I am only teasing."

"Yes, I should hope so," came Jack's drawling voice from the staircase. We glanced up to see him and Ginny descending the steps arm in arm, both with matching grins. "I would hate for Ginny to learn I married her for her fortune."

"Shocking, to be sure," Ginny said mildly. "Drat, I am trapped now. But I suppose what's done is done."

She always surprised me with her dry humor, and I saw even more why Jack had fallen head over heels for this woman.

Elizabeth joined us a minute later, looking pale but a little better than she had when we'd arrived. As the others went ahead, I walked alongside Elizabeth.

"How are you?" I asked softly.

She exhaled a shaky breath. "I do not think I shall get any sleep tonight."

I could not blame her. She would face her parents tomorrow, and Lord Blakely. She would have to tell them everything. And besides that, we had our plan to put into action. Anyone in their right mind would be nervous.

"They will understand," I told her and prayed desperately that I was right. "They love you. You have nothing to fear."

She shook her head. "Do not say that. I am not as brave as you, Verity, and I know very well that my situation is a precarious one indeed. I cannot guess what my parents will say, and Lord Blakely . . ." She swallowed, and her voice trailed off.

"I will be with you," I whispered as we neared the dining room. "Every step of the way."

She squeezed my arm, her eyes watery.

Nathaniel had reached the drawing room door and glanced back. His eyes fixed on me, as though looking anywhere else were a hardship. A shiver traced my spine—a rather pleasant shiver. I should not enjoy having his eyes on me, especially when my friend endured so much. But Nathaniel gave me strength. He gave me confidence. And I very much needed both, considering what we would be facing in London. So I let myself enjoy the way he looked at me.

A girl could get used to such a thing.

CHAPTER 23

The clock was chiming eleven o'clock at night when I made my way back down the stairs, stepping lightly to avoid any creaking steps. I wasn't certain whether anyone was still awake. Elizabeth had gone to bed early, and I'd gone with her to try to set her at ease. She was asleep now, and I was in search of some paper and pencils. I had an idea for a new sketch—Nathaniel in the golden light of the meadow in Bibury—and wanted to try my hand at it before the image slipped away.

But as I crossed in front of the drawing room, the door slightly parted and firelight shining through, I heard male voices. Jack and Nathaniel were still awake.

I hesitated at the door. It was abominably rude to even consider eavesdropping, but then, I had never been a good student of social etiquette. Why begin now?

I moved closer to the door, careful not to step into the stream of light that slipped through the opening.

"—keep an eye on her," Jack was saying. "Very rarely do I wish myself back in London, but tonight, that is the case."

"Understandable," Nathaniel said, and just the smooth, deep ribbons of his voice made me breathe easier, as if my lungs grew tighter whenever he wasn't near. "But I do not think you need to worry. She is quite capable of taking care of herself."

They were speaking of me. They had to be.

"Indeed." Jack sounded amused. "I can only imagine what transpired for you to learn that yourself."

Nathaniel chuckled, the sound full within his chest. "Let us simply say that I have no plans to startle her from behind. She would likely take me down before I had any chance to shout for help."

It was Jack's turn to laugh. "She remembers what I taught her, does she? She was always a quick study. Kept me on my toes."

I crossed my arms over my chest, smiling as I leaned against the wall. I hadn't thought that hearing these two men speaking of me would bring such contentment, yet here I was, beaming like an idiot. My brother and Nathaniel had been rather quiet through dinner, letting Ginny and me carry the conversation, but the fact that they now conversed—and that they seemed to get along—meant a great deal. It was ridiculous how much I liked it.

There was a short silence, then Jack spoke again. "How long have you been at Bow Street?"

"Just over four months," Nathaniel answered. "Promoted from the day patrol."

"How do you find the new magistrate?" Jack questioned. "Etchells, is it?"

"He's a fair man," Nathaniel said. "Though I don't know him well."

"I daresay he is relieved to have such men as you and Rawlings and Drake," Jack said. "I was always the troublemaker."

"You did leave something of a legacy."

I could not see their faces, but I could sense the tightening of the air in the room, as if Jack were sizing up Nathaniel.

"The price I paid for my arrogance," Jack finally said. "I don't deny that."

Another pause. "Do you miss Bow Street?" Nathaniel quietly asked.

A sigh from Jack. "Yes. But only in the way one lingers nostalgically over the past. I am far happier now."

"Your wife is a diamond," Nathaniel said. "You are the most fortunate of men."

"A fact I am well and truly aware of, no matter my teasing." I could tell Jack was smiling by the lightness in his voice. "I highly recommend falling in love with a determined, headstrong sort of woman. That way when she makes up her mind to marry you, there'll be no talking her out of it."

"Ah." A chair creaked as if Nathaniel had adjusted his weight. "But how do you convince such a woman to want to marry you in the first place?"

My heart stilled in my chest. I should not listen to this, yet I could not have torn myself away for a thousand pounds.

Jack pondered this before speaking. "I haven't a good answer for you, Denning," he said finally. "I stumbled upon my own future rather stupidly. But if you do find a woman like that, all I can tell you is to keep trying. She will be worth it."

"I have little doubt of that," Nathaniel said, and I finally gave in to temptation, peeking around the corner of the door. The two sat before the fireplace, and my eyes went straight to Nathaniel's face. He stared pensively at the glowing coals, as if deep in thought.

"I do have one suggestion," Jack said, and my attention turned to his wide grin. "If you can save a lady's life—if at all possible—it certainly helps to encourage feelings of romance."

Nathaniel gave a short laugh. "And if she continues to insist on saving herself?"

Jack shifted so his gaze was directed toward the open door—toward *me*. I drew back into the shadows. "Then perhaps she needs to learn that independence is not everything," he said sincerely. "There is no harm in relying on those we love for help."

His words struck me hard—not like a bullet or arrow but like a sweeping river. The truth of it was startling, and I did not like what I saw in myself because of it. An indifferent, aloof soul, intent on doing things her own way, in her own time. Alone.

I pulled away from the door and slipped quietly back upstairs.

"Are you certain I should not come with you?" Jack asked doubtfully as we prepared to leave the next morning, all of us milling about the front drive as our bags were loaded onto the carriage. "I could be of use, I am certain."

Ginny laid a hand on Jack's arm. "Mr. Denning and Verity have things well in hand, I am sure," she said. "Besides, you are needed here."

Jack sighed. "I've no doubt in their abilities, but an extra set of hands is always useful."

"We shall call upon Drake and Rawlings if we need help," I assured him.

"So long as it's not Nettleton," Jack muttered.

"Never Nettleton," I agreed, hiding a smile.

Ginny stepped to Elizabeth's side and took her arm. She whispered, and Elizabeth listened intently. A moment later, Elizabeth hugged Ginny. What had my sister-in-law said to her?

Nathaniel went to help load the carriage, and Jack moved to stand beside me, arms crossed. "I like Denning," he said quietly.

"I do too."

He looked at me then, his bright, blue eyes—just like mine—piercing straight through me. "Promise me you'll take care."

"Of course I will, Jack," I said. "I've learned that lesson quite thoroughly."

"Yes, but you are too much like me," he said, his expression softening. "Sometimes we need to learn a lesson a few times before it sticks."

Then he surprised me by wrapping his big arms around me and hugging me. Just a brief embrace, but considering the last time Jack and I had hugged was his wedding day, it caught me off guard.

I hugged him back until he pulled away and clasped his hands behind his back. "Off with you," he said gruffly. "And take your troubles with you."

I laughed and went to bid farewell to Ginny, thanking her with a tight embrace. Nathaniel waited to help me inside the carriage, and I took his hand so naturally, so easily, it seemed as if we'd always been a part of one another.

As the coach started off, I looked back. Jack and Ginny stood before Wimborne, waving as they moved to each other's side like two magnets. Two forces unaccountably pulled together.

I glanced at Elizabeth beside me, and I was surprised to see she looked remarkably calm, her cheeks with more color in them than I'd seen in weeks.

"What did Ginny say to you?" I asked quietly. I did not mind if Nathaniel overheard, but I wasn't sure if she would speak if he did. He pointedly turned away, looking out the window and allowing us a modicum of privacy.

Elizabeth gave a half smile. "She said she knew what it felt like to have one's life upended, to face a future that seemed impossibly bleak." She looked at me, her eyes holding a new spark of light. "She said that our greatest trials often come before our greatest joys and that I should hold fast to those I love. That they would see me through." She grasped my hand tightly. "Thank you, Verity, for seeing me through."

We were able to travel much more directly than a mail coach, so only a few hours later, our coach stopped in front of Harwood House, the weather drizzly and cold. Elizabeth stared up at her home, apprehension in her every aspect. But she set her shoulders and opened the carriage door, stepping down onto the street. I moved to follow her, but Nathaniel caught my arm.

"You'll come to Bow Street as we planned?" he asked.

"As soon as I can."

We'd decided it was best for me to see Elizabeth home while Nathaniel went directly to Bow Street. It would be a difficult enough conversation without an officer present.

"And you'll make sure the Harwoods know what to do?" he pressed.

I smiled. "Rest assured, Sir Chivalry. We will put the plan into motion."

Still, he did not release my arm, though his hold on me was gentle. His eyes found mine, intent and entirely captivating. If Elizabeth had not stood a few feet away, he might have kissed me again. A soft, sweet, simple kiss. Just imagining it sent a wave of desire curling through my stomach.

"I will see you soon," I promised.

He nodded. "Be careful."

He closed the door after I descended, and the coach was soon rattling off down the cobblestones.

I faced Elizabeth. "Are you ready?"

"I am," she said, her voice surprisingly steady. "I've been dreading this for so long that I am almost relieved to have it over and done with."

She went up the steps and opened the front door. I moved inside after her, and we both removed our bonnets, our footsteps echoing.

"Mother?" Elizabeth called out tentatively.

A thud came from the nearby parlor. Then rapid footsteps and the door was yanked open. Lady Harwood braced herself in the doorway, dressed in a simple morning gown, face pale and eyes wide.

"Elizabeth," she whispered. She took a step forward, then another, then she ran to her daughter and threw her arms around her. "Oh, darling, my darling."

Both women were weeping, clutching each other.

"I was so worried," Lady Harwood cried. "Where have you been?"

But Elizabeth shook her head, unable to speak.

"Reginald!" Lady Harwood shouted. "Reginald, come quickly!"

"What is the fuss all ab—" Sir Reginald came striding down the corridor, but he stopped short when he saw Elizabeth in Lady Harwood's arms. He said nothing, only stared, then swooped forward, throwing his arms around his daughter.

"Father," Elizabeth murmured, holding him tight. "I am so sorry."

He shook his head, still pressed into her shoulder. "None of that," he said hoarsely. "I never thought to feel such relief."

I stood to the side, bonnet in hand, smiling at the reunion even as my heart ached for what was yet to come. Their reaction, at least, made me feel confident that the blackmailer hadn't yet revealed Elizabeth's secret. They would have greeted their daughter much differently if they'd known.

Lady Harwood turned to me, eyes tearful. "We surely have you to thank, Verity, for bringing her home."

I shook my head. "All your thanks should be given to Mr. Denning. He made it possible."

Lady Harwood shook her head. "I shall give you a goodly share, and you mustn't deny me. Our gratitude knows no bounds."

Elizabeth pulled back, brushing the tears from her cheeks. "I truly am sorry," she said again. "I know I have caused so much pain and worry."

Lady Harwood took her hand. "But why, my dear?" she asked. "What on earth drove you to run away?"

"I have much to tell you," Elizabeth said. "Perhaps we might sit down."

Once we were all seated around the fireplace in the parlor, Lady Harwood and Sir Reginald looked at Elizabeth with expectant curiosity. Elizabeth clasped her hands in her lap and took a shuddering breath.

"The reason I ran away," she began, "was that I received a threatening note. The sender knew a secret about me and warned that he would reveal it if I did not comply with his demands."

Lady Harwood leaned forward. "The secret from the letter Verity told us about?"

Elizabeth nodded. "Last year, when I was with Aunt Augusta, we weren't traveling. That is, we traveled to the Cotswold Hills, but we remained there for the majority of the six months I was gone."

"What on earth do you mean?" Sir Reginald said, baffled. "Why?"

"We could not travel," Elizabeth said, somehow managing to raise her gaze to meet her parents'. "Because . . . because of the baby."

Silence greeted her, her parents staring at her in bewilderment.

"*My* baby," she finally said, eyes red. "I have a child, a little girl."

She hurried to explain everything she'd told me two days ago, her voice shaking but determined. But even with her practiced words, she was often overcome with emotion and frequently had to stop to regain her composure.

Lady Harwood and Sir Reginald sat in stunned silence, simply staring as she spoke. They said nothing, did not even look at each other, and my heart sank.

"I am so terribly sorry," Elizabeth whispered when she finished, a solitary tear slipping down her cheek. "You must know how difficult this was to keep from you."

The room was quiet for a long minute. Then Lady Harwood shifted forward in her seat, her eyes red and watery. "I've a granddaughter?" she asked, her words barely audible.

Elizabeth nodded. "I named her Rose, after the cottage where she was born."

Finally, Lady Harwood looked at her husband, but Sir Reginald seemed to be in shock. He stood suddenly and moved to the window to look out over the dreary street, the stone townhouses wet with rain. He said nothing.

"I cannot believe this." Lady Harwood spoke as if in a daze. Her shoulders drew down around her, her face stark white. "Why would you not tell us? Why would you not tell *me*?"

"How could I?" Elizabeth's voice trembled. Her father's reaction had shaken her. "We had such plans, such grand aims for my future. But I ruined everything." Her face softened. "That is, I assumed everything was ruined. Until Rose was born."

Lady Harwood stilled, her eyes on her daughter.

"How I love her, Mother," Elizabeth whispered. "It is pure misery to be apart from her. I worry every moment of the day for her, wondering if she is well, if she's fed and warm and content. If she misses me as I miss her."

A rustle to my left indicated that Sir Reginald was listening as well.

"Knowing now the strength of a parent's love, I am even more sorry for what I have put you both through." Elizabeth looked at her father near the window. "I have worried you. I have disappointed you. I've ruined the Harwood name and my reputation, and I've no right to beg your forgiveness. But I shall beg all the same."

Another pause, then Lady Harwood stood. My heart stopped, thinking for one second that she was leaving, too distraught at the news to stay in her daughter's presence a moment longer.

But she knelt before Elizabeth, taking her hands. "You do not need my forgiveness," she whispered. "But perhaps I need yours, for being the kind of mother you were too afraid to come to when you needed one the most."

Elizabeth's eyes filled with tears yet again. "Oh, Mother."

"I am only glad you are home and well," Lady Harwood said fiercely. "We shall manage all the rest."

I thought Elizabeth might smile, glad to have her mother's support, but she baffled me by shaking her head.

"But that is just it," she whispered. "'It is because of 'all the rest' that I cannot sleep at night. Because during the last few days, I have come to realize that I cannot be without my daughter. I cannot be without my Rose."

Lady Harwood pulled away slightly, mouth parted.

"What do you mean?" Sir Reginald's voice came from across the room, and we all turned to look at him. He gaped at her, genuinely shocked. "You are engaged to an earl. You cannot have a daughter."

Elizabeth's lip trembled, but she met his eyes. "I still wish to marry Lord Blakely, if he will have me after I tell him the truth."

"And if he will not have you?" he asked, moving one sharp step closer.

She seemed to collect every ounce of calm remaining to her. "Then I shall live in happy obscurity with my child, tucked away in the country where no one knows us."

Now it was my turn to stare. I hadn't had any idea she'd harbored such plans for herself and Rose. She would truly give up a life as a countess, with wealth and status and an adoring husband?

"Of course you cannot do that," Sir Reginald said, aghast. "Elizabeth, be reasonable. This is not how things are done. Please, we will find a family for . . . for . . . the child. You can still marry, have the life you planned for."

"But if it is a life without Rose," she said softly, "then I do not want it."

Sir Reginald looked as if he wanted to take her by the shoulders and shake some sense into her. But Lady Harwood stood suddenly.

"Now is not the time, Reggie," she said in a tone that refused to be argued with. "We will speak of this later. We have more immediate concerns."

"What is more concerning than my only daughter choosing to throw her life away?" Sir Reginald snapped.

"The fact that your only daughter is being blackmailed," I said quietly.

He seemed to have forgotten I was in the room. He stared at me, catching his breath. "Blackmailed?"

Elizabeth closed her eyes, her energy spent.

I spoke for her. "Yes," I said. "The threatening note Elizabeth received made it clear that the writer knew about Rose."

"What could this fellow possibly want?" Sir Reginald took a few steps toward us.

"He demanded that Elizabeth bring him *The Woman in Red*." I glanced at the portrait above the mantel. The woman looked out over the room, ignorant of the drama unfolding just beyond her gilded frame.

"*The Woman in Red*?" Sir Reginald shook his head. "Why?"

"No doubt he wishes to sell it," I said. "All of London is aware of its value, considering how much you paid for it."

Lady Harwood sat back down beside Elizabeth. "What are we to do?" she asked. "We cannot let such a vile man win."

"Of course we won't," I said firmly. "First, I must ask if anything strange has happened in our absence. Any curious notes or occurrences?"

Sir Reginald shook his head. "Nothing. It has been quiet."

I turned to Elizabeth. "It would appear your scheme worked. The blackmailer has likely been biding his time, waiting for your return."

She nodded. "But we will be ready for him."

Lady Harwood looked between the two of us. "What do you mean?"

I sat forward. "We have a plan, together with Mr. Denning, to catch the blackmailer. For your safety, the less you two know about it, the better. But the sooner we enact your part in it, the sooner we can have it over and done with."

"What is our part?" Sir Reginald asked doubtfully.

"Spreading the word that Elizabeth has returned," I said. "We must tell as many people as possible so the blackmailer will hear of it. We expect he will contact her again, thinking she's come to her senses."

"But really, we shall be laying a trap for him," Elizabeth said, her voice hard. "One he will never see coming."

"What sort of trap?" Lady Harwood asked, brow lowered in concern. "Nothing dangerous?"

"Not to you or your family," I assured her. "That is why Mr. Denning has gone straight to Bow Street, to ask the magistrate for help."

Lady Harwood and Sir Reginald looked at each other, neither seeming terribly convinced this was a good idea.

But then Elizabeth spoke again. "This is the only way we can be sure that my secret won't be leaked," she said softly. "The only way I can protect my reputation and that of my daughter."

Sir Reginald opened his mouth to speak, perhaps to insist yet again that Elizabeth see reason, but Lady Harwood laid a hand upon his arm, silencing him.

"Then of course we will help," Lady Harwood said with a steady gaze. "In any way we can."

Sir Reginald blew out a long breath but then closed his eyes and nodded his agreement. "Yes. We will help. Tell us what we must do."

"Oh, thank you, Father." Elizabeth reached one hand toward him, then drew it away, no doubt fearful of his rejection.

Sir Reginald hesitated a long moment, then reached over and grasped Elizabeth's hand. She clutched at him, tears falling from her eyes.

"I am sorry," he whispered. "I have spent the last three days fearing I might never see you again. I am only trying to protect and guide you as a father should. I am trying to find my way."

"I know, Father," she said, voice shaking. "I have not made it easy on you. But Verity and Mr. Denning will catch the culprit. I know they will."

I could not help but feel her confidence in me misplaced. But she did not need to know my doubts and fears—she had enough of her own. The plan was a good one, after all. So I nodded firmly, trying to reassure them all.

I would not let Elizabeth down.

CHAPTER 24

All I wanted to do was go straight to Bow Street. I wanted to see Nathaniel, tell him what had happened, and learn if there had been any developments while we'd been apart. But I had to go home. I needed a change of clothes, and that meant facing Mama.

I walked from Harwood House, the bustling streets doing nothing to distract me from the whirl of my thoughts. Would Mama be angry with me for leaving? Would she try to keep me from continuing with the case? I braced myself as I stepped through my front door.

"Verity?" That was Grandmama's voice, calling from her room down the corridor. I sighed and removed my bonnet as I approached her room.

She glanced up at me from her chair near the window, a book in her hand. "I see the bezoar worked. Still in one piece."

She was quite serious. I nearly laughed but contained it as best I could.

"Yes, thank you for that," I said, pulling the pendant out from beneath my fichu. "I'll keep it a few days more, if it's all the same to you." I could use a little more luck.

She made a humming sound, turning back to her book. "You need to go see your mother."

"She is not here?"

"Of course she isn't. She is rehearsing." Grandmama glared at me. "Do you think we just sit around, waiting for you day in and day out? No, she asked me to tell you she needed to speak with you as soon as you returned home."

She had? Mama considered the theatre sacred space. She loathed interruptions and distractions. The fact that she insisted I find her there meant . . . something. "I can speak to Mama tonight," I said. Perhaps I was lucky after all and could avoid her for a little while longer.

"And will you be home tonight?"

I hadn't any idea. If our plan worked as we hoped, I couldn't guess where I would be in a few hours.

"What does she need to speak to me about?" I asked hesitantly.

"I imagine you can guess." Grandmama closed her book. "Just as I see everything that goes on around this house, I hear everything too."

I leaned against the wall, suddenly very tired. "You heard our argument?"

"The neighbors likely heard it too," Grandmama said wryly.

I rubbed my forehead. "I . . . I said some things I shouldn't have."

She eyed me. "Your mother is many things," she said. "She can be filled with her own importance, grandiose, and ambitious. Heavens, after a performance the woman is downright unbearable."

I smiled at that. How many times had Mama come home after performing, bursting with energy, her eyes sparkling, her laugh filling the house?

"But she is more than you can imagine," Grandmama said. "You do not know her as I do. I know every choice she has made and every consequence she has suffered. People are allowed to make mistakes. Even mothers. Especially mothers. Do you know how hard it is to raise children?" She scoffed. "It's a trial, it is."

"Have you a point to this, Grandmama?" How easily her monologues veered into strange territory.

"Yes." She frowned at my impertinence. "All that to say, you ought to hear her out. She told me that if you were to come home while she was out, I should send you directly to her at the theatre."

I sighed and glanced at the clock on the nearby table. It was only midafternoon. I hadn't planned on meeting Nathaniel for another hour at least.

"Very well," I grumbled. "You win yet again, you old harpy."

"Music to my ears," she said, opening her book. "Now leave this old harpy in peace so she can finish her book."

I changed my clothes quickly, splashed water on my face, and fixed my hair. I waffled for a moment in indecision before adding a touch of rouge to my lips and cheeks, then dabbed perfume behind my ears. Nathaniel had seen me first thing in the morning, with my hair in a tangle and sleep still in my eyes. It seemed only fair that I be allowed this chance to fix a new image in his head.

It was a walk of but a few minutes to Drury Lane. I stopped before the doors of the Theatre Royal, took a deep breath, and went inside.

Mama still had several performances of *The Grecian Daughter* remaining but had begun practices for the upcoming production of *Henry VIII*. Not quite *Macbeth*, in her estimation, but close enough.

The long saloon was quiet when I entered, though I could hear the echo of voices reverberating from the stage. I took a back corridor that led to the rooms behind the stage. There I found the hubbub I was searching for—actors milling about in costume, scenery stacked against the walls, and the dramatic pull of voices.

I moved to the edge of the stage and spotted Mama in an instant. She wore a deep-blue gown, edged in pearls and trimmed with fur, and stood at the center of the crowded stage. The actor playing King Henry sat beneath the cloth of state, surrounded by cardinals and advisers. The trial scene, I gathered, a thought confirmed when Mama began her lines.

"Sir, I desire you do me right and justice," she said, her voice appropriately meek even as she projected to the entire theatre, "and to bestow your pity on me. For I am a most poor woman and a stranger born out of your dominions."

She swept toward King Henry, hands clasped to her chest. "Having here no judge indifferent," she cried, "nor no more assurance of equal friendship and proceeding. Alas, sir, in what have I offended you?"

Mama turned and saw me standing in the shadows. She blinked in surprise, then held up a hand briefly, urging me to wait. I nodded, and she continued the scene. After delivering Queen Katherine's parting lines, she exited the stage.

"I shall need a few minutes," she called over her shoulder, her skirts sweeping across the floor with a dramatic rustle. "Run through the rest of scene four while I am gone. It was positively dreadful yesterday."

I nearly laughed, a smile climbing my lips. Only Mama.

But then she reached me, and her eyes tightened, her mouth settling into the barest of lines. "Let us speak in my room."

I followed her as she wove through the organized chaos that was the Theatre Royal. When at last we reached the relative quiet of her dressing room, she ushered me inside and closed the door behind her.

I turned to face her. She looked me over from head to toe, then gave a great sigh. "I am glad to see you well," she said. "I hardly knew what to expect after reading your note."

I bit my lip. "I am sorry, Mama. I did not think you would let me go."

"That is just the thing." She moved to her dressing table and sat in a swirl of skirts. "I truly might have if you'd come to me in open honesty. Traveling to the country is likely safer than wandering the docks at night. And I know how desperate you were to find Elizabeth." She paused. "You did find her?"

"We did," I said. "She is well."

"Thank goodness for that," Mama said with a sigh of relief. "And Mr. Denning kept an eye on you?"

I sighed. "He did, though I cannot like being compared to a wayward pet."

Her lips twitched for the first time. "Wayward pet indeed." Then she sobered again. "We need to talk, Verity."

"I know."

Mama gestured to the chair beside her table, and I sat, watching her all the while. She did not look nervous to broach the subject of our argument. Instead, she looked only resigned.

"I've told you a great deal about your father and my past," she said quietly. "But I haven't told you everything. Or rather, I haven't explained everything."

She sat back in her chair. "I was desperately in love with your father when we first met," she said. "It felt like a dream that I, an actress in a country troupe, had caught the eye of the Earl of Westincott. I imagined him marrying me, raising me from obscurity, and whisking me away to London." She smiled wistfully. "When I learned I was expecting your brother, I was more certain than ever that he would marry me. But while he was pleased, he insisted the time was not right, but soon—*soon*—we would marry."

I sat in silence, listening closely. I'd heard this before. But I could tell it was leading somewhere new.

"You came along a few years later," she said, "and I was still trapped in the same web of lies. You were just a baby when I learned—from the newspaper, of all places—that your father planned to marry. But not me, of course. I was not good enough for him, for his family."

Her voice held no bitterness, only sadness.

"Reality caught me," she went on, "and it became clear that he had never intended to marry me. I think he cared for me, in his own way, but it was nothing compared to what I felt for him. And I was tired of him breaking my heart. So I confronted him and told him he must choose between me and his betrothed." She paused as if the memory were still painful. "He chose her. I was angry. I said some foolish things, and he responded in kind. He cut me off financially, and you as well."

I stared at her, mind trying to comprehend. "But he still sends money. I know he does. He paid for my schooling, for my clothing, everything."

She smiled sadly. "No. He paid for Jack's schooling and his commission in the army. But not yours."

"Why?" I asked in shock. I'd always assumed I was financially obligated to my father. It was why I worked so hard to find independence.

She shook her head. "He wanted to hurt me in return, for the things I said. He knew how I loved you."

"But he still supported Jack."

"Jack was a boy," she said quietly. "A girl was of no consequence to a man like him."

"But you had your career," I insisted. "We did not need his money, surely."

"Oh, but we needed it then," she said. "I did not have the fame I have now. After our argument, I never received another penny from him. And that was when the lie began."

I met her eyes and was stunned to see a glaze of tears there. Mama never cried, save for on stage. Now a tear trickled down her cheek as she gazed at me, though her chin still held strong.

"When we traveled the country," she said, "it was easier to simply tell everyone my husband had died rather than open our lives to gossip. But after we moved to London and my name began to be worth something, the lie took on a life of its own. We needed it, to protect your reputation. I was determined to provide for you and give you every opportunity in life."

"Why didn't you tell me?" I whispered. "All along, I assumed that *he* was paying for everything—that he still did."

"I was too ashamed," she said. "My anger and pride had lost you your future. How could I admit that if I'd held my tongue, your father would have paid for your every need? I might've been the mother you needed, not the absent one you had. You might've worn the finest dresses, socialized with only the best families. But because of me, you wore secondhand dresses and grew up amongst traveling troupes."

She spoke as if these were terrible things, but I was beginning to see it all so clearly. "Yes," I said quietly. "You are right. Because of you, I was fed and clothed and cared for. You made something of yourself, provided for us both." A lump formed in my throat.

"Oh, darling." She dabbed at her eyes with a handkerchief as she gestured around her dressing room, lavishly decorated and richly furnished. "I never imagined it would lead to all this. When I found success, I admit that I enjoyed it. I relished the attention, the acclaim. I still do." Her eyes found mine again, pleading. "But how I hated missing so much of your childhood. It broke my heart to leave you so often. I had to work so hard, Verity. The late nights, the long days. Yet it was only ever for you. For us."

We sat in silence for a few moments. I considered what she'd told me, thinking over the long years where she'd been but a sometimes mother, always rehearsing, always working. Yet I saw it differently now. Because she was right. Only in the last decade had she gained her popularity. Before that, it had been smaller theatres and country circuits. I had thought she was chasing fame and fortune, but she'd worked those endless hours and sought those opportunities for *me*. So I could have whatever life I wanted. So I could choose.

"I wish I had known," I whispered. "I am sorry, truly, for what I said the other night."

Mama smiled gently. "You needn't be. This is a conversation we've long needed to have. I simply wasn't sure how to broach it."

"Thank you, Mama," I said. "For everything. For things I am sure I don't even know about. I simply wish I could have done more to help over the years."

"That was not your responsibility." She sent me a meaningful look. "I regret so many of my choices. I was young and foolish and had no idea how my actions would affect you and Jack. But I brought you into this world, and I was determined to give you the best life I could."

"Does Jack know?" I asked. "I cannot imagine he would not have tried to help."

She shook her head. "I never wanted him to feel guilty for having more than you. And by the time he was old enough that he might have helped, I'd found the success I'd hoped for."

"Still," I said, a slight edge of bitterness entering my voice. "The earl should not have abandoned you."

"And yet, I am glad that he did," she said. "If I'd continued to depend upon him, I never would have pushed myself to such lengths. I would have remained lost to a man who did not love me. I would not have learned who *I* was." She reached out and took my hand. "I hope we might start anew, Verity. I've already told Mr. Webb that I plan to pull back at the theatre. I don't want to lose what time we have left."

"I am not dying, Mama," I said with a watery laugh.

"No, but you're grown. You have a life of your own now," she said. "I've too many regrets already."

I squeezed her hand. "You needn't sacrifice your career for me," I said. "I know how you love it. Our lives may have taken different paths, but that does not mean we cannot travel them together."

She gave a short laugh. "What a smart child you are. You must have a wonderful mother."

"Beyond measure," I said, smiling.

She patted my hand, and I knew then that Mama and I had formed a new relationship, one of honesty and trust. And I would not take it for granted.

$\mathcal{C}$HAPTER 25

I checked my tiny pocket watch as I approached No. 4 Bow Street. I'd told Nathaniel I would meet him at four o'clock—I was a few minutes late. He would be worried.

My steps quickened. I was eager to hear what news Nathaniel might have, but more than that, I was anxious to see him. As I stepped inside the magistrate's court, my eyes immediately went in search of him.

I found him easily, speaking urgently to Drake in the corner of the main office. Nathaniel's hair was in disarray, and his eyes were intent as he spoke. And yet, something settled inside me. As if a cloud had moved from the sun, and I could feel its warmth yet again. How quickly I'd come to know him, to depend upon him, to care for him. But that was the way of life. Sometimes a relationship of a fortnight could be infinitely deeper and dearer than one developed over many years. Nathaniel and I had faced so much during our time together, learned so much about each other, that it felt as though I'd known him a lifetime or longer.

As if he could sense me, his gaze flicked up, and he stopped midsentence. He looked me over in a second, as if to reassure himself that I hadn't come to any harm in the few hours since we'd parted, then he said something to Drake and started directly for me. Drake crossed his arms, eyes amused as he nodded a greeting at me from across the room.

"Everything went well?" Nathaniel asked when he reached me, one hand coming to touch my elbow.

I nodded. "The Harwoods have their instructions. I assume we have Mr. Etchells's approval for our plan?"

"Yes," he said. "Rawlings and Drake and an entire patrol stand ready when we need them."

I exhaled. "Now we wait."

"Not quite yet," he said, a new gleam in his eyes. "Come, I've something to show you."

He started back toward the entrance I'd just come through.

"Nathaniel, where are you going?"

"You'll see."

We were out the front door and across the street before I realized our destination. The Brown Bear, a tavern Bow Street officers often frequented. My brow furrowed even deeper as Nathaniel held the door for me and ushered me inside. He raised a hand at the barkeeper, then led me through the taproom and down a narrow back stairway.

"What are we doing?" I asked impatiently. We should be preparing for tonight.

"This morning," he said, his words trailing after him in the confines of the steep passageway, "Bow Street received a message."

"A message?" I repeated.

"Yes," he said. "An unsigned note that revealed the location of a man wanted in connection with a robbery on Drury Lane."

My heart skipped a beat. "You don't mean . . ."

We reached the basement, which revealed a long corridor filled with barred cells. I remembered then that aside from being the preferred watering hole of Bow Street men, The Brown Bear also contained several holding cells since No. 4 had grown too small for the expanding operations of Bow Street.

"I tracked him down while you were with the Harwoods," Nathaniel went on. "I've only just brought him in, and I thought you'd like to be present for my questioning."

But my eyes were already focused on the man in the first cell, seated upon the pallet bed on the floor. He glared back at us, hooded eyes just as I remembered, revealed by the dim afternoon light creeping through the barred window high above him.

"Tobias Higgs," I said, my voice hard.

He gave a short laugh. "Everyone round here seems to know my name."

"You don't recognize me?" I shouldn't have been surprised. He likely hit a dozen marks a week. But the fact that his face was emblazoned upon my mind while he could not recall holding a *gun* to me—

Higgs watched me with a bit more curiosity now. "Should I?"

My eyes narrowed to slits. "I am one of the ladies you robbed the same night you attacked Sir Reginald Harwood."

"I'm afraid I don't recall doin' any such thing," he said, his voice unconcerned. "And this don't look like a court. What evidence could you have?"

"Plenty," Nathaniel said with a threatening rumble. "With several witnesses, including Miss Travers here and the honorable Sir Reginald, I've little doubt you'll be found guilty and sentenced as you deserve. Transportation at best. The gallows at worst."

Higgs's expression lost some of its smug confidence, and he paled slightly.

"That is," Nathaniel said, "unless you choose to help us find the man who hired you. Then perhaps the magistrate would be willing to lessen your sentence."

My eyes widened right alongside Higgs's. I turned to face Nathaniel. "Is that something we should promise?" I whispered. "This man is guilty."

"Yes, he is." Nathaniel matched my quiet tone. "And he'll get what's coming to him. But if we play our cards right, we might fill two of these cells tonight instead of one."

I did not like it. I understood precisely what Nathaniel's aim was— Higgs could give us information about whoever was blackmailing Elizabeth. But letting the thief off easy made my veins flush with anger. He did not deserve leniency.

"What are you sayin' over there?" Higgs asked suspiciously. I turned to face him again, steeling my expression.

"Tell us what you know about the man who hired you to attack the Harwoods," Nathaniel said, moving directly in front of the cell.

"Wait now," Higgs protested. "I never agreed. How do I know you'll hold up your end of the bargain?"

"You don't." Nathaniel's voice was flat, harsh. I nearly shivered at the sound of it. "But you don't have many options at the moment, so I would suggest helping the one person who can help *you*."

Higgs twisted his face into a scowl, but clearly, he was considering it. "Fine," he muttered. "I'll do it."

I wasted no time. "Do you know the man's name?"

Higgs chuckled, a rough, gravelly sound. "Yes, he handed me his callin' card," he said sarcastically.

"Then do you know where we can find him?" Nathaniel pressed, crossing his arms. "Any clues as to his identity?"

Higgs shrugged. "He dressed well, though he tried to hide it under a ratty cloak. Spoke like a gentleman."

A gentleman? I exchanged a glance with Nathaniel, whose eyes echoed my surprise. I'd been imagining someone like Higgs, a desperate, conniving thief.

"Did he tell you why he wanted you to steal from the Harwoods?" Nathaniel asked. "What did he want with them?"

"I haven't a clue," Higgs drawled. "Didn't care either."

"How many times did you meet him?" I asked.

"Twice," he said. "Once when he hired me, and once when I delivered the goods. We met on a street corner."

I eyed him curiously. An idea began to brew in my mind.

"Did you not hesitate to take such a risky job?" Nathaniel braced one arm on the cell door. "Robbing a family of rank so near the theatre *and* Bow Street?"

"For what the fellow was offerin' me?" Higgs smirked. "Even you would have taken it."

"Doubtful."

My idea came full circle, and I stepped forward.

"You've seen him," I said to Higgs. "The man who hired you. Could you describe him to me?"

Higgs furrowed his brow. "I suppose. Not sure what good it would do. You aim to knock on every door in London?"

But I turned to Nathaniel, and he was already nodding. "I'll send someone for pencils and paper," he said, moving toward the stairs.

"You're goin' to draw the man who hired me?" Higgs said with no small amount of amusement as Nathaniel left.

"Yes." I did not have to explain myself to him. It was a long shot, but perhaps it would give us a chance at discovering Elizabeth's blackmailer.

"I recognize you now," Higgs said, putting his elbows on his knees as he sat forward. "That little spark in your eyes. Dangerous, that is. You'd best keep to needlepoint, Miss Travers. This ain't a lady's world."

"A little spark, you say?" I leaned toward him, my voice thin. "You underestimate what a little spark can do, Higgs. It burns. It grows. And I would not want to be you when it does."

He sat back, eyes wary, mouth pressed into a line. I'd unnerved him. Good. It was easier to weasel information from someone who was off-balance.

And I needed to get every ounce of information from this man that I could.

"Come now," I said in frustration two hours later. "You must remember if the man had dark eyes or light."

Higgs threw his hands in the air. He'd been pacing the small cell for the last half hour, no doubt regretting his decision to help us. "I told you," he growled. "It was night, and I couldn't have cared less what his eyes looked like."

I blew out a breath. "Fine. We'll come back to it."

"We've come back to it twice already," he muttered, lacing his hands behind his neck as he stared up at the ceiling.

I peered down at the sketch in front of me, tapping the pencil against my forehead. We'd made some progress, but the face in front of me was still irritatingly vague. The only truly helpful detail Higgs had given me was the man's nose, sharp and short. But there were a thousand men in London with sharp noses. It didn't help us in the least.

I was about to rip my drawing to shreds, thinking this was useless, when Nathaniel came down the stairs. He beckoned to me, and my heartbeat sped up. I set down the sketch on my chair and went to meet him.

"Elizabeth's maid just arrived," he said. "They received a letter."

I followed him back upstairs and across the street. We'd been waiting for this, hoping for this, but now my chest did not seem to know what to do with the emotions racing through me.

We entered Bow Street, and Marianne looked relieved to see me, surrounded as she was by Drake and Rawlings. I gave her a reassuring smile as I joined the group.

"Tell us exactly what happened," Nathaniel said, leaning back on a desk and crossing his arms. I was distracted for a short second—how easily this man commanded a room.

"It must've been about six o'clock," she said, clutching her reticule nervously. "A knock on the door and note left on the step. I have it here."

She held out a folded note, with *Miss Harwood* written across the front. I recognized the hand immediately from the note Elizabeth had shown us in Bibury.

Nathaniel took it and read aloud.

My dear Miss Harwood,

I cannot imagine what you were thinking, leaving Town as you did. Did you think I would not follow through on my threats? Fortunately for you, I have decided to give you one last chance. Deliver the painting to the park, as I specified in my first letter, by midnight tonight, or everyone will know about your little problem.

Tell no one. Come alone. This is your last chance.

I'll be watching.

I looked up at Nathaniel when he finished reading. "Tonight," I breathed.

"Tonight," he said, eyes fixed on mine.

It took a moment to remember that we were not alone, and I tried not to flush as we turned back to the group. Drake eyed us with a knowing twist of his lips.

"How is Elizabeth?" I asked Marianne to deflect the attention.

"Shaken," she said. "But determined. She wanted to come herself but worried that she would be followed. But she trusts you all to find this man."

Elizabeth's confidence settled like a pit in my stomach.

"The plan seems obvious," Drake said. "We plant a fake painting at the park, then wait for the blackmailer to collect it. We surround him, and that's that."

"It is not so simple," I said. "He said he will be watching. If he sees anyone besides Elizabeth deliver the painting, he will know something is wrong."

Marianne shook her head. "I do not think Elizabeth will do it."

"Of course not," I reassured her. "I never intended for it to be her."

A moment of silence, then Nathaniel stood, dropping his hands to his sides. "No," he growled. "You're not coming, Verity. This is a Bow Street operation."

"I'm the only one who can impersonate Elizabeth," I deflected. "We're nearly the same height. If I wear a hooded cloak, I'll look enough like her."

"You're not coming," he said flatly. "I can deliver the painting."

"You?" I made a sound of amusement. "That would fool no one."

Indeed, the idea of Nathaniel's shoulders and tall figure crouched under a lady's cloak was so ridiculous, I nearly laughed. But the look in his eyes made the smile fall right from my lips. He stepped closer, his gaze fierce and stubborn.

"Then we will find another way," he said flatly.

I could almost see the workings of his thoughts. He wanted to protect me, and I loved him for it. But he also had to trust me.

"I hate to be the voice of reason," Drake said, looking positively delighted to do so, "but we may have no other choice, Denning. We haven't any other leads, and Verity is right. If the blackmailer sees one of us leave the painting, he'll know it's a trap, and we'll never catch him."

Nathaniel put his hands on his waist, his jaw tight.

"I'll deliver the painting and leave," I insisted. "I'll be in no danger."

"That does nothing to reassure me," he muttered. "You attract danger like flies to honey."

"I can do this," I said firmly.

His eyes burned into mine, and I knew he was thinking of what I'd told him that night at the inn. How close I'd come to death just a few short months ago. I could not help but think of it too. But it was Nathaniel himself who had told me I must be brave enough to choose my own path. I straightened my shoulders and held his gaze.

"This is our only chance." My voice was soft but steady. "Please let me help."

I thought he would argue more, insist on me staying behind. But something in his expression shifted, and his eyes closed. "Fine," he said roughly. "You'll deliver the painting. But then you'll return directly to Harwood House."

Perhaps I should have been irritated by his authoritative tone, but I was so relieved he had agreed that I nodded. "Of course."

Nathaniel checked his pocket watch. "It is nearly seven o'clock. We haven't much time for details." He blew out a breath as he returned his watch to his pocket. "First, we need a false painting."

Marianne cleared her throat. "Harwood House has dozens of paintings. I'm certain we can find one of a similar size to *The Woman in Red*."

"Won't it be terribly obvious it's a decoy?" I asked.

"We can wrap it in paper?" Drake suggested.

Nathaniel crossed his arms. "I'm not sure that will be enough."

Rawlings spoke for the first time, his Scottish brogue slightly softening the bluntness of his words. "There's nothing we can do about it. Either he will take the bait, or he won't, though having Miss Travers deliver the painting will help with the deception."

Nathaniel considered that, then nodded. "We don't know how the blackmailer will be watching, so we must assume he has eyes on the house. Verity should leave from there as if she were Miss Harwood." He turned to Marianne. "We will need the Harwoods' cooperation. You should return home now and inform them of our plan."

"I'll follow from a distance," Drake said. "To be sure you're safe, miss."

Marianne's cheeks turned pink. "Thank you."

"I'll bring Verity along around eleven o'clock," Nathaniel said, drawing our attention back to him. "She will enter through the servants' door. The blackmailer can't watch every entrance."

Marianne nodded in agreement.

"Once I leave Verity," Nathaniel said, "I'll join Drake, Rawlings, and the patrol in St. James's Park. We'll form a perimeter around the tree, though we'll have to be careful. No horses or carriages—they'll draw attention—and we'll have to be far enough not to be seen. Verity will deliver the painting and return immediately to Harwood House. Then it will be up to us to corner the blackmailer when he comes."

A sudden quiet fell over the group as we all considered the plan, trying to imagine any pitfalls or failings.

"It has every chance of working," Drake said optimistically.

"You say that about every plan," Rawlings muttered.

"It will work," Nathaniel said, though he looked at me as he said it. "It will."

I had to believe him. I had to have faith in my friends. If I didn't, then the fear that rapped at my door would take full control of me. I exhaled and set my jaw.

We had our plan. And by the end of the night, we would have our blackmailer.

CHAPTER 26

Night had descended in full when I hurried across to The Brown Bear once again, the streetlamps glowing against the encroaching dark. I had only a minute to return to Higgs's cell to gather my things—Nathaniel would be waiting to walk me to Harwood House.

We'd spent the better part of the evening going over the plan again and again. Everyone knew their part. And for the first time in months, I felt confident in mine. I could do this. I could play my role and help Elizabeth and put a dangerous man behind bars. My determination was a heady stream through my veins, and it kept my body moving even though it was after ten o'clock at night.

I slipped inside The Brown Bear, loud and lively, and descended the back stairs. I had thought Higgs might've fallen asleep waiting for me to return, but he still sat up on his pallet, eyes peering at me through the dark.

"Decided to come back, eh?" he grumbled.

"Not for long." I began gathering the sketch and my pencils.

"Why the hurry?" Higgs looped his arms over his knees. "Don't you want to know what I remembered while you were off flirtin' with your Runner?"

I paused, my hands in midmotion. "What are you talking about?"

"I remembered somethin'," he said, lip curling up in a distasteful smirk. "About the man who hired me."

I scowled. "What did you remember?"

He raised his chin, enjoying lording this over me. "You're clearly in a rush. Pay me no mind."

I blew a curl from my face. "For heaven's sake, just tell me."

He relented, though he kept that superior smile. "The man. He had a beard."

"A beard?" I repeated suspiciously. "I questioned you for two hours, and only now you happen to recall such a prominent feature?"

He shrugged. "The mind works in funny ways, Miss Travers. Because I do remember it now. Trimmed short, but yes, a beard."

I gave a vague shake of my head. It did not matter. We were leaving even now to intercept the blackmailer. "Thank you kindly," I said, stuffing my things into my reticule. "I'll take that into account."

"Into account?" Higgs huffed behind me as I started for the door. "I've given you valuable information, and you're just goin' to—"

"Leave?" I called over my shoulder. "Yes, yes, I am."

He shouted after me as I clattered up the stairs, but I wasn't listening. Higgs had no place in my thoughts anymore. My mind was already focused ahead, concentrating on everything we had to accomplish tonight.

Nathaniel waited for me outside the tavern, arms crossed. "Ready?" he asked.

At my nod, he shoved his hands into his pockets and started up the street.

I frowned and hurried to catch him. Nathaniel had been rather clipped during our hours of planning, but I'd assigned that to him focusing on the case. Now it seemed like more.

"Are you angry with me, Nathaniel?" I asked.

He blew out a long breath. "I wish I were."

"What is it, then?"

He shook his head. "It won't do any good to discuss it now."

"But—"

"Please, Verity." The shortness in his words left no room for argument. And yet I wanted to argue. Why was he acting so?

We walked to Harwood House in silence, nearly twenty minutes of unbroken quiet that seemed to fill my chest the longer it endured. When we reached the entrance of the mew that ran directly behind Harwood House, Nathaniel held up a hand to stop me, glancing up and down the dark street before hurrying me forward and into the shadows.

"I don't think we were seen," he said, his hand warm on the small of my back as we approached the servants' entrance.

I said nothing, my heart fighting with every ounce of logic inside me. We needed to focus on the task at hand. And yet . . .

I took Nathaniel's arm and pulled him to a stop in the deepest shadows across from the door. "I believe you're not angry," I said. "But why, then, will you not look at me?"

He closed his eyes. "This is not the place."

"Seeing as I won't be going inside until you tell me, I rather think it is," I retorted.

"Heavens, Verity," he said under his breath as he finally met my gaze, his eyes aglow in the moonlight. "You want to know why I cannot look at you?"

"Yes," I said stubbornly.

He swallowed hard, his eyes tracing over my face. "Because I cannot bear to," he said, his voice low and rough. "We don't know what we will face tonight. Anything could go wrong. Anything. You are running blindly into a fire, and I cannot even run beside you. How am I to look you in the eye? It is my job to protect you, not to put you into more danger." He was breathing hard, and his obvious pain tore through my heart.

I touched his waistcoat with my fingertips, the slightest brush. "Do you think I do not fear for you as well?" I whispered.

His head lifted slightly.

"I am terrified to think of you in harm's way," I said, my voice barely audible. I closed the distance between us and pressed my face into his jacket, my arms wrapped around his waist. I tried to memorize his scent, the feel of his breath warm on my cheek. "And yet we have both made our choices. We are choosing to help. To make the world a better, safer place. Of course it will be dangerous."

"I know that," he said, and the gravel in his voice made my heart skip a beat. "But it is one thing to plan an operation. It is entirely different to see it play out before me. How can I watch the woman I love—" He stopped.

I stood frozen a second, then tipped my head up to look at him. He stared back at me, eyes suddenly uncertain.

"Love?" I repeated softly. *Love.*

"I'm sorry," he said, pulling back. "I shouldn't have said that. I know you're not ready to—"

I kissed him. I did not stop to think. One second we were speaking, the next my lips were on his, my hands encircling his jaw. I only knew that I did not want him to go another moment without knowing what I felt for him, and I'd never been terribly good with words. Kissing seemed the best way to go.

Nathaniel apparently agreed. His arms wrapped around my waist, pulling me up to him until my toes barely touched the ground. Our mouths melded together, a fierce connection that marked me at my very core. My heart pounded wildly inside my chest.

He loved me. *Me.*

I did not know what had changed since we'd spoken that warm evening on the bridge near Rosemont Cottage, when I'd been so afraid of the strength of my feelings for him. It was as though every moment I'd spent with him reminded me of whom he was. Of whom I could be. Of what we could become *together.* And it was enough to break the ice of aching distrust that had stolen over my heart in the last few years. It was enough for me to reach for what I wanted, even as fear tugged at me and doubt clamored at the back of my mind.

Nathaniel kissed me passionately, fully. He gave all of himself to me, and I felt in his kisses a new hope, a hope that grew within my own heart with every brush of our lips and caress of his fingers. Our kiss at the inn had caught me off guard, had made me reevaluate everything I had thought I believed. *This* kiss felt like an answer. A declaration of all I'd been too afraid to say before.

When we parted, Nathaniel smoothed a curl behind my ear, his eyes tender. I looked up at him in dazed disbelief. I had told myself for years that this could not be my future. That I would not be subjected to the whims of love. But this was different from anything I had ever imagined. What I felt with Nathaniel was real and true and so boldly ours that I pressed a hand to my stomach, overwhelmed by the flood of emotions that swept me up in its wake.

"I—" My voice caught. I tried again. "Nathaniel, I—"

He pressed a kiss to my knuckles, stopping me. "You needn't say anything. We haven't the time. You're already late."

Just how long had we stood there kissing in the stillness of the shadows?

"Go now," he said. "I'll be waiting in the park when you arrive, near the entrance. I'll be watching you the whole time."

He started to move away, but I grasped his hand. "Be careful," I said desperately. "Please."

"I am always careful." The corner of his mouth tipped up. "But perhaps I will be even more careful if you promise to kiss me like that again."

He spoke teasingly, but I was all soberness in my response. "I promise a hundred such kisses," I whispered. "A thousand."

I meant it. I wanted each and every one.

His gaze took on a new fervency. "And I shall be there to claim them."

I took one last look at him, the shadows and planes of his face that had become so dear to me in so short a time. Then I pulled away and hurried across the alley to the servants' door. When I glanced over my shoulder, he was already gone.

At my knock, the door opened, and Marianne ushered me inside. "It's nearly a quarter after," she said as she closed the door behind me. "Where have you been? We were growing so worried."

"I am sorry," I said. "I was . . . delayed."

That was certainly not how I'd ever thought to describe a clandestine kiss in the moonlight, but I could hardly go into more detail now.

"Come," she said. "Everyone is in the drawing room."

I heard lowered voices as we approached. When we entered, Sir Reginald, Lady Harwood, and Elizabeth all looked up, expressions serious. Had they been discussing Elizabeth's future again? Or simply the task we faced tonight?

Elizabeth stepped toward me. "Verity, are you sure about this? Marianne told us what part you are to play, and I cannot in good faith allow you to—"

"I am sure," I said firmly. "The blackmailer wants the painting. He doesn't want to harm me—or you, rather. I shall be perfectly safe."

"Until he realizes the painting isn't real," Sir Reginald said.

"I shall certainly be well on my way before then." I moved toward the wrapped frame on the table before them. "Is this the decoy?"

I lifted the wrapping slightly, peering inside at an angle, then froze. I looked up at the three of them.

"What is this?" I managed.

"*The Woman in Red,*" Sir Reginald said, eyes daring me to argue with him.

"But it is meant to be a decoy," I protested.

Sir Reginald shook his head. "I hardly care about the painting anymore. I'll not send you off on this madcap scheme without doing everything I can to keep you safe. If it helps you in any way, it will have been worth it."

My eyes stung with unexpected tears. *This* was what a father was supposed to be like. Sacrificing without expectation of reward simply because he wanted to keep me safe. Because he cared. I replaced the brown paper around the painting, my throat dry. "Thank you," I said, my voice frail. "But as an artist myself, it pains me to put this painting in any sort of danger." I would never have dared call myself an artist a few months ago, but Mr. Allett's words from our first meeting echoed through my mind. *If you create, you are an artist,* he'd said.

"I am confident," I went on, "in Bow Street's ability to capture the blackmailer no matter what I deliver. Please, we needn't risk such a masterpiece. I will take the decoy."

Sir Reginald's frown suggested he meant to argue, but Lady Harwood put a hand on his arm. "As you wish, Verity," she said. "We prepared another just in case."

Elizabeth brought forward a different wrapped frame and placed it beside *The Woman in Red.* They looked identical in size and shape, small enough to carry without it being unwieldy. My confidence in my decision was renewed. This would work.

Lady Harwood glanced at the clock anxiously. "You had best be off, my dear."

Marianne brought me a rich woolen cloak that I knew to be Elizabeth's. She draped it around my shoulders and pulled the hood forward over my face.

"There," she said. "No one will know you are not Miss Harwood."

Elizabeth crossed her arms, looking away.

"Please do not worry for me," I said, touching her shoulder. "Do not feel guilty. I do this because I believe in law and order. We will catch this criminal, and he shall have no more hold over you or Rose."

She swallowed hard, meeting my eyes again. "I very much hope so."

I picked up the decoy painting and fitted it neatly under my arm. I glanced toward her parents speaking quietly and lowered my voice. "Has your father relented at all toward Rose?"

"He has . . . tried to see my way of thinking," she said. "I think it is simply the shock of it all. I've disappointed him." She bit her lip. "But I hope he will soften in the coming days."

"He will," I assured her. "He is a good father. He wants only what is best for you."

"I know." She released a trembling breath. "Godspeed, Verity. We shall be praying for you until you return."

Sir Reginald nodded, and Lady Harwood offered a watery smile. I took a deep breath and made my way to the front door, then out into the cool night air. I ducked my head, keeping the hood of the cloak low over my eyes as I came down the steps. Was the blackmailer watching even now?

I could have walked to St. James's Park, but Nathaniel had insisted that the blackmailer would expect Elizabeth to hire a hack, so that was what I did. The jarvey seemed curious about me, eyeing me as I waved him down, but he only nodded when I gave my destination. I climbed inside the coach and sat in the darkest corner, keeping my hood in place. We started off, and I set the painting gently on my lap, holding tight to the wrapped frame. I wasn't sure what painting *was* inside, but knowing the Harwoods, it was likely valuable still. I would take care.

The coach moved through the night, and my mind flew ahead of it to where I knew Nathaniel was waiting in the park. I'd been to St. James's Park many times, but I could not picture which tree precisely the blackmailer had detailed. I would have to search for it.

We passed a man on the street, and he glanced toward the hack. I did not recognize him, but it sparked an idea in my mind. I opened my reticule and pulled out my sketch of the blackmailer. I held it up to the passing lamp light, wanting to memorize the face as best I could in case I spotted him and could somehow alert Nathaniel.

He had a beard. Higgs's voice came back into my head, insistent. I frowned. Had he truly remembered? Or was he simply desperate for leniency? Still, I set the painting on the bench beside me and fished a pencil from my reticule. Though the road was bumpy, I set about filling in the man's jaw with a short, trimmed beard, as Higgs had described.

It was the work of a minute, and when I finished, I held the drawing away from me. My eyes traced over every feature, willing myself to recognize the face.

I didn't, of course. For all I knew, Higgs was lying about everything. There was no reason this face should be familiar to me.

And yet . . .

I stared closer. The eyes. I rubbed with my fingers, lightening them as I smudged the graphite. If his eyes had been lighter than the black I'd drawn them, then—

I gasped. My pencil flew over the page again, adjusting the line of the jaw, the curve of the brow, the turn of the mouth. When I finished, I clutched the sketch, my fingers wrinkling the page. They had been such small changes, the beard and the eyes. But once I'd started, I could not stop. I could not unsee it.

The man that stared back at me was Lucas Allett.

$\mathcal{C}$HAPTER 27

My rapid breaths did nothing to fill my lungs as I gaped down at my sketch. It could not be. It made no sense whatsoever. Mr. Allett had no reason to—

The coach came to a jolting halt.

"Here, miss," the jarvey called out.

But I did not move. I had to tell Nathaniel, had to tell someone. But I couldn't. He and the other men were hidden, waiting.

What was I to do?

"Miss?" he called again.

I managed to calm my breathing. "One moment!"

Lucas Allett was somewhere nearby, waiting for me to deliver the painting. I wasn't even sure the information I had was terribly useful—Nathaniel would catch him no matter what, surely—but if there was some small advantage to informing him and the men about who they were watching for, I had to try.

Working quickly, I scrawled Allett's name across the bottom on the paper. I quickly folded it into a messy square and tucked it up the sleeve of my pelisse. Then, picking up the painting and tugging my hood over my eyes, I opened the door and stepped down.

"I'll only be a few minutes," I said to the driver. "Will you wait for me, please?"

He eyed me, scratching his rough jaw. "For an extra shilling."

"Yes, all right," I said. "I'll return shortly."

I started into the park, eerily devoid of its usual occupants. The moonlight painted the landscape in silver and shadows, making the familiar unfamiliar. I located the path mentioned in the letter Elizabeth had received and followed it, keeping a close eye for the tree with a lightning scar.

I also searched surreptitiously for any sign of Nathaniel. He'd said he would be near the entrance of the park, but I saw nothing and heard no one. Wherever he and the other men were, they'd done a good job of hiding themselves.

I saw the tree when I was a hundred feet away. Its trunk was split nearly down the center, jagged edges pointing to the star-filled sky. I wrapped my arms tighter around the decoy painting and crossed the lawn, my veins pulsing with energy and awareness as I approached. I stopped before the tree, pretending a hesitation that I imagined Elizabeth might feel, then leaned the wrapped painting against the trunk.

That was it. I'd done my part.

I hurried back the way I'd come. Again, I saw no one, but I knew Nathaniel was watching. My hope was that wherever Allett was, he was now paying less attention to me and more to the painting.

Under the guise of adjusting my sleeve, I slipped my sketch free and tucked it in the palm of my hand. I looked for the best spot and found it just ahead—a bend in the path near a stand of trees and bushes. I let the folded page fall from my hand, and it landed on the grass. I did not look back as I continued toward the waiting hack. I could only hope Nathaniel had seen me drop it and was able to retrieve it behind the cover of those trees.

If not, I reassured myself, it did not matter. These men were professionals. They could handle the likes of Lucas Allett, an artist turned criminal.

At least, I hoped they could. I climbed into the hack, absently directing the jarvey back to Harwood House as my thoughts tumbled about. What did I really know about Mr. Allett, a man I'd met only twice? I'd never felt threatened in his presence, after all. He'd been all that was charming and disarming. Had it been a deception? Was his portraiture business simply a front for more lucrative—and illegal— dealings?

For a few minutes, I debated turning back. But I did not know if Allett was watching me still. I had to keep up the act, even if my heart tugged me to where Nathaniel was surely in danger.

I told the driver to stop a block from the house, paid him, and then continued on foot. I approached silently, my mind still back at the park.

Then I came to a sudden halt.

An empty carriage stood unattended right outside Harwood House, its two horses dancing anxiously. It was plain and well-used, nothing like the equipages normally used by the wealthy residents of Mayfair.

My eyes darted to the house. The white front door was open, the black gap swallowing the moonlight. Then I heard voices. A shout.

Someone was inside the house.

I immediately ducked, crouching beside the front steps. Blood pounded in my ears. It took every bit of willpower I had to stop myself from barreling inside. I did not know who was there, if they were armed, what their intentions were. I had to gather as much information as I could.

"How dare you," came Sir Reginald's voice, hissed as if he spoke through a clenched jaw. "How dare you come into my home and—"

"I haven't time for this." This voice was unsteady but familiar. Lucas Allett. "The painting. Now."

"Give it to him," Lady Harwood said desperately. "Let him take it."

Allett must have a weapon. They would not sound so afraid otherwise, nor would they give in to his demands. And if *he* had a weapon . . .

I fumbled with my reticule, my fingers ripping open the cinched top. I emptied its entire contents on the ground—my pistol, powder flask, several lead balls, and a tiny ramrod. Running around with a loaded flintlock was a quick way to lose a limb, so I hadn't dared load my pistol beforehand. Now I wished I'd chosen the more foolish path.

"Step back now," Allett ordered, his voice clearer. He must have the painting—his footsteps moved toward the door. "Except for you."

A scuffle, then a small shriek from Lady Harwood. What was happening? I tried to focus. I poured a measure of powder inside the barrel, then grabbed the ramrod and a bullet.

Footsteps sounded inside the house behind me. Panic rose inside my chest. I wasn't fast enough. I wasn't ready. My fingers slipped on the narrow rod as I shoved down the lead ball.

I tipped my head so I could just see the open front door, where a figure now appeared. Elizabeth. And behind her came Allett, the painting in one hand and a pistol in the other, pointed directly at my friend's back.

He'd taken Elizabeth hostage.

"Do not send Bow Street after us," he said over his shoulder, "or Miss Harwood here will pay the price. If we are not pursued, I shall release her when my escape is assured."

I froze, my hands clutched around my pistol and the ramrod. Of course he would take her. Allett needed leverage, after all. He'd played *all* his cards by coming directly to Harwood House. If he simply ran, there would be officers after him in minutes, and his chance of escape would be slim indeed. Elizabeth was his ticket out.

I pressed my back against the side of the steps as the two of them came down to the carriage. I dared not finish loading my pistol; Allett might notice me. I heard Elizabeth's gasped breaths and could not stop myself from glancing upward. Her face flashed white and frightened in the lamplight, and then she was gone, Allett prodding her toward the carriage.

Time came to a halt. My heart stuttered even as my thoughts crystallized. I had to stop them. I could not let him leave with Elizabeth. But how? I would only put my friend in danger if I confronted them.

With Allett's pistol at her back, Elizabeth climbed into the carriage. He hissed something at her that my ears could not comprehend—a threat, no doubt—and slammed the door. He climbed into the driver's seat and set the painting at his feet.

A fully formed plan leaped into my mind. It was preposterous, desperate.

I dropped the ramrod, snatched up my powder flask again, and dumped a small amount into the pan, snapping the frizzen into place. My motions were suddenly smooth and confident. I had no other choice. Because I knew what I had to do.

Allett took the reins and whipped them against the horses' backs. The carriage jolted forward, rattling past me on the cobblestones. Pistol in one hand, I took a step, two, then I was darting forward. It would never work. It couldn't work. The rear of the carriage was just a few feet from me now, and its pace quickened with every second. I took a running step and lunged, catching the handle on the rear and pulling myself up to the small seat where a servant might have ridden. The carriage lurched slightly under my weight, but the left wheel hit a rut at the same moment, and we dipped together. I ducked, praying Allett hadn't noticed. But the carriage continued, faster and faster, and no shouts came from the driver's seat.

Allett directed the carriage through the streets of London. I kept my head bowed, though I peeked up every now and again to get my bearings. We soon left Mayfair and crossed through Covent Garden. I spotted the facade of the Theatre Royal, still lit at this late hour. Mama had likely already returned home after her performance and was wondering where I was.

I hoped I would have the chance to tell her.

The lights of the theatre faded away, and Allett pushed the horses, only slowing to make turns. I tried to imagine what Elizabeth was feeling inside the carriage. Would she try to escape? I did not think so. Not with Rose depending on her. Elizabeth would do everything possible to return to her daughter.

Eventually, we made our way onto a street running alongside the Thames. I could see the moon and stars glittering on the surface of the river, wide and dark. We traveled for twenty minutes or so, my back aching from my awkward crouch behind the carriage. When I felt the carriage slow beneath me, I stiffened.

We came to a stop, and my stomach jolted along with the carriage as Allett alighted from the high step, his boots just visible through the spokes of the back wheel. He opened the carriage door.

"Come along, Miss Harwood," he said, his voice like ice.

"I won't go with you," she said, and pride welled in my chest for my friend. I knew she was terrified, yet she defied him. "You've escaped. You don't need me now."

"I will decide that." He grabbed her arm and tugged her down to the street. He tucked the painting under his arm, then grabbed an overstuffed valise from the floor of the carriage. Of course he'd packed for a quick escape. One did not return to normal life after accosting a baronet and his family in their own home. But why had he done it? He'd gotten the painting, but he'd ruined his future. He could never return to the comfortable life he'd had before, painting the elect of high Society. All for one painting. How could that be worth sacrificing *everything*?

They walked toward the glistening waters of the Thames, Allett once again pointing his pistol at Elizabeth's back. I peered around the carriage after them. He did not seem at all concerned about abandoning his horses and carriage, indicating he must have a second method of transportation.

I eased myself down from my tiny seat and took in my surroundings. Masts and sails filled the night sky around me, the hulls of ships bobbing in the Thames's current. I stood among the Wapping docks now abandoned by its workers for mugs of ale or warm beds. Nathaniel and I had come here only a few days ago to search for Higgs. Was it a coincidence?

I did not have time to wonder. Allett and Elizabeth were vanishing into the dark. I secured my hood around my face once more and started after them, keeping to the shadows alongside the buildings.

Allett glanced back every minute or so, and I folded myself into ill-lit doorways and corners, evading his searching eyes. Finally, he paused, head turning to ensure no one was watching, then guided Elizabeth down a set of stairs.

I crept after them, keeping low until I reached the stairs. They led down to a dock with a few berths. The boats here were smaller, with single masts and narrow hulls. My heart pattered faster. Was this how he planned to leave London?

Allett moved Elizabeth along the short dock until they reached a square-sterned wherry. He tried to urge her inside, but she balked, backing away. A not-so-gentle nudging with his pistol made her step from the dock down into the boat.

I carefully made my way down the stairs, pressing myself to the rough stone at my back. Was this Allett's boat? Or was he stealing one?

It did not matter; my object was the same. I had to stop him. Once he fled on the river, we could lose his trail—and Elizabeth's. He might land anywhere along the Thames or even escape to the sea and beyond.

I held my pistol carefully in both hands as I moved along the dock, pausing behind the boat that swayed between me and Allett's. I peeked around the side. There was movement aboard the wherry—he was tying Elizabeth's hands. I had to surprise him now, while he was distracted.

I darted forward. Allett was crouched before Elizabeth, tightening a knot around her wrists, but at my footsteps, he spun. Before he could do anything, my pistol was leveled directly at his chest.

"Don't. Move." My voice was a sharpened edge, a dagger in the night.

Allett blinked as though he thought me an apparition. "Miss Travers," he said in disbelief. "How . . . ?" Then focus found his eyes again, and he shook his head. "I never thought to see you again."

"Then perhaps you should reconsider your current line of employment." I took one step closer, my pistol steady. "I am not one to let thieves go free."

My eyes flicked to Elizabeth. She watched the exchange with wide eyes, her golden curls trailing over her shoulders. She'd been gagged, a handkerchief pulled tight across her mouth.

Allett gave a hard laugh. "I am no *thief*."

Every thief had a plea of innocence on their lips. "Then I suppose you are going to deny that you currently possess a valuable painting owned by Sir Reginald Harwood?"

"I don't deny that I have it," he said, his blazing eyes catching the moonlight. "But *The Woman in Red* does *not* belong to him."

What on earth was he talking about? But it did not matter. He was at my mercy. I knew the Thames River Police had a station near the Wapping New Stairs, not far from here. Elizabeth and I could walk him there through the docks, but it wasn't ideal. I would feel much better if his hands were restrained. I did not know where he'd stowed his pistol.

"Throw your pistol onto the dock," I ordered Allett. "And untie Miss Harwood." I would use the rope to bind him.

"I'm afraid I have no intention of obeying you, Miss Travers," he said evenly. "Though I applaud your efforts."

"I know how to use this pistol," I said, my voice hard.

"Yes," he said. "I am sure you are quite proficient. Only, I don't think you'll be holding it much longer."

Elizabeth stiffened and shouted against her gag. A warning.

A shadow rushed at me from my right. I swung my weapon around. My brain had only a half second to recognize the threat—a large man, menace in his eyes—before I acted.

I pulled the trigger.

CHAPTER 28

My pistol fired with a blinding flash and a deafening roar. The man's fist caught me almost at the same moment, striking me hard across the jaw. I dropped, barely catching myself on the splintering dock as my pistol skittered over the edge and into the river below. My vision filled with bright lights, swirling through the sky above me, and my head flared with an intense, throbbing pain. I cried out, ears ringing.

The man who'd attacked me staggered to the side, one hand grasping his arm, cursing loudly. "She shot me!" he shouted.

"Quiet," Allett hissed, leaping onto the dock. He pulled his pistol free, pointing it at me. "Don't move, Miss Travers."

I couldn't have even if I wished to. My limbs felt like jelly, my thoughts scattered.

Allett quickly examined the man's arm. "A graze. We'll wrap it on the boat."

"We'll wrap it now," the stranger growled.

"Any second, these docks could be swarming with Runners," Allett insisted. "We have to go. Now, tie her up, and keep her quiet."

My wits came back to me as rough arms hauled me to my feet. For the briefest of moments, I prepared to act. I could spin away, break his hold, and knee him sharply between the legs. He would drop like a load of rocks. Then I would run back up the dock and escape. Allett had his pistol, but I doubted he was anything close to a crack shot. I could get away, I was certain.

But . . .

If I ran, I would leave Elizabeth. And I could not—would not—abandon her to these men.

So I formed a new plan.

My assailant pulled my arms in front of me none too gently, and I felt the scratch of rope around my wrists. My eyes managed to focus on the man above me, short and barrel-chested, with a stubbled jaw and mangy hair. And even though my thoughts still whirled chaotically, instinct kicked in. How many times had Jack warned me about such a situation?

I fisted my hands, pressing my knuckles together, and pulled them toward my chest. The smallest of movements, but I knew they could make a world of difference.

When he finished tying the knot, the stranger hoisted me up. My legs wobbled beneath me.

"This wasn't part of the deal," he hissed at Allett. "You didn't tell me we'd be snatching women. I'm no kidnapper."

"Neither am I," Allett replied. "But if we are pursued, we *need* something to bargain with, Barlow. We'll let them go once we're safely away."

"So they can run and report me to the magistrates?" Barlow looked incensed. "I've a life here. I can't just up and scurry off like you."

Allett threw up his hands. "Then lie low until the search dies down." His voice had gone a bit wild, his plan coming apart at the seams.

Barlow muttered obscenities under his breath and shoved me forward. I stumbled down into the wherry, my knees hitting the rough wood. "Stay there," he ordered, his voice irritated. "Say nothing."

I did as he said, crawling to Elizabeth, the boat rocking beneath me. Her bound hands came to clutch mine, eyes frightened, the gag a white slash across her face.

"It's all right," I whispered. "It will be all right."

Barlow found a bandage in a small chest, and Allett quickly tied off his wound. I cursed my luck that my shot had missed anything more vital—Barlow seemed barely hampered by the bullet's graze. The two men prepared to cast off. I watched them, determined to stay alert despite the insistent ache in my jaw from where Barlow had struck me. To my surprise, Allett seemed strangely competent in his tasks. He tied off lines and adjusted the sails as quickly as any sailor I'd ever seen. I hadn't imagined he had any experience in such a trade. He was a painter, after all.

When I thought neither was watching, I glanced down at my bound hands. I pulled against the rope and—just as I'd hoped—there was the tiniest of gaps between my hands. I breathed a sigh of relief. Now I simply had to work the rope until my bindings were loose enough to slip off. I began wiggling my wrists, rotating them back and forth.

Elizabeth noticed what I was doing, and her mouth parted in surprise. I shook my head, and she immediately tore her eyes away, looking in the opposite direction. Barlow moved behind us, readying his oars. Allett, however, finished tying off his line and sat on the forward bench, against which he'd leaned the wrapped frame of *The Woman in Red*. I paused my work on the ropes and watched as he slowly began unwrapping the painting. I expected glee to cross his face. He held a fortune in his hands, and no small one. But instead, when he unwrapped the final layer of paper, his eyes filled with tears. Anguish twisted his features, and his hands clutched the frame until they turned white.

And then something became abundantly clear to me. This painting was more than just a fortune to him.

"Why did you do this?" I asked him, my voice low. "What is that painting to you?"

He looked in my direction, eyes still glistening. He said nothing for a long moment before returning his gaze to the painting. One hand released the frame to hover over the woman's face, as if he wished to trace a finger over her haunting features.

"I cannot begin to explain." He spoke with a rasp in his throat. "There are no words."

"There are *always* words," I shot back. "When you threaten the future and safety of my dearest friend, there must be a reason."

His eyes flashed toward Elizabeth. "Your friend is a spoiled lady of the *ton* who ruined her future all on her own. Privilege should not make one immune to consequences."

Elizabeth's face crumpled, and I knew she still felt the weight of her choices and the responsibility toward her daughter. I wanted to tear the gag from her mouth, allow her to defend herself.

"That is quite ironic for you to say," I retorted, "considering you are on the run from the law even as we speak."

"I told you," he said through gritted teeth. "I am no thief. This painting does not belong to Reginald Harwood. It belongs to the artist."

I furrowed my brow. "Romano? But he is dead."

"No, not Romano." He wrapped his hands possessively around the ornate gold frame. "The true artist."

My thoughts connected like a bolt of lightning. "You," I said in disbelief. "*You* painted *The Woman in Red?*"

Allett set his jaw. "I never gave permission for it to be sold. It is mine and always has been."

I had a dozen more questions, but Barlow called impatiently from the stern. "We're ready."

I tried not to panic at his words. Once we cast off, my options would be limited. I'd only ever swam in still, shallow water. This was the Thames, wide and swift, black as freshly brewed coffee. If I were desperate enough, could I swim it?

Elizabeth moved closer to my side, and I abandoned that plan immediately. I knew Elizabeth could not swim. Tears streaked down her cheeks, her eyes red and puffy, and the gag cut against the corners of her mouth.

"Remove her gag, please," I begged Allett. "It is hurting her. She won't scream, I promise."

He pressed his lips together, then moved to us, the boat rocking beneath his motions. He untied the gag and yanked it free. Elizabeth gasped, coughing a little.

"Not a sound from either of you," he muttered, "or you'll both get one."

I did not entirely believe him. It was becoming clearer and clearer that Allett was no hardened criminal. He only wanted to escape. Elizabeth and I were but a means to an end.

Allett untied the mooring lines and pushed us from the dock. Barlow began to row, sending the wherry slipping silently through the lapping waves. Allett returned to his bench—and the painting.

Now was my chance to learn more. What strange hold did the painting have over Allett?

"If you painted *The Woman in Red*," I said, "then why did Romano claim it?"

Allett did not look at me. I almost thought he would not answer, but then he spoke.

"Romano was jealous of me," he said bitterly. "I was just a sailor with a love of painting when I went to Florence to study under him."

That explained his comfort on the boat, his working knowledge of sailing. Besides that, Higgs and Barlow both clearly worked the docks. Was that how Allett had found them?

Allett went on. "It did not take Romano long to realize my talent, and he did everything he could to keep me from realizing it too. He claimed my paintings as his own and sold them for ten times what he paid me for them, insisting it was his name that garnered the price, not the painting itself. I was glad. Grateful, even. He gave me a place in the world, money in my pocket."

"What happened?" Elizabeth asked, her voice weak.

"Isabella," he whispered, his gaze returning to the woman in the portrait. "She was engaged to Romano, a forced arrangement." Allett's words were distant, like he was trapped in memories I could not see. "When we met, it was love from the start. She was beautiful, intelligent, kind. But for some reason, she chose me. She loved me.

"She allowed me to paint her, and I poured myself into every stroke. It was my finest work. When Romano discovered the painting, I thought he would be angry that I had painted his betrothed. But he did not care. He did not love her. He only knew it would fetch an enormous price and wanted to sell it. I refused. He grew angry with me, and Isabella was frightened for my safety. We decided to run away together. But there was a storm. Isabella tried to find me, even in the rain and wind. She went too close to the cliffs, and—"

Allett's voice broke. My insides twisted. How could I feel sympathy for this man who had blackmailed Elizabeth and now held us both hostage?

"Romano insisted I was to blame, that I'd lured her from the safety of her home to marry her for her fortune." He shook his head. "Lies. We both knew it. But who were the authorities to believe? A respected artist, a native of Florence? Or me, a traveling Englishman with no money and no connections?"

I said nothing, only listened. Elizabeth also watched him, brow pulled into a deep furrow. I could not imagine what she thought about him. The man had been painting her portrait for weeks, a rather intimate affair. I could not imagine the betrayal she must feel.

"I fled," Allett said. "I returned to England, changed my name, and started my career anew. I promised myself I would become so great an artist that no one would remember Romano. But I could not escape him. His work—*my* work—gained new fame after Isabella died. He claimed they'd been in love, knowing the price he could fetch for such a story. And it worked. *The Woman in Red* became his most famous work."

His voice grew so sharp, I wondered that he could speak at all. "My painting of the woman I loved became his legacy. A legacy that has passed through half a dozen owners in the last two decades, each more corrupt and greedy than the last. Just as Romano was."

I did not know why he was telling me this. Perhaps he'd never told anyone this story and wanted someone to know, to understand. There was the slightest unsteadiness in his voice, his movements, that put me on edge. He was not fully in control, no matter that he tried to seem so.

"That is why you stole it," I said quietly. "You do not think anyone deserves the painting."

"Certainly not." Allett's eyes narrowed upon Elizabeth. "Least of all a family like the Harwoods. Wretched and selfish and full of their own importance."

"You do not know my family at all," Elizabeth said, the fierceness in her voice surprising even me. "How dare you judge us."

He snorted. "I judge you as you deserve."

"And what of your actions?" she challenged. "Should you not be judged as well? Did you not hire a criminal to attack my father?"

"I did what I had to," he said tightly. "I needed to frighten you into helping me steal the painting. I planned to send you a token, something that Higgs had stolen, along with a threat against your father, the robbery being proof that I would follow through. But when I read your letter and learned about your *indiscretion*, I knew I'd found a better bargaining chip."

My mind raced, trying to put together the pieces still disconnected from the rest. "You knew the park was a trap. How?"

Allett waved that off. "I had my note delivered earlier as a test. I watched the house, and once I followed Miss Harwood's maid to Bow Street, I knew the Runners were involved. I never planned to go to the park."

"Because you knew the real painting remained at Harwood House."

"Yes," he said. "The Harwoods would never let it out of their sight. And it was time for me to reclaim it."

But he was wrong. Sir Reginald and Lady Harwood had intended for me to take *The Woman in Red*. If I'd listened to them, would Allett have taken Elizabeth? Would we be in the midst of this fiasco?

"And will it be worth it?" I asked. "Hurting an innocent family? Sacrificing everything for a painting?"

Allett gazed again at *The Woman in Red* on the bench beside him. "Yes," he said. "It is worth it."

If I'd learned anything over the years, it was that love could be both a blessing and a curse. It was obvious to me what his love had turned out to be.

"And to think I admired you," I whispered. "I wanted to be like you."

He gazed toward the far shore, holding himself steady against the rocking of the boat. "It is a pity."

"What is?" I took the chance to work on my bindings again. I worked my wrists together, and I had to push down a leap of excitement when I felt the rope stretch, the gap between my hands growing with every movement.

SO TRUE A LOVE

"That I shall not get to see your own talent bloom," he said, and I almost thought him sincere. "I am not like Romano. I do not feel threatened by rising talent. I truly wished to help you."

I set my jaw. "Then, I shall thank the heavens you chose lawlessness and extortion before I was duped into apprenticing with you."

He chuckled, the sound of it making the hair on my neck stand on end. "Believe what you will, Miss Travers. Believe what you will."

He continued to look away, and I set myself even more fervently at my task of twisting my ropes. Then, suddenly, one of my wrists slipped loose. Elizabeth saw, her breath catching. I pressed my knees to my chest, hiding the fact that my bonds were barely draped around my arms. I was free. But what good was my freedom now, trapped on this boat in the middle of the Thames, with Elizabeth unable to swim?

"Allett," Barlow snapped from behind us. "The sail."

We'd moved to the middle of the river, our path clear and a stiff wind at our backs. Allett pulled an oil-skin bag from his valise and carefully tucked the painting inside. He leaned it gently against the bench before he moved to the mast, steadying himself as he worked to release the sail. Barlow stowed his oars and sat near the tiller, ready to steer.

They were distracted. Now was my chance. But what could I do? Even if I convinced myself that I might escape and go for help, I sincerely doubted my ability to swim the distance to shore, especially in my dress and boots and cloak. But could I trust Allett's word that he would release us after he escaped? Perhaps, but I certainly did not trust Barlow. He did not want us turning him in to Bow Street.

No, I could not depend on any goodwill from our captors. I had to act.

My eyes landed on the painting. The oil skin had fallen slightly, and *The Woman in Red* stared at me, her eyes tortured. And I knew what to do.

I gathered my legs beneath me, slowly, quietly. Elizabeth watched, alarm in her eyes, though she dared not speak. I waited, eyeing the sail. Not yet. Not yet.

The sail unfurled. Allett caught the corner and turned to secure it, his back to me.

Now.

I shot forward, scrambling over benches, stumbling as the wherry lurched.

"Halt!" Allett shouted behind me. He'd seen me.

But he was too late. I snatched up *The Woman in Red*, its protective bag falling free, then grasped one of the taut lines of rope reaching toward the mast. I hauled myself up onto the forwardmost bench.

"Stop," I ordered, holding the painting with one hand over the black waters of the Thames. "Stop, or I will drop it."

Allett stumbled to a halt, staring at me in disbelief. "Please," he whispered. "Please, no."

"Why should I show you any mercy?" I asked, my words biting. "You have none for those around you, though you are as imperfect as they. I have no sympathy for you."

And yet I did. Small though it was, the pain in Allett's eyes when he stared at his beloved Isabella was enough to slip through the smallest cracks in my heart.

"I'll do anything," he said, sounding as if his throat were lined with broken glass. "Please, do not harm her."

As if the woman still lived and breathed. As if she were not simply captured in oil and canvas.

"Take us to shore," I demanded. "Release both of us."

Allett twisted to face the stern. "Barlow!" It was a wild, desperate sound.

I glanced toward the barrel-chested man sitting at the tiller.

He glared at us in disgusted disbelief. "Don't be daft," he growled. "We can't take them ashore. They know who you are, who I am. I'm not giving up my life for a blasted *painting*."

"Now," I said firmly. "Now, or I drop it."

Barlow kept a tight grip on the tiller. "Drop it if you like."

"No!" Allett stood frozen on the middle of the deck, his eyes moving between me and Barlow. Then he shifted, as if he'd realized something. In the next moment, his pistol was in his hands—but not pointed at me. He did not dare put Isabella at risk. No, he pointed at Barlow.

"Steer toward shore," he spat out. "Now!"

Barlow slammed one fist against the wherry's hull. "This is insanity."

"Then, I will do it." Allett moved forward. "Do not test me. Step aside, or I will shoot."

Barlow cursed under his breath even as he released the tiller. Allett pointed with the barrel of his pistol, and Barlow climbed toward the bow of the boat, nearer to me.

"Neither of you move," Allett ordered. He kept the pistol pointed in our direction as he jerked the tiller. The boat slowly shifted, turning toward the northern bank of the river where a few lonely docks waited.

"Who goes there?"

The shout flew across the water, coming from behind. We all froze, stunned.

"This is the river police," the same voice called. "Declare yourself, and prepare to be boarded."

I clung to my rope, still holding the painting over the water, but I managed to peer back the way we'd come. A boat followed us, perhaps a hundred feet away, its oars flashing in the moonlight as two men propelled it forward. Another boat was directly behind the first, with more men.

But my eyes were locked on that first boat, on the man who leaned over the bow, a lantern lighting his familiar face. My heart leaped.

"Nathaniel," I shouted, my voice breaking. "Nathaniel, I'm here! And Elizabeth!"

The boat rocked beneath him as he surged upward. "Verity!" Relief and desperation tangled in his voice. "Are you all right?"

I opened my mouth to respond, but Allett swung the pistol to aim at me, his eyes wide with fear. "Quiet," he shouted.

I did not think he would shoot, not while I still held his beloved painting over the water. But there was a frenzy in his eyes that made my voice die in my throat.

"Straighten us out," Barlow hissed at Allett. "The wind is in our favor. We can outrun them."

The police boat drew nearer and, with it, the lantern light. I could tell the moment Nathaniel saw my precarious position as I perched on the edge of the wherry. His mouth dropped.

"We are coming aboard," a man in the boat behind Nathaniel's yelled. "Drop your weapons."

Allett did not move, panic filling every inch of his face. Would he set the pistol down and go peacefully? Or would he die rather than let anyone else take the painting of his long-lost love?

I need not have wondered.

"I'll not be hanged for your sake," Barlow shouted at Allett.

Then he barreled at *me*, his eyes filled with hate.

My mind slowed. What was he doing? It connected a moment later—he wanted to be rid of me, of the painting, so he could convince Allett to escape. I made to leap back down into the safety of the wherry, but he was too fast. He shoved me with all his strength. The back of my knees hit the railing.

And I went tumbling into the black.

CHAPTER 29

I plunged into the river. The water swept over me, hungry and greedy, and then came the cold. I felt it to my bones, the shocking ice that enveloped me. The painting—gripped in my right hand—was torn away.

I rolled in the current, kicking my legs and flailing my arms. I needed air. I forced my eyes open.

All I saw was blackness. Vague shadows but no light. No moon or lantern or boat.

My arms tangled in my cloak, so I scrambled to release the clasp at my throat. My cloak disappeared into the deep, a floating wraith.

Fire raced through my veins. I could swim well enough to make it to the police boats, but I did not know which way the surface was. I was trapped in this endlessly swirling river.

I forced myself to focus, though my lungs already screamed inside me. I closed my eyes, then opened them again. There. Was that passing darkness a boat?

It was all I had.

I kicked, throwing my hands before me and propelling my body toward the shadow. Every inch of me was a battleground, my body fighting the cold, the panic, the fear.

I pushed myself, my skirts wrapping around my legs, my boots clinging like anchors to my feet. My muscles burned. My head grew clouded.

So close.

A numbness settled into my limbs, and they moved clumsily. I forgot what I was trying to do. *Inhale*, a voice inside me said. *Inhale, and this will all be over.*

Something tightened around my neck, a sharp line against my skin. I was tugged to one side. Was that . . . a hand?

Then an arm came around my waist, strong and sure. I was pulled through the roiling waters and reaching depths.

My head broke the surface. I inhaled and coughed, water streaming over my face. I clutched at the arm around my waist, terrified of going under again.

"Verity." Nathaniel's voice was a broken sob in my ear. He pulled me closer, his free arm working wildly to keep us both afloat.

"Nathaniel," I gasped. Relief poured through me, fighting the panic and dread that had overcome my body.

Men shouted from the boats nearby, and Nathaniel kicked, dragging me with him.

"I can swim," I insisted, though my limbs felt weak and numb.

"I don't care," he said, his breaths coming in short, tight gasps. "I'm not letting go of you."

The side of the police boat loomed over us, and arms reached for me. Someone pulled me from the water—and from Nathaniel, despite his words. I collapsed onto the bottom of the boat, water pooling around me. Two men I did not recognize hovered over me, unsure what to do.

The boat tipped again as Nathaniel pulled himself over the side, bringing another rush of water. He righted himself and stumbled to my side, dropping to his knees.

"Blast it, Verity," he said, his eyes like midnight. "You'll be the death of me."

"I—"

He gathered me into his arms and held me against his chest so tightly I could hardly breathe, let alone speak.

"Thank God," he whispered in my ear. "Thank God."

I clutched him closer, my throat aching. My clothes were soaked through, and the chill night air pierced through me, yet I couldn't feel it. My heart filled every inch of my chest.

"I could not have lived . . ." he said into my hair, his voice cracked and faded. "I could not have lived if you had not." He pulled back, and his hands roamed my shoulders and arms as if searching for an injury. "Your necklace," he rasped. "It was a miracle, I swear."

I looked down, and there hung Grandmama's bezoar pendant, winking in the moonlight. I remembered the sharp tug around my neck, the murky hand.

"You grabbed the chain?" I said, dumbfounded. "That was how you found me?"

"Good fortune indeed." He exhaled, shaking his head.

I gave a disbelieving laugh. "I shall never doubt Grandmama again."

But he did not laugh. He only took my face in his hands, cradling my jaw as though I were priceless porcelain, the most breakable glass. His eyes shone, his breathing haggard. "It happened so quickly," he whispered. "I thought I was too late."

I grasped his hands around my face, holding him there even as tears streamed down my cheeks, hot against the dripping river water. "I am here," I said fiercely. "You are here. That is all that matters."

His lips pressed into mine. His kiss was desperate—boundless—yet he tethered me to reality, to life and love. He kissed me with all that he was, with every good part of him, and I clung to him. I needed him.

Like I needed air or food or shelter, I needed Nathaniel Denning.

A distant shout barreled through my thoughts, and we parted with a jolt.

"Denning!" came the shout again. "We have them both secured."

Drake stood aboard the wherry a dozen feet away, holding a lantern. I could see two river policemen standing guard over Allett and Barlow kneeling with their hands bound. Barlow glared across at me, but Allett's expression was empty. Broken. He simply stared at the river.

Where *The Woman in Red* had sunk.

Where I'd nearly drowned as well.

Elizabeth stepped forward into the light of Drake's lantern and grasped the side of the wherry. "Are you all right, Verity?" she called, her voice desperate.

"Yes," I managed, though I'd begun shivering from the cold. "Alive, at the least."

"Return Miss Harwood to her home," Nathaniel ordered Drake. "Then take the prisoners to Bow Street. I will join you shortly. I must see to Miss Travers."

"I am certain you must." Drake grinned but turned with a parting wave to follow Nathaniel's instructions.

The river policeman sitting behind me spoke. "Where to, sir?"

"Take us back to the Wapping station," Nathaniel said. "We can take a hack from there."

"Take a hack to where?" I struggled to sit up, and Nathaniel helped me to the middle bench beside him. "I want to come to Bow Street."

Nathaniel blew out a breath. "You nearly drowned, Verity. I am taking you home."

"But I—"

"Please," he said. "Please let me take care of you. You need dry clothes, a fire, and a bed. There will be time tomorrow to go to Bow Street."

His eyes held mine, so fervent and true, and my fight melted away. "All right."

He wrapped a long arm around me, though it did little good. We were both soaked. One of the river police offered his coat to me, which I gladly accepted.

"Did you find my sketch?" I asked Nathaniel as the men began rowing us back up the river, the lights of the city once again encompassing us. "Of Allett?"

"Yes," he said. "I could not believe my eyes. Drake and I left Rawlings and the patrol at the park and went immediately to Allett's home. I had little hope he would be there, but luck was with us."

"How so?" My teeth chattered.

He pulled me tighter against his side. "We were returning to Bow Street for reinforcements when a man stopped us. He told us what happened at Harwood House and that he saw you go after Allett and Miss Harwood. He followed you enough to see Allett was heading for the docks, then he came for us. We went straight to the Wapping station, and the river police agreed to help us search for you." His voice cracked, and he turned his face from me. "I thought it was a lost cause. I thought we would never find you."

I looked up at him, starlight casting the side of his face silver and black. He held me in his arms, but the fear of the last hour had yet to release either of us.

"When I saw you," he whispered, "it nearly broke me. I would have done anything to get to you. To see you in such distress and to be unable to help—"

I slipped my hand into his, raising our joined fingers to my lips and kissing them. I did not reassure him. I knew precisely how difficult it was to rid oneself of awful memories. But I could hold his hand. I could stay at his side, and we could help each other through this.

Then I realized what he'd said. "The man who found you. What was his name?"

Nathaniel shook his head. "He wouldn't tell us, though he said he was a friend of yours. He dressed strangely, in the brightest colors and patterns."

I stared at him. Wily? It had to be. But . . . he had helped Nathaniel find me?

"You know him?" he asked curiously.

I nodded. "I believe I do. Where did he go?"

Nathaniel shrugged. "Once he gave us his information, he vanished."

"Ah, yes," I said. "He is rather good at that."

"And you won't tell me who he is?"

My lips curled into a grin. "You can hardly expect me to give up an informant, Sir Chivalry."

Behind my levity, my mind whirled. I could not believe it. Wily had risked a great deal in aiding Bow Street. They knew his face now, if not his name. Why had he done it?

Nathaniel's arm tightened around my waist. "I suppose I can settle for knowing only some of your secrets."

I knew he was teasing. But my heart pattered more quickly, and my mind agreed. I was ready. "One day, Nathaniel Denning," I whispered, "I will tell you all my secrets. Because I know you will keep them for me, and I know you will love me even still."

He said nothing for a long moment. Then his throat bobbed, and his eyes met mine. He knew what I was finally saying.

I trusted him. I loved him.

"I will," he said hoarsely. "I swear I will."

He kissed me again, so sweetly and lightly that it could have been a brush of the wind against my lips. Then he held me close as we skimmed over the river, the brilliant stars lighting our way.

The gentle light of dawn woke me. I rolled over in bed, peering at the mantel clock above my banked fire. Six o'clock in the morning.

Memories from last night rushed into my mind. Allett. The boat. The painting. Nathaniel. They felt like snatches of a dream, warped and unreal.

Nathaniel had brought me home last night, I remembered hazily. I could see Mama's white face in my mind's eye and her relief when I'd assured her I was all right. Nathaniel had explained everything to Mama as he'd guided me inside. Then he'd bid us farewell, hurrying to go change before heading to Bow Street. He'd made me promise to sleep a few hours.

Four was sufficient, I decided. I threw off my covers and went to my armoire, selecting a deep-blue walking dress. I had to learn what had happened after we'd parted from the others on the river. I had to speak with Elizabeth and reassure myself that she was unharmed.

And I had to see Nathaniel, because every inch of me yearned for him.

After dressing, I looked in my mirror and touched the bruise on my cheek where Barlow had hit me, then the red welt on my neck. I'd never believed in any of Grandmama's superstitions before last night, but I could not deny that Nathaniel's grabbing my necklace had been serendipitous. Or perhaps something more. All I knew was that I certainly wouldn't laugh at her beliefs in the future.

I slipped from my room and started for the stairs but stopped when I heard footsteps in Mama's room. I pushed open her door. "Mama?"

She stood near the fireplace, one hand cupped around her neck. She smiled wearily as I stepped inside. "Good morning, dear. How are you feeling?"

"Perfectly well," I said, though my body ached with exhaustion.

She sent me a wry look. "Of course."

I moved to stand beside her, welcoming the warmth of the fire. I still felt a chill in the center of me, though I hoped it was only the memory of the icy waters rather than any lingering physical effect. "I am sorry to have worried you last night," I said softly. "I wish I could claim ignorance of the danger of our plan, but . . ."

"But you knew it very well." Mama sighed. "I stayed awake all night, Verity, thinking of you. Praying for you. And I have come to a realization."

I could not look away. "Yes?"

"I realized that I have been selfish," she said. "I've wanted to keep you safe for my sake, but I have never considered the lives of all those you can help. Where would Elizabeth be now if not for you?"

She wrapped her arms around me. I slid my hands around her waist and held her tight, my eyes already welling with tears.

"You are a wondrous person, Verity," she whispered. "I am so proud of you and all you have done."

"Thank you, Mama." My voice cracked.

She pulled back and straightened my spencer. "Now, off with you," she said with a knowing smile. "No doubt Mr. Denning is anxiously waiting."

My cheeks pricked with heat. "I meant to tell you about us. Only, before last night, I wasn't entirely sure what we were."

Mama laughed. "I saw how he acted when he brought you home, Verity. It was perfectly clear what you are to him. But what is he to you?"

I kissed her on the cheek. "The world, Mama. He is the world."

I left the house with a smile. Mama was right. I could be a force for good, use my talents to help others. And no matter what obstacles I faced, I knew that knowledge was something I could hold to for the rest of my life.

I tied my bonnet and set off down the street. The sun was just rising, reaching toward me with its warmth and light. I tipped my face up and closed my eyes briefly. Considering how black last night had been, the sun felt particularly soothing today. I'd been so lucky. How differently things might have gone.

"Dropping your guard, Miss Travers?"

I jumped a little as Wily fell into step beside me, dressed in a garish orange jacket.

"You ought to keep a weather eye at all times," he said, hands in his pockets as he matched my pace. "Never know when some scoundrel will surprise you."

"Indeed." I managed to recover. "Like last night when a certain scoundrel aided in the capture of a wanted criminal?"

"Odd, that is."

I wouldn't let it go that easily. "Really, Wily, what were you doing at Harwood House last night?"

He shrugged. "After turning in Higgs, I was somewhat invested in the outcome."

"*You* informed on Higgs?"

"Of course," he said with a saucy grin. "As if the Runners ever would have found him. In any case, I was watching Bow Street last night when I saw you and Denning leave. Got my suspicions up, that did, and I followed you to the house. I saw the whole thing."

"And you found Nathaniel and told him."

"Aye."

I paused there on the street, and he did as well. "Thank you," I said quietly. "I know what you risked by helping me."

"Ah, well." His cheeks, already ruddy, flushed even more. "I owed you."

He had, but that did not mean I couldn't be appropriately grateful. He'd likely saved my life—and Elizabeth's—when he'd decided to intervene.

"I also happened across these," he said, holding out a hand. The sunlight winked on the familiar gold setting of a pair of pearl earrings. I stared, then looked up at him. "Wily, you are positively sentimental. Jack will never believe it."

"Then let it be our little secret," he said with a wink, dropping the earrings in my palm. "I've a reputation to uphold."

"Very well," I said. "Friends?"

Wily chuckled. "If you like, Miss Travers."

"Verity," I said with an answering smile. "My friends call me Verity."

He tipped his hat. "Until next time, Miss Verity."

With a jaunty nod, he melted back into the early morning crowd. I smiled to myself as I tucked my earrings into my reticule. Jack had been right. I'd needed to learn for myself whom I could trust, and I had.

CHAPTER 30

"After Barlow tied you up," Drake asked, consulting his notes, "what happened?"

"We cast off," I said, "and started down the river. I worked the ropes around my hands and managed to free myself."

"And that was when you decided to grab the painting?"

"Yes."

Drake laughed. "Brilliant. Truly brilliant, Verity."

I grinned. "Why, thank you."

He leaned back in his seat. "Though you might have avoided being captured in the first place."

I waved that off. "All part of the plan, of course."

"Of course," he said, eyes twinkling.

As he jotted down a few more notes, I allowed myself to peek past him out the open door of the interview room. No. 4 Bow Street was as busy as ever, but not for my handsome Sir Chivalry, who paced the main office. Nathaniel had wanted to interview me himself, but Mr. Etchells had insisted Drake do it to ensure as unbiased an account as possible.

Besides, Nathaniel knew everything already. I'd told him all that had happened on the carriage ride home last night, including what I'd learned from Allett about his past and his reasons for stealing the painting.

But selfish though it was, I liked knowing that Nathaniel worried for me. That he wished to be at my side, holding my hand even though I could do this well enough on my own.

Perhaps that was the crux of it. I *could* do this alone, and he knew it. But he wanted to be there for me even still, lift my burdens if he could. And it made me love him all the more.

Drake questioned me a while longer, but when he at last seemed satisfied, he let me go.

"What will happen to Allett," I asked as I stood, "if he is convicted?"

He sighed. "His charges are not light. It is likely he will see the gallows, along with Barlow."

Sentencing in England was harsh and decisive, that I knew well. I was simply glad I was not responsible for such a task.

"See if you can stop Denning's incessant pacing," he said, tidying his notes. "The lad is as edgy as a fox during the hunt."

"What happened to 'Sir Chivalry'?" I asked as I stood. "Has the nickname run its course?"

He sighed. "It's lost its appeal. He doesn't seem to mind it anymore."

I hid a smile.

I left Drake in the interview room, but before I could take more than two steps toward Nathaniel, a voice spoke behind me. "Miss Travers."

I turned to see Mr. Etchells at the door of his office, spectacles glinting.

"Might I have a word?" he asked, gesturing back inside his office.

I exchanged a surprised look with Nathaniel, then I followed after the magistrate. He sat behind his desk and gestured for me to sit across from him. He smiled as I smoothed my skirts, easing some of my nerves.

"Miss Travers," he said, steepling his fingers above the desk. "I have been informed of your involvement in the Harwood case, and I must say I am rather impressed."

I blinked. That was not what I'd expected. "I—well, thank you, sir."

"I daresay I am quite tempted to hire you as an officer." His eyes twinkled. "But I am not sure London is ready for that yet."

I smiled. "Likely not, sir."

"Though, in any case, I've heard you have ambitions of your own outside of Bow Street," Mr. Etchells said. "Your brother was just as slippery."

"Jack?" I straightened. "What do you mean?"

He sat back. "Why, that I offered to reinstate him as a Bow Street officer. About a year ago now. But he kindly turned me down."

I stared at him. Jack had been given the chance to return to Bow Street and had turned it down? Why? It was all he'd ever wanted.

No, a voice said inside. It wasn't. He'd found something better. His life with Ginny.

"I hadn't realized," I said. "I apologize that we Traverses are a somewhat difficult lot."

He smiled again. "Not in the least. In fact, I thought to offer you a different position."

"Position?" My brow furrowed.

He sorted through some of the papers on his desk, unearthing a familiar-looking sketch. Allett's face leaped from the page.

"Mr. Denning said you drew this," he said. "Just from a witness's description."

My heart quickened. "I did."

"That is incredible." Mr. Etchells set the sketch down. "Such a talent could make a world of difference for Bow Street, and for police work in general. As such, I've a proposal for you. I hope to call upon you as a sketch artist should we have need in the future."

I gaped, my eyes wide. Did he mean it?

He took my reaction the wrong way. "It would be a paid consultancy, of course," he added quickly. "We would happily work around your own cases. But I imagine we could keep you fairly busy, especially once the other offices get wind of you."

"I . . ." I almost laughed, such was my shock. Me, work for Bow Street? This offer could be everything I'd ever wanted. I could use my skill with a pencil to catch criminals. I could work with Drake and Rawlings . . . and Nathaniel.

I looked up at Mr. Etchells. I tried to be professional, but the smile that burst onto my lips could have lit the sky. "I gladly accept your offer. I can think of nothing I'd like more."

He stood and bowed. "Then I look forward to our continued partnership, Miss Travers."

I was still dazed when I left his office. He'd offered me a job. A Bow Street magistrate wished to work with me.

"Verity!"

I looked up to see a head of blonde curls rushing at me, and then I was wrapped in Elizabeth's embrace. I hugged her back, so glad to feel her warmth and strength, to reassure myself that she was well. Sir Reginald and Lady Harwood waited near the front door, speaking with Rawlings, who had been conducting their interviews. I'd known they were all here somewhere, but I hadn't yet seen them.

She pulled back, inspecting me. "Oh, what a relief," she exclaimed. "Mr. Denning insisted you were all right, but I had to be sure."

I laughed. "I am perfectly well, Elizabeth. It will take far more than a little dip in the Thames to do me in."

Her smile faded, some of her joy slipping away. "I cannot believe it, Verity," she finally said. "I cannot believe you followed Allett and me. It was so dangerous."

"I could hardly let him steal you away." I tried to speak lightly, but my voice caught in my throat. We both knew how desperate things had become last night, how close we had come to not seeing today.

Elizabeth squeezed my hands, then looked over her shoulder at her parents, still distracted near the door. She turned back, her expression sober. "I saw Lord Blakely this morning."

I straightened. "Oh?"

"I told him everything," she said. "I told him about Rose."

"What did he say?" My heart clenched.

"He was shocked, to say the least," she said. "He could not speak for a long while. When he did manage to, he . . . well, he told me he did not think that marrying was the best option at present. That perhaps we ought to postpone the wedding."

"Oh, Elizabeth." I hurt for her, but I also hurt for Lord Blakely. I certainly did not know him well, but he'd seemed to love my friend. She'd kept this enormous secret from him, and he had to feel pained, hit on his blind side.

"I knew he was only trying to be kind," she said with a sad smile. "So I released him from our engagement. We parted on . . . well, I cannot say they were *good* terms, but perhaps one day, we might be friends."

Though her voice twisted, she did not seem quite so heartbroken as I would have imagined. "And you are all right?"

"I am," she said, sounding rather surprised at herself. "Truly, I am. I care for Lord Blakely, but our entire engagement felt like something of a sham. He did not know the real me. When we parted, I felt pain, yes. But also relief. I did not have to lie to him anymore."

I knew something of that. How well I remembered Nathaniel's simple acceptance of my past in the golden meadow at Bibury. How it had felt to realize he knew all of me and still loved me.

"But besides that," Elizabeth said, her voice quiet but steady, "what I feel for him pales in comparison to what I feel for Rose. I want to be with her, Verity. That is all I want."

Oh, how I wanted this for her. "And what do your parents say?"

Elizabeth smiled. "Mama is on my side. She insists that we can re-tire to our country house with Rose, live quietly there. Little towns care far less for reputations than London Society."

"And your father?"

Her eyes took on a calculating—and slightly mischievous—look. "He has yet to agree, but I *have* managed to convince him to meet Rose. I've little doubt she will win him over in the end."

"She will," I assured her. "Undoubtedly."

She took my hand again, holding it tight. "You'll come visit us when we are settled?"

"Of course I will." I swallowed. "I hope you will find such happiness."

"I hope that for you as well." Her eyes searched my face. "And may I guess that your future happiness might involve a certain Bow Street officer?"

"It might," I admitted.

Elizabeth squeezed my hand. "Good. You need someone to look after you while you take on the world."

There was a new peace in her expression, reminding me for the first time in weeks of the girl she used to be. I could only hope that her heal-ing would continue. And perhaps in her new, quiet country life, there might be a gentleman willing to love every part of her, including Rose.

Sir Reginald and Lady Harwood joined us, and when I tried to apologize for losing *The Woman in Red*, Lady Harwood hugged me so fiercely that my lungs were nearly crushed.

"You saved Elizabeth," she whispered. "That is all that matters."

Sir Reginald nodded behind her, his eyes glassy. "Without a doubt."

After thanking me so profusely that my face turned red with embar-rassment, they left with Elizabeth, and I finally had the chance to seek out Nathaniel.

But he'd vanished. I rose on my toes, looking over the heads of the men in the room, and still, I could see no sign of him. Perhaps he'd gone outside. I started for the front doors and—

Someone caught my arm and pulled me into a darkened interview room. I gasped, instinctively raising my hands to defend myself until I saw Nathaniel's dancing eyes and wide grin.

"Dash it all," I breathed. "Why did you have to scare me like that?"

He closed the door behind us. "Because you are constantly sur-rounded by people, and I was desperate for a moment alone with you."

Instead of calming, my pulse took off like a bird in flight as he approached and stopped just an arm's length away.

"You hardly need to steal me away," I said, trying to sound unaffected. "I am more than willing to make time for the handsome officer who saved my life."

"Are you?" Nathaniel asked, a sly look in his eyes. "As I hear it, that is the quickest way to a lady's heart, and I am quite intent on yours."

A pleasant tingle skittered up my spine as I remembered Jack's words of advice to him that night at Wimborne. "It certainly does not hurt. Although it seems it is becoming a habit of yours. Wasn't that how you earned your nickname in the first place, pulling a woman from the river?"

"Ah, well," he said, the corner of his mouth twitching. "So many ladies are falling into the Thames these days, I can hardly keep up."

I made to smack him on the shoulder, but he grasped my hand instead and pulled me against him, grinning playfully. I let him, relishing the solid feel of his chest beneath my gloved hands and the way his gaze slid slowly down to my lips.

"How shocking you are, Mr. Denning," I whispered. "Do you plan to kiss me right here in the office?"

"I am generally a man of restraint, Miss Travers," he replied, leaning in. "Except . . .

"Except . . . ?" I tilted my face up, tempting him.

"Except when it comes to you." He let his lips brush the curve of my ear, and I shivered. "Every minute I spend with you tests my self-control. It only takes one look, and I'm consumed by my need to kiss you."

Heavens. It did not seem fair that Nathaniel was attractive, intelligent, *and* had a way with words. But I was not about to complain. Not when his lips were tracing a line along my jaw, from my ear to my mouth, and I forgot what words were altogether.

He pulled back suddenly, brows lifted. "I'd almost forgotten. What did Etchells want with you?"

I stared dazedly up at him. "Good heavens, man, you cannot threaten to kiss a girl and then not follow through."

"*Threaten?*" He pulled back farther, eyes narrowed in jest. "Is that really the right word for this situation?"

I laughed, my head tilted back. "It is your fault. You've stolen my words. I haven't any left."

"Perhaps just a few to tell me about Mr. Etchells?" he said in a teasing voice.

"Very well." I allowed myself a smile. "He wishes me to work with Bow Street as a sketch artist."

Nathaniel's mouth dropped open. "Truly? Verity, that is wonderful."

"I know," I said, my voice softening. "It's more than I could have imagined for myself." I tugged the lapels of his jacket straight. "Every part of my life right now feels like more than I could have imagined." I looked up at him. "Especially you."

His throat bobbed, his eyes searching. "You are everything to me, Verity Travers," he whispered, brushing his knuckles against my cheekbone. "Everything I could have hoped for, and everything I never dared dream of." He moved me against the wall as he slid his arms around my waist. My hands tightened around his lapels, and my stomach floated like a feather on the wind.

"I want to ask you a question," he said quietly. "And you must answer honestly."

My eyes widened. Did he . . . did he mean to propose? I knew I loved him, but was I ready for more? For *marriage*?

He seemed to sense my panic, because he smiled gently. "Will you let me court you, Verity Travers?" he asked, his voice like velvet. "Danger is all good and well for falling in love, but I want to know you in every facet of your life. I should like nothing more than to take you to assemblies and laugh over dinner and bring you flowers."

I could not help my smile, and I certainly did not try to stop it. "It is fortunate, then, that you already know my favorite flower."

"But of course," he said, grinning wickedly. "I made sure to secure that information long ago."

I tugged on his cravat, pulling him close. "If you should come courting," I whispered, "then I should be the happiest of women."

I'd never felt like this. Like spring after a long winter. Like a rainbow after a storm.

Like a woman absolutely and completely in love.

He kissed me, his lips capturing mine so fully and deeply that I had to cling to his jacket. I felt the trueness of this, the surety that even if the world around us twisted and tore apart, I would have Nathaniel, and he would have me.

And *that*, I realized as Nathaniel swept me away in yet another dizzying kiss, was love.

$\mathcal{E}$PILOGUE

I walked down Tottenham Court Road, a large basket on one elbow, glancing in shop windows with interest. False interest, as it happened, since I'd never been one for shopping. But if anyone were to pay me any undue attention, I wanted to appear as innocent as possible.

I swept my gaze up the street, searching as nonchalantly as I could, and found Nathaniel immediately. He cut quite the figure, leaning against the aged stone of a dress shop, one leg propped behind the other as he inspected a copy of the *Times*. He was effortlessly handsome, the late afternoon sun brightening the auburn of his hair, his pose a model of easy masculinity.

A young lady passed him, eyeing him with unmistakable interest. I could hardly blame her—the man certainly knew how to lean on a wall—but I still glared at her back. Nathaniel Denning was not hers to gawk at. That was *my* exclusive privilege.

I moved closer to him, hefting my basket on my arm—a basket far heavier than might be expected from a window-shopping lady. I knew he saw me, felt his eyes flick over me, but he said nothing, only turned the page of his newspaper. I stopped not five feet away, peering in the dress shop window.

"Very convincing," I said under my breath.

"You as well." I could hear the smile in his voice. "Is your mother an actress, by any chance?"

I had to bite my lip to keep from laughing, though I recovered quickly, clearing my throat. "Focus, Sir Chivalry." I began to move past him, my skirts brushing the tips of his boots.

"You look beautiful today," he whispered.

I whipped my head to look at him, my cheeks flushing. He grinned, his eyes crinkling at the corners. He liked teasing me—especially, it seemed, when we were working together.

I attempted a disapproving look, my brows lowering. Then Nathaniel winked. The smallest of actions, but there was such a familiarity and lightness to it. I had no defense. I turned away quickly, a smile pulling at my lips. The scoundrel.

Moving up the street, I lingered outside a milliner's shop, pretending a fascination with flowered silk hats. But I was much less interested in the latest fashion trends than in the silversmith who happened to be located next door.

We had to wait only five minutes before our suspect arrived, walking down the street toward me. I eyed the man in the reflection of the window as he passed me, keeping my bonnet low to block my face. He was short in stature, with shaggy brown hair and a slight limp. But it was the large bag he held over his shoulder that I focused on. Based on his ragged breaths and slow steps, the bag was incredibly heavy. As we'd expected.

The man went past me and entered the silversmith. I waited a few seconds, then slowly meandered past the window, glancing inside with bare interest. I spotted Mr. Durham, the silversmith, in a second. He stood behind the counter, where the man hefted his large bag. When the man bent over his bag, Mr. Durham looked at me and gave a quick, tight nod.

This was the thief we were looking for.

My heartbeat quickened, but I did not hesitate. I carefully switched my straw basket from my right arm to my left, signaling Nathaniel up the street.

I moved past the silversmith, fighting to keep from looking behind me. But when I heard Nathaniel's familiar footsteps, I couldn't help but turn. He had paused outside the silversmith and watched me seriously, all teasing gone from his face. Then he gave a short nod, an acknowledgment of the danger we faced and a reminder of why we did this. To make the world a better, safer place. To help.

Nathaniel opened the door and went inside. The door caught before it closed completely, leaving the slightest gap.

"Ebenezer Croft?" Nathaniel's voice drifted back to me.

I couldn't resist. I crept forward again until I could just see inside the silversmith.

The man froze, one hand going to his bag on the counter. "Who's asking?"

Mr. Durham backed away. He had been willing to help us by identifying Croft, but that didn't mean he wanted to be caught in the middle of a confrontation.

"My name is Mr. Denning," Nathaniel said firmly. "I'm an officer of Bow Street, and I've come to arrest you on charges of theft, fraud, and damage to property. If you come willingly—"

Croft did not wait for him to finish. He darted for the back of the shop, abandoning his bag on the counter. It appeared he would not be coming willingly. Nathaniel was after him in the blink of an eye.

Of course the lout had run. They never could make it easy for us. I hesitated for all of one second. I was *supposed* to stay where I was, keeping a lookout on Tottenham Court Road in case Croft had any accomplices who might interfere. But I could hardly leave Nathaniel to apprehend the thief all on his own, could I?

I turned on my heel and ran to the street corner. Unfortunately for Croft, I knew this neighborhood well, including the precise location where the alley behind the silversmith met the main road. I grasped my straw basket in both hands as I ran, feeling its comforting weight.

I reached the alley entrance and stopped just out of sight, listening carefully. Then I heard quick, thumping footsteps, heavy breaths, and gasped swearing. I peeked around the corner. Croft ran wildly toward me, throwing a glance over his shoulder at Nathaniel. The man was right to have such panic in his eyes. Nathaniel was fearsome, so close on the man's heels.

Croft was almost to me. I pulled back, energy coursing through me. I counted to three, then swung my basket as hard as I could around the corner.

It whacked Croft squarely, and he went down hard. He hit the street, stunned, the barest wheezing moan escaping him.

I stepped into the alleyway as Nathaniel reached us. He stared at me, then put his hands on his waist, breathing hard. "Blast it, Verity. You were supposed to remain as the lookout."

"Was I?" I asked, unperturbed.

He reached for the pair of iron fetters in his jacket pocket. "I really should stop being surprised when you refuse to listen," he muttered as he bent over Croft and yanked his arms behind his back. The thief groaned in response, barely coherent.

"And here I thought it was something of an ongoing lark between us," I said, crossing my arms. "You insist I stay behind. I come anyway and save the day—"

"A lark?" Nathaniel said dryly. "Yes, such fun to never be sure when you'll actually keep to our plan."

"That is why we work so well together," I replied with a saucy wink. "You plan; I improvise."

"Is that right?" He was clearly exasperated, but even he couldn't deny that I *had* helped. Croft would have likely fought him, but now the man slumped against the wall, expression dazed and body slack.

I hefted my basket back onto my elbow, and Nathaniel eyed it suspiciously. "What exactly do you have in there?"

I assumed a look of pure innocence. "Just my coin purse and handkerchief."

He raised an eyebrow.

"And perhaps five or six of my heaviest books."

He gave a short laugh, shaking his head. "Only you, Verity."

"Me?" I asked, holding a hand to my chest in mock outrage. "You are the one who insists we must be prepared for anything. Today I happened to be prepared for a bit of light reading."

"Light," he said, still grinning. "Indeed."

"Come on, then," I said with a few jaunty backward steps. "We need to take him back now, or we'll be late for dinner, and Mama will have my head."

Nathaniel grabbed Croft's arm and hoisted him to his feet. The man should have been a bit more concerned about being arrested, but instead, he stared at me with a bewildered expression.

"Who is *she*?" I heard him ask Nathaniel as I turned to lead us from the alley.

"That, sir," Nathaniel said in amused resignation, "is a woman the likes of which you will never see again."

I grinned.

We left Croft in a holding cell at The Brown Bear and reported our success to Mr. Etchells at the office. It was a fairly simple case, and I doubted the magistrate would have any difficulty finding Croft guilty. We'd caught him red-handed with stolen silver, which he'd intended to have melted down until the crest and initials were unrecognizable.

"My client will be pleased," I said as we started back down Bow Street. "He had thought the silver lost forever."

"I hope you are rewarded appropriately," Nathaniel said pointedly.

I slipped my arm through his. "It was only the one time."

"It shouldn't have happened even once." His voice was gruff. He had yet to forgive the man who had refused to pay me for my services a few weeks ago, even though I had returned his lost dog. "You did the work, and he owed you."

"Champion of women, indeed," I said as I tightened my hand on his arm. "Thank you, Sir Chivalry."

He gave a smile. "You hardly need a champion, Verity."

My chest filled with a familiar warmth. His confidence in me was a continual source of strength, and how grateful I was to have found such a man.

"When do you leave for Devon?" I adjusted the heavy basket on my arm. Books made for excellent weapons but were not entirely pleasant to carry in large quantities.

"Tomorrow," he said, taking the basket from me. "Rawlings wants an early start."

I sighed, perhaps a bit dramatically. "Call me selfish if you must, but I am always rather put out when Mr. Etchells sends you away for a case. There is plenty of crime in London, is there not?"

"Yes, but that is what *you* are for," he said, teasing. "You must keep the criminals in line while I am gone."

"You know I shall," I said. "But that will not make me miss you any less." My hand tightened around his arm.

Nathaniel slowed our steps and turned to face me. "It's only a week," he said softly.

I absently toyed with the buttons of his waistcoat. "A week without you is an eternity," I said, my voice delicate.

I meant it. The last three months together had been something of a dream. Even though we were both busier than ever with cases, Nathaniel had been quite serious about courting me, and we'd spent every spare second together that we could. He had become a steady, easy part of my life—laughing with me, sharing my fears and dreams, holding me, and kissing me.

He had been patient and understanding during our courtship—he knew my apprehension about love and marriage. But that apprehension had faded with every day he stayed at my side. He loved me in a way that both shook me and grounded me, so raw and beautifully real. And

I loved him, too, so much so that it was difficult to understand. But love was not something to be understood, I'd learned. It was something to be trusted.

I'd come to love him while we worked the Harwood case, but now, after spending so much time together, I was more certain than ever that he was all I ever wanted. And anytime we were parted was a physical pain to me, one of aching want.

Nathaniel's eyes moved over my face, as if he sensed my thoughts. He opened his mouth, stopped, then firmly set his jaw—as if deciding something. "You could come with me," he said simply.

I lifted my head. "Come with you?"

"That is, not tomorrow," he clarified. "But if I were to ask Mr. Etchells, I do not think he would refuse me next time." He cleared his throat. "If you were my wife."

I stilled, my eyes fixed upon him. "Nathaniel, is that—is that a proposal?"

Nathaniel grimaced. "Not a terribly good one."

He glanced around, then pulled me with him through the bustling crowd to a nearby mew, lit by the setting sun. It gave us an illusion of privacy, though the noises of the street still rang through the air, and passersby walked not ten feet from us, ignorant of our life-changing conversation. My heart was pounding fiercely in my chest. Ever since our first kiss at the inn, I'd pictured this moment—dreamed of it—even when I'd refused to admit it to myself.

He set my basket down at our feet and took both of my hands in his. He tugged me closer until our knees touched, and I was forced to look up at him. "Shall I try again?" he asked softly.

I nodded, my throat inexplicably dry.

"I know very well how different we are, Verity," he said, thumbs brushing over my knuckles. "If you wished it, you could marry a wealthy man, any of your choosing, and live a life of comfort and plenty."

"Don't be ridicu—"

He put one finger to my mouth. "But if you are determined to marry beneath you," he said, his voice softening, "let me put forth my suit."

I pressed my lips together to hide a smile, then nodded. He lowered his hand, and his gaze swept over me, tender and sweet.

"I want to be with you always, Verity," he said, tightening his hold on my hands. "I cannot promise an easy life, but I can promise you laughter and love. I can promise you hope and happiness. If we are together, we cannot help but have those." He allowed himself a smile. "I do not care if we are chasing criminals or children, I only wish to do it with you."

A small bubble of laughter escaped me, though my eyes were glassy with tears. Nathaniel tucked back one of my ebony ringlets. "My heart is yours, Verity Travers, to do with as you wish." He lowered his head to whisper in my ear. "But if you trust me with yours, I will cherish it until the day I die."

I pressed my forehead against his, eyes closed, heart full. "You do not realize it, do you?" I managed, my voice hoarse. "You do not even realize how you've saved me. I was lost, and you found me." My hand slid to his jaw, holding him there against me. "You have helped me remember who I am, but even more so, you have helped me understand whom I wish to be. There is no one I trust more with my heart, and I give it willingly. I wish to be yours, Nathaniel. Your wife, your friend, your home."

Nathaniel kissed me, his hands finding my back and holding me against him. He had kissed me countless times, but never had it felt like this. There was a new intimacy between us, soft and unspoken, and I knew he felt it too. The promises we made echoed back with every caress of our lips. This was it. Our beginning. Our future.

When we finally pulled away, I sighed and leaned my cheek against his chest. "You have timed this abominably, you know," I said cheerfully.

He chuckled. "How so?"

"We still have to attend Mama's dinner party, and I have little inclination to do anything but stay right here with you."

"And I thought I'd done well," he said. "Do you not want to tell everyone right away that you will soon be Mrs. Denning?"

"Hmm." I lifted my head to look at him, resting my chin on his jacket. "Are you sure you do not wish to take *my* name? You did make such an excellent Mr. Travers."

He laughed out loud, tipping his head back. "If that is what it takes to get you to the altar."

I grinned. "Never fear. I rather like the sound of Verity Denning. She seems a happy and contented sort of person."

"I very much hope she will be," he said, kissing my forehead.

We stood there in an embrace, the busyness of the city surrounding us. I ignored it all. There was nowhere better than *here*—in the arms of the man I loved.

$\mathscr{A}$CKNOWLEDGMENTS

I am feeling so incredibly blessed as I sit down once again to write a note of thanks to the people who make my books possible. I am surrounded by the best—the best family, the best writing friends, the best publishing team, and the best readers—and I will never take any of them for granted.

First, to my readers: thank you for supporting *all* my books, but *A Heart Worth Stealing* especially. It was my first foray into suspense and mystery, and because of your excitement and love and cheerleading, it made me believe I could write more in this world! Verity and Nathaniel's story would not exist without you, and I am forever grateful for the opportunity to write for the most incredible readers ever.

A mountain of thanks to my wonderful publisher, Shadow Mountain (pun intended). To Heidi Gordon, for believing in this series and in Verity's story. To Sam Millburn, for your detailed and insightful edits that made this book the best version it could be. To Amy Parker, Haley Haskins, Ashley Olson, and the rest of the marketing and sales team, for your expertise and enthusiasm in helping my books find homes with new readers! And to Heather Ward, for the most beautiful, perfect cover for Verity and Nathaniel.

I will never be able to feel fully confident in a book until it has been read by my critique partners (AKA my writing lifelines)—Heidi Kimball, Megan Walker, and Arlem Hawks. I breathe a sigh of relief every time you all tell me a story is worth telling, and that I'm not ruining it too terribly. Thank you for being the best of friends and the best of women, and for being there for me when I need it the most. I'm continually inspired by you, and it's a rare day that our texts don't make me laugh out loud. So grateful for you all!

A huge thank you to my fabulous beta readers—Cassy Watson, Jessica Christian, Jan Lance, Jillian Christensen, and Deborah Hathaway! You are all the unsung heroes of this book, and I am incredibly thankful for all of your time and talents.

To my kids, for thinking my writing gig is cool sometimes, for asking me what my book is about, for reading over my shoulder, for coming to book signings to see me, and for forgiving me when I have to miss bedtime to hit deadlines. I love you!

To Cody, who knows if I'm drafting or editing just based on my mood, all I can say is that I could not do this without you. My brain would break, the house would be a disaster, and my books would be forever unfinished. Thank you for taking up all the slack I leave you, and for being the best daddy and hubby ever.

JOANNA BARKER firmly believes that romance makes everything better, which is why she has fallen in love with writing Regency romances. When she's not typing away on her next book, she's listening to podcasts, eating her secret stash of chocolate, or adding things to her Amazon cart. She thinks being an author is the second-best job in the world—right after being a mom. She is just a little crazy about her husband and three wild but lovable kids.